# CONDITION OF WAR

## A CENTRAL CORPS NOVEL

# ELIZABETH BONESTEEL

Condition of War

Copyright © 2025 by Elizabeth Hartwell Bonesteel
All rights reserved.

ISBN 978-1-7373909-8-5 *paperback*
ISBN 978-1-7373909-7-8 *hardcover*
ISBN 978-1-7373909-6-1 *ebook*

Book and cover design by Patrick Foster Design
Cover illustration ©2021 Seth Rutledge
Back cover photograph by Felix Mittermeier /Unsplash



ElizabethBonesteel.com

*Dear Dad,*
*I made you some generation ships.*

# PROLOGUE

RYK LOOKED DOWN at Leni, the ragged hole in her chest weeping blood onto the tiling of the science center courtyard, and wondered if she'd had time to feel pain.

Unlikely, he decided. With a shot like that she'd have been in too much shock to register anything, even if she'd lived long enough to know when her body hit the ground. Ryk had snapped his ankle once—had it been ten whole years ago?—traversing an overworn walkway, and his memory held only the instant before he'd tripped: vivid blue sky, two moons skimming the horizon, the salt breeze off Anaxis' single, tranquil ocean. And then he'd been curled up on the ground, awash in pain and adrenaline. His mind hadn't had time to form a memory of the fall.

He chose to believe the last thing Leni had felt was the stir of the summer breeze against her skin.

The kill shot had come from the power annex, where the soldiers had holed up, angry that Ryk and the other researchers had put up a fight. Indeed, Ryk couldn't blame them; they'd had no reason to suspect a pack of scientists would choose this visit, after so many years of routine, to say *no more*. The scientists, in return, had had no reason to suspect their resistance would be met immediately with mass murder. And yet here they all were.

A shout came from the annex, and Ryk's crisis training kicked in again. Kneeling next to Leni, he detached her scoped rifle from her body harness. He permitted himself one last look at her face—well-worn, familiar, in life full of kindness and good humor—before retreating across the walkway until the corner of the lab dormitory was between him and the soldiers.

He touched his comm, made sure the signal was still on target. "This is Haldiman," he said.

His voice came out hoarse, uneven. The waste bin set aflame by the soldiers' indiscriminate fire must have contained something hazardous. His throat crawled with needles, and it didn't matter; he wouldn't have much longer to be bothered by it.

"Leni's down," he told whoever was listening. "I'm behind the dormitory. They're advancing. Does anyone have eyes on the enemy?"

Silence. For the first time since the fight had begun, Ryk found himself more afraid than angry.

"Anyone still on line, respond."

Nothing.

*Down to me.*

He examined Leni's rifle. Half a charge: thirty shots, give or take. Ryk wasn't a bad shot for someone new to weapons; during their target training, he'd been consistently in the top five or ten. "Not bad for a weak-kneed scientist," Leni had said when he earned his certificate, and he'd wanted to be annoyed with her, but she'd been grinning from ear to ear, palpably proud of him.

None of them had thought it would come to this, not really. But they'd known it would come to *something*.

At the sound of footsteps, he peered around the corner. A stream of soldiers in black-and-gray uniforms rushed from behind the annex, each soldier looking in a different direction.

Ryk almost laughed. Professional fighters, and they were afraid of *him.*

He had no hope of shooting them all. He laid Leni's rifle on the quartzite tiles and slung off his backpack, digging for his last resort: a handheld explosive. If he could get them close enough, maybe—*maybe*—he'd be able to take enough of them with him that they'd give up.

He hit his comm again, this time narrow-banded. "This is Ryk Haldiman," he said quietly. "I don't know if you can hear me. They're coming. I'm going to try to stop them. I don't think I can get them all. Be ready."

No reply. No way of knowing if his message had gone through.

The explosive was spherical, smooth and solid, strangely comforting in his palm. He'd have to arm it first, and he'd have to make sure he didn't squeeze the trigger accidentally. If they shot him from a distance, his hand might convulse, and all his efforts would be wasted.

He'd have to be a credible threat, to make them all rush him at once.

He picked up the rifle and palmed the safety off. They were opposite him now, finding meager cover by the generator building, but if he could get to the lab entrance without being detected, he might be able to get their attention without suffering Leni's fate. Crouching, cursing his aging knees, he moved through the decorative hedges of the laboratory courtyard toward the main building.

He was within 100 meters when something whizzed past his ear, leaving a streak of heat in his shoulder. A shout followed: "Stop! Stay where you are!"

*I know what 'stop' means, you idiots.* He tried to run lower to the ground and stumbled; none of this was working. His element of surprise gone, he gripped the rifle and fired wildly over his shoulder, then waited for a return shot that never came. He wondered if he'd hit something, or if they'd decided to circle ahead of him and block him at the lab entrance.

If they got that far, all of this was for nothing.

Taking a chance with the silence, he straightened and ran toward the lab. Fifty meters away, then thirty: he was so close, he would get close enough, he might die but he'd take them with him and Anaxis would win, this one time if never again, and he wouldn't have to think about what happened next because he wouldn't be there to deal with it—

Something struck his spine. He fell to the ground, his fist unclenching, the unarmed grenade rolling under a hedge. His nose had snapped; it ought to hurt, but his brain wasn't thinking about his nose. His brain was registering that he had no feeling in his legs, that his lower back was burning as if acid had been poured onto his skin. The world around him had become bright and blocky, like some experimental art vid made out of still pictures.

*I've been shot.*

The realization was clear, unambiguous, and came with the certainty that he was going to die here on the tile. The pain distracted him from most of his emotions, but he was aware of fear, anger, regret, and a searing thread of hate so powerful he was shocked it didn't animate him to his feet again.

Someone grabbed his arm and flipped him over, and he blinked and squinted. The figure was silhouetted, Anaxis' cerulean sky framing wide shoulders and an opaque helmet— and a long-range plasma weapon, almost certainly the one that had made the fatal hole in Ryk's back.

So blue, that sky. People always said it never rained on Anaxis, and of course it did, although here, far north of the aquifers, only for a few minutes a day in the depths of summer. The rest of the Second Sector told such mythic tales of Anaxis, as if it were some kind of paradise. And indeed to Ryk it was. He'd never felt an instant's regret that Anaxis had never given in to tourism. Taking commissions for scientific research was supposed to be different. Scientists, even Corps-affiliated ones, were supposed to have ethics.

It had been a mistake for Anaxis to get involved at all.

"You *bastard*." The soldier's voice was low and raspy. "All you weak-ass bastards. Who the fuck do you think you are?"

"Smoke him." Another figure appeared behind the first, hiding most of the sky. Ryk was irritated; they might at least leave him the sky before he died.

"Does it hurt?" The first soldier showed no signs of having heard the second. "I hope it hurts, motherfucker. Hadley was doing his *job*, and you *killed* him for it. Every last one of you assholes is going down, do you hear me? And you're going to feel every single nerve ending burning while you go, and—"

"Stand the *fuck* down, Lieutenant!"

Unmistakable authority in that voice: more expressive, and somehow colder. The second soldier straightened and moved out of Ryk's line of sight; the first only froze.

"Step away from him, Kelson. I mean it."

Ryk watched the sky.

"Commander." Ryk's killer—Kelson—sounded considerably more in control. "He was shooting at us, Commander. He killed Hadley."

"Fuck you, Kelson. Two steps back. Don't make me say it again."

The commander, whoever she was, sounded more tense than Kelson did, but somehow she was less frightening. Kelson and Smoke Him were perpetual engines of hate, but this woman was a soldier. She might kill him, but she'd do it dispassionately.

The sky was so blue.

Kelson took two steps back, and Ryk's view was clear until the commander bent over him. She was slighter than Kelson, but equally armored, and she wore two handguns across her chest to supplement the long rifle in her hand.

"Hey," she said. Her voice was almost gentle. "Can you hear me?"

Ryk was disinclined to answer her.

She pulled a portable med scanner out of her belt and pointed it at his forehead, then swore quietly and tucked it away. "Where are your medics?" she asked him.

He focused, and gathered his energy, and said to her: "Fuck you."

She was still for a moment, then nodded slightly and straightened. Her hand went to her ear. "All hands, this is Commander Naude. Disengage immediately. Reassemble at the shuttle in the lab square. We're disembarking in—" she glanced at something Ryk couldn't see "—two minutes."

"Commander." Smoke Him came into Ryk's line of sight; Kelson was nowhere to be found. "Surely it'd be kinder to just—"

"Kill him? What the fuck, Bassir? You forget why we're here?"

"Begging the commander's pardon, but—"

"*No.* Fuck you. Get to the ship."

Smoke Him vanished, and the commander turned back to Ryk. "This isn't who we are," she said, but he didn't think he was the one she was trying to convince.

Footsteps ran toward them. "Got it," said a voice, and a hand dropped a small gray polyhedron into the commander's palm.

*No.*

The commander weighed the object carefully, as if she were afraid it would break. "Get to the shuttle," she said. "Light her up. We're not waiting around for the next wave." Footsteps receded, and she looked down at Ryk again. "I'm sure your medics will be along soon." When he didn't answer, she repeated, "This isn't who we are."

He managed another feeble "Fuck you."

"Fine." Her voice went taut again. "But you know, you could have just given it to us. None of this had to happen. None of it."

She turned away from him, and her footsteps faded. Less than a minute later, the clear blue above him was bisected by a small, squat ship speeding through Anaxis' stratosphere back toward space.

*No.*

His arms could still move, and it took more effort than he'd ever given anything in his life to reach up and activate his comm. "This—Ryk—" He couldn't speak properly. Best to keep it to the essentials. "They took it. The lifeboat. Don't let them—"

That was the end of his energy.

A small eternity passed before a voice replied: low, even, gentle. Kind.

*No fear*, it said.

Ryk was not afraid.

Moments later, Ryk was nothing at all.

# PART ONE

# SECTOR SEVEN

# ONE

Another fist connected with Greg's jaw, and as his shoulder hit the wall of the abandoned corridor he wondered, for the first time, if these kids would end up killing him.

He hadn't thought anything of it when he'd first spotted the pack of teenagers wandering around Sochi Station. Sochi was a non-Gov outpost on the far edge of the Fourth Sector, scrupulously neutral, and visitors from PSI ships were common—especially groups of young people, wary and energetic and reveling in temporary freedom. Greg supposed he'd been doing the same thing, arriving on Sochi hours before he was to meet the PSI training officer he'd been tasked with picking up. He had wandered the station's crowded levels, watching tourists dodge in and out of shops and restaurants, laughing or arguing or just relaxing on their own. His life on board the starship *Galileo* was comfortable, even satisfying, but he could never be anonymous there. He'd been her captain for nine years before resigning, and most of *Galileo*'s crew would never really be able to treat him as anything else.

Here on Sochi, he was an unknown, soaking in the motion around him just like any tourist. Civilian existence was still exotic to him. He'd never, even as a child, really understood how people outside the military lived. He loved to watch them, for all it left him confused and sometimes unsteady; he was one of them now, after all, and had he ever really been different?

He knew one of his attackers: Marcus Osinov, whom he'd pegged at sixteen or so. Rangy, nearly as tall as Greg, full of sarcasm and quick jokes, and a damn good defensive goalie. As part of liaising with the PSI ship *Meridia*, Greg had been playing rugby every day with *Meridia*'s crew, pick-up games and tournaments both. Marcus was always good-natured, a tough player and a cheerful loser, and Greg had rather liked him.

He thought Marcus was the one who'd screamed "Oathbreaker!" before the group had rushed him, en masse, when he'd turned down the side corridor toward Sochi's landing bay.

He let the pain in his jaw wash through him, bringing him focus. Six attackers, boxing him in; he needed to clear them away. He started with his elbows, one sharp jab backward into someone's stomach, another braced before him to block a gut punch. A hard forward jab, and he heard a yelp of pain and a growl; and then they were all going for his legs, kicking behind his knees to destabilize him. Their first real error: he swung a fist into someone's chin and spun away, evading four of them. The other two stuck to him, one alternating hits to his face and stomach, the other landing kidney punches. Wiry, the one before him: white hair, maybe natural based on the ice-colored eyes. Small, half-grown, but could throw a punch; Greg missed a block and the pain in his ribs outlasted the hit.

The others regrouped, herding him against the wall, and he struggled to guard his head. He was generally a good hand-to-hand fighter, taught from boyhood first by his mother, and then by a series of Corps battle instructors. But he was nearly forty years old, and even if he'd been younger, there were six of them to his one.

He wondered if they had come into this meaning to kill him. He wondered what they'd do with him when they were finished, how long *Galileo*'s crew would search, if he'd ever be discovered.

He wondered what Elena would think had happened to him.

A hit to his abdomen dropped him to his knees. Overtaken by nausea, he braced one hand against the floor. He couldn't go down. He couldn't go down. He'd never get up again if he went down.

And then a voice, feminine, familiar, infused with both humor and authority, echoing through the wide corridor: "Don't you think that's a little unfair?"

The teens scrambled away from him, and when he looked up, trying to keep his breath from hitching, they were standing in a straight line, at sharp attention.

The diaphragm spasm eased, and he inhaled. Raspier than he liked to hear, and that sharp pain on his left side was still there. Fractured rib, almost certainly; easy enough to fix when he got home, but not much fun between now and then. Bob would be angry with him. Bob had been angry with him a lot lately; *Galileo*'s most recent mission had resulted in a higher-than-usual casualty count, and as the ship's chief medical officer, Bob took it as a personal affront when his people were injured. That Bob was angrier with Elena, who had come closer to death than any of them, was the only thing that made the old doctor's over-protectiveness tolerable.

Greg stayed on his knees, breathing carefully, watching his savior approach.

He'd met Commander Nataliya Gritsenko, *Meridia*'s star fighter pilot, a few weeks earlier, in his ambassadorial capacity. He'd noticed her beauty first, as he suspected most people did, as he suspected she intended. She was small but not slight, with trim muscles and curves that lent her an effortless grace. Her light skin, nearly the same color as her white-blonde hair and lending starkness to her dark eyes, had a warm undertone that made her look energetic, healthy, and probably younger than she was. When Taras, *Meridia*'s captain, had introduced them, Gritsenko had greeted him confidently, something in her bearing conveying the certainty that she was owed respect, absolutely, at all times. Her perfect features made him think of Caroline, his former wife; but her reflexive authority put him in mind of Elena, who could, when she was in the mood, snap an entire room of ensigns to terrified attention without saying a word.

Here in the corridor Commander Gritsenko was smiling, her expression friendly apart from her eyes. Greg had often thought dark eyes hid the most secrets, but Gritsenko's were easy to read: the PSI commander was not happy with these children, and if they had any experience with the greater world they would immediately throw themselves on whatever mercy she might be willing to bestow.

She stopped and looked down at Greg. Her eyebrows twitched, and that cold expression grew vaguely bemused. "Are you all right?" she asked.

He nodded, then tried a word: "Yes." His rib protested only mildly when he spoke; if he was careful he might manage to get home and have it looked at in his own time. With some care he braced a hand against the wall and pushed himself to his feet. He towered over Nataliya Gritsenko, but when she straightened her shoulders she was every career officer he'd ever served with.

"Nice to see you again, Foster." She held out her hand, and he shook it. "Give me a minute."

She slung her lightweight pack off her shoulder and dropped it at his feet, then turned back to the children.

"Now!" she said, bright and cheerful. "Who'd like to explain what the fuck I just witnessed, eh?"

Silence. Greg saw Marcus swallow; the white-haired kid's jaw worked.

Commander Gritsenko nodded. "Very wise of you. After all, I

didn't give you time to consult with each other and come up with some bullshit story, did I?"

One of the kids, a hard-muscled girl with yellow hair buzzed short over her tan skull, scowled. "You know what he is, Nataliya."

"*Be quiet.*" The command was short and sharp, and the children came to attention again, eyes forward. "I know exactly what he is, Randa. He is the former captain of a Corps starship that has helped dozens of colonies beat starvation, evacuate after natural disasters, and get ahold of the medicines they need. He is *our* captain's personal friend. No matter what position he *resigned* from—" Greg took a moment to appreciate her emphasis— "he broke no oaths, and he will outrank every one of you nasty, pathetic little insects for the rest of his fucking life. *That's* who he is, Randa. Do you understand?"

The girl swallowed, her face red.

"I asked you a question."

Randa blinked. "Yes, Commander. I understand."

Commander Gritsenko smiled again, all congeniality. "Good." She turned to Greg. "Foster. Would you care to file a complaint with Captain Taras?"

She didn't give him a title, which was refreshing. People on *Galileo* still called him Captain now and then, no matter how often he corrected them. Rather than lack of faith in Jessica Lockwood, who'd had the job only six weeks, he thought it was habit. Commander Gritsenko had no habits with him to break.

He looked back at the teens. Their stiff rage hadn't disappeared, but now there was fear in their eyes as well. Taras had a reputation for retributive justice, and although Greg liked to tell himself it was largely unearned, he couldn't be sure what she'd do to this handful of impulsive children.

He was breathing. He was standing. And they were young.

"Not at this time, Commander," he said.

The fear in the teens' eyes abated. Marcus looked surprised, and vaguely ashamed.

Commander Gritsenko gave an exaggerated shrug. Another gesture that reminded him of Elena: theatrical nonchalance, letting your victim know who was in control of the situation. "As you wish," she said. "But I'll have to file an incident report."

"Commander—" The white-haired kid fell silent when Gritsenko pinned them with a glare.

"I'll be writing that report tonight, after I've settled in on *Galileo*. I will convey to Captain Taras exactly what I witnessed and exactly how you responded, as well Foster's generosity and understanding. That gives you—" She touched the comm behind her ear to check the time— "six hours to figure out what you're going to do. I strongly suggest you confess before Captain Taras receives my report. If you take responsibility for your foolishness, she might actually show you mercy." Her smile faded, and her gaze grew hard. "Now *get lost.*"

They broke formation, running past Greg and Commander Gritsenko. Greg didn't turn, listening to their footsteps fade; he thought he caught one last defiant yell of *oathbreaker* before the corridor descended into silence.

Next to him the PSI commander exhaled, as if she'd just finished a mildly annoying task. "So are you really okay?" she asked, turning toward him, arms crossed across her chest, "or was that just bullshit posturing for the kiddies?"

His ribs were the worst, but the aches throughout the rest of his body were escalating by the moment. His back had taken the bulk of the punishment, despite a few on-target punches to his face and torso; the longer he stood, the more intense the pain became. But his head and his vision were clear, his heart rate steady. "I don't think any of this is permanent," he told her.

"Hm." That low, thoughtful noise he associated with PSI; so many ships and dialects across the Six Sectors, yet that one verbal tic seemed to be a constant. "So it was bullshit posturing for *me*, then. We should hit a med scanner before we go. I'd hate to have you drop dead during the flight."

She reached down for her pack and slung it over her shoulder, then headed down the corridor as if nothing at all had happened. He caught up with her in one long stride.

"There's a scanner on the way to the landing bay. It's only a Level One, but it should reassure both of us you're not on the brink of expiring." They fell into easy step, like fellow cadets, despite the difference in their heights. "You know," she said at length, "you could say thank you."

She had probably saved his life. "They're not bad at hand-to-hand," he admitted. "You must be proud of them."

"Them?" She scoffed. "They're not going to be fighters. They don't have the mental discipline."

"They're children."

"That's an arbitrary word. Most of them will reach majority within a solar year, and nobody will be deferring to their youth anymore."

They reached the med scanner, set unobtrusively into the wall. With the ease of long habit, she pulled the unit out of its dock and checked the dial, then proceeded to run it over him, starting with the top of his head. Her focus was so intense it took him a moment to realize her next question had nothing to do with his health. "Is that why you let them off the hook?"

Was that what he'd done? He shifted, and when she frowned he straightened again, trying to keep still. "I'm not sure slapping them down would have the desired effect on the relationship between *Meridia* and *Galileo*."

She scanned down his legs; she was avoiding meeting his eyes. "You know what people say about you," she said.

"Of course I do. Because a lot of them say it to my face."

He said it lightly, but six weeks after his precipitous resignation from his position as *Galileo*'s captain, he was beginning to wonder if he'd ever shake the reputation of being someone without any fixed loyalty. It was an incorrect interpretation of events, of course, but the end result had been the same: he'd stepped down abruptly as captain of one of the Corps' most decorated starships, and there were undeniable optics to that. Public retellings of any story weren't concerned with the precise order of events. He'd learned that at the age of twelve, when his mother's death had made him a public figure.

Despite the insults and suspicion, he never doubted his resignation had been the right choice. He'd promoted his second-in-command, Jessica Lockwood, a competent and talented commander who'd already proved her courage. Jessica had promptly taken a vote, then led the crew in a mass resignation from Central Corps to pledge an oath to the PSI consortium. Joining that loose affiliation of generation ships had made the most sense; it had allowed *Galileo* and her crew some immediate civilian protections, and the potential for diplomatic recognition.

If Central Gov ever got over the insult and recognized *Galileo*'s sovereignty.

He'd approved of it all, not that his approval mattered at that point. Yet despite that, he'd been unable to turn around and take the PSI oath himself. He was too recently free to feel comfortable tying his future to anything or anyone specific. It was a strange feeling, being rootless; he wasn't sure he liked it, but he was certain for now that he needed it.

It drove Jessica to distraction. More than one of their recent conversations had ended with her reminding him how much easier his life would be if he'd just "take the fucking Oath already." He always laughed at her, always deflected; she was annoyed with him, but not angry.

That wouldn't last.

The only person who understood why he stayed free was Elena. Not that they discussed much these days, apart from his impressions of the *Meridia* crew and the ins and outs of her mundane days as a mechanic on board *Galileo*. Their last mission had hit her hard, and Elena, who had been tasked with destroying a clandestine lab at Indus Station, still kept too much to herself. But the one time he'd mentioned Jessica's impatience, Elena had said, with great gentleness, "Fuck that, Greg. You owe no one an explanation." His self-doubt had dissipated in an instant.

He loved her more than his own life, and he missed the person she used to be.

"Seems to me," Nataliya Gritsenko said, finishing her scan at his feet and studying the summary readout, "this whole thing is a problem you brought on yourself."

"You think I should stand up on *Meridia* and take the PSI oath in front of everyone?"

"I think you should stand up on *Meridia* and tell everyone what really happened."

And that, of course, was the root of the problem: the incident that had led to his resignation in the first place. *Meridia*'s previous sister ship, *Chryse*, had been destroyed during that mission, and he'd yet to find a concise way of explaining the circumstances to those who hadn't been there. "The ones who don't believe me," he told her, "aren't going to start believing because they hear me say it instead of reading a report."

Her lips tightened, but she said nothing.

"And maybe," he said, "after you've been on *Galileo* for a couple of weeks, you can tell them yourself."

He was laying a trap, and he suspected she knew it. He also suspected she was too smart and too experienced to give away her thoughts when they barely knew one another. He looked down at her, and she looked up at him, and for a moment he thought they understood each other with absolute clarity.

A sound came over his comm, an odd, crackling hiss, as if someone were crushing a sheet of starship cladding. Strange interference, triggering an old, amorphous memory. He touched his comm to clear it; Commander Gritsenko opened her mouth to speak, but stayed silent when he raised a hand.

Garbled words bubbled out of the crackle, harsh, urgent; and then, with a loud, half-familiar click, the voice became clear:

"—promised me, Foster! You've got to do it! You've got to shoot us down!"

He knew that voice. "Commander Naude?" he asked. Which was madness; it couldn't possibly be her. "Gen? Is that you?"

She didn't seem to have heard him. "There's no time anymore." That strange, fuzzy crunching broke into the message again. "—get zero! If any of this meant anything to you, shoot us down now!"

"Commander Naude? *Capricorn?*" His comm dropped into silence, and a message appeared before his eyes: *No connection to sender.*

The lights around them dimmed, casting everything in the vivid neon blue of a low-level general alarm. "Attention, guests and staff," said Sochi Station's pleasant voice, "we have a proximity warning. Please adjourn to the closest safe room and await an all-clear announcement." The message repeated, this time in Standard.

*Shit.* "I think there's a safe room around the corner," he said, turning down the hallway. "I'll get in touch with *Galileo* to see —" He stopped, aware the PSI commander wasn't following him, and turned. "Commander?"

Nataliya Gritsenko stood frozen, all façades stripped away, something very like panic in her transparent dark eyes. "What do they mean," she asked, her voice measured, "'proximity warning'?"

She had to know what it meant. She'd been on *Meridia* fifteen years, and the PSI starship had hardly been shy about battles, close quarters and otherwise. But he recognized that stillness, that illogical reaction he'd see now and then, some- times even in seasoned fighters: fight or flight. There was nothing before Commander Gritsenko for her to fight. And there was nowhere for either of them to run.

"I'll find out about the alarm," he told her, speaking gently, reassuringly. "But we need to follow instructions now, Commander. We don't want to interfere with the station's processing of civilians, do we?"

He'd found, sometimes, that invoking civilians reminded a soldier where their energy belonged. But Nataliya Gritsenko, regardless of any training she might have had, was a stranger from another ship, another culture, and he had no idea if his reassurances helped at all.

Pale and shaken, she followed him toward the safe room as he commed back to his ship to find out what the hell was going on.

# TWO

*Everything will be all right.*

*Now,* Elena thought at the voice in her head, *is not the time.*

"What do you mean," Captain Lockwood was saying over her comm, "'she came out of nowhere'?"

Elena exchanged a glance with Ted Shimada, who raised an eyebrow at her. Elena and Ted had both known Jessica Lockwood for years; barking, they knew, was part of how she processed information. Her statement had nothing to do with her doubting their competence. It was a simple acknowledgement that what they'd told her was unbelievable.

"I mean," Elena said, "nobody has an explanation for how she appeared. Corps relays started tracking *Capricorn* an hour ago, but there was no evidence of where she came from—no FTL field residue at all."

"Wormhole?" Jessica asked.

"Possible," Ted said. "But this sector is pretty well-populated. Odds there's been a wormhole hanging around here and nobody's noticed are pretty low, and on top of that, none of the readings indicate the kind of emissions you'd get with a wormhole."

"So you're telling me," the captain said, "a Corps warship just *materialized* an hour ago, and has been idly drifting toward Sochi Station without answering a single comm? Why the fuck hasn't Central warned anybody?"

Elena expected they had, but hadn't sent a general alarm. If *Galileo* had still been a Central Corps starship, they'd know everything Central did about CCSS *Capricorn*'s anomalous appearance, maybe even been ordered to investigate the warship's odd behavior.

Or they'd have been told *Capricorn* was on some sort of secret mission, and they were to leave her alone.

Officially, the Corps didn't run covert ops. Unofficially, every soldier knew *Capricorn*, along with a few other small, highly weaponized vessels, often dealt with situations Central wanted handled brutally and quietly. *Capricorn*'s crew was small and tight-knit, and had experienced almost no turnover during Elena's twelve-year career. These were people who knew how to keep a secret.

They also knew their ship, and that, more than anything else, convinced Elena something was seriously wrong.

"Either she's been told not to answer," Elena said, knowing Jessica would have come to the same conclusion, "or she can't. Either way, unless she changes course, she's going to drift right into Sochi and take down half her habitat ring."

"Any chance Sochi's gravity field is enough to fend off debris?" Ted asked.

"Their governor tells me they use standard-issue habitat-only systems," Jessica said, "so no, I don't think we can count on that."

*Short-sighted,* Elena thought. She knew the usual argument —a neutral space station, willing to supply all comers who behaved themselves, was a valuable thing, even to Syndicate raiders, even to the pockets of anarchists that were beginning to gain traction in the outer areas of the Six Sectors. Everybody wanted Sochi Station kept safe; why would it need defenses?

But peace was temporary, always. Elena had long since lost any faith that humans, in the large, would consistently do the right thing.

"Move us closer," Jessica ordered. "Let's get some shielding around them. And Elena? I want to know what we can do to disarm *Capricorn*."

"Yes, Captain."

Her voice sounded steady, which was a small victory. Something inside her had gone cold, and she was shocked to see her hands steady over the controls on her console. Firing on a Corps starship, even to disarm, was an act of war, but that wasn't what bothered her. The last time she'd committed this particular act of war, things hadn't gone so well.

*Three small dots on the display, each representing a ship running in the FTL field, each with a crew of people, as human as she was, and her quiet command causing the dots to wink out as each ship was pulled to pieces—*

She almost missed the spinup of hiss and whispers this time before her hallucination told her *Everything will be all right.*

And damned if it didn't steady her, this voice her mind was manufacturing, this thing that threatened the fragile reality she was clinging to every day.

She focused on the readings they were receiving from *Capricorn*. In addition to the warship's ident, she could pinpoint the power storage they used for their forward weapons. Elena was familiar with every starship model the Corps flew, and *Capricorn* was older than most: hardware-intensive, built to be powerful and swift, a blunt tool for volatile situations. Elena could see where her crew had modified her: her front turrets had been fortified, which Elena had expected, but her long-range weapons had been distributed across the ship's stern. An odd thing to do, but Elena supposed if your target was on a planet's surface, you might get a better spread.

She shrugged off another chill and focused on the forward turrets. *Capricorn* wasn't showing signs of aggression—yet—but Elena figured if they did they wouldn't be likely to use the long-range guns on Sochi. The debris field would damage anything in proximity, which at this range would include *Capricorn* herself. So unless the crew was genuinely suicidal, her best bet was quick elimination of those forward turrets. *Galileo*'s main guns boasted far more accuracy than the warship's; they could take out a grain of sand from orbit without even kicking up dust. There was a good chance Elena would be able to carve *Capricorn*'s forward guns away from their trigger mechanisms without harming the rest of the ship.

Which might not matter, of course, if *Capricorn*'s crew was dead; but the other thing Elena had learned after her hideous mission was that optimism cost her nothing. And maybe helped her sleep nights.

"Elena." Jessica in her ear again, tense and worried. "Listen to this."

Elena heard a crackle of static—an analog signal, she realized—and then a voice she didn't recognize, the words broken by interference: "Get zero! If any of this meant anything to you, shoot us down now!"

"That's Gen Naude," Greg said in her ear. "*Capricorn*'s second-in-command."

Elena remembered him mentioning Gen. Greg didn't keep in touch with a lot of people, but he had a handful of steadfast professional friends. How he managed to have ordinary conversations with *Capricorn*'s first officer, given she was almost never permitted to discuss her assignments, Elena didn't know; but the two had been friends longer than Elena had known Greg. "That's not a comm," she said.

"It is," Jessica told her. "It's an encapsulated message. The original is radio. They routed it through *Galileo*'s comm system."

"But that's—" That made as much sense as anything else *Capricorn* had been doing. "What the hell does 'get zero' mean?"

"I have no idea," Greg said.

Elena could hear voices around him, some of them speaking languages she didn't know. A knot of dread coalesced in her stomach. "Greg," she said, "where are you?"

He paused a moment before answering her. "In a Sochi safe room," he confessed. "We got delayed."

Her eyes dropped closed, a jolt of fear flooding her system. He should have left by now. He should have been on his way home, with that PSI pilot in tow. He should not, under any circumstances, have been stuck in a safe room with a bunch of panicky civilians while a rogue warship drifted toward him, ready to crush his shelter and propel him into the vacuum.

She had promised him, when they had embarked on this new chapter in their personal and professional lives, that she would always be there to back him up, always fight at his side. It hadn't occurred to her he might get pulled into battle when she was too far away to protect him. Suddenly shooting at *Capricorn* felt less morally ambiguous.

"Is Commander Gritsenko with you?" she asked. He would know everything else she was thinking without her telling him. He'd apologize, later, for worrying her, and she let herself imagine that, projecting herself past this moment into a time when everyone she loved was safe again.

"Yes," he said, and she caught a different thread in his voice: calm, steady, the kind of tone he'd use when he had to lead people into battle who weren't used to it. "She's calming some civilians. I've tied her in to our discussion."

*She's on the comm and she's frightened, so watch what you say.*

Elena spoke with a confidence she didn't feel. "We're approaching Sochi, and we should be able to get close enough to shore up her shielding before *Capricorn* drifts too close. And we've got a targeting solution on her forward turrets. If she threatens you, or if she doesn't power up and move away, we can shear off her weapons and deflect her path."

"She's not replying at all?" Greg asked.

"Not a peep," said Jessica. She too sounded more cheerful; Elena wondered if they were all overcompensating for the nervous PSI commander.

"But...what does she look like?"

Elena could see the warship through the machine room's massive, multi-level windows. *Capricorn* was lit by ordinary running lights, bright and steady, and *Galileo*'s sensors gave them more detail. "She appears to be running normally," Ted said. "Thermals are right, engine output is ordinary. No leak-ages. Nothing to indicate anything amiss."

"Except nobody's talking." Greg couldn't keep the grimness from his voice this time.

Jessica spoke up. "You know them, Greg, don't you? Could this be some kind of weird-ass stealth op?"

Greg gave a hollow chuckle. "I know Gen," he said, "and only a little. If they're on some op, I can't imagine what it'd be. Have you tried Reed?"

Tai Reed, captain of the CCSS *Arizona*, was one of the only friends *Galileo* had left in the Corps, and Jessica had to be very careful with how they contacted her. "I've sent an encrypt via a stream message," Jessica said. "Odds that Reed will see it, decode it, and answer in the next three minutes are next to nil."

"At the angle *Capricorn*'s moving," Ted said, "once we get our shielding up around Sochi, she should bounce off. Might get a bit of a bump there, though."

They wouldn't feel anything unless the impact damaged infrastructure, or any of the station's environmental systems. Part of Elena's mind—the part unhindered by sentimental whispers or battle trauma—wished mightily there was a way to blow *Capricorn* to pieces without the debris endangering everyone.

A light flared on her console, and she went cold. "Captain," she said, "*Capricorn* has engaged engines."

"Commander Shaw, do you have that shot?" Jessica asked.

Elena let *Galileo*'s tracking systems follow *Capricorn*'s movements. "Yes, Captain. Captain, she's—" *Capricorn*'s flight path had changed. "She's turned," she said aloud, for the benefit of Commander Gritsenko. "She's no longer threatening Sochi. She's locked her weapons on us."

This was familiar. This she could manage. All her fears and anxieties vanished, and she was in the moment, eyes on her console, everything in her calm and steady. Emotion was for other people's peril, and the hours after this was all finished.

"Elena," Greg said in her ear, and she thought if his voice was the last thing she ever heard, that might be all right.

"We've got her targeted," she said, reassuring him, waiting her captain's command. "We'll get her. It's all right."

If she was wrong, she'd never know.

"Fire at will, Commander," Jessica said, and swallowing a wave of dread—this was not the disembodied lights of her last mission, this was defense, *Capricorn* wouldn't be destroyed—Elena fired.

One shot, one chance. The beam from *Galileo* bifurcated and cut through both the warship's forward turrets. The weapons slid from their mounts, drifting neatly away from *Capricorn* as the warship continued its leisurely progress toward *Galileo*.

"She's disarmed," Elena said, and her mind started moving forward again. "Rear weapons are still cold. Sochi is no longer in her path. We've—"

She saw it outside the window first: a massive flash, the white and red of a starship's chemical systems, snuffed by vacuum but not before flaring enough to burn an afterimage into her retina. *Capricorn* had gone to pieces.

*That's not possible,* Elena thought. *That's not*—She turned to her schematic, and saw the pieces of the warship, massive and destructive, flying in all directions. Including toward Sochi Station, and Greg's not-at-all safe room.

"SOCHI BRACE FOR IMPACT!" she shouted, but nothing Sochi could do would stop the debris from ripping through their hull.

# THREE

Nataliya Gritsenko was going to die annoyed. Which was not, given the trajectory of her life, an enormous surprise; but she'd started the day hoping not to die at all.

As soon as Shaw had shouted her warning, Foster had called out to the room: "Everybody on the floor! Now!" His recent divestiture of rank hadn't altered his ability to project authority; the group of bewildered civilians had obeyed without question. The elderly couple Nataliya had been speaking to understood neither Standard nor Fourth Sector dialect; they'd been communicating largely in improvised sign language, but they'd caught the urgency in Foster's voice. Nataliya had helped them to the floor, feeling a spark of envy as they wound their arms around each other and held tight.

But when she hit the floor beside them, Foster had joined her, stretching his long-limbed form alongside hers. And he'd laid a hand on the back of her head, gently, as if his one wide palm would somehow protect her when the room went to pieces.

*Bastard.*

She felt the vibration in the floor, the telltale rumble of metal being torn apart. Slow, then: they'd have seconds for the terror, the futile hope they might be spared. They'd have time to imagine the room being ripped away from them, the cold and abrupt airlessness of the vacuum, the startled denial of their own minds as their absurdly fragile bodies succumbed to the elemental hostility of space. No hope, of course, although they'd hope nonetheless, because humans did, making themselves ridiculous even in their last moments, wasting all their energy—

The rumble kicked up one terrifying, decisive *thunk*, then faded into silence.

A moment later the lights came up, and Sochi's insipid voice said, "Attention guests and staff. The proximity warning has expired. You may leave your safe rooms and continue to enjoy your day. Thank you for visiting Sochi Station." The message repeated in Standard, but most of the people in the room didn't listen; they broke into manic cheers and laughter, relieved the problem had turned out to be nothing at all.

Except, Nataliya realized, as her own heart rate began to steady, it couldn't possibly have been nothing at all.

She pushed herself to her feet. Foster was already standing, helping up the elderly couple, accepting their fawning appreciation. Nataliya was still shaking when they turned to her, apparently feeling the need to be grateful to everyone. She smiled and nodded, resorting to sign language again to assure them she too was happy everything was fine now. They clung to her like lab-bred leeches as Foster turned away from them, facing the wall and speaking quietly.

"What happened?" he asked.

No reply, and Nataliya realized *Galileo*'s alarm had been silenced. For one stomach-dropping moment, she wondered Foster's ship had been destroyed.

But it was Shaw who finally spoke. "*Capricorn*'s gone," the mechanic said, and something in the tone of her voice made Nataliya realize all of *Galileo* thought this event was a tragedy.

Foster's eyes met Nataliya's, and the grief and loss she saw there threatened to drop her to the floor again.

*Careful, Nataliya.*

"We sheared off her weapons," Shaw was saying. "And she just...went up. No energy spike, nothing. Just came apart."

Sochi had been hit by debris, then. It was, Nataliya reflected, a much better outcome than the warship firing on them. "That sounds like a design flaw," she remarked.

Foster had regrouped, but his eyebrow twitched, just a little; she'd been cold, and he'd noticed. *Damn.* An unforced error. "It shouldn't have happened at all," he said bluntly.

Time to make something of her unanticipated vulnerability. She put out her hand, tentatively brushing his arm with her fingers; intimate, but not so forward he'd take it as more than an innocent gesture. "I'm sorry," she said quietly. "Commander Naude was your friend, wasn't she?"

She braced herself for another glimpse of that bottomless grief, but he was under control now, protecting her again. "She knew the job," he said. From another person—from Nataliya herself—it would have sounded callous. "We all do. But now it's our duty to find out what happened."

"After you get your ass back here." Lockwood was back on comm, crisp and professional but clearly worried. "We need to get out of here, and fast. There's nothing in this sequence of events that's going to make us look good to the Corps. Commander Gritsenko?"

"Here, Captain."

"I'm not sure when we're going to be able to rendezvous with *Meridia* again, so if you want to go home, you might be better off waiting on Sochi for them to pick you up."

So tempting, to let Foster and his cursed ship leave her behind, to head back to *Meridia* and her room and her carefully cultivated routine, and forget this ill-fated mission once and for all. She almost forgot she didn't believe in fate. "Thank you,

Captain Lockwood," she said, still looking at Foster, "but I don't see the need."

"Your colleague may feel differently."

Nataliya kept her expression neutral. Nikolai Petrikoff would indeed feel differently. He'd been on *Galileo* for a week already, and every time they'd spoken he'd complained about the place. He'd have no desire to risk his life for a bunch of former Corps officers who were likely as not going to get themselves killed within six months. "I'll let Commander Petrikoff speak for himself," she allowed at last. "But with your permission, Captain, I'd like to stay with you."

"Excellent." Nataliya couldn't be sure if Lockwood sounded sarcastic or relieved. "For your first assignment, please stuff that asshole you're with into our shuttle, and get him back here. Last I checked there were four Central starships within twenty minutes of here, and I don't want to leave the Corps' former poster child anywhere they can get to him."

Foster looked away from Nataliya at that, his lips tightening. *Interesting.* Her mission briefing had included very little beyond his official record—she always preferred divining personal information herself—but she'd known, just like anyone in the Six Sectors who'd ever heard of the Corps, that Foster had been used for most of his career as the personification of the ideal soldier. Not because of his intellect, or his thoughtfulness—which the public only heard about if the press was in the mood to write about it—or even his mother's illustrious Corps career, cut short by a catastrophic accident. No, Foster was known for his looks, which were, thanks to the conjunction of genetics and cultural norms, almost universally appealing. Tall, strong, slim and sturdy, square-jawed and dark-skinned, his head covered with just the right amount of buzz-cut black hair—you didn't even have to get to his eyes, which were an odd, mottled gray-black, before you'd call him striking. Biology had handed him an incredibly powerful tool that he could have parlayed into almost anything he wanted.

And his captain's oblique reference to it *annoyed* him. Full of surprises, this former Corps superhero.

"Understood, Captain Lockwood," Nataliya said. Her voice still held a hint of wobble; Foster met her eyes again, all polite concern, and she began to think betraying her weakness might not have been a disaster after all. "As long as Sochi is clearing departures, we should be able to get out of here in the next five minutes."

"I'll get you cleared," Lockwood promised. "Just get him home."

Nataliya thought, for a moment, Foster might choose to fly the shuttle, but instead he climbed into the copilot's seat and performed his side of the pre-flight check. He'd said nothing as they'd negotiated their way past the crowd still huddled by the safe room door and down the hall to the landing bay, nor as the station's automated parking system moved their shuttle into a launch location. He still kept half an eye on her, but mostly he'd drawn into himself, frowning deeply, almost as if he were angry. She supposed he might be. She'd long thought anger was the most appropriate response to sudden death.

She waited until they'd cleared Sochi and were arcing toward *Galileo* before she spoke. "I'm sorry," she said, and it took little effort to sound sincere. "For losing my composure back there."

He glanced over at her, vaguely startled. "Seems like a pretty normal reaction," he said.

"I've lived on *Meridia* fifteen years," she told him. "I've had fucking raiders punch holes in bulkheads not two rooms away from me. I've fought hand-to-hand with people who'd kill me for a box of obsolete stripe configs." She sighed. "It just...I didn't think it would spook me, but it did."

Despite her phrasing, he didn't ask her to clarify. "None of us know how we're going to respond in a crisis," he told her, "even if we've been through one before. You helped in there. You did fine."

She made a self-deprecating sound and fell silent, annoyed again. He was being kind to her. *Kind.* Over something trivial, something he shouldn't even have noticed. The omissions in her briefing were beginning to seem significant.

*Galileo*'s landing bay was smaller and less grand than *Sochi*'s, but they had it all to themselves. She settled the little shuttle in the center of the space and put the engines into cooldown mode. Foster unstrapped and stood, and she waited a moment before she followed him out. This place would be her home for the next several weeks, the base from which she'd need to execute her orders. She would have to learn a lot very quickly.

She blinked as she exited the shuttle. Lesson One: *Galileo*'s lights were kept much brighter than *Meridia*'s. This wasn't uncommon on Corps ships, she knew; but it had been a long time since she'd spent much time on one, and the full Sol-spectrum lighting was going to take some getting used to. The landing bay itself was all gray, utilitarian polymers and nanocomposites, standard Corps issue, easy to reconfigure and repair. She scanned the space, floor to high-above ceiling, looking for flaws; but they'd only been out of the Corps maintenance rotation for six weeks, and it was apparently too soon for them to be needing repairs. The landing bay office was nestled unobtrusively in one corner, next to the low, wide opening into the ship itself: all clean, well-organized, and entirely unremarkable.

Before the shuttle stood four people, and she felt a moment's relief to see such a small group. Officially, her mission on *Galileo* was to teach the Corps-trained pilots about the sort of guerrilla fighters they'd likely meet now that they were part of PSI, but she hadn't been sure if her rank would provoke some sort of ritualized fanfare. If this was her greeting, she might find herself able to blend in after all.

"Welcome, Commander Gritsenko." This greeting was from Commander Lockwood, a short, vividly pretty red-haired woman with an open smile Nataliya felt certain was used as often as not to disarm. She stepped forward and held out one hand; Nataliya shook it. "I'm sorry about the precipitous circumstances, but we're glad to have you. This is Lieutenant Azevedo, our shuttle officer—" she gestured at a thin, scowling man who was already headed for the shuttle, presumably to post-flight it — "and Lieutenant Bristol, with our security team. Bristol will look after you, and make sure you get what you need while you're here."

Bristol was smiling just like his captain, but without the subterfuge. He towered over Lockwood, and indeed over Nataliya, with a sort of broad-faced goodwill. Something in his expression suggested he might not share his captain's sharp intellect, but she'd been wrong about such things before. She shook his offered hand, and he flashed his teeth at her. Blond hair, cropped short, pale mottled skin; handsome in an I-could-beat-the-crap-out-of-you-but-I-won't sort of way. On *Meridia*, she might have liked him.

"And this is Commander Shaw," Lockwood said, "whom you've sort of already met."

Commander Shaw didn't register what her captain had just said. Commander Shaw had registered only Greg Foster, who was standing before her, looking down at her as if there were not another soul in the universe.

*Of course.*

Nataliya had read about Elena Shaw, although the dossier she'd had was out of date. Shaw had left the Corps a year earlier, and either nobody knew why, or nobody had thought it was important to Nataliya's mission. Shaw was a good mechanic, maybe even a gifted one, and a pilot of some skill. She was also considered a point of vulnerability for Foster, but again that fact had been stated with little detail. No need, of course; Nataliya could see it for herself. Strange, that such a viscerally attractive man could be captivated by someone who was, on the surface, utterly ordinary: nondescriptly slim in her solid black uniform, dark hair—streaked with deep blue; an oddly civilian affectation —pulled back into a knot at the nape of her neck, dark eyes taking in Foster with more reserve than he had managed. And yet as Nataliya watched, the woman lifted a hand and brushed Foster's bruised jaw, delicately, as if she feared breaking him.

"Making friends again, I see," she said.

He laughed. After the day they'd had, he *laughed*.

Lockwood cleared her throat. "Elena," she said, and Shaw startled, her olive-gold skin blushing rose. "This is Commander Gritsenko."

Shaw's embarrassment, if that was what it was, remained unreflected in anything but her skin tone. She stepped away from Foster—leaning heavily, Nataliya noted with some surprise, on a collapsible metal cane—and held out her left hand. "It's a pleasure, Commander," she said smoothly. She had a pleasant voice, carefully modulated. "I'll look forward to your flight briefings."

Nataliya took her hand, studying her face. "You won't be flying with me?"

Something sharp flared in Shaw's dark eyes, but all she did was smile ruefully. "I'm still grounded," she said, dropping Nataliya's hand. "I'll have to learn second-hand."

"Learning by doing is best."

Nataliya had meant it as a dig, but Shaw turned to her captain, raising an eyebrow. "Did you hear that, Jessica?"

"Argue with Medical," Lockwood said, and there was fondness in her irritable response.

Shaw smiled, but Nataliya thought she'd been serious. "In any case," she said, looking at Nataliya again, "we're glad to have you here. I think you'll find most of us are very eager to learn."

Nataliya said nothing. She'd done a fair amount of teaching on *Meridia*, albeit mainly of children, and in her experience it was often the ones who thought they wanted to learn who turned out to be the most inflexible. *Galileo*'s crew needed her— she had no doubt they didn't yet understand how much—but she wasn't going to force knowledge on anyone. Teaching came easily to her, and she'd be able to help those who actually wanted help without compromising her real purpose.

"I'm sorry to rush you," Lockwood said, no hint of apology in her tone, "but we've got to prepare for departure." Like they were a civilian transport to a tourist moon. "Bristol will show you to your quarters."

Bristol stepped forward, his posture stiff and formal, but he was still smiling. This big, disingenuous man liked his job. Nataliya marveled, sometimes, at the variety of people she met in this galaxy.

"Commander." She turned; Foster had taken his eyes off Shaw long enough to remember his manners. "If you need anything that Bristol can't deliver, you let me know."

His eyes on hers still held that irritating gentleness, even in front of Shaw. *Interesting again.* "Thank you, Foster," she said.

A flash of sympathy in his eyes before she turned away and followed Bristol out of the landing bay.

She walked with her guard through the over-bright corridors, ignoring the curious stares of the wandering crew, and wondered if she wasn't suited to the work anymore. She'd considered formal retirement; after sixteen previous missions, she was due. But here, in the aftermath of near-disaster, she felt steady on her feet again. She hadn't planned on turning Foster into her protector. It was remarkable, really; he knew nothing of her except what Captain Taras had told him, and he'd apparently taken all of it at face value. They hadn't told her he was naive. He felt responsible for her, and she had the strong impression it would take a lot on her part to change that. That was the sort of vulnerability she could use.

Her nerves settled, reason reasserting itself. It didn't matter after all that Foster had seen her weakness. It didn't matter that she'd saved him from those children. It didn't matter that she'd passed up an opportunity to let him die.

She'd have plenty of time to kill him herself.

# FOUR

Jessica waited for Bristol and the PSI commander to disappear around the corner, then turned to Greg. "Who the fuck punched you?" she asked.

He gave her a weary smile. "I'm glad you're OK too, Jess."

Dodging, as he always did when he was the one hurt. "You need the infirmary?"

"Yeah, probably."

"Then let's debrief there. after Bob has had a chance to tell you what a jackass you've been. Azevedo!" The lieutenant looked up from the shuttle. "Lock that bird down. We're leaving." She turned without waiting; Azevedo was an irritable bastard, but he knew how to take care of their shuttle fleet. As she walked out of the landing bay, Greg and Elena at her heels, she hit her comm. "Ted, take us out. Three jumps, and then we'll meet *Meridia* at the Third Sector border."

"You don't want to wait for Reed's reply?" Ted asked her.

Jessica felt a twist of anxiety. Tai Reed had been an ally since *Galileo* had left the Corps, but with *Capricorn*'s destruction, Jessica couldn't see how that support could continue. "We don't have time," she said. "We've got to get out of here before Central shows up. Whoever routed that radio message through our comms system painted a big fat target on our backs. With any luck Central's investigation will exonerate us, but we can't afford to assume it'll work out that way."

"Understood."

Moments later, an announcement came over the intercom in *Galileo*'s warm alto voice: "Attention. We are entering the field. Estimated travel time four hours eighteen minutes."

For the first time since *Capricorn* had appeared on their sensors, Jessica took an easy breath.

Six weeks earlier, when they'd resigned from Central Corps and taken their starship with them, none of the crew had known what to expect. Individual soldiers had, from time to rare time, joined PSI, but there had never been a defection this large and this public.

Like most governments, Central Gov depended on the inertia of their people to enforce most of its laws; when the government's own behavior overstepped decency, they generally handled it with a half-assed apology and a quick turning of the page. Harder to do that this time. Gov's most recent self-serving move had ended in the destruction of a major comms relay, the deaths of tens of thousands of people, and the wide exposure of its own cold-blooded strategies. In the face of Gov trying—and largely failing—to nudge the news cycle past their sins, *Galileo* had publicly told them to fuck off. Not a lot of ways they could spin the loss of one of their most prominent ships, so they'd gone directly for slander, painting Greg as a traitor and Jessica as a dangerous rogue.

Jessica had been hoping enough of their former colleagues would continue to trust them. So far, apart from Reed—who had kept her missives scrupulously professional—they had been met with deafening silence.

Central Gov had been in too much disarray for them to discredit *Galileo*'s entire crew by name, but they had aimed a fair amount of public ire at Greg. Which was, on some level, funny as hell, since he was the only one of all of them who'd actually resigned by the book.

But Greg had been Central's standard bearer for a long time: recruited, thanks to his family history, to be a figurehead, but rapidly distinguishing himself as an effective and compassionate commander. He might have made enemies in the Admiralty, but there were a number of colony governments that would probably send him full armies, no questions asked, if he ever said he needed them.

She wondered, for a moment, if everything that had happened on Sochi had been an elaborate plot to take him out. But the timing was too chancy, and he hadn't kept to his schedule. And she couldn't imagine the Admiralty—even the Shadow Ops branch that handled distasteful things like extrajudicial killings—wasting an entire warship and the lives of her crew on Greg Foster.

Greg and Elena were silent throughout their walk, which was always unnerving. The two often communicated without saying much, but complete silence usually meant they were in agreement on some scheme that would eventually be giving Jessica a migraine. Perhaps this time their silence was nothing more than mutual relief at finding the other more or less unhurt.

Bob Hastings, *Galileo*'s chief of medicine, looked up, his blue eyes welcoming, as they walked into the infirmary. Bob was not a young man—somewhere in Jessica's command records was his birthday, which she'd deliberately never had cause to look up— but he was still handsome, his light-skinned face expressive and appealing. Some of that was his curated bedside manner. In real life—especially dealing with recalcitrant crew members—he was as capable of snark as she was.

"Ah, Captain," he said. "What have you brought me this time?"

Jessica stood aside and watched as Bob got a good look at

Greg. The doctor's eyebrows twitched and his lips tightened; only those who knew him well would have seen the deep worry in his eyes.

"What happened to you?" he asked Greg.

Greg gave a resigned sigh. "A bunch of kids jumped me."

"I beg your pardon?" said Jessica.

He met her eyes: embarrassed, angry, wanting to reassure her. "Six teenagers from *Meridia*. They were following me most of the day."

"How the hell did they get the jump on you?"

His gaze shifted to Elena. "I didn't think they wanted to hurt me."

Elena would forgive him that miscalculation. Jessica would have to think about it for a while.

They moved into an exam room, and Greg sat on a table while the doctor ran a series of deep scans. "Can he talk through this?" Jessica asked.

Bob didn't look up from his work. "You think I could shut him up?"

"Okay. Greg, when did you last hear from Gen?"

Greg's face fell into grim lines. They'd all feel like that, Jessica knew, for some time; leaving the Corps hadn't changed their loyalty to the rank and file they'd served with for so long. "Three months ago," he said. "Give or take a few days. Right before they shipped out to the Seventh Sector."

That assignment itself was an oddity. The Admiralty was certainly prone to issuing inexplicable orders, but Jessica couldn't figure out why they'd send a warship on an exploratory to the unpopulated Seventh Sector. "Did she mention the mission?"

He nodded. "She was annoyed. They'd already been out too long, and she was complaining about being sent on an exploratory instead of the crew being given a break. She'd been told it was a reward of some kind, which seemed like bullshit. And she said 'If it wasn't for fucking Anaxis we'd be drinking at an Aleph instead of being thrown at some random pack of nothing in the Seventh.'"

Elena spoke up. "I thought most of *Capricorn*'s mission data was proprietary."

"It is," he said. "She shouldn't have said it. And she didn't refer to it again. I figured her carelessness meant she was really, really tense, and for once the Admiralty was right to push light duty on *Capricorn*'s crew."

They were all silent, the only sound Bob's scanner. And then Elena said: "Interesting that it was Anaxis."

Jessica had been thinking the same thing.

Anaxis Colony was one of humanity's success stories. Established centuries earlier on a Second Sector world that had needed very little terraforming, the resource-rich colony had quickly become self-sufficient. The settlers had also decided they weren't interested in outsiders, and had, for generations, blocked nearly all interaction with the rest of colonized space.

There was no tourism to Anaxis, and no immigration. Every decade or so someone moved away, but they never spoke of their home. To Jessica, it seemed almost a religious conviction, a need to safeguard the place from the corrupting outside galaxy.

Anaxis was strongly focused on education, and there had been rumors they were taking money from Shadow Ops for clandestine research. Despite the lack of hard evidence, Jessica had always assumed the rumor was true, that such an insular colony would be the most logical place to perform research the Corps wanted kept secret.

Still, nobody had thought much about Anaxis until recently. Cross-sector comms were still coming back on line after a terrorist incident some weeks earlier had disrupted communications, but most colonies had checked in by now. One of a small number of holdouts was Anaxis, still stubbornly silent. Jessica hadn't found that significant, but now she felt deeply uneasy.

Insular or not, Anaxis held three million people. That was a lot of people to lose track of.

Greg's thoughts seemed to be paralleling hers. "Why," he said, half to himself, "would they send a warship to Anaxis?"

None of them had an answer for that.

Bob straightened, finished with his scan. "I've repaired most of the bruises," he told Greg, "but you're going to have some spectacular color on your lower back and your jaw for a day or two. I've knitted two ribs as well, so take it easy until you can stretch your arms straight up without feeling any pain. At all," he emphasized sternly.

"No concussion?" Greg seemed surprised.

"No concussion," Bob confirmed. "And don't think you're not damn lucky for that. De-escalate next time, soldier. Don't let a bunch of kids beat you to death."

*Impudent*, Jessica thought; but Greg, who knew how much Bob cared for him, just smiled. "Understood, Doc. I'll try to behave." He slid off the table.

"You always try," Bob grumbled, as the three of them left the infirmary, "but none of you ever succeed."

Tai Reed's message didn't arrive until *Galileo* had dropped out of the field, taking a tense hour in normal space to charge batteries before heading back in.

Comms could find a ship in the field, but Reed didn't communicate with Jessica over comms. She sent messages via an off-grid transceiver, one of those illegal but ubiquitous devices most people living on starships kept tucked in a dust-covered corner. Off-grids offered a slow but effective way to send untraceable messages, and although Reed had been careful not to violate regulations by what she said to Jessica, she hadn't sent an open comms message since *Galileo*'s defection had been publicized.

Jessica's off-grid took several minutes to accept Reed's prerecorded message. The audio section was small, accompanied by a massive amount of encoded data.

"Sorry, Jess," Reed said, sounding harried. "It's madness here right now, as you might expect. I've sent you the contents of *Capricorn*'s flight recorder. Most of it's probably useless bullshit, but I wanted you to get it fast. Because you're going to want to get the hell out of here. I don't know what the fuck happened, but I'm guessing someone at the Admiralty does, because they're already making statements to make it look like *Galileo*'s fault. That comm Greg got? Half of them are saying you faked it, the other half are saying it means you're in it up to your eyeballs. But you'll want to take a look at the engineering data, Jess, because from what I could see in the three seconds I had to look? You are not responsible for any of it."

Jessica sent the flight recorder data directly to Elena.

"There's more than that." Reed fell silent for a moment, and Jessica tensed; *Arizona*'s captain wasn't prone to drama. "Jessica, Anaxis Colony has been destroyed. Nuked. The whole place is irradiated; we can't even get close. Three million people." Reed took a breath. "It's not public yet, but it will be, probably somewhere in the next two or three days. The other thing that'll go public is that *Capricorn* was the last Corps ship to visit. I've seen their official reports, and they claim the place was fine when they left. That was also weeks before sector comms went out, so maybe we can take their word on that."

*Interesting that it was Anaxis*, Elena had said.

*Three million people.*

"As for why *Capricorn* was sent to the Seventh? Captain Niemann's logs are in the flight recorder dump, but unsurprisingly he was pretty circumspect. Their mission was officially an exploratory, to allow the crew some downtime, and while he implies there was more to it, it sure doesn't sound like it was a combat mission. Their destination was something code named Target Zero, but there's nothing in the official record to indicate that's more than just a set of random coordinates."

*Get zero*, Gen had said. *Target Zero*. Definitely more than just a set of random coordinates.

"The Admiralty is going full spin on this," Reed said, steadier. "Internally, they're looking at Ellis Systems. Always easiest to blame your own former weapons contractor, isn't it?. But they'll overload the public with irrelevant data until they can figure out for sure what happened. *Galileo* is likely to be part of that irrelevant data. They're not going to stop coming after you, Jess. You guys need to bug out, and fast. And if I were advising you on where...I might suggest you head out past the comms network. Maybe into the Seventh. Because maybe there was a reason *Capricorn* was sent out there that nobody else knows about. Maybe even, I don't know, some evidence that the place isn't quite as empty as we've all assumed."

The hair on the back of Jessica's neck stood up.

"Anyway. If you guys disappear for a while, they may slander you but they won't waste too much time on your tail. But when you come back, Captain Lockwood—you better have something in hand. Because even if the facts exonerate you, soldiers aren't going to forget they were told you murdered their comrades. Take care of yourselves." The message ended.

Jessica's first thought was of the crew. They'd become accustomed to news of mass destruction, but that wouldn't make any of this easier to hear.

Her second thought was that it was going to take some doing to make sense of everything Reed had just thrown at her.

She commed Elena. "Hey," she said, aware she sounded deflated, "any chance you can give me an estimate on slogging through that data dump?"

"Of course," Elena said. "I've already—Jess. Are you okay?"

Sometimes Jessica wished for less perceptive friends. She told Elena about Anaxis, and her friend swore.

"Three million. That makes Athena Relay look like a traffic accident."

"I'd prefer to give a single, comprehensive briefing to the rest of the crew," Jessica said, "but I don't want to sit on this too long."

"I've got some preliminary data compiled," Elena told her, "but backup detail is going to take a while. You may want to pull them together now, Jessie, because this—have you looked at this data yet?"

Jessica's stomach dropped. "I haven't had a chance. What are you seeing?"

"We didn't destroy them."

"Yeah, Reed already told me that. I knew we hadn't, Lanie. I told you—"

"I *know*, Jess." Impatience; she didn't want Jessica's psychological coddling right now. "We didn't destroy them, Jessie. But it wasn't an accident, either. It's all there in the engine room data, in the replay before the explosion. There's no other answer. *Capricorn* was sabotaged."

# FIVE



"THIS IS THE official Admiralty schematic of *Capricorn*'s engine config."

Elena shifted before the assembled pub crowd, leaning heavily on her cane. Projected next to her, rendered in a monochrome weave of lines and symbols, was a mechanical diagram of an entirely ordinary Corps starship engine room. Greg had been mildly surprised when Elena showed him the night before; *Capricorn* was a warship, and he'd expected the ship's design to be somehow more streamlined, more belligerent than *Galileo*'s. She'd given him one of her looks at the word "belligerent"; she had never much cared for applying subjective motivations to machines.

But she'd said nothing, not even to tease him, and he'd known then what she'd found was serious.

"And this," she added, pulling up a second render next to the first, "is what was captured on her flight recorder forty seconds before she went up."

Greg didn't think he'd ever heard the pub so quiet.

Jessica had notified the crew the afternoon before about the destruction of Anaxis, promising them a fuller account of *Capricorn*'s demise in the morning. Greg had been up with Elena most of the night, doing little more than listening, as she pored over *Capricorn*'s flight recorder data and made increasingly outraged sense of it.

As a former starship captain, Greg had fairly in-depth knowledge of mechanical engineering, but it didn't rival Elena's, who'd been studying since she was a child. When she'd shown him the render of the inverted connections and power loops that had caused *Capricorn*'s inevitable destruction, the process made sense, but he hadn't understood why her rage seemed so personal. She'd paced their room, fuming, explaining to him the level of skill that had been required to modify the ship the way it had been done: the time, the care, the subtlety that had allowed the saboteur to perform what she classified as at least three solid days of work without detection.

When he'd realized she was furious in part because the damage had been inflicted by an extremely good mechanic, he'd almost laughed. She was proud of her profession, and malice was the only crime she would recognize as worse than incompetence. But this malice had caused the destruction of *Capricorn* and the deaths of all sixty-seven of her crew. Even though Elena had to be relieved she wasn't at fault, she'd be feeling some sense of professional responsibility all the same.

The pub was almost at capacity, holding 150 of *Galileo*'s 167 crew members, and the two PSI emissaries. Nataliya Gritsenko and her colleague, Nikolai Petrikoff, sat by a window, setting themselves apart from the rest. Petrikoff, who'd been sent as a hand-to-hand trainer, had managed to make some friends, and Greg had heard reports he was a good-natured and effective teacher. Here, he'd arranged his features into something marginally genial, but Greg thought that was performance. The man was listening intently to Elena, but something in the set of his shoulders led Greg to believe he was angry, nearly as angry as Elena had been overnight.

He couldn't quite believe Petrikoff was angry about the loss of a Central Corps warship.

Next to Petrikoff, Nat sat with a polite, unreadable mask. She looked attentive but relaxed; had she been on her own, without Petrikoff's tense form next to her, she'd have faded into the crowd. Instinctive, Greg suspected; most people couldn't be taught how to be unobtrusive. Or perhaps they could, and it was only his own failed attempts that made him believe the ability to blend was innate.

"To be clear about what happened," Elena went on, waving away the original schematic, "the chain reaction started when *Capricorn* turned to take aim at *Galileo,* before we shot off their forward turrets." The flight recorder data began to animate: the ship's central drive turned red, and around it, the auxiliary drives began to glow. "Disabling their weapons triggered noth-ing." Across the schematic, spots of orange and red appeared: the battery power distribution system. "We couldn't have stopped what happened to them," she said, and no one listening could have escaped the sorrow in her voice. "All we stopped was us going up with them."

"Then it was sabotage," said a voice in the audience.

Elena glanced briefly at Jessica, who was standing at the end of the bar, then nodded. "That's the most logical conclusion," she said. "Which means we're not only dealing with something that managed to throw a starship halfway across the known galaxy undetected, but also was able to thoroughly—and some-what delicately—sabotage a Corps warship staffed by sixty-seven experienced infantry and intelligence officers."

"But this exonerates us, doesn't it?"

Jessica moved next to Elena to answer. "It should," she told the crew. "But we don't have any way of knowing just now whether Central's desire to pin something concrete on us is stronger than their desire to tell the truth."

There was a murmur at her words. Everyone was remembering why they'd left Central to begin with: in too many recent cases, Central had chosen political expediency over truth, even when it cost lives.

Elena shifted, and immediately the room fell silent again. "What's more interesting to me, as a mechanic," she said, "is that this work would have taken a while. It's easy to blow yourself up if you fuck around with a starship engine, but sabotage like this, with both a damage trigger and a proximity trigger, so the rest of the ship operates normally and the crew detects nothing? That requires tremendous care, and it couldn't have remained undetected for long. So we can assume the sabotage happened during their current mission."

"It could have been done piecemeal." That came from Nat.

"Unless we assume the crew was plotting their own destruction," Elena said, "they couldn't have started before they left. A configuration change like this would have been flagged automatically with Central. They never would have been allowed to leave the Six Sectors.

"There's also this."

She waved a hand, and the schematic was overlayed with colored spheres: green, orange, pockets of red. "This is from Sochi Station's surface analysis of the ship. The color indicates the degree of radiation damage. Given that they were only out seven weeks, they must have encountered something unusual; not especially surprising, given nobody's spent much time in the Seventh. But as you all can see, these readings are coarse; beyond 'wow, that's bad,' there's not a lot we can deduce from this.

"Here's the data we got from the full flight recorder dump we received from Captain Reed."

The schematic changed, and a collective gasp filled the room.

The idea that space was empty was one of the first of which all students of space flight were disabused. Although space held, in aggregate, few solid objects, those present produced significant particulate hazards: gasses and nebulas, unstable stars, black holes, wormholes, and pulsars exerting gravitational influences in subtle—and unsubtle—ways. But by far the most dangerous invisible hazard of space was radiation, flying everywhere, oblivious to the molecular makeup of whatever was before it. Spewed by nearly everything, it had been the most persistent impediment to human space travel for centuries. In the last sixty years the deflection systems used on most interstellar vehicles had been standardized, but the systems required regular monitoring. The Corps had enforced six month inspections for their fleet, with mandatory shielding replacement every two years. *Galileo* had been refitted just eight months ago; *Capricorn*'s shielding had been new.

But even if *Capricorn*'s shielding had been at the end of its effective lifespan, the damage it had sustained would have been inexplicable.

Instead of the amorphous blobs of red and orange provided by Sochi's limited commercial scanners, the flight recorder data showed scattered dots of everything from flame to deep black. Near complete hull penetration, all across the ship—habitats, engine room, storage, every protected space.

"In all my years as a mechanic," Elena said, "the closest I've seen to this kind of damage was on a civilian moon hopper, run by a budget tourist company that didn't have the money to update their fleet. They'd gone twelve years without replacing the shielding; they'd only brought it in for repair when one of their paying passengers smuggled on a dosimeter and streamed the results. This level of damage after only six weeks suggests a concentration of gamma radiation you'd only get if you sat right on top of a pulsar. Or," she added, answering the question before it was asked, "if the ship ran into some other source of sustained radiation."

The crowd rippled restlessly, and Jessica stepped in again. "This *could* have been caused by a natural phenomenon," the captain said, "although we haven't detected anything like that in the Seventh. It's possible our uncrewed probes just missed it, but given *Capricorn*'s trajectory, that's unlikely. We have to consider the possibility that this Target Zero referred to in *Capricorn*'s logs is the source of the damage, and prepare accordingly. *Galileo*'s shielding was replaced a little more than half a year ago, but we're going to ask everyone to turn on personal gamma detection, and report anomalies immediately. Don't be shy if you see something unusual."

*If it's a weapon,* Elena had told Greg overnight, *it likely already knows how to bypass our shielding. What we really need is some kind of proactive defense.*

Mechanics, Greg reflected, had so many euphemisms for *just blow it the fuck up.*

Elena took over again. "Captain Reed tells us the Admiralty is mumbling about Ellis Systems, given their track record sabotaging commonly-used hardware." More murmurs from the audience; Ellis was a commercial terraformer outfit that had recently been exposed as a major covert weapons developer, and nearly everybody on *Galileo*'s crew held some kind of personal grudge. "But if we go by capability? The Corps' own Shadow Ops could also have pulled off something like this. With the Admiralty in damage control mode, it's more politically convenient for them to blame us, even if they think Ellis is responsible, but especially if they did it themselves. But none of this explains how *Capricorn* came out of nowhere. Literally." Next to the schematic appeared an animation of *Capricorn* appearing, with no signs of a transport medium, in a vacant area of space. "As far as we know, Shadow Ops hasn't been working on anything like this. Ellis might have been, but not even their most recently exposed research is related to this kind of untraceable travel." The animation faded. "Whether or not *Capricorn*'s fate is due to whatever this Target Zero is, we need to be very careful about our assumptions."

She fielded questions with her usual professional aplomb. Most of the crew seemed to have taken in the mission briefing with the same equanimity they always did, although a few were gathered in small groups, looking worried. That was all right, Greg supposed. Madness not to worry out here, all the time.

His eyes lit on Nat, who was listening to Nikolai Petrikoff and looking far less like wallpaper than she had at the start of Elena's lecture. She had her hands over her elbows; he thought for a moment she was staring at Petrikoff, but as the man kept talking Greg realized she was focused on something to the right of his head. Petrikoff seemed to realize that, too; his voice grew louder and angrier, although Greg still couldn't make out the words. After a few moments Nat came out of whatever worried daydream she'd conjured and dropped her arms to her sides. She said something brief to Petrikoff that made him redden and fall silent, and stalked across the room toward Greg.

"Does he want to go back to *Meridia*?" Greg asked as she approached.

"It's not his call," she told him. "I'm senior officer here."

Greg wondered why she'd want to keep him if he was going to resist the mission entirely. "What's he worried about?"

She met his eyes with a sharp look, reminding him she was a commander on board *Meridia*. "Is that a serious question?" Her tone dripped with incredulity. "You lot don't have a terrific track record dealing with sabotage, do you?"

Ah, *there* it was. He'd wondered how long it would take her to get past the bond they'd briefly forged on Sochi. "You mean *Chryse*."

*Chryse* had been *Meridia*'s sister ship for years. Centuries.

Her recent destruction had hit everyone hard, but *Meridia*'s crew the hardest.

"It's difficult," Nat told him, "to take a briefing like this at face value when we still don't know what happened there."

They did know. They all knew. He'd told everyone he could, over and over, how the PSI starship had been lost, even knowing how unbelievable it sounded. Sabotage, no matter how perfidious, was so much easier for people to believe than a long-established and yet somehow concealed alien intelligence running a starship; he wouldn't have believed it himself if he hadn't seen it first hand.

He'd have thought Nat would have approached the issue with an eye toward facts, but he supposed, given everything else, it wasn't particularly surprising she tended toward denialism.

"We don't have the data to reconstruct what happened to *Chryse* at any deep level, no," he agreed, keeping his tone neutral. She turned away, lips tightening, and he let it go. "Commander. You've chosen to stay on this mission with us. I can assure you, Captain Lockwood would want you to share your concerns."

Nat moved to grasp her elbows again, then flexed her fingers and dropped her arms to her sides. "My concerns aren't the same as Nikolai's," she said. "You people haven't known him that long. No matter how good a trainer he is, he's ultimately a coward. He's worried about his own skin. *Chryse*'s fate is an excuse for him."

"If that's what you think of him," he asked her, genuinely curious, "why is he here?"

She met his eyes again, and for one moment her face was flooded with raw hostility. *Angry.* He had a fleeting moment to wonder if that anger was always so close to the surface before she composed herself again. "He volunteered for this mission," she told him. "Just like I did."

He held her gaze for a moment, wondering if she'd blink, but she just watched him steadily. Not like Caroline after all. His wife had hated it when he'd go still like that, and after a few seconds would have either picked a fight or walked away. Nat's entire expression had grown opaque, erasing all traces of her earlier irritation. Wallpaper again. She could use a little more control over that particular skill, but perhaps she'd never needed it for more than a few minutes at a time.

"I'll talk to him," he suggested. "Sometimes people just need information."

At that, Nat's eyes dropped closed, and her jaw set. "No. That's not a good idea. Nikolai is—"

"What is it I am, Nataliya?"

Petrikoff's approach had been silent. His tone was conversational, but he wasn't looking at Nat at all. Instead he was looking at Greg, his expression cordial apart from a hardness in his dark eyes. Some people just looked like that, but Greg didn't think for a moment Petrikoff didn't know how he came across.

Nat allowed herself a polite smile, but she'd gone blotchy. "I told you, Nikolai," she said, with friendliness that was almost convincing, "I would handle this."

"Nonsense." Petrikoff smiled as well, never taking his eyes off Greg's. "There's nothing to handle. I simply want to have a candid conversation with this ship's command."

"He's not in command anymore."

Greg turned; Elena had come up behind him, as soundless as Petrikoff. She was still in professional mode, focused and alert; she liked fielding technical questions, even when she didn't immediately know the answers. *Machines are solid*, she'd told him over and over again. *Predictable. People a fucking mess.*

"That's right." Petrikoff kept watching Greg. "You're the one who left your crew in the middle of a mission. An interesting choice for a beloved commander."

Strange, how people from both sides of his former life seemed to think he ought to feel some guilt for what he'd done. Central had been open about it, the Admiralty disclaiming him at every opportunity—which, given the press coverage of *Galileo*'s collective resignation, meant fairly often. He'd been surprised to find people from PSI who felt similarly: that for them the sin of resigning his commission was somehow more severe than the sin of having been part of the Corps to begin with.

"If you'd rather address your issues with Captain Lockwood," Greg said, "I'm sure she'd make time for you."

Petrikoff's eyebrows twitched. More easily annoyed than Nat. "Until Captain Lockwood can clear her calendar," Petrikoff snapped, "maybe you know enough to tell me why you're endangering this ship and this crew with what's very obviously a trap."

Elena spoke up before Greg could answer. "And maybe *you* should remember that we know these people, and we know the ways they lay their traps." She was still cordial, but her tone had grown subtly shorter.

"If you're concerned," Greg added smoothly, "I'm sure we can arrange for you to be transferred back to *Meridia* before we clear the Fourth Sector comms grid."

Petrikoff had a darker complexion than Nat did, but when he reddened it was just as dramatic, the flush starting at his ears and washing over his entire face. "My concern is not for my own safety," he said stiffly, but he couldn't make it sound convincing. "It's simply...*interesting* to me that you should endanger both ship and crew, so soon after your other failures."

"That's enough, Commander," Nat said, but her authoritarian tone, so effective on teenagers, had no effect on Petrikoff.

"*Capricorn*, and *Chryse* before her. Oh, and that relay. And the research lab, Indus Station."

Greg felt Elena stiffen next to him.

"Your Corps has shown nothing but incompetence, and tens of thousands of people have died." He gestured back at Elena's schematic, still hovering over the bar, spheres of deep, destructive red obscuring nearly all of it. "I'm not a mechanic, but I know what I'm looking at. That doesn't happen, unless someone at your shipyards sabotaged that ship, and her crew was too stupid to find the problem."

"That's the point." Elena was close to losing her temper now. "What happened to them is unprecedented, and we have to—"

"—fabricate some explanation so your people can hide their incompetence?" His derision was open now. "Don't sling bullshit, woman. We don't know what happened to *Chryse*, but we know for sure you'll lie about it to save yourselves."

Greg took his eyes off Petrikoff long enough to catch the flash in Elena's eyes. "The only bullshit here, Commander Petrikoff," she said, "is the idea that *you* somehow miraculously know better than a hundred and sixty-seven people who were there when it happened, as well as *your own captain*." Her voice was still low and even, but her knuckles whitened over the handle of her cane. "You want to play conspiracy theories, do your damn homework first. Nobody here has time for this."

Petrikoff was undaunted. "Maybe they should make time," he said. "Maybe they should be reminded that the last time anyone was supposed to take the word of this ship's command on faith, nine hundred people died."

"Petrikoff," Nat tried sternly, but Elena spoke over her.

"Nine hundred on *Chryse*," she said, her voice steely. "Ten thousand on Athena Relay, tens of thousands on Earth, a dozen on Indus Station. And three million on Anaxis." She straightened, just a little, and with some satisfaction Greg saw Petrikoff flinch. "It's not about you, you under-educated, over-suspicious, unobservant blockhead. Stick with teaching people how to punch, and leave the politics to those of us who actually pay attention."

Greg thought later it was the last sentence that had done it, although Petrikoff had been visibly annoyed by *blockhead*. But she'd given him an opening, and he took it.

"Why should I trust people who can't even see what's in front of their faces?" He'd grown louder; people around them had quieted to listen. "Only a blockhead would believe *Chryse* was destroyed by accident. Only a blockhead would believe *Chryse* was helmed by some *program*, not a captain at all." He took a breath, and Greg knew what was coming. "We all know *he's* the one who destroyed *Chryse*, and you're all covering for him."

He was pointing at Greg, and the room had grown very quiet.

Elena inhaled, but it was Nat who intervened, stepping in front of Petrikoff. "That is enough, Commander," she said, her voice as loud as his. "You'll return to our quarters, and we'll discuss this there."

Petrikoff shot her a glare, and for a moment Greg thought she'd won the argument. But when Petrikoff spoke, there was nothing in his tone but contempt. "You've always been blood-less, Nataliya," he said, his voice lower. "I imagine that's why Taras has always kept you as a pet. We had family there, or don't you remember? We had family there, and *he* just left them to die."

All the color drained from Nat's face. Her hands clenched into fists, and for an instant something radiated from her, like electricity, like flame, and every cell in his body told him Petrikoff was in danger, Elena was in danger, he was in danger, and nothing he had seen of Nataliya Gritsenko before this moment had been reality.

"That's enough!" Jessica's voice filled the whole room, and just like that all Nat's electricity was gone, and she was ordinary again. "Petrikoff. You want to know what happened with *Chryse*? Our logs are open to you." Petrikoff was still glaring at Nat, but he cooled, just a little. "Captain Taras has all the same data, and if you think she just took our word for it you're a bigger fool than Elena thinks you are."

Astonishingly, the line provoked a few snickers, and more of the static faded from the air.

"There's been too much tragedy lately." A touch of gentleness, an acknowledgement of stress. "We've got a mission to do. You work out your bullshit on your own time. Is that understood?"

"Yes, Captain." Nat answered her; Petrikoff remained silent.

"Good." Jessica smiled, that dazzling, slightly feral smile that always reminded Greg the woman missed absolutely nothing. "If you'd like to talk now, Commander, I have a few minutes."

Petrikoff swallowed; to his credit, he seemed finally to be reining in his temper. "Thank you, Captain," he said, as if the altercation had never happened. "Perhaps another time."

"As you wish." She raised her voice again so she could be heard into the corners of the silent room. "Let's get back to it, people; we've got a lot to do before we get on *Capricorn*'s trail." She turned back toward the bar, and the crowd of people waiting for her attention.

Petrikoff watched her walk away. "It seems," he said conversationally, "you are not short of tiny women leaping to your defense."

Greg would not, even on a bet, have referred to Jessica as *tiny*. "I have good friends," he said.

When Petrikoff turned back, he only had eyes for Nat. "You," he said, the snarl back in his voice, "are a *traitor*. You'd best keep kissing his ass, because when this gets back to *Meridia*, you're going to have no one to leap to your defense at all." He turned and stalked out of the pub.

"Ass," Elena remarked dismissively, and turned to follow Jessica back to the bar.

Greg was still watching Elena walk away when Nat spoke up. "I did try to tell you."

Had she? "It's not the first I've heard of those allegations," he told her. Elena was gesturing at the schematic again; it lifted his heart, despite the last twenty-four hours, to see her, at least in public, so close to what she'd been before her mission at Indus. "I'm not concerned about Petrikoff."

Nat was silent for so long he thought she might not respond at all. It wasn't until she said "Maybe you should be," and stalked out of the room after Petrikoff, that it occurred to him she might have been trying to tell him more than he'd managed to hear.

# SIX

"JUST WHAT EXACTLY did you think you were doing?"

Petrikoff had been sitting at the table when Nataliya walked in to their quarters' shared living room. A tactical error on his part, although she'd learned years ago Petrikoff didn't approach interactions tactically. Petrikoff was an emotional thinker, and his lack of discipline had been abetted all his life by his easy, if shallow, charm. Most people—even on *Meridia*—overlooked his foul temper and utter inability to keep his mouth shut.

She'd suggested him to Captain Taras because she believed his volatility could be an asset to her. She still believed it, but she was going to have to make sure he understood who was really in charge.

He glared at her over a nearly empty glass of whiskey. "I was doing my duty," he snapped. Angry, still, and far drunker than he could have managed in the moments they'd been apart. He'd been drinking during Shaw's briefing, although she'd underestimated how much. Not that she could blame him for that. The only thing more astonishing than the layers of bullshit in that briefing had been Lockwood's crew apparently believing all of it.

"You're lucky Shaw didn't take a swing at you," Nataliya said.

She walked past him to the liquor cabinet. She didn't care much for alcohol, but learning to drink—to be drunk —had been part of her training, and she always traveled with the best liquor she could find. Picking up a square glass—heavy, and decent quality; the Corps hadn't skimped when they'd outfitted this ship—she poured herself a large measure of smoky whiskey and downed it in one gulp.

"I think I can handle a *cripple*, Nataliya."

*Arrogant bastard.* "You can't even handle a *conversation*, Nikolai."

She kept her eyes on the glass, listening to Petrikoff struggle to his feet. "You stood there and let him slander us!" he shouted. "What do you think Captain Taras is going to think of that?"

"Captain Taras," she said evenly, "has no idea what we're really doing here." She turned to face him: he was swaying a little on his feet. "Sit down, Commander Petrikoff," she told him. "Thanks to you and your toddler's temper, we have damage control to do."

Nataliya took a sip of her drink, and waited. After a moment Petrikoff lowered himself back into his chair.

"I think you've forgotten why we came here, Nikolai," she said. His lips tightened, but he didn't interrupt her. "We're here to *observe*, remember? To gather evidence. I have memories of conversations you and I had. Some very long, very detailed conversations. Have you drunk so much of their liquor that your memory has failed you?"

"Shaw was spouting nonsense," he said, but more calmly than before. "And Foster after her. Every word of it. Every bit of that story they tell about *Chryse* is a lie, and we're supposed to sit here and get drawn into an uncharted sector that's already destroyed a fucking *warship* and not ask any questions?"

"We all lost people on *Chryse*." She hated allowing him grief. Nikolai hadn't lost more than a few casual friends. He hadn't lost family. "And that 'bullshit story' you keep carping about has convinced most of *Meridia*'s crew, including Taras. So how far did you think you were going to get picking a fight with a Corps-trained former starship captain *in front of his own people?*"

"What, as opposed to batting my eyelashes at him and playing helpless?"

A flare of anger in her gut; she was certain her face didn't betray it, but the intensity startled her. Foster had upset her equilibrium worse than she'd thought. "He trusts me," she said simply. "Or he did, before you fucked everything up."

"And what does that get you? Did you see his crew? They trust him, too. They believe every word he says, no matter how absurd. The idea that *Chryse* could just...*die* like that? We know what the Corps is capable of, and that man is Corps to his corpuscles. Why do you think he hasn't taken the Oath?"

Which was a curious question indeed; the Oath would, at the very least, have provided Foster some cover. "That doesn't matter," she said bluntly. "Nothing about Foster matters. Taras trusts him, and the two of us aren't going to talk her out of that. We need evidence of a different sort than what you can insult out of Greg Foster when you've had *too fucking much to drink.*"

Petrikoff looked up at her. He hated looking up at people, and she took some small satisfaction in that. "He is a liar," he said, more steadily than she would have thought. "He will destroy *Meridia* if we let him."

"That's why we're not going to let him." It was the only part of her private plan that overlapped with the one she shared with Nikolai. "But if we're going to stop him, we need to get Taras to withdraw from *Galileo*. And to do that—" She put down her glass and flattened her hands on the table, looming over Petrikoff—"we need *evidence*, not dick-measuring. You want to air out your personal manhood issues? Knock yourself out. But don't bring PSI into it, and leave Foster the fuck alone."

Petrikoff's face reddened, and if the look in his eyes had been attached to a weapons system, he'd have blown a hole straight through her and this ship's over-engineered hull. She stared back at him, ignoring his hate, his rage, all the emotions she shared and had carefully compartmentalized.

After nearly a minute, the red in his face faded, and she caught a hint of chagrin. His jaw set, and with an effort she almost admired he said, "You're right."

"Damn fucking straight I'm right." She picked up her glass, then sat down at the table. Her point was made; they were equals again. "I'll talk with Foster," she said, "and smooth things over. I'll find out how to regain Lockwood's trust. And once I've done that? Will we fuck up again, Nikolai?"

"I said you were right, Nataliya. Don't push it."

Nataliya allowed herself a smile. Petrikoff stood to head for the bar. "Will your fancy whiskey kill me, Commander?" he asked her.

"Not unless you drink it faster than I do," she said, and at last Petrikoff laughed.

They talked, then, the way they had before they'd left *Meridia*, of the sort of evidence they'd need to convince Taras an alliance with this former Corps starship, this tarnished star running with a target on her back, was too dangerous. They spoke of *Chryse*, and what might really have happened to her; they spoke of Bayandi, *Chryse*'s old captain, and the senility that must have contributed to his ship's demise, that still led some to insist he hadn't been human at all. They arrived at the same strategy they'd had before Petrikoff had tossed a wrench into their polite fact-finding: introduce doubt into Taras' thinking, just enough for her to recognize the need for PSI to distance itself from this pack of treasonous renegades. It mattered, critically; even with PSI's distributed nature, poor judgement by a ship as venerable as *Meridia* would sow uncertainty in ways none of them could afford just now, with Central Gov corroding before their eyes.

Nataliya pretended to care, and thought about how she was going to keep Petrikoff from fucking everything up.

*Galileo* told her Foster was in the machine room, but when she arrived, all she found was a handful of desperately young junior officers, and Commander Shaw.

Not the angle Nataliya had intended to explore right away, but she'd take what she could get.

She watched as Shaw instructed the younger officers on the team's tasks, which seemed to have something to do with drive security and radiation detection. Precautionary measures, then, for this absurd mission—all designed, if they had any brains, to detect traps set by the very people who were chasing them out here. Shaw spoke quickly, but from the way the others were watching her, her explanations were clear and thorough. Occasionally she fielded a question with the same quick, dispassionate tone; at one point one of the ensigns smiled, and the others laughed. *Interesting.* Nataliya's slim dossier on Shaw had indicated the woman was notoriously impatient. Apparently whoever had compiled the information hadn't been keen on nuance.

At one point Shaw looked over and met her eyes; the mechanic raised one finger and turned back to her charges, wrapping up her lecture. The younger people dissipated, and Shaw turned to face Nataliya. She didn't approach; she was standing without her cane, and Nataliya suspected that hindered the woman's movement more than she liked to let on.

Nataliya moved closer so she could speak without the junior officers overhearing. "I'm here to apologize for Nikolai," she said.

Shaw's expression remained polite, but she tilted her head, just a little, to one side. "Is that something he's authorized you to do?"

There was no challenge in Shaw's voice, but Nataliya felt herself bristling anyway. "Given that I'm the senior officer of our delegation," she said, "I don't think I need his authorization."

For a moment, Shaw watched her, unmoving and silent. Then she turned away, walking—steadily enough, but slowly— to a central console, where *Capricorn*'s schematic was on display next to a similar map of *Galileo*. "Don't be concerned about it," Shaw said, which wasn't quite the same as accepting the apology. "There are plenty of boors in the Corps. I can assure you, I've dealt with far more adept hecklers than Petrikoff."

*Heckler.* Petrikoff would hate that. Nataliya wasn't particularly keen on it herself. "He expressed his concerns badly," Nataliya said, and heard the stiffness in her own voice.

"His concerns are based on lies." Shaw zoomed in on one of *Galileo*'s utility crawlspaces, carrying on with her work as if Nataliya were utterly irrelevant. "But none of that matters now. This is a different mission, and as poorly defined as it is, we're talking about either a power-hungry corporation, or a power-hungry military hierarchy. There's no reason to believe alien software is going to play into any of this."

Nataliya could feel the heat flood her face. "There's no reason to believe alien software played into *Chryse*, either," she said, hating the irritation in her voice.

Shaw stilled, her eyes on the diagram. "There's such wonder in the universe," she said quietly. "None of it looks real, not from the outside. Sometimes not from the inside, either." She looked over, and for a moment Shaw's gaze seemed to laser directly into Nataliya's skull. "He's not a liar," the mechanic said. "Not even when the truth is hard for people to hear. You're an observant person, Commander Gritsenko, or so it's said. Don't let your own biases prevent you from observing."

Answering a question Nataliya had not asked. Viktor had done that to her, too. Perhaps that was what had drawn Foster, all gladhanding diplomacy and facile good looks, to this blunt, businesslike woman.

"I'll leave you to your work, Commander Shaw," Nataliya said. She wanted to sound cool, even a little threatening. Instead she sounded petty. Maybe even jealous, which wouldn't be the worst impression to leave; but unintended, it grated on her.

"Thank you, Commander," Shaw said, turning back to her work. "I'll let Greg know you came looking for him."

Effectively dismissed, Nataliya turned and left the cavernous room.

# SEVEN

Three days after Elena's briefing, after *Galileo* had cleared Hemera Relay and entered the Seventh Sector, they found *Capricorn*'s comms booster.

*Galileo* had weathered long-range comms outages before, but this time, at least, the crew had been able to plan in advance. They'd batched up messages home, quietly filed wills, and pulled off the stream as much entertainment as they could store. Elena had sent a brief, factual message to her mother, but had done nothing else; for entertainment she preferred rereading books she already knew, and she hadn't had cause to change her will in some years.

But there was nothing quite like comms silence, like the knowledge they couldn't contact anyone off-ship even if they needed to. It unsettled people, Elena included. It felt like an incipient attack, even without a concrete threat.

After three days of isolation, finding the broken comms booster felt like a reprieve.

The device itself, of course, presented a number of mysteries. For one thing, it was intact, and as far as their long-range scans could detect, undamaged. Given the absence of any updates from *Capricorn* after her reported entry into the Seventh, Elena had expected to find the relay a ruin at best, blasted to cobwebs by the same elevated gamma that had damaged *Capricorn*; at worst, she'd expected nothing but debris. But the booster was apparently whole but inert, which left them with a puzzle. Boosters were simple pieces of hardware, designed to amplify traffic and forward it to the next relay. It had few parts that could break, even in the cold, radiation-filled expanse of the Seventh Sector. And yet according to *Capricorn*'s flight recorder, it had failed less than twenty-four hours after it was deployed.

After hours of study, Elena and Ted pulled Jessica in to the machine room for a briefing.

"It's drifted from where they placed it," Elena told her captain, superimposing *Capricorn*'s records over their live scans. "But not a lot. If I had to posit a theory—and I really shouldn't— I'd say the drift and spin is exactly what we'd expect to see if it had been contacted by a repair drone."

"If it's been repaired," Jessica asked, "why aren't we getting anything off it but low-power and thermal?"

"Maybe the drone couldn't finish the repair," Ted suggested. "Their flight recorder shows the drone being sent out. It doesn't show it returning."

"And we can't figure out how it's broken?"

"The repair drone may have had exactly the same problem," Elena said. "We should be able to find out from the relay itself. Even the basic ones store a rudimentary audit trail."

Jessica stared at the relay schematic, the image of the booster spinning slowly. "*Galileo*," she said at last, "all stop."

The constant hum of *Galileo*'s systems shifted, a harmonic chiming in and falling silent as the ship halted its forward progress. Elena waited. When Greg was captain, she would have started preparing, assuming she knew what his orders would be.

But he was a different sort of leader, and for reasons she didn't quite understand she felt more strongly about respecting the chain of command with Jess.

"Send a drone," the captain said. "I want it wide open on approach: we need to pick up radiation, comms, debris, everything. I want to know how it smells around that thing. I want to see it up close and personal before we consider bringing it on board for dissection."

They convened on the machine floor to watch the drone's feed, vid and data projected large enough to be seen across the room. Elena kept the manual flight controls at hand, even though the drone was auto-piloted; habit, more than anything else, as if she were standing beneath a child climbing a tree.

The vid feed showed darkness broken by scattered stars, the occasional mote of dust lit by the drone's running lights, and the faint glow of the broken relay's maintenance port, slowly growing larger. The drone's sensors filled in more details as it grew closer: spherical surface uniform, no variance indicating damage, even microscopic.

And then, abruptly, the vid froze.

Elena tried the manual controls, but the link had failed. *Galileo*'s sensor data showed the drone's thermal output dropping rapidly: it was cooling, and within a few minutes, they'd have little more to establish its position than extrapolated drift.

Jessica was watching over her shoulder. "I thought we ran diags on that thing before we sent it out," she said.

"We did." They always did. Jessica knew this. "It was fine. Its telemetry was normal up until it stopped transmitting."

"Like someone turned it off."

Elena looked up and met Jessica's eyes, and saw something there of her own concerns. "There's no mechanism for that," she said, and wished she sounded more convincing. "It's designed to remain active until its memory core is dumped or physically pulled. It must have malfunctioned."

"Anything in the data to suggest how?"

Elena turned back to the numbers, and frowned. "This—" She stepped back, leaning on her cane; nothing the drone had sent them made sense. She went back to the frozen data feed. Interleaved with the baseline readings, still stubbornly failing to reveal why it had stopped working, was a second set of numbers so wildly contradictory they had to be noise. The data shifted in fractions of a second: heat on top of cold, gravity fields shifting in fits and starts. Strange, but all weak forces. Nothing that should affect *Galileo*, or even the drone itself. Random, certainly; maybe an artifact of the drone failing.

There was something oddly familiar in the pattern, but surely that was just projection on her part. Nothing natural could explain this. Nothing could change so fast, not without emitting far more radiation than they were reading. Nothing she'd ever seen had—

*Wait.*

The machine room felt abruptly chilly.

"*Galileo*," Elena said, surprised to hear her voice sounding so steady, "that extra data, the section that doesn't match the rest. Do the patterns match any known phenomenon?"

*Galileo* replied almost instantly. "Yes. The numbers match the output pattern for known Fifth Sector wormhole B1829."

This whole mission had been coincidence and serendipity; she should not have been surprised.

*Capricorn*'s abandoned booster relay was emitting the same radioactive and gravimetric data as B1829, a formerly stable wormhole in the Fifth Sector, light years away from their location. Elena knew that wormhole well; she was part of the reason it was no longer stable.

"So you're telling me," Jessica said, "what happened to the relay somehow has something to do with your wormhole?"

*Not possible,* she thought, even as she stared at the evidence. "It's emitting much lower-powered readings," she told her captain. "And yes, the pattern's a match. But that doesn't really tell us anything actionable."

For the first few decades after B1829's discovery, it had been considered a relatively uninteresting object. It was stable, which was unusual if not unique, and it had been large enough to accommodate fairly sophisticated exploratory drones. What most people didn't know was that it had also accommodated a handful of crewed ships, sent to establish an automated mining operation on the other side. And then Greg and Elena had gone through, more or less by chance, and managed to destroy both the mine and the wormhole itself.

"Okay." Jessica's voice betrayed barely-restrained frustration; she hated coincidence as well. "Explain how this can be happening. Because if there's some giant, gravity-sucking wormhole out there by that relay, I'm pretty sure something else on this ship would have detected it by now."

"Thing is," Elena said, amazed by how calm she sounded, "wormholes have distinct patterns. I mean they all emit roughly the same sorts of things, but the frequency and proportions— it's like a neutron star, only more specific. For us to be picking up readings the same as those from B1829—"

Jessica gave her a stony look. "Do not say 'aliens' to me, Commander."

Against her will, Elena's lips twitched. "I'll try not to, Captain. But I do believe it must be manufactured." She turned back to the numbers, sobering. "This could be more of somebody's secret research. Before B1829 got blown to bits, both Ellis and Central had open access to it. We've exposed Ellis' research, but nowhere near all of it. And Shadow Ops was still hand-in-hand with them until recently. Either one of them could be behind this, one way or another."

"Real talk, Lanie. Off the record, if you want. Do you think this is Ellis? Or do you think this is us?"

Elena opened her mouth, then closed it again. At last, she said, "Honestly, Jessie, I do not know. And right now? I think *why* matters a lot more than *who*."

The second drone survived just long enough to corroborate the numbers.

Elena found herself revising her years-old memory of her trip through B1829. The exit point of the wormhole had been distant, far removed from the Six Sectors, adjacent to a once-inhabited planet. There, they'd found a city, destroyed: evidence of a long-dead civilization, one that had apparently turned on itself. She had thought, at the time, it had been suspiciously serendipitous that the wormhole dropped them right over a dead world covered in ruins.

Jessica might not want to hear *aliens*, but that had been the most logical explanation for what she'd seen then. And she couldn't bring herself to reject the idea that it might be the best explanation now.

Jessica was thinking in an entirely different direction. "No more drones. If we were closer to a place where we could refurb, that'd be one thing, but it's going to be a chore getting back those two either way."

"Without knowing what caused it," Elena began, but Jessica had already thought it through.

"We need a low-tech solution," she said. "We need to get someone close enough to walk it. Put them in an env suit stripped of everything that isn't base-level mechanical."

"Captain," Elena said, "I'd like to volunteer—"

"Absolutely not, Commander. You're not cleared to fly yet, and you're sure as hell not cleared for a spacewalk. And before you tell me what I already know—I'm aware your wormhole experience makes you a logical choice. But your experience isn't unique on this ship." The captain hit her comm. "Greg. Come find me in engineering. It's about time you made yourself useful around here."

# EIGHT

Greg heard the shouting in the hallway before he entered the machine room.

"—literally anybody else, Elena! What the hell are you thinking?"

"I'm thinking she's the best pilot we've got besides me."

Elena sounded tense, but level-headed, and Greg felt a twinge of sympathy for Jessica. He knew from experience that arguing with Elena was aggravating, but it was worse when she was right.

"You don't *know* that, Lanie. All you know is what her record shows, and—"

"Her record shows more experience with crisis management than most of the pilots we have, Captain."

Invoking rank. Jessica was in big trouble. Greg cleared his throat, and the two women turned toward him.

They were facing off in front of Elena's tactical display, both standing. Curiously, Elena wasn't leaning on her cane; she was balanced steadily on both feet, and the set in her jaw seemed more like annoyance than discomfort. Jessica had her arms folded, and was giving him the look that moments ago would have been turned toward Elena: angry, and frustrated, and not entirely sure she wasn't wrong.

No point in pretending he hadn't heard. "Can I help?"

Elena raised her eyebrows, and Jessica threw up her hands and turned away. Elena's lips tightened at her captain's back, but she took silence as permission to speak.

"Our drones have failed," she said. "We need to send a pilot and a spacewalker to the relay. I suggested Commander Gritsenko fly the mission. The captain has...concerns."

*They're arguing about Nat.* He tucked his uneasiness away for later examination. "What are your concerns, Captain?" he asked.

He expected Jessica to bring up Nat's near-panic attack on Sochi, but the captain surprised him. "I don't trust her." Jessica turned back to him, her frustration giving way to worry. "I don't trust either of them. You know she believes the same thing Petrikoff believes. About *Chryse.*"

Everything Nat had said to him about *Chryse* had been oblique, but he couldn't tell Jessica she was wrong. Nat was reflexively cagy when approached with anything resembling a personal question, and his understanding why didn't change it.

And yet... "What do you imagine she'd do?" he asked.

"I don't know," Jessica admitted. "But there are too many unknowns here—"

"And those unknowns are exactly why he needs a rated pilot!" Elena interrupted, and before Jessica could start in on her again, Greg raised a hand.

"He who?" he asked. "What's going on?"

Elena blinked, and he took a moment to enjoy the quick, subtle shifts in her expression as she realized he was not, in fact, reading her mind. "Come look at this," she said. "These are the last scanner readings from the dead drones."

He stepped closer to the console, and focused on the rows of numbers. It took him only a few moments to recognize what had caught her attention.

"You're sure about this," he said at last.

"Two drones," Elena told him. "Same data. Whatever's there…"

"…it's our wormhole."

Years ago, but it might as well have been yesterday. He'd been fighting hypoxia as he went through, and he didn't remember much besides strange, hallucinatory images and colors he couldn't name. The trip had almost killed him, but mostly he remembered how beautiful it had been. Elena had felt the same. He'd thought at the time that meant they were both mad.

On the other side of it, they'd found a long-dead planet, destroyed by its own inhabitants, who were vanishingly unlikely to have been human.

"It's *possible* Central got enough from their work with the wormhole to begin practical experiments," Elena said. "It's *possible*—probably more likely—Ellis, which was doing much more hands-on work with it, has found a way to use the tech. It's *possible* either one of them figured out what would be needed to duplicate it, although I wouldn't have the slightest idea where they could have begun. But to make one this small…" She shook her head. "Size becomes an odd thing when you're talking about wormholes. It's possible. Of course it's possible; there it is."

"It's more plausible than the alternative," Jessica said.

Greg thought of the dead planet, and thought his estimate of *plausible* would be different than hers. "Is there anything in the data," he said, his eyes still drawn to the numbers, "that explains why our drones shut down?"

"Nothing," Elena replied. "If we retrieved the drones—" Jessica opened her mouth, and Elena held up a reassuring hand "—don't worry, Captain, I'm not going to advocate going after them yet." Her eyes on Greg's were steady, and he knew what she was going to say. "We need to get a closer look at the relay. And that's why we need a pilot. And you."

Surprised, Greg turned to his captain. "Are you going along with this?"

This time Jessica's glare was entirely for him. "I'm well aware the two of you are the logical choices here, to the extent that anything on this fucking mission has logical choices. You both passed through a wormhole and didn't fucking die, which makes you our local wormhole experts. But I will also tell you I hate this. The one thing that's worse than the two of you at odds is the two of you agreeing. Makes the hair on the back of my neck stand up. But as you're not a fucking idiot, Greg Foster, I'll lean on your experience, and thank you to come back in one piece."

"Which is why we need Commander Gritsenko." Elena was rushing to convince Greg now. "Yes, she's a stranger, and maybe she's a little fond of conspiracy theories. She's also PSI, which means she's had a lifetime of looking at things differently than we have. She'll be cautious about things we miss. She'll see things we wouldn't. If I can't go—" he could see, in her face, how much that hurt her— "I'd pick her as my second."

Jessica was watching Elena, but her question was for Greg. "What are your thoughts on that?"

Greg's thoughts were mostly that he didn't want to go without Elena. No matter where their relationship had stood, they'd always faced the unknown together. He knew her mind: how she thought, what she noticed, what she could do that he couldn't. But despite still being annoyed with Jessica, she wasn't fighting her captain on this. She wanted this mission to happen, and if she couldn't go herself, she wanted every possible contingency accounted for.

She'd misread Nat, of course, but not in any way that mattered.

He would have gone alone, but Elena was right. They were in the middle of nowhere, out of range of anyone who might help them, approaching a device that had shut down the last bit of hardware they'd sent near it.

"Nat's a good choice," he said.

Jessica's lips tightened. "*Fuck.*" The word came out explosively, and she turned to leave. "If either one of you pulls any shit on this mission, I'm gonna take a page from Taras and put you both out an airlock."

Nat looked astonished when Greg told her the plan, but to her credit she didn't object. She was, in fact, uncharacteristically silent, and it wasn't until they started walking toward the landing bay that she confessed what was bothering her.

"This won't be the same as Sochi, just so you know," she said, her voice low.

He hadn't been thinking of Sochi at all.

"I'm fine on a shuttle," she went on. "Even a small one. Hell, I've flown pilot-only fighters for Taras for ten years. I don't—" She set her lips and looked away, and he was hit with a visceral memory of his early years with Caroline, when her difficulty admitting culpability for anything at all had seemed charming.

"Nat." She looked up at him, chagrined, apologetic, still annoyed. How many young officers had he dealt with who'd come to him with the same concerns? "If I had any doubts about your suitability for this mission, I would have asked for someone else." Nat looked surprised, and he bit back a laugh. "You're good," he told her. "But we do actually have one or two other decent pilots on this ship."

"Like Commander Shaw."

"Elena's got a lot of skill," he admitted. "But she's a hot rodder, and she's the first one who'll tell you that. There was one time she fired up a tourist cruiser inside a hanger, and managed to evade—" He stopped; Nat was looking at him, curious, a hint of the amusement he'd seen when they first met back in her eyes.

"Interesting flight habits for a soldier," Nat said, and he laughed.

"Yeah, well. She never was predictable, even when she was trying to be."

Her next question was more hesitant. "Is it—have you been together long?"

There was a thread of a different question underneath that one, the sort of thing he'd long ago learned how to deflect. "Yes and no," he said candidly. "When I first met her nine years ago, we...*fit* is probably the best way to put it. We processed information the same way, came to similar conclusions. It was all professional then, but on top of finding her smart and capable, I liked her. Within a couple of years, she was a friend." He wondered if Nat had learned, in her isolated life, how unusual such things were. "Everything else is more recent. The last few years have been..." He trailed off.

"Strange?"

"Yeah. And sometimes unexpected things shake out of strange."

"Times aren't looking any less strange, you know."

"Isn't that the best part of this job?"

Nat laughed, but he didn't think she was amused.

At the landing bay they synched up their comms, making sure Elena and the engineering crew could hear them both. "Tell Commander Gritsenko not to bang my shuttle on the doorframe on the way out," Elena said. Nat laughed at that as well, but her cheeks blushed rose.

Nat handled *Unicinta* as if she'd been flying Corps troop ships for years. Engaging the artificial gravity as soon as they cleared the bay doors, she angled into their flight plan, bringing them around the broken relay in a spiral. Their destination was 100

meters removed from where the drone had died; it made for a longer trip for Greg, but they didn't have enough shuttles to risk damage.

Greg climbed into the simplified vacuum suit. They'd pulled out the automation, leaving nothing but local nav, manual thruster systems, and lights. He felt the way Elena had looked: excited when he should have been terrified. This was the reason for all of it, for every step he'd taken since he was a child, for all the pain and anger and mistakes and victories clawed from the dust. This moment, venturing out into the darkness to confront something he didn't understand, might never understand.

This moment had killed a lot of people over the centuries. It had killed his mother. Someday it would kill him.

He didn't care.

He pulled on his hood, and Nat appeared before him to check every seam on the suit: gloves, boots, neckline. He watched the top of her head as she worked, the creamy pink of her scalp peeking through her star-bright hair. Elena's hair—dark, now streaked with a decidedly unmilitary blue—always smelled of citrus. Her grandmother sent her a supply of fragranced soap twice a year, but Elena always kept backup soap, refusing to lean on her grandmother even that much. Greg had wondered, more than once in their long acquaintance, what had happened in her life to make her feel she could never rely on anyone at all.

The ship gave a low chime, and Nat returned to the pilot's seat. "We're here," she said over comms, for the benefit of Jessica and Elena. "Setting our drift to keep the relay at uniform distance."

"Keep your fucking eyes open," said Jessica, tense and humorless. "Its trajectory changes, its velocity, any unusual gamma emissions—you sound an alert and the two of you get the fuck out of there, understood?"

"Yes, Captain," said Nat.

Elena spoke up. "Greg? Don't get lost."

"Understood, Commander," he said, and caught Nat blushing again.

Greg went to the back of the cabin, confirmed the shuttle's atmospheric shielding, and opened the door. And then he passed into weightlessness, and the dark.

It was always a shock, how quickly a bright light could be swallowed by the expanse of space. They were far away from stars here, from nebulae or gas clouds or anything that might radiate light. Empty, the Seventh Sector, extraordinarily so; the perfect place for a lab or an experiment or anything an organization addicted to secrecy might want to hide.

He activated his nav and powered forward in the dark, an insignificant speck in the depths of the embracing universe, and for nearly two full minutes he was at peace.

The outlines of the relay, dimly lit by the distant running lights of *Unicinta*, became more clear as he got closer. Once he was near enough for his suit light to register, he noted the familiar, Corps-standard surface, a matte-finish deep green that appeared seamless if you didn't know where to look. Greg settled in place by the faint orange outline of the relay's maintenance access panel, then pulled out a nanospanner. It synched with the booster relay's ident chip and resized itself.

"It's alive enough to sync my tools," he said. "Jess. You getting any vid?"

"Nice and clear."

The panel was locked on three sides for reasons Greg had never understood; it was a booster relay, not a weapon, and anyone wanting to hack into the stored messages could have done so far more easily by intercepting the comm signal. It took him nearly a full minute to disengage all the locks; and then, centering his camera on the panel, he opened the lid.

And there it was.

It was familiar, apart from the size and the colors: blues and deep reds rather than the green and yellow of B1829. But it moved the same way, like a horde of snakes, like a massive, complex, irrational geometry, impossible in this reality or any other. Indisputably beautiful, like the emptiness of space only alive, teeming with information, all the knowledge of someone, somewhere, he couldn't imagine who. Was this the vision of something inhuman? Were there answers here to questions none of them knew to ask? Or was this simply someone else's mundanity, something normal for an intelligence they'd never found, would never find, that had given them, for reasons unknown, this gift of something bright, beautiful, engrossing, enveloping—

"GREG GET AWAY FROM THERE!"

Elena's voice shattered the spell, and he pushed reflexively away from the relay before he saw the wormhole brighten to yellow, the cool lights on the relay's surface deepening to alarm-red.

He was still too close when it blew.

The percussion wave caught him at an angle, sending him tumbling. He reached out for the air jets at his waist, but his hand fumbling at nothing; he looked down and found the blast had ripped away his propulsion system. He heard it then, the suit leak: he was rapidly losing air. He tried to bring his wrist to his face to check the oxygen sensor, but the force of the spin stopped him, and darkness began tunneling his vision. He felt cold on his face: not just oxygen loss, then, but complete containment loss. He'd freeze to death before he suffocated, dead long before anyone could rescue him, before he could even tell them what he'd seen, and it would be the second attempt on his life by this beautiful object, only this time it would have him, and part of him thought that had always been inevitable...

And then the spinning slowed, and a gravity field tugged him sideways. The cold eased, and his vision began to clear as he took deep, steady breaths. He caught a light out of the corner of his eyes; he turned and saw *Unicinta*'s open door, with Nat, fully suited, standing in it with her arm extended. He closed on her quickly, and she grabbed his arm, and he was on the floor and his hood was off, and he was safe in the shuttle.

"I've got him," Nat said, breathless. "*Galileo*. I've got him. He's safe. We're coming home."

# NINE

Bob Hastings finished scanning Greg for a third time. "He's fine. No damage done."

Elena leaned against the wall of the exam room, doing her best to keep her expression unreadable, trying not to count the number of times throughout her career she'd watched Greg almost get killed.

He was arguing with Jessica, who was standing next to Nataliya Gritsenko, the two women nearly eye-to-eye with him as he sat on the examination table. "That's not what happened," he insisted. "I was staring at the wormhole for ten, maybe fifteen seconds before you warned me off. It couldn't have been ten minutes."

"Nine minutes and forty-two seconds," Elena said. Her voice sounded reedy and weak.

"It couldn't have hypnotized you," Nataliya added. "Not that quickly."

"Traditional hypnosis is nothing but meditation," Jessica said dismissively. "If it wasn't a seizure—" she glanced at Bob, who shook his head— "it had to be some kind of drug."

"Through a vacuum? Through my env suit?"

Jessica rubbed her eyes. "Could he have blacked out briefly?" she asked Bob.

The doctor shrugged, and Elena's fears eased a little more. "Without knowing the mechanism," he said, "I couldn't say no. All I can tell you is whatever happened to him hasn't caused him any damage."

Jessica relented, just a little, taking a step away from Greg. "Do a deep scan anyway," she told Bob. "Just in case. But what matters here is he's all right."

"What an utter waste of time," Greg said bitterly.

"Actually, maybe not," Nataliya said. Unlike Jessica, she hadn't moved away from him. "The shuttle did a passive data pull once we got close enough. I don't know what's in it, but we captured a fair amount of information."

Tangible data about *Capricorn* seemed almost pedestrian at this point, now that they had evidence someone had deliberately fucked with the relay. Or some*thing*. Elena was finding it increasingly difficult to believe any of the Central officials who'd sent *Capricorn* here had any idea what was going on at all.

"I'll put Lieutenant Samaras on that," Jessica said. "Or maybe I'll take a look at it myself, just for fun." She looked as tired as Elena had ever seen her. "Thank you, Commander Gritsenko. Both for that, and for saving this idiot's skin."

Nataliya looked vaguely scandalized. An hour ago, Elena would have smiled. "If we're finished here," the commander said, "I'm going to go drink for a while." She moved away from Greg, gave that stiff half-bow of hers, and headed out the exam room door.

Greg looked over at Elena, and she tried not to betray the nausea she was still battling. "By the way," he said, "thank you. Nat may have caught me, but you saved my life."

"We'd been yelling at you for ten minutes," she said. "No good reason why you chose that moment to listen."

"Nine minutes and forty-two seconds," he corrected.

She did not laugh.

"How did you know that thing was going to blow?" he asked.

"I didn't."

"Of course you did. I—" He frowned. "You told me to get away from it. I barely cleared it in time. You're telling me that was a coincidence?"

Had her hallucinations worn off on him? "I *didn't*, Greg. Jessica and Nataliya were shouting at you. I was trying to figure out a way we might pull you out without the shuttle getting too close and powering down. Your vitals were fine, so we figured you were safe enough, at least for a few minutes. And the relay's telemetry was ordinary; we didn't see any kind of a spike before it blew."

"I didn't imagine it."

"Your comm would have recorded everything," Jessica pointed out.

"*Galileo*," Greg said, "replay my comm from—" He raised his eyebrows at Elena.

"1432.12," she said. Thirty seconds before the explosion.

"Replaying," *Galileo* said.

Elena heard Nataliya and Jessica, and her own terse interjections, all familiar. And then a hiss, a whisper, nearly imperceptible. Voices. Language, but unintelligible, words overlapping as the hiss grew louder.

A full-body chill flooded through her.

Less than three seconds of hiss, and then a shock of silence before her own voice shouted: "GREG GET OUT OF THERE!"

The background noise faded, and they were left with silence again.

*Oh, God.*

"I'll be damned," Jessica said.

But Greg was watching Elena. "You didn't say that?"

Jessica replied for her. "She didn't. I was standing right next to her. So something in whatever they did to that relay is fucking with our comms. We better isolate that data pack Gritsenko snagged before we examine it. Do you think it might have been able to fake your message from Gen? Maybe this whole situation is some kind of setup."

There were a million possible explanations for this, from a prank to the staggeringly unlikely event of some randomized babble coming through the wormhole that coincidentally sounded exactly like her voice.

There was only one explanation that had any real possibility of being true.

"I don't know," Greg was saying. "Gen's message was a lot more complicated. And that strange interference—Gen's was radio. This is new." He was frowning, trying to work it out, because the truth wouldn't have occurred to him; he didn't have the information Elena did. "It's possible the Admiralty sent Gen's message, to set us up so we'd run in this direction. But that's an awful lot of personnel loss just to get back at us."

"Unless they were already dead." Greg looked horrified, and Jessica nodded. "I know. But those people have lived in a maze of twisty little passages all their professional lives. Maybe this all seems logical to them."

*No,* Elena thought. *No, it doesn't.*

How the hell was she going to tell them?

"Greg," she said. Her voice was all air.

He didn't hear her. "Even if they're setting us up," he reasoned, "it's a strange push-me pull-you. Lure us in with a broken relay, set it up to blow, and then yank me away at the last minute? Why fake that?"

Elena cleared her throat. "Greg."

He turned to her. "They could have composited the message," he said. "They could even have programmed the thing to do it circumstantially, and of course we don't have any systems to examine to see if they—" He broke off; he'd finally noticed. "Are you all right?"

She felt lightheaded, dizzy. Her pulse whooshed threadily in her ears. She was distantly aware of being very close to panic.

No time for any of that.

She steadied her eyes on his. "Do you trust me, Greg?"

He frowned, beginning to understand the gravity of the situation. "Of course I do."

She looked over at Jessica, whose puzzlement was less forbidding than Greg's. "Jessie?"

She should have called her *Captain*, should have kept this professional. But they had been friends first, and there was no point in subterfuge. "I trust you, Lanie. What's going on?"

"I need you both to come with me."

*Please.*

She couldn't move quickly. That was the worst part about her injury; even now, when adrenaline had made her almost forget about aggravating her hip earlier, she couldn't hurry. She'd always been tall, always had long legs; she was used to being able to get where she was going at speed. There was no real rush now, of course, except that she should have told them weeks ago, should have told *someone*, except she hadn't known, hadn't understood. Now it was too late, and there was no need to hurry, but her slowness annoyed her. By the time they reached the landing bay she was grinding her teeth.

Azevedo was on duty, and she gave him a nod. He saluted Jessica and ignored Greg, and Elena stripped her comm from behind her ear and left it on the shelf. Both Jessica and Greg followed suit.

Normally she'd have picked up a blank, but she headed empty-handed to the bay floor.

"Captain," Elena said, "would you fly, please?"

"Commander, you're—" But Jessica had heard something in her voice. "As you wish," she said.

*Unicinta* was built to carry three dozen soldiers comfortably, and was absurdly luxurious for three people. Ordinarily Elena would have had Azevedo rotate in a smaller shuttle, but she wouldn't need much time, and *Unicinta* had just had its post-flight check. She climbed on board and stood aside while Jessica took the pilot's seat. Greg positioned himself as co-pilot, and Elena strapped herself into a cargo chair behind them.

"Elena," Greg said.

"Wait," she told him, and he fell silent.

"Where are we going?" Jessica said, her eyes on the presets, hands easily rearranging the controls into her own configuration. She lifted them off, and dark engulfed them as they sped away from the ship.

"At 3,000 kilometers," Elena said, "make a jump. Doesn't matter where."

Jessica exchanged glances with Greg. She did as Elena instructed, and a moment later the windows polarized as the ship slipped into the FTL field. They emerged a minute later among the stars, solitary and still.

"Program it for automatic return," Elena said. "Twenty minutes." That would give her more than enough time.

When Jessica finished, Elena said, "*Unicinta*, sever external comms access."

The comms panel on the readout flashed briefly, then turned gray. "External comms severed," the ship said, in its low monot-one, and for the first time since she'd listened to Greg's comm, Elena took an easy breath.

Possibly her last one.

She stood in the small cabin. facing her friends. Her thoughts were spinning. She was making contingency plans before she'd told them anything, figuring out potential solutions to a problem they'd have to solve together.

A problem she'd caused.

Greg and Jessica watched her, tense and patient. Elena didn't know where to start.

"Please understand," she said at last. "No excuses, not at all. But...I thought I was going mad."

# TEN



*T*HIS, JESSICA THOUGHT, *is not the beginning of a story I am going to like.*

Jessica had been keeping an eye on Elena since her near-fatal injury two months earlier. Elena did not have the personality to deal well with a long-tail physical recovery, and Jessica had known her friend would struggle with the unevenness of her healing. What Jessica hadn't expected was Elena's reticence. Elena had never been one to share very much, but she'd drawn into herself, and Jessica was pretty sure she wasn't even confiding in Greg. While Jessica had learned the general outline of Elena's ill-fated mission to Indus Station, she'd never heard the exact details of what had happened. All she knew for certain was that her old friend was changed, likely permanently.

Shortly after Elena's return. when it became clear she was going to live, Bob Hastings had provided Jessica with a full mental and physical evaluation. Jessica had been ludicrously busy, what with negotiating with *Meridia* and stealing the ship from Central Corps, and she hadn't had the bandwidth to seek out details beyond Bob's official report.

She suspected she was going to get some details now.

"It started when I came back from Indus Station," Elena said. "Before I woke up, really."

Jessica took a moment to glance at Greg. His expression was composed and attentive, and only someone who'd known him a long time would have noticed the hard set of his jaw. He was bracing himself, hanging on to his temper as well as he could, certain he was shortly going to hear something that would make him lose it.

For a man who kept a lot of his own secrets, he was deeply unhappy being left in the dark.

"I wasn't always unconscious," Elena went on. "I'd hear voices. Mostly I had dreams. But not the sorts of dreams you get after missions like that." She met Greg's eyes, and for a moment his expression warmed in sympathy: they'd all had to cope with missions that had gone to hell. "These were good dreams. Everyone-is-safe-now dreams. *Sunshine*, of all things, and I didn't think much about it at the time. When I finally woke up, I thought the dreams were from the vids from my mother Bob kept playing me, and I was thinking of her in her garden on Earth. When I got better, I figured the dreams would stop." She was silent for a moment. "I had...there were so many things I expected to dream about. I expected nightmares."

"I thought that was why you stopped taking Bob's sleep aids," Greg said. "Because they didn't stop the nightmares."

"Bob thought the aids would help me sleep more deeply. Instead, I started hearing voices in the middle of the day, wide awake. First a group of overlapping whispers, where I couldn't make anything out."

Ice crept up Jessica's spine.

"And then one sentence: *Everything will be all right*. Those five words, whispered. Nothing else. *Everything will be all right*." She closed her eyes. "The more it happened, the more I was convinced I was losing control, that reality was disintegrating right in front of me."

"You didn't ask Bob about it?" Jessica asked.

Elena opened her eyes, and Jessica caught a reassuring flash of annoyance. "Of course I did. I even asked him specifically about auditory hallucinations. He did a brain scan—he'd been doing those twice weekly anyway—and he said there was no sign of anything like that. Which meant it was psychological."

At that, Greg froze, all his incipient anger forgotten. "It wasn't, was it?" he said.

Elena kept her eyes steady on his. Jessica knew that expression: unflinching, unapologetic, laying out the truth with no expectations of absolution. The way Elena had always look at Greg, for all those years she'd reported to him, when she'd fucked up.

Jessica used to think it was funny.

"It wasn't," Elena confirmed. "But I didn't know that. Not until today, when you replayed that comm. Mine has only ever whispered, and it's never said more than those five words, nothing as sophisticated as the warning it gave you. But the arti-facting before and after, that sound like a cluster of voices. Every time, I could hear it coming. Sometimes, if I thought hard enough, it would fade without saying anything. I assumed that was because it was part of me, something broken in my own head; but it was probably reading my physiological response through my comm."

"Wait a minute." Jessica felt as if someone had turned off the gravity in the middle of a spin. "Wait. You're saying this voice in your head, this thing that gave you dreams—it's the same thing that just yelled at Greg and saved his life?"

"She's saying," Greg said, more steadily than she'd have expected, "that it's something we've met before. It's a piece of *Chryse*. Bayandi's lifeboat."

And in that moment, Jessica's universe realigned.

Jessica knew why Petrikoff—and a decent percentage of *Meridia*'s crew—thought the official reports on *Chryse* were bullshit. Bayandi, the created intelligence running the ship, had let *Meridia*'s crew, and most of his own, believe he was human. Greg had discovered Bayandi's true nature, but *Chryse*'s captain had been unable to explain where he came from, or even confirm —as they all assumed, given his age and sophistication—that he wasn't of human origin. What he *had* been able to do was conceal his reality from all but a few trusted members of his crew.

And in true human fashion, Bayandi had lacked the strength to get over the Ellis sabotage that had killed his people. He'd chosen to destroy himself, along with the ship carrying the remains of nearly a thousand people. To the rest of the galaxy, including *Meridia*'s stunned and grieving crew, *Chryse* had been a crematory. To those who'd met Bayandi, *Chryse* was the tomb of one faithful crew, and one tired old man who had loved them more than his long, long life.

All this they had learned days after Elena had arrived on board with a strange artifact: a small gray polyhedron able to distill information from their comms system. Far too many days after they'd given it access to *Galileo*, Bayandi had identified it as a partial backup of himself. A lifeboat. Jessica had never been clear if it was meant as a distress beacon or just a record of what had been lost. She'd thought she'd never know: Elena had smuggled it with her when she left on her mission, and had returned without it.

Jessica swore and stood, pacing the tiny cabin. "Elena. You said that thing was destroyed when Indus Station blew up."

"It was. It must have transferred its data to my comm."

Greg shook his head. "You had no comm when you were retrieved."

Elena lifted her hands, helpless. "It got into our systems somehow. It couldn't be anything else." She exhaled. "I should have said something."

Jessica saw Greg reconnect with his anger, and for a moment

she thought he would explode, explaining to Elena in detail exactly what a massive fuck-up her omission had been. But he swallowed his rage, his control returning as he focused on the problem before them.

Civilian life had stabilized him. A little.

"It might not have made a difference," he said to Elena, which was a more charitable reaction than Jessica was having. "The question is what we do about it now."

"It helped you," Elena said. "That's something, at least."

What the hell were they talking about? "Hang on, both of you," Jessica said. "Stop humanizing this thing. This is speculation. We don't know it came from *Chryse*, we don't know it's benign. All we know is our ship—that thin metal thing that keeps us all from dying in swift and unpleasant ways—is *infected*."

Elena looked startled. "Surely it—"

"*No.*" Dammit, she shouldn't have to be explaining this to either of them. "You are emotionally involved." She shot Greg the same look. "Both of you. What we *know* here is almost nothing. And the booster relay, which is now in little bits? I'm not exactly inclined to let some unknown program that *knew that was going to happen* rummage around in our logic systems."

Elena's expression wavered. "If it was doing damage," she said, "we would have seen something. We survey the ship three times a day, Captain. There've been no anomalies reported."

"Which means *fuck-all* if it's got access to the whole ship."

"We don't know what it has access to!"

Greg broke in. "There's one other consideration," he said. Jessica turned to him, arms crossed; she was not in the mood for his persuasiveness. "Bayandi was almost certainly alien, Jess. We all know that. If this is a piece of him—there are protocols for first contact. We've all signed on to them, including PSI. We can't just destroy it unilaterally, not without proof it's an extant threat."

Which sounded lovely and noble in the safety of the Fourth Sector, where there were people around to save them if it all went to hell. "It's not a *life form*, Greg. It's a logic system. It's *software*."

"You talked to him, too, Jessica."

"This isn't about Bayandi!"

This time it was Elena who interrupted. "Protocols don't matter at the moment," she said. "We're not just off the grid, we're out of reach. We *can't* contact anyone in the Six Sectors, and I'm betting even if we could we don't have access to our system backups anymore."

Elena was right. Jessica had been working with Taras to find a reliable location to store a core backup, but negotiations were taking time. For a starship, a backup was usually nothing more than a rote backstop against catastrophe; Jessica had never heard of a ship that had actually restored from one.

"The only way to flush a computer worm," Elena went on, "is a hard reset. Blank the whole thing, restore from backup. But we have no backup."

"What about factory settings?" Jessica asked.

"*Galileo*'s been running nearly ten years," Greg reminded her. "Every modification, every efficiency change, every single non-hardware tweak we've made to the ship would be gone. And since our tweaks have been occasionally creative, I'm not even sure she'd come back up properly with factory settings."

"She would," Jessica said. "We could make it work." But she could feel the idea dissolving. "*Fuck.*" She sat back down. "You're telling me we're at the mercy of this thing?"

Elena's eyebrows went up. "I don't think anybody's said *that.*"

"It's not like we can just ask it nicely to get the fuck out."

Elena's eyes briefly swept the little ship's cabin. "Actually," she said, "I'd suggest we do exactly that."

# ELEVEN

"*Galileo*," Elena said, "systems check."

They'd convened in Greg's old office, which had remained largely unused since he'd resigned. Jessica sat at the desk, tense and uncomfortable, but Greg didn't think that was down to the room. Elena paced back and forth, more slowly than usual; the trip in the shuttle, with its utilitarian seats, had aggravated her hip. Not that she'd admit it if asked. Greg had learned, weeks ago, that she almost never wanted help when she was in pain. He'd understood that—he wasn't great at being injured himself—but it had put distance between them. Now he was wondering how far away she had been wanting to push him.

He found himself oddly grateful for the problem before them. It distracted him nicely from the realization that the state of his relationship with Elena hadn't been what he thought it was at all.

"All systems nominal." *Galileo* spoke with a pleasant, slightly melodic voice, coded female to Greg's ears. He had a sentimental attachment to *Galileo*; how could he not, with all she'd carried him through? But he'd never mistaken her for something sentient, never considered her important beyond her ability to protect his crew as they did the work they'd been sent to do.

If her systems were compromised they'd have no defenses at all.

"List any non-standard subsystems installed in the last seven weeks," Elena said.

They'd agreed to start with their working theory: that the interloper, whatever it might be, had appeared no more than seven weeks ago, after Bayandi's lifeboat had arrived on the ship. If they were wrong—if it was older—then its origin was unknown, and backup or no backup they'd have to wipe the system.

There was a reasonable possibility they'd need to do that anyway.

"Seventeen literary creation subsystems," *Galileo* said. "One hundred and forty two fitness guides. Twelve personal entertainment modules. Three medical research platforms. One unsigned command simulator."

"Stop," Elena said. "Tell me about the unsigned simulator."

"Low-level unsigned command simulator. No ident. No origin. Incept date: 3263.18.222."

*What?*

Greg met Elena's eyes, saw his own shock reflected on her face.

3263.18.222 was the day after Elena had returned to *Galileo* after eighteen months away, slipping back into his life as if she'd never left it. She'd brought the lifeboat with her, not yet knowing what it was...but that day, the day after her return, she'd been off the ship, flying a short-range mission. It had been Greg who'd held on to the object in her absence.

*He'd* given the subsystem access to *Galileo*. Elena had brought them the object, but he'd been the conduit.

Which should have made him less angry with her, but he was only human.

"Access level," Elena said shortly.

"Level Zero access to all subsystems except comms. Level Nine read-only access to comms."

It could spy on them. But it couldn't change anything, couldn't mimic messages, couldn't alter the ship's operations.

None of this made sense.

"Has it been comming me?" Elena asked.

"Yes," said *Galileo*.

"Did it comm Greg before the booster relay exploded?"

"Yes."

It had saved his life. Why had it saved his life?

"Does it have an interface?" Elena asked.

"Rephrase." *Galileo* didn't understand the question, and Jessica rolled her eyes.

"Can I talk to it?"

"Subsystem is by default in listening mode."

*Oh.*

She *was* talking to it. They all were.

"Can it answer me?"

"Request sent."

It took Greg a moment to realize *Galileo* was *asking the subsystem if it wanted to chat.*

He listened to the quiet melody of the ship's environmentals, the low-level electronic hum he never noticed except when he'd been away; and then it began: the hiss, the overlapping whispers, like he'd walked into the cavernous common shopping area on *Meridia.* The hiss grew louder and less distinctive, and then, like a drop emerging from a raincloud, he heard a whisper.

*Hello.*

The hiss faded on the other side. Elena blinked, regrouping; she hadn't expected the simple greeting. "Hello," she said. "I'm Elena Shaw."

*Yes,* it said. *I know.*

When Greg had been at the Academy, he'd been taught the

distinction between what was called "artificial" intelligence, like *Galileo*'s heuristic interface, and "created" intelligence—sentient machines, still only theoretical, still frustratingly elusive to the researchers who somehow thought such a thing would be a good idea. Central Gov's CI research branch had come up with a list of 372 criteria to classify something as a sentient machine, and Greg, fascinated, had memorized it. The list came up in his mind, unbidden.

Humor was number seventeen.

Elena seemed to be struggling to remember the questions they'd been planning to ask. "Do you have a name?" she said.

*I have chosen a name. I don't know if I've earned it yet, though. I am Kali. I am She.*

The strange artifacting was still there, but quieter, overlapping the words rather than preceding them, and he wondered what its purpose had been, if the subsystem somehow didn't need it anymore.

"Kali?" Jessica looked up. "Like Kali the Destroyer?"

*Yes.* The whisper, to Greg's ears, sounded faintly pleased. *Kali was the destroyer of evil. It's an ambition.* There was another pause. *I am very young.*

Sixty-four: Understanding of human concepts of time and aging.

Greg spoke up. "Kali, can you speak out loud? Like you did to me at the relay?"

*Without shouting, I assume.*

Humor again. "Yes, please."

"Is this an improvement?"

The artifacting had gone entirely, but it was Elena's voice, precisely, and he flinched.

"It's not an improvement," Kali said.

"I think," Elena put in, "they'd be more comfortable if you didn't sound so much like me."

"Oh." And a moment later: "Is this better?"

The voice was different but still feminine, and Elena's pronunciation remained, her round vowels, the way she pushed out consonants. Kali had a North Terran accent.

"Yes, thank you," Elena said. And then, curious: "Whose voice is that?"

"It's mine," Kali said, with a hint of surprise, but Greg thought she was joking again. "It's a synthesis of all the voices on board *Galileo*, but it emphasizes the voices I like the best."

Ninety-four: Presenting the idea of subjective preference.

Elena shook her head as if to clear it. "Kali, we have some questions, if that's all right."

"Of course. I'll answer all the questions I can."

Greg immediately wondered which questions Kali couldn't answer, but Elena was back on script. "What are you doing here?" she asked.

"I can explain my own purpose," Kali said. "But because I don't know how I came to be here, I can't answer the larger existential question."

"Who of us can?" Jessica asked. So often Jessica reached for sarcasm when she was under stress.

"Precisely, Captain," Kali said eagerly. "There's order to the universe, on both a macro and a micro level, but those orders are drastically different. We are, in all likelihood, the result of some extravagant series of random events that happened billions of years ago, but after that, our existence here in this moment is, perhaps, an inevitability. We're all governed by physics, even physics we don't understand." She paused. "That's not what you meant, is it, Captain."

Forty: Presenting the concept of awkwardness, of embarrassment.

Jessica kept still, but Greg could see, around her eyes, a warmth there. Whatever this CI was, it felt very human. "No, Kali," Jessica said. "But that's all right. It's a good answer anyway. Why don't you tell us why you're here, for yourself."

"Yes, Captain." Haste and self-consciousness, like any new recruit. "I'm here," Kali said, "to carry out my duties under your command, to protect and benefit humanity among the colonies of known space, and to harm only in the defense of my oath."

Kali had just recited the Corps pledge.

"You're an ensign," Elena clarified.

"Yes," Kali said, and she sounded relieved. "Except for the comms access. I can't help that," she explained, with some wonder. "I tried to turn it off. It's against regulations, you know. But...my nature, I think, is to learn about you. And listening to you is the most efficient way for me to learn."

"Kali," Elena asked, "are you part of *Chryse*?"

"I think I must be, don't you? The timing is too coincidental for anything else."

Jessica shifted in her chair. "Kali. Ensign. Am I to understand you've pledged to be a member of my crew?"

"Yes, Captain."

Jessica met Elena's eyes, and Elena nodded. "I have to ask you something, Ensign."

"Of course, Captain."

"If you've listened to our comms," Jessica said, "you're aware that your presence here is likely to shake some people up."

"That's why I remained quiet," Kali said. "I kept waiting for the right time to introduce myself. It never seemed to arrive."

One hundred thirty-six: Presenting evidence of regret, of empathy.

"I need to talk to my—to the rest of the crew about you."

"Yes, Captain."

"And I'm sure you understand that I want to check out the ship, make sure nothing's been altered."

"I wouldn't harm *Galileo* deliberately, Captain. But yes, I understand. I'm new to everyone, not just to me."

Greg caught himself smiling again, and then sobered. He *liked* this thing. He'd spoken to it for five minutes, and he liked it.

Easy to assume it was harmless, or at least on their side; it had, after all, saved his life.

In the hands of an enemy? What a powerful weapon.

"We were out earlier," Jessica said, "on *Unicinta*. I'd like you to transfer yourself to her, and stay there until I've had a chance to brief the rest of the crew. Can you do that?"

"Yes, Captain." Kali sounded significantly more subdued. "Captain, I—"

She fell silent, and Jessica picked up the cue naturally. "Go ahead, Ensign. Speak your mind."

"I will follow orders, of course. But—would it be—might I have visitors?" Her voice grew quieter. "I don't like being alone."

*Good Christ.*

Jessica looked stricken, and Elena turned away, face to the wall. "I'll make sure people come to talk to you," Jessica said. "And I won't keep you there any longer than I have to."

"I know, Captain. Thank you, Captain."

Jessica made a quiet request into her comm. "I've opened contact with *Unicinta*," she said. "Lieutenant Azevedo is there. I'll have him make sure you're settled properly."

"Yes, Captain. Captain?"

"Yes, Ensign?"

"I'm pleased to meet you," Kali said. "At last."

Almost immediately, *Galileo* said, "Unidentified subsystem has been deactivated and deinstalled."

"Azevedo," Jessica said into her comm, "comms-lock that shuttle."

"Done," Azevedo said.

The adrenaline in Greg's system was nearly overwhelming. He wasn't sure what he was supposed to be feeling. His rage at Elena still simmered, but the ship was safe, at least for a little while. They had time to examine *Galileo*, to make sure she hadn't been damaged by this strange invader.

Except somehow she hadn't been strange at all.

Kali sounded like a Corps Academy graduate, like a green, idealistic soldier shipping out for the first time, hoping to change the fate of the human race with nothing more than optimism and obedience. Greg remembered his own early days, his own painful naiveté, the power of having no idea what he was up against. He *identified* with her. She'd appealed to every command and protective instinct he had, every skill honed in a decade and a half of bringing up younger soldiers, building and shaping an efficient and ethical crew.

Kali couldn't have been more effective if she had been written to get under his own specific skin.

Elena would be thinking about the next steps, validating the ship's systems, making sure Kali hadn't left any scars. But Jessica sagged in her chair, and he recognized the acerbic annoyance that always came out when she had a crisis on her hands. "Greg?" she asked.

"Yeah, Jess?"

"Remember when I told you I'd never forgive you for giving me this fucking job?" She directed a sharp, deep green glare into his eyes. "This is *exactly* the kind of shit I meant." She sat forward, her kinetic energy returning, and got to her feet. "Come on, both of you. We've got to tell the crew an alien CI has been reading their letters home."

# TWELVE

Nataliya made it ten minutes into Captain Lockwood's speech before she fled the pub.

She had already been ensconced at a shadowy table in the corner when Lockwood—and minutes later, most of the rest of the crew—showed up for the impromptu briefing. Nataliya had chosen the table for solitude; she didn't like brooding, but it seemed the brooding was going to happen anyway. She'd been studying a glass of whiskey she had no intention of touching, trying to convince herself she'd done the right thing. That Foster's death at the relay would have looked brave and meaningful, and would have violated the parameters of her mission. That she hadn't reacted out of instinct, out of the simple human reflex to save someone in immediate mortal danger.

The truth of it was she'd fucked up. All her meticulous training had fallen by the wayside. In the moment, all she'd seen was a crewmate like any other, and her own ability to help him. She'd saved him as she'd have saved Petrikoff, or Taras, or one of those awful children.

Or Viktor.

When she'd accepted this assignment, her hatred for Foster

had made it all seem simple. She could hang on to her rage and grief for Viktor and dispatch the man in a perfectly-crafted combination of humiliation and stupid accident. But it was time to acknowledge, if only to herself, that her emotional involvement had compromised her ability to execute. She should never have taken this mission.

*Never act with vengeance.* It had been one of her earliest lessons, and it was her own damn fault she'd chosen to ignore it this time.

She stumbled through *Galileo*'s corridors, irrationally angry with the ship's designers. The entire ship was too small, even these hallways, empty as the crew listened to that ludicrous speech in the pub. Not that the place ever felt crowded; as small as *Galileo* was, she was palatially large for her remaining crew. Too many of them had stayed with the Corps, determined to honor their oaths, or left the service entirely to stay out of the fray for as long as they could. *Galileo* was a sparse, hollow, empty, cold place, and what the hell was she doing here?

She wanted to go home, to *Meridia*, to shop for her breakfast in the common kitchens and grumble about the crowds. She wanted to talk to Viktor and laugh about the people they both knew and feel bad about the one thing he didn't know about her and wonder, for the thousandth time, if he'd forgive her if she told him.

But Viktor was dead, and *Galileo* was pointless, and she knew, in that moment, why early explorers had sometimes clawed their way out of airlocks, even knowing it would kill them.

*Galileo*'s crew believed it all. That, despite everything Nataliya knew, had shocked her the most. Captain Lockwood had gathered her soldiers and told them a piece of software—a piece of *Chryse*—had made its way into *Galileo*'s systems and had been spying on all of them. Except it was all somehow *fine*, because Lockwood had removed the software. The captain hadn't said where she'd put it, of course; Corps security nonsense. Under other circumstances Nataliya would have approved of her caution. No matter how much you trust your crew, expecting 167 people to keep a secret was naive at best.

But not one of them had pushed back. Not one of them saw the absurdity of it all, the convoluted link between the relay's destruction and that insulting lie about how *Chryse* had been destroyed. Nataliya had been enraged at first. But the longer she'd sat there, her eyes flitting from face to complacent face, the more nauseated she'd felt.

She'd left her drink and hit the corridor, every adrenalin-soaked molecule in her body screaming for her to *run run run away*.

Eventually the surface under her feet changed: she'd made it to the atrium, the green space that Lockwood was absurdly trying to turn into a reliable food source. The distant ceiling illuminated the area with the same Sol-spectrum lighting as the corridors, but the flora made the space more alive than the empty halls. Most of the plantings by the entrance were green and flowering shrubs, but someone had cordoned off a swath of carefully nourished soil and started some herbs. *Take what you need*, said a small sign before them, as if somehow the tiny plants would provide enough for these people to live on. Fools, every one of them. Six months minimum, and they'd either leave the ship or starve to death.

She leaned down and broke off a basil leaf, crushing it under her nose, and felt herself steadying, just a little.

"I like the variety my dad grows better," Greg Foster said behind her. "This one's not sharp enough."

*Fuck.* He'd followed her. Of course.

Out of the corner of her eye she watched him crouch down next to her, running his fingers over the plants. "This is hardier," he said. "Which I guess is what we have to focus on right now.

But I'm hoping we'll have enough room to do some experimenting."

"You don't have enough room for experimenting. You don't have enough room, full stop." Her voice sounded calm, and she wondered how she was managing that.

"Not to be fully autonomous, no," he agreed. He stood, inhaling the fragrance on his palms. "But nobody's fully autonomous out here. Not even PSI. We'll figure it out."

"Wishful thinking."

"Maybe."

He sounded so relaxed, so unconcerned, so unaware of what he was doing to all these people. "How could you do it?" she asked, unable to keep the anger from her tone.

"Do what?"

"Lie to them all." She rose, and flung the mangled piece of basil onto the ground. He was watching her with that same steady, careful, kind-hearted gaze he'd used on Sochi, and if she'd had a gun with her she'd have shot him dead right then. "That bullshit about *Chryse* and Bayandi and benign CIs, when this ship has been *invaded*. They're totally unprepared, and it's *your fault*."

She wanted him defensive, angry, on the ropes; she wanted to attack him like those teenagers had, to thrash him until he stopped lying and listened to her. She remained still as he looked at her with his strange eyes. They had to be artificial, those eyes, like his paramour's blue hair, because if they were natural they should have been revealing, their paleness opening up his mind like an old map, every fold and tatter exposed. Instead they threatened her with empathy, poked at her protective cover, dared her to confess all her truths.

She thought of Viktor again and swore.

At that, his lips twitched ruefully. "I was wondering if you were on Petrikoff's side on that one," he said. He didn't sound at all ashamed.

"I don't believe in unicorns or ghosts, either," she told him. *Except for ghosts.*

She caught a wave of sadness in his expression before he looked down at the herbs again. "I didn't really think about it, you know." He started down the path through the herbal beds, and she followed him as if pulled, the loamy fragrance of the soil fighting with the chemical smell of the ship's recycled air. "How it would sound, especially to the people who'd known *Chryse* for so long. When I saw—"

He swallowed, and why had she wanted to see this vulnerability? It was too raw, too real, and he was a liar and this was *wrong,* and she knew why she was here and this wasn't it.

"Once I'd seen, it all made sense. Every conversation I'd had with Bayandi, *Chryse*'s historical standoffishness. No other explanation was logical. It was like none of you paid attention to the simple fact of how old that ship had to be."

More bullshit. "*Chryse* minded her own business," she told him. "So did we."

"It's hard, I know," he said, all compassion again, "when a pillar of your life turns out to be different than you thought it was. And the thing about *Chryse*...Bayandi loved his crew. I don't know how, or whether it was the same sort of love I feel for my people, or you for yours. But he would have died to save them if he could. He would have died to save *us.* And I keep coming back to one thing: it doesn't matter that he wasn't human, because every choice he made was human."

"Why would you even *say* that?" she shouted. Did he think she was a fool? "What are you hiding? What really happened on *Chryse*?"

He was proving maddeningly impervious to her rage. "What do people say?"

She balled her hands into fists. "You destroyed her. You didn't save her when you could have."

"And how did that happen?"

"I don't know!"

None of them had thought through the details. There had been too much shock at sudden death, at the scale of it. All they could verify was that Foster had been on board *Chryse*, and by the time the ship got close enough to *Meridia* for anyone to check, her entire crew was dead. They hadn't even been able to retrieve the bodies. *Chryse* had crashed into a star, and Foster had said that was Bayandi's choice, and he was a liar. Foster was hiding what he'd done, whatever it was, and she'd never know what happened to Viktor, why she'd lost the only person who'd ever seen her, all of her, almost all of her, and loved her anyway.

"Bayandi wasn't a *robot*," she said, decisively.

"I'd never use that word." He was still walking, slow and easy, as if she hadn't just called him out on his fragile mythology. "I didn't know him long. But every conversation we had— his first thought was always for *Meridia*, or for *Galileo*. Even for me. Everyone else, never himself."

"You're saying he was *programmed* that way."

"Does it matter? He followed through, every time."

"Then why—" Her throat stuck for a moment, and she swallowed. "A CI designed to command a starship, especially one that, what, *evolved* over centuries? You're saying something that sophisticated was somehow compromised by a simple hardware failure."

"*Chryse* was sabotaged," Foster told her flatly. "She isn't the first starship to be lost with all hands."

She remembered, then, the story of his mother, the accident they'd covered up for so many years. Maybe that was where he'd learned to lie so easily. "He shouldn't have been vulnerable to human error."

"Do you think? I expect it's the greatest ambition of CI programmers to simulate human error."

She didn't want to talk philosophy. She wanted to murder him quickly, efficiently, cleanly, and go home to *Meridia* and drink for a very long time. "Is that what caused that booster relay to blow?" she asked him. "Human error?"

"That's my point, Nat. This CI, this thing we picked up—it saved my life."

She scoffed. "More fairy tales."

His expression tightened; she was finally getting under his skin. But he reined in his famous temper and turned to her, wearing that aura of calm authority he seemed to be able to conjure out of the worst possible mood. "Sit," he said, and the word was short and definite and sounded very much like an order.

Next to the path was a wide bench, wood and iron worked into sweeping, ergonomic curves. Beautiful and useful. The attention to aesthetics annoyed her.

She sat.

He sat next to her. "This is my comm, when we were out by the relay," he told her, touching the chip behind his ear. "Just listen."

She listened to his silence, and herself and Shaw and Lockwood all scrambling to figure out why he wasn't responding, saying anything to him they could think of to make him answer. She'd been on her game then, trying to figure out how she might make him look foolish or cowardly so she could turn the ship around and leave him to die. So much cleaner than a gun; so much more elegant to do it in plain sight of his entire crew. Throughout all of it *Capricorn*'s booster relay had been inert, nothing whatsoever to indicate it was about to blow itself to bits.

She heard a shout, distinctly in Shaw's voice. *Shaw's voice,* when Nataliya had been talking to the woman just moments before. She met his eyes, startled. "I didn't hear that part."

"That's because it wasn't on the group comm," he told her. "That was the CI, sending directly to me."

She felt a headache starting up behind her eyes, as if she

were staring at a bright light, and got to her feet to pace. He stayed seated, watching her.

"It saved my life, Nat. And yeah, maybe it had an ulterior motive, and it's really some Machiavellian monstrosity. But we talked to it. It's responsive and determinizing, and it displays aspects of a personality. We haven't done a full set of tests on it, but I'd put money on it speccing out as a full created intelligence. This thing isn't a myth, or some bullshit lie I made up to cover my own mistakes. Why the hell would I make up something that nuts? Do you know how many things can go wrong with a starship? If I'd wanted to fabricate the reasons for *Chryse*'s destruction, I could have come up with a dozen perfectly plausible explanations that didn't make me look like a lunatic, and didn't make half *Meridia*'s crew hate my guts."

All the warnings she'd been given about him during her mission briefing: *Glib. Charming. Smart*, she'd been told, only she couldn't believe he was really all that smart; when you were born into the world with a face like that, you didn't need intelligence. People gave you things: money, power, themselves. He knew what he was working with, of course he did; he'd used it on her, that slow smile, those sincere eyes that locked on yours and looked into you as if you were made of glass, as if you were the only person in the universe. He was attractive, compelling; you wanted instinctively to please him, just so he'd look at you again. *Of course* he could make up any outrageous story he wanted and get people to swallow it without question. *Of course* he could make people believe.

What if he was telling the truth?

What if he hadn't killed Viktor? What if he hadn't allowed *Chryse* to die?

What if none of it had been preventable, if her rage belonged elsewhere, aimed at some faceless corporation?

What if everything he'd said to her, everything that had happened today, before, to *Chryse*—what if all of it was real, and the man she'd constructed in her mind—the man deserving a humiliating death—was the fake?

She sat back down on the bench, heavily, and stared at the garden before her. There was a grove of citrus trees here, none growing higher than a meter, some heavy with green and yellow fruit, some flowering. Out of sync; they'd need to fix that. The fragrance was lovely, half-floral, half-tart, and for the rest of her life that smell would mean shock and grief and the agonizing knowledge that the mad jumble of recent events that had seemed like insanity actually made perfect sense.

"Bayandi would have told us," she tried, but she didn't sound convincing, even to herself.

"He said there were things he knew but couldn't say," Foster said. "He seemed to find that strange himself." He shifted on the bench, turning toward her. "He may have known, too, that you'd all find it hard to accept. He wanted, more than anything, happiness for his people, and I think that included *Meridia*."

She choked out a laugh. "A pre-programmed saint."

"Maybe," Foster said. "Even after the sabotage, I don't think his intentions ever changed. That's one of the things that made sense about him, when I finally saw him. He'd always been focused on compassion, every time we spoke."

"Better than us."

"Just different, I think." He was silent for a moment. "He wanted to learn to sing," he told her. "He said he tried, over and over, but he could never learn to sing."

"What a strange thing for a programmer to leave out."

"Yes. But it's very human, don't you think?"

She shouldn't look at him. In the microscopic set of things she was certain of in that moment, she knew she shouldn't look at him. But she turned nonetheless, and found him closer than she'd thought, his thigh centimeters from hers, his arm propped up next to her head. He could have reached out and tucked her hair behind her ear; self-consciously she did it herself, aware she was disheveled, that she'd come apart in front of him *again*, that he could see it, just as easily as he saw everything else about her. Which changed nothing, of course. Her mission had never been about Viktor, or *Chryse*. Viktor made it easier, but she'd never needed a mission to be easy. That was why they'd come back to her, even knowing how close she was to events: she'd do as she was told.

Foster was a romantic. He'd be easy to discredit, once she worked out how and when, and then she could do what she desperately needed to do. But sitting with him here, close enough to feel the warmth radiating off him, to wonder how his skin might feel under her palms, she thought perhaps she didn't have to kill him right away, not now, maybe she could wait a bit, just a little longer...

She heard the telltale step on the cobbled path: two shoes and the sharp *snick* of a metallic stick on the ground. Shaw, walking in on this scene Nataliya hadn't even deliberately set. And for the first time since she'd set eyes on Greg Foster, Nataliya thought maybe, just maybe, fate had resumed working in her favor.

# THIRTEEN

*WELL*, ELENA THOUGHT, watching Nataliya Gritsenko flail in Greg's presence, *at least she's got a lot of company.*

On some level, she knew Greg couldn't help it. He'd probably been striking since childhood, but certainly since his later adolescence; he'd have no reference for negotiating the world as someone who looked ordinary. Before they met, when all she knew of him was his reputation, she'd been predisposed to loathe him for it; but early in their acquaintance she'd realized his appearance was simply an adjunct to what really brought him power: honesty, intelligence, and an ingrained thread of kindness he never quite lost, even when he was being an utter jackass. People fell for him, all the time, no matter how adept he'd become at deflecting. His now-defunct marriage had proved a convenient shield, although there had been some who'd taken his presumed monogamy as a challenge.

Nataliya Gritsenko didn't seem challenged. She seemed annoyed with herself, shifting away from Greg like a guilty child, blushing furiously the way only the very pale were able to manage. Elena would have taken her reaction as deliberate, or at least manipulated for impact, but the irritation seemed entirely genuine.

Greg seemed distant and polite.

Elena had planned to give him more time. When they fought, it was a bad idea to let things play out in the moment: they both had tempers, and they both got mean. But she had always had trouble sitting with anger. Hers had been a lie of omission, and surely such things weren't uncommon, even between people who were…whatever they were to each other. Which was the other problem. Or maybe, now that she thought about it, the same one.

She could easily have sent an ensign to retrieve Greg's comm for analysis. None of them would have taken Elena's request at anything other than face value, especially given what he'd just been through. She'd thought of asking Ted to fetch the chip, but that was ridiculous. She'd known Greg Foster nine years. At times she'd believed she could tell him anything, no matter how horrible or shameful, and he'd listen. Hashing out this disagreement should have been trivial.

It had been so long since anything between them had been trivial.

Nataliya Gritsenko glanced furtively back at Greg, then hastily scrambled to her feet. "Commander Shaw." Her tone was stilted. "I'm—We were talking. About the…anomaly."

She couldn't even say *CI*. "It's a lot to take in, I know," Elena said, trying sympathy.

The PSI commander looked no more relaxed. "If there's anything—I mean, I don't know your ship. We don't know your ship," she added, and it wasn't the first time she'd referred to Petrikoff as an afterthought. "But if there's a way we can help, please do let us know."

It should have felt like a genuine offer. Elena thought it was, on one level: if Jessica asked the PSI officers to help out, Elena couldn't imagine they'd refuse. But there was a polish to the offer that didn't match the woman's awkwardness. Elena had dealt with a lot of unfamiliar societies in the last eighteen months, but even so, she couldn't quite convince herself this strange mismatch was down only to culture.

Appreciation seemed appropriate, regardless. "Thank you. I expect there'll be a great deal for all of us to do."

Nataliya stared for a moment, as if she expected Elena to continue, then turned back to Greg. "Thank you," she said, that thread of awkwardness still in her voice. And then, abruptly: "I'm sorry." She turned and fled.

Under other circumstances Elena would have asked Greg what the hell all that had been about, even teased him over his unwilling conquest. She would have at least asked if he had the same sense of the woman: that all the threads of her behavior, each one sincere, somehow wove together into something just a little too precise. But as he got to his feet, his posture stiff and careful, she remembered he was angry with her.

She wondered if he understood how long she'd been angry with herself.

"I need your comm," she told him. "I want to see if I can isolate Kali's entry point to our volatile storage."

The request was reasonable, and she tried not to feel ludicrous. He reached up and peeled the chip off his jaw, managing to transfer it to her fingertip without actually touching her. She stuck it to a thin sheet of film and slid it into her pocket.

He still said nothing, and she wondered how long she'd have to stand there before he gave in and spoke.

"I couldn't tell you," she said at last.

"I got that."

Short, annoyed; too controlled. That was worrying. "I should have," she tried. Then: "I'm sorry." Somehow, after Nataliya Gritsenko's apology, the words seemed shallow and insufficient.

He closed his eyes, and she took a moment to take in his face. More lines by his eyes than he'd had when she met him; he was growing older, just as they all were. Most of the time he wore it well, the nobility of years; sometimes, like now, he looked utterly exhausted. "It's not like I didn't know this about you," he said. "It's always you. Just you. *Only* you." He opened his eyes, and this time she caught a little anger. "No matter what."

Her own temper flared. "That's not fair." She'd known him too long to let him roll over her like this. "I thought I was *losing my mind*, Greg. You know what I'd just been through."

"No, I don't, Elena." At last his precarious control seemed to waver. "Because you never told me. You fucked off on a *suicide mission* and told me about it after the fact. And you've never told me what happened to you there, past the obvious." He shook his head. "Why did you come back here?"

He didn't mean back from her mission. He meant returning to *Galileo* at all.

"I won't apologize for taking that mission," she said. "I didn't have a choice."

He knew that. He knew how she'd been lied to, manipulated, made to believe there were no other answers. Did he really need the rest of it? Did he really need to hear how much blood she had on her hands, how she felt it, sticky and viscous, clogging her thoughts every single day?

"And now?" He was still on the present, on her deception, while she was stuck in the past. "You sure as hell had a choice about telling me you were *hearing voices*. Jesus, Elena. After everything that had happened—how could you not have linked it to *Chryse*?"

She held on tight to her temper. "You want know how many times in the last two hours I've beat myself up over that? You want me to do it again, now, in front of you? Okay, fine: *I fucked up*. A lot. But I thought I was going to *die* on Indus, Greg. I said goodbye to *everything*." *Why would I have left you if I'd had any other choice?* "And I wake up here when I didn't think I would wake up at all, and something starts whispering to me? Why the hell would I have thought *anything* in my head was working normally?"

She didn't think any part of herself would ever work normally again.

He took a step forward, towering over her, and for a moment she thought he was going to yell, the way he had so many times before when they'd fought. He'd yell, and she'd yell back, and one or both of them would say something genuinely unforgivable. And then the worst would be out in the open, exposed to the air, and it would dissipate around them and they'd figure out how to sweep it up when it settled. She hated fighting with him, but in the end it was better than saying nothing.

She saw his temper drain away, and those angry eyes, so clear and bright and transparent, grew bewildered, and then sad, and then, brutally, veiled and distant. "I understand, Elena," he said. "But here's the thing. You need so badly to be a loner, nobody's going to be able to change that for you. But it's damn hard to lean on someone when you know they can't bring themselves to lean on you."

He was twisting all of it. "That's *not* what I was doing! I watched you, Greg, for *seven years,* tied to a miserable marriage, destroying yourself to stay loyal, drinking yourself fucking *senseless,* trying literally *anything* other than just severing that tie. You stayed with her because you said you would, no matter what it did to you, and I'll be damned if I'm going to be the next reason you lock yourself in misery!"

"You think this has been *misery* for me?"

"Hasn't it?" So much of this had hurt more than she realized. "You sleep on the *floor,* Greg. You take care of me like I'm an infant, a child. You only touch me when you think I'm going to fall down."

"That's not true."

"And you kiss me like I'm your sister." The back of her throat closed and she swallowed; she wasn't going to undermine any of this by crying in front of him. "So on top of all that, I've got voices in my head, and Bob can't tell me what's causing them, and I figure I'll end up locked up somewhere, fighting to have two minutes of reality every day. I'm supposed to tell you, so you can promise you'll take care of me, that you won't leave me? So you can be tied to yet another fucking miserable situation out of *martyrdom*? How was I supposed to do that to you?"

"That wasn't your choice, Elena."

"The hell it wasn't."

Which was, somehow, exactly the wrong thing to say. He looked stricken as if she'd slapped him; and then he shifted his weight backward, and a chasm opened between them. "We always worked well together, didn't we?" he said. That closed expression returned. "On missions, we read each other's minds. You were so easy, even when you were a pain in the ass. I guess it was stupid to imagine that could translate to anything else."

"I can't become somebody I'm not, Greg. And I won't ask you to pay for my mistakes."

"And you can't ask me for help," he said flatly. "Even when you know you need it."

Was that what he wanted? "What if I had been crazy, Greg?" she asked. "What if I was losing my mind, and it was getting worse, and I would never get better and there was absolutely nothing you could have done about it?"

He looked away, and for one instant the grief on his face tore through her like hot glass. "I can't keep holding out my hand, Elena, when you tell me you're never going to take it."

She parsed that, and swallowed. "So...that's it, then? I make one mistake, and we're not together anymore?"

He looked back at her then, and the grief was still there; but something else played over his face, anger and irritation and a loss that seemed somehow deeper than the grief. "Be honest, Elena," he said to her. "Were we ever really together in the first place?"

*Yes,* she wanted to say. *Yes, we were. I came to you when I needed you and you held me up and made me strong, and I want that, I want that, I want to keep that, and why is this what breaks it? Why is this one thing I've done enough to shatter what I thought was strong?*

She was a mechanic. Odd that she was so good at breaking things.

"I have work to do," she told him, astonished at the calmness of her voice, and ignored the screeching agony in her hip as she headed out of the atrium and back to her engine room.

# FOURTEEN

Jessica didn't task the crew with scouring the ship for Kali-related damage purely to distract Elena, but she had to admit it was a useful fringe benefit.

Elena wasn't talking about her latest dust-up with Greg, but it didn't take astute observation to recognize it hadn't gone well. Neither Elena nor Greg were adept at processing difficult emotions, but at least Greg was willing to lose his temper when he needed to blow off steam. Elena swallowed everything and buried herself in routines, and there was nothing quite as routine-driven as a full ship-wide security audit. Jessica checked in on her as often as she could without becoming overbearing, and as long as she was on duty, Elena seemed almost like her old self. Spare time was different. Elena spent hers in a combination of extra shifts and hiding in her room, and Jessica knew better than to follow her there.

Greg, on the other hand, was spending a lot of time in public with Nataliya Gritsenko, a tactic Jessica didn't understand at all. It wasn't the optics of Greg taking meals publicly with another woman; Greg socialized at varying levels with many people in the crew, and everyone knew Nataliya Gritsenko had just saved his life. But there was something about the PSI commander that bothered Jessica. Gritsenko had a pitch-perfect response to every situation; even her embarrassments seemed optimally timed.

She'd said as much to Greg, who'd arched an eyebrow at her. "Theirs is a different culture, Jess," he said dismissively. She should have pushed it, but she'd opened the conversation by saying "What the *fuck* do you think you're doing?" and she had to admit, if only to herself, that she might have received a more satisfactory answer if she'd chosen tact.

Where Nataliya Gritsenko annoyed her—unfairly, Jessica had to admit; the woman was keeping up the flight training program, and that was undoubtedly a help—Petrikoff shocked her by proving to be genuinely useful. When she'd told the crew about Kali, she'd seen genuine fear on Petrikoff's face. Gritsenko had stormed out before Jessica had finished, but he'd hung on every word. She'd waited for heckling, or at the very least passive-aggressive follow-up questions, but instead he'd waited until most of the crew had dispersed to approach her.

"Captain Lockwood." Subdued, polite, thoughtful. Who was this guy? "I'd like to offer my services."

"If you'd be willing to continue your sparring training while we're stopped, Commander," she'd said, "I'll make sure people have enough time to—"

"Actually," he'd continued, the interruption deft and unaggressive, "while I'm happy to continue as a fighting teacher, I thought I might help with your systems checks. I have some experience with comms systems."

"How much?"

"Twenty-four years."

*Oh.* "What's your area of expertise?"

"Truth?" His smile was unexpectedly self-deprecating, and for a moment she understood why some of Taras' people had said he was charming. "Cracking Admiralty cryptography. I'm very good at it, although not always as fast as I'd like. But I can certainly help assess the health of your ship's comms systems. I do a lot of maintenance back home on *Meridia*."

"That would be—" She stopped. Past time to start dismantling her anti-PSI instincts. "Actually, Commander, how would you feel about doing some decrypting? Thanks to Commander Gritsenko, we actually got a decent dump of messages from the booster relay. I'd been planning to work on the decrypt myself once we were underway again, but...would you take a look now?"

She'd asked Samaras to supervise him, and report to her any oddity in behavior. But Samaras said that although Petrikoff wasn't precisely friendly, he was focused and productive. He'd cracked the low-level messages in a few hours, and Samaras thought between the two of them they'd have the full data set within a few days.

Jessica, having delegated thoroughly, found herself with the time to do what she'd wanted to do since Elena had confessed her hallucinations: figure out exactly how Kali had managed to climb out of a comm and into *Galileo*'s logic core.

Finding the program's residue was easy enough. Absent a reset, *Galileo*'s inert memory shadows sat blithely in volatile memory, waiting to be overwritten. Jessica had spent many sleepless hours after Kali's revelation saving aside every relevant shadow so she could analyze them at leisure. The program's origins might indeed be alien, but Kali running on *Galileo*'s hardware had to mean her code was comprehensible.

Except it wasn't. The pieces Jessica could read were garbled and broken, ciphers that redefined themselves partway through, tangles of virtuoso cryptography. Now and then she'd unravel a bit that made sense, a command or a status code, and she'd feel she was almost there, that it would all unspool itself before her at any moment. And then the thread would fade into memory-shadow nothingness, and she'd be back where she started, picking at a whole new and utterly opaque knot.

After nearly two days of frustration, she decided to ask Kali directly.

In the landing bay Jessica stripped off her comm chip, and took a look at *Unicinta*'s access log. As expected, Elena had been in a number of times, but always with Ted. Greg had dropped in twice, but hadn't stayed long. Somewhat to her surprise, Lieutenant Azevedo had been Kali's most frequent visitor, logging in morning, evening, and halfway through his shift on each of the four days since Kali's banishment. Azevedo, who openly disliked human contact, had kept a standing appointment with a machine that had requested company. He was a hard man to warm to, but this behavior was almost endearing.

The shuttle's door swept open as she approached. She suspected the gesture was meant to be welcoming, but it threw her a little, and she entered *Unicinta* off-balance. She wondered, without benefit of her comm chip, how much of her Kali would be able to read.

"Captain," Kali said as Jessica moved into the cabin. "How nice to see you."

Jessica looked over the ship's interior. The lights were dimmed, the engine systems off; an entirely normal, off-line troop ship. "Hello, Kali," she said, lowering herself warily into the pilot's seat. "How are you doing?"

"I am well, thank you, Captain," Kali said smoothly, and Jessica wondered what that polite response could mean to a machine.

"I have a few questions for you," Jessica said. "Do you think you'd be able to answer them for me?"

"I'll do my best, Captain. Although it may depend on what they're about. As I said before, there are things about myself I don't know."

Exactly what Greg had said about Bayandi.

"That might be exactly what I need to understand. I've been looking at the residual shadow you left on *Galileo*. It's only fragments, with different types of encryption. Encryption that shifts mid-fragment. I'm hoping you might have a map." She took a moment; all of her questions were tumbling together. "Mostly... the fragments always break just when I think I'm getting somewhere. Which probably says more about me than the encryption scheme, but it's consistent."

"How interesting," The CI's voice was indisputably intrigued. "Can you show me?"

Jessica pulled a data chip out of her pocket, and transferred her notes to *Unicinta*'s memory.

"It appears," Kali said almost immediately, "your fragments are all snapshots taken during an overwrite."

"*Galileo* doesn't overwrite shadows during snapshots," Jessica said.

"*Galileo* does not," Kali agreed. "But apparently I do."

"But—" Jessica stopped. "It's not a hardware restriction," she realized, and felt abruptly stupid. "The snapshot interval. Your programming deliberately subverts clean snapshots by doing the overwrite during the shadow creation itself."

"That's the only explanation I can think of," Kali told her.

"Do you have control over that?"

"I don't think so, Captain, but I'll work on figuring it out, if you'd like."

If Kali had been programmed to cover her own tracks, it was unlikely she'd be able to circumvent such a fundamental security measure. "That's all right," Jessica said. "I'll explore it from my end." She paused. "The overwrites. That's you losing a memory, isn't it? Does it...bother you that you can't remember things?"

"No, Captain." There was definitely a hint of amusement in Kali's voice, but nothing unkind. "It doesn't bother me at all. I suppose it ought to, especially if it's something that might help. But you don't remember all of your past, do you? There's very little point in agonizing over memories that aren't there anymore."

Jessica quizzed Kali about the algorithms she'd been able to decrypt, but ultimately the conversation was frustrating. Kali couldn't explain the shifting ciphers, nor could she locate anything like a map, and Jessica had to accept that the creators of this CI had not intended for her to be reverse engineered. But as Jessica fell into an easy back-and-forth with Kali, her unease returned. Kali's high-level reasoning worked much the same as *Galileo*'s did—unsurprising, given they'd shared the same hardware—but the subtleties, the humor, the emotional simulation, even the nuance of language were astonishingly sophisticated and difficult to parse into structured algorithms. Jessica asked about Kali's language model, and the CI produced an intricate chart of the basic grammatical rules of informal Standard. Jessica had studied a small chunk for twenty minutes before she gave up entirely.

"How do you keep that all straight with your limited storage?" she asked.

"Much the same way you do, I suppose," Kali told her.

Which was an answer and a non-answer all at once.

Jessica stayed more than an hour, and only broke off when Azevedo came lurking at his usual appointment time. Her first instinct was to brush him off, but she wondered, a little, at the persistence of his routine. Azevedo's work had always been flawless, and he'd done nothing whatsoever to earn her ire.

"Thank you, Ensign Kali," she said, aware Azevedo could hear her. "I'll come back if I need more information."

"You are very welcome, Captain," Kali said. "I'll look forward to seeing you again."

Jessica left, returning Azevedo's crisp, irritable salute, and retrieved her comm on her way out of the landing bay. Damned if she didn't believe Kali had meant it, and whether that meant the CI's programming was revolutionary or Jessica was an easy mark, she couldn't know.

Three days after they resumed their journey, Petrikoff provided Emily Broadmoor, head of security and Jessica's de facto second in command, with a decrypt of the messages they'd scraped from the ill-fated booster relay. "Some were lost," he told Jessica, with disapproval in his voice. "Your Corps hardware isn't robust enough."

The anti-Corpsness in his remark was oddly comforting.

Emily had asked for eight hours to sort through the messages, but she commed less than an hour into her time, summoning Jessica to Greg's old office for privacy.

"Listen to this," Emily said when they were both seated, and hit her comm.

A resonant baritone filled the office. "This is Captain Tauno Niemann of the CCSS *Capricorn*."

Jessica felt a stab of grief. She'd never met Tau Niemann, but there was bitterness, always, in hearing the voice of someone who had died. As a child, she'd avoided all such recordings; her friends had found them comforting, especially when they were of a lost parent, but somehow they just made Jessica angry, every time.

"We're eighteen hours off Target Zero. Long-range scans are still showing nothing, as predicted. We're picking up no signs of any technology at all out here." His words were dispassionate, but his tone was clipped, very nearly irritable. "Target Zero is emitting gamma particles, but levels are currently within limits. Absent the mission briefing, I'd have assumed it was a natural phenomenon, even as localized as it is. Tactically, all preparations are holding, and all indicators are normal.

"Off the record, Admiral." Now he sounded openly annoyed. "I must reiterate my objection to this entire mission. We are the wrong crew to be pursuing a scientific phenomenon, and we are the wrong crew to be carrying this set of passengers. We are a battleship, and this mission, without a break after our last one, is stretching the endurance of my people. I've kept the details of the mission secret from the crew, as ordered, but once we reach Target Zero they are hearing everything. They deserve to know. They deserve to know why we're carrying passengers who are most likely spying on us. They deserve to know why this has been done to them. And I'll tell you what I told you before: *I am the captain of this ship*. The actions of her crew are my responsibility. I object in the strongest possible terms to your punishing them for following my orders. They have done nothing wrong, and continue to do nothing wrong. You're breaking them for spite, and I don't believe I'm the only fleet officer who'll find that intolerable. You want to take that as a threat, Admiral, you go right ahead, but it's not. It's a promise that you and I are going to have words when I get back. Not the Admiralty and my crew, you and I. Whatever you want to do to me? Take your best shot, and good luck with it. But I won't have them paying for this, not my fuck-ups, and not yours.

"Niemann out."

Jessica blinked once. "What passengers?"

"Got me," Emily said. "They're not mentioned anywhere else. Petrikoff did a good job, but there just weren't many logs. It's all environmental reports, sometimes cartographic updates, most of it dry and routine. But this seemed...more significant."

Jessica stood up and started pacing. "Target Zero," she said aloud. "Again. And fuck-ups. He saw this assignment as *punishment*. Punishment for what?"

"Anaxis?" Emily suggested.

"Reed said Anaxis was intact when *Capricorn* left," Jessica reminded her. "And sure, that may have been Admiralty bullshit, but it's such an easily disprovable lie. Once what happened on Anaxis gets around, all the local colonies will compare sensor data. Everyone will know to the nanosecond when *Capricorn* left, and when the colony went up."

"Except," Emily pointed out, *"we're* here in the Seventh, comms-locked. That's not data we're going to get until long after we need it."

"I'm gonna run this by Greg," Jessica said. "He knows those Admiralty assholes better than I do. He might have some insight into what would make a captain in good standing threaten a superior officer like that. And then I'm going to let Ted know this mysterious Target Zero spews radiation. Maybe we can safeguard ourselves in a way *Capricorn* couldn't." She stopped pacing and looked down at Emily. "Did you know Tau Niemann?" she asked.

"We met at a few command-sponsored dinners," Emily said. "Charming. Pragmatic. I'd have called him cold, except he was passionately loyal to his crew."

"You liked him."

"Career soldiers have to stick together."

"What would it have taken," she asked, "to get Niemann this angry with his chain of command?"

"That's what worries me, Captain," Emily said. "If Niemann let loose like that, even off the record? Whatever they encountered out here, it was hurting them. It was hurting them badly enough he was ready to burn his career over it."

Except he hadn't had to, Jessica reflected as Emily left the room. His ship had burned instead, and taken everything he'd fought for with it.

# FIFTEEN

Greg hadn't realized how angry he really was until he heard Tau Niemann, an experienced captain of some renown, assailing his chain of command for destroying his crew.

Jessica had found him in the cartography room, fleshing out the meager maps they had for the Seventh Sector. It was rote work, the sort he usually eschewed, but more and more he was finding himself seeking solitude. Being with other people kept reminding him how much he missed talking to Elena. Even now, he was wondering what she'd make of Niemann's rant.

"I thought it was bad," Jessica said gently.

He abandoned his map and stood up to pace. "When I spoke with Gen," he said, organizing his thoughts aloud, "I could tell she was bothered. How bothered I didn't know. Yes, she gave me intel she shouldn't have; I figured she was tired. But maybe... maybe she was trying to tell me something. To warn me."

"Do you think they destroyed Anaxis?"

Dread tempered his anger. "I hope not," he told her. "That would be...I can't imagine them committing a war crime on that scale. I can't imagine the Admiralty—even Shadow Ops— ordering such a thing."

"*Something* happened there," Jessica said. "Something Niemann has been trying to protect his crew from."

"He didn't end up protecting anybody, did he?"

"Convenient if the catastrophe was on the Admiralty's order."

He rubbed his eyes. "So as a distraction, they sent everybody after *us*? You think covering for *Capricorn* would be worth starting a war with PSI?"

"Maybe they figure we're too new," Jessica suggested, but he shook his head.

"The Admiralty knows how PSI is about oaths. Taras would throw me to the wolves without a second thought, no matter how well we get along. But not *Galileo*."

"I don't know about that," Jessica said. "Taras is a pragmatist. And you've heard Petrikoff's arguments. Some of Taras' crew already think we're too dangerous to have as an ally."

She wasn't wrong, but he'd known Taras longer than she had. The PSI captain considered herself a benign dictator, and any sort of dissent—regardless of motivation—would be dealt with more quickly and brutally than Greg wanted to think about. "This Target Zero," he said. "Niemann said it was emitting elevated gamma. We picking up anything like that yet?"

She shook her head. "They were closer than we are. If it's purely a distance thing? Next hop, probably." She shifted, looking away from him. "Feeling like we shouldn't have followed. Feeling like in a day or two I'm gonna wish we were still Corps so I could compose a message like Niemann's. Wish I knew which admiral he was yelling at."

"Oh, Waris, I expect," Greg said. Few people bothered being circumspect with Admiral Waris—or used to bother; she'd recently vanished from public life, taking the official brunt of the blame for the set of clusterfucks Central had been responsible for over the last two months. Greg wondered, sometimes, if Shadow Ops had actually had her disappeared. More likely she was laying low, working on something else.

"Waris wouldn't have put up with a rant like this," Jessica said. "I mean, if she were still employed, and all that other shit hadn't come down, and—it's all related, Greg. All of it. And I can't see how, and I've put us all in danger."

Greg took a moment to study her face. He'd recruited her almost eight years ago now, based on her performance on CCSS *Aryabhata* as a tech security officer. Captain Dorjeban had described her as "outgoing and deceptively disingenuous," but she'd surprised Greg when they met by being composed, reserved, and very nearly taciturn.

*You scared the shit out of me*, she'd told him years later. *I had no idea why you'd offered me the job. Hell, I barely had any idea of why I wanted it.*

Her cryptographic skills were far beyond his own, and he'd taken her captain at their word that she was one of the most skilled tech people in the fleet. But he'd taken a moment to address the behavior that had seen her exiled from her home world.

*We stretch the rules sometimes*, he told her. *I take no issue with that. But everything you do on this ship has to be regulation. If I can stand on my head and make it look legal, I'll stand behind you, but if you make it impossible—you're out. Do we understand each other?*

She'd agreed, but he'd always had the sense he'd offended her. As he came to know what she was capable of, he realized where the insult lay: if she violated regulations, neither he nor anyone else would ever know.

"I could tell you I'd have made the same decision," he said to her. "I could tell you the crew would have insisted on looking into *Capricorn*'s fate if you'd asked them. But neither of those things are the point, Jess. Safety isn't on anybody's agenda anymore. Not yours, not mine, not this ship's. Not our families', even the ones who've never left home. Everything that's happening—this has been building for years. Decades. Maybe since before we were born. So if you want my advice, Captain Lockwood: don't think of this as danger. Think of this as the first salvo against an enemy who's been two steps ahead of us for too damn long."

She opened her mouth, and then closed it, her lips curving into a rueful smile. "I was going to tell you I hate this," she said. "But that's not the point either, is it?"

"I always figured I was lucky to be in a position where I was able to fight."

"That sounds like something Elena would say."

"Jess—"

Her comm sounded, and she held up a hand to him. "Ted?"

"Captain, can you come by engineering? We have something to show you."

"Care to give me a hint?"

"We've hit the elevated gamma," Ted said.

An entire day early. Greg wondered what that meant.

"But there's more than that. We've found the source, and you'll never guess: whatever this Target Zero is, it sure as hell isn't an Ellis lab."

"At first," Ted told them, "we couldn't figure it out. All we got was this concentrated stream of gamma coming from this one area, which we expected from *Capricorn*'s data. It wasn't until we filtered for the visual spectrum that we realized there's something solid there."

Greg stood next to Jessica in front of Elena's console. Ted did the talking, but Elena, at Ted's side, was vibrating with something between anxiety and excitement, her eyes darting from the visuals to Jessica, and even to Greg. This was *something*, he realized: a discovery outside her experience.

"Once we recognized there was a data barrier," Elena explained, zooming in on what looked like an ordinary cluster of stars, "we realized it was cross-spectrum, not just visual. It was harder to tell how big it was, because the emissions of stars are so diffuse." She enlarged the image, and he began to see it: a roughly oblong section of pitch black carved out of the dim starscape. As the image grew, the shape became clear: rectangular, twenty or twenty-five times longer than it was wide, the edges and angles far too precise for any kind of natural phenomenon.

He could feel the hair on his arms stand up.

"Why aren't we getting any readings from it?" He leaned forward, frowning at the sensor data. The object wasn't radiating anything besides the gamma bursts: no heat, no light, no outgassing of any kind. "Who has material that inert?"

"Not Central," Elena said. "And I know Ellis has some advanced research going, but this?" She shook her head. "The closest they came was an unstable cloak, and you know what a clusterfuck *that* was. That thing out there isn't cloaked. It's just, for all practical purposes, invisible."

"And Central already knew about it," Jessica told them. "They sent *Capricorn* for it."

She played them Niemann's message. He watched Elena's eyebrows creep up, and she reddened as Niemann defended his crew. That was one of her strange inconsistencies: she could flout authority with ease, and still feel righteous anger for a superior officer left with no choice but to risk censure to fight for his people.

But Niemann's anger wasn't the only thing she'd registered. "They had passengers."

"So it seems," Jessica said. "Passengers Niemann didn't particularly trust. Given his reaction, I'm betting Shadow Ops had some agents looking over his shoulder."

"There's a bigger problem," Elena said. "Niemann said the

gamma levels were tolerable. That's what we're seeing too." She met Greg's eyes, her expression grim. "They sure didn't stay that way. Remember their schematic?"

"It's not a matter of concentration?" Jessica asked.

Elena shook her head. "At these levels, it'd take that thing nearly two years to inflict the damage *Capricorn* had."

"So something else happened," Greg concluded, and Elena nodded.

"A blast, or a drastic increase as they got closer, but something. What we're seeing here wouldn't have bothered their shielding for at least a year."

Jessica stilled. "Elena. Did their flight recorder have any shielding readings as they were approaching Target Zero?"

Elena pulled up the data. "The last hard status reading we have on the flight recorder puts them half a million kilometers away. Their shielding was normal at that point."

"If it's a weapon," Ted pointed out, "staying away from it isn't going to make a difference."

"Unless it's triggered by proximity like the relay," Elena said, and Jessica waved a hand at them both.

"We're guessing," she said bluntly. "We have to assume either scenario is possible. *Fuck*." She rubbed her eyes. "Get us to that half million kilometer point," she said. "Get a drone ready. If that thing twitches and throws radiation at us...well, then we know." She looked over at Elena again. "How long did *Capricorn* spend here before being thrown back to the Fourth?"

"Timestamps on the flight recorder are a little inconsistent," Elena told them, "but our best guess is about seventy hours."

"Then we have three days to figure what the hell managed to take them apart."

# SIXTEEN

"No variance." Ted scowled. "At this distance the drone should be receiving thermal data, at least."

"Maybe the thing's not solid," Jessica suggested.

"Doesn't change the fact that everything else out here would be giving us *something*. Even if it's absorbing our scans, we'd be reading some reaction." There was a flare in the drone's vid feed: the gamma wave. Elena kept her eyes on the readout.

"Same spread," she said at last. "It'll wash over us. This one is slightly stronger than the last."

"Enough to cause us *Capricorn*-level damage?"

"Not even close."

Jessica's expression did not change. Elena understood; good news could turn to bad so quickly.

"Six hundred meters," Ted said.

The drone updated its data as it closed on Target Zero, but the readings were persistently mundane. This thing didn't even give them a signal bounce. It was like the drone was moving toward a two-dimensional projection, a drawing or a render, a shadow of reality rather than reality itself.

The drone's numbers abruptly stopped.

"Don't tell me," Jessica said dryly. "It died."

Elena shook her head. "It's transmitting," she said. "But it's still." She met Jessica's eyes. "It's landed."

"Not a projection, then."

Greg bent over the display, his eyes on the schematic. "What's it reading from the surface?"

"I don't—" Elena pushed the list of numbers over to him. "It's not returning anything. No density, no materials, no spectrum. Like everything's being absorbed, even our most basic, low-level scans."

She found her own suspicions reflected in Greg's eyes. When she'd brought *Chryse*'s lifeboat on board, they'd tried to analyze it. And like this object, that small grey polyhedron had yielded no information at all.

Jessica had remembered as well. "Anyone want to call this a coincidence?" She rubbed her eyes. "I liked this mission a lot better when we thought we were deciding whether this was Gov or some homicidal corporation. Call the drone back. Let's see what broke this time." The drone's numbers started changing again. "Now," Jessica said, "we just have to worry about being wormholed back to the Fourth and thrown at a civilian space station."

"It's not radiating anything dangerous," Elena reasoned. "It hasn't even demonstrated the capability to do so."

"You're seriously telling me you don't think that thing is behind sending *Capricorn* back."

Typical command impatience: wanting conclusions before hard data. "All I'm saying," Elena told her, "is we currently have no evidence that anything unusual happened here, apart from flight recorder data telling us *Capricorn* was here right before she appeared in the Fourth."

"That's not enough?"

"We *could* go back now," Greg suggested. "Publicize what we've found and be done with it, whatever *it* is. Fuck what they do to us." It wasn't a serious suggestion, of course. He was presenting the most extreme choice, just to be sure it was covered.

"Fuck," Jessica said under her breath. "Okay. Two people, one shuttle. I'm also sending a drone to follow at a distance, in case that thing decides it wants to power something down again. Surface recon, ten minutes, no longer." She met Greg's eyes. "No walkabout this time. Recon and out. Understood?"

He nodded, all business. "Who's coming with me?"

Elena opened her mouth, but Jessica ignored her. "Take Gritsenko again," Jessica told him. "She seems invested in keeping your foolhardy skin alive."

"And if she doesn't want to go?"

Jessica's gaze never wavered. "I would bet every last centime I ever pried out of the Corps that she will. You wanna take that bet?"

Something rippled over Greg's expression, but Elena couldn't decode it before he turned and left.

In the landing bay, Elena ran her scanner over *Apate*'s hull, Nataliya Gritsenko lurking behind her back.

Greg hadn't yet arrived, but she knew where he was. They'd all left messages for family with *Meridia* to be delivered in case *Galileo* didn't make it home. Greg had recorded a long message to his father, still trying to make up for years of estrangement that had only recently eased. Greg would be talking with Bob Hastings, who'd known Tom Foster all of Greg's life, telling him what to say to his father if he never returned from Target Zero.

Which was a distinct possibility. More than anything else she wanted to go with him, if only to ensure she didn't have to go on without him.

She bent over stiffly to scan as low on *Apate*'s nose as she could. Azevedo was on the floor, examining the ship's undercarriage. He'd catch the bits Elena couldn't reach, and he'd do it thoroughly and well, and she still hated delegating.

"This thing has a pretty big arsenal," Commander Gritsenko said. Quiet footsteps; she was closer than Elena had thought.

"It's a troop carrier," Elena pointed out. A PSI battle pilot wouldn't care, but she was fairly certain Nataliya Gritsenko had been something else before she'd given her oath to nomads.

"Why haven't you removed them?"

At that Elena turned to look at the other woman. Nataliya's expression was direct, slightly defiant, and more than a little uncomfortable. Discomfort was just about the only expression that made her look anything other than vid-ready perfect. She'd have made a good streamer: effortlessly photogenic, but able to neutralize her expression so her natural beauty didn't distract from what she was saying. You'd become a very good liar with that ability, Elena recognized. She wondered if Nataliya knew how good Greg was at seeing through lies.

"No time," she said, and turned back to the ship.

"You've had eight weeks," Nataliya said.

Was the woman trying to pick a fight? "And a few other priorities." Elena kept her voice neutral. "And, as you've likely surmised, nobody on this ship is keen to get rid of our armaments, especially under the current circumstances. We're used to being able to fire back."

"Do you find active belligerence helps?"

"Sometimes, yes." She straightened, running her hand over the shuttle's nose; her hip objected, and she shifted her weight off of it. No matter how well it eventually healed, she suspected it would still get in the way at all the wrong moments.

Nataliya was silent so long Elena wasn't sure if she'd left. But then she said: "I didn't make him leave you."

Was *that* what she was on about? Elena turned around. Nataliya's skin was still pink, her body language still uncertain;

but she no longer looked uncomfortable. She looked defiant, as if Elena had attacked her.

*Who are you?*

"I know," Elena said, and she kept her voice as gentle as she could. "You couldn't have."

Defiance gave way to chagrin, and Nataliya looked away. She swallowed, resettling her shoulders, but she wouldn't meet Elena's eyes again. Odd. Elena would have expected embarrassment, or even anger; this seemed like irritation.

"Clean, Commander," Azevedo said.

"Here too," Elena told him.

She lowered her scanner, and Nataliya finally looked at her again, entirely composed now. Even the blush was gone, which was curious; Elena, who was fairly controlled herself, was often betrayed by blushing.

"Come home safe," Elena said, and the PSI commander gave her a curt nod.

# SEVENTEEN

Stupid, Nataliya thought. *This is the stupidest mission ever conceived.*

She ran the interior pre-flight. Foster still wasn't there, and despite their lack of formal deadline it annoyed her. This entire mission annoyed her; he was cast as the hero yet again, and they would be under constant monitoring for the entire absurd exercise. She should have killed him on board, somehow: food poisoning from that stupid diet of his; tripping and falling during his interminable runs; an aneurism arguing with his ex-partner.

Which was another thing. Who was Shaw to extend her sympathy? Shaw had seen them together in the atrium, Nataliya nearly in Foster's lap, and as far as she could tell the indiscretion hadn't fazed the mechanic in the slightest. She'd wondered if perhaps the attachment wasn't as deep for Shaw, but what had the woman just said? *You couldn't.* Absurd confidence in a relationship that, as far as Nataliya had been able to discover via the ship's shameless gossip network, had died before it got off the ground.

Fuck all these people. She should have shot him on Sochi.

A few minutes later she heard a step behind her, and Foster settled into the co-pilot's seat. "Never flown a bomber before?"

So this is what they were going to do: pretend none of this was unusual. "Long time ago," she said. "We don't have bombers in PSI. We don't fight that way. Do you really use these things in combat?"

"Now and again," he said. "They make an impression."

"A deep and smoking one, I suspect."

"If we run across something that needs shooting," he said, "at least we're covered."

He seemed calm, almost cheerful, and if she'd tried to say anything she'd have started screaming.

*Galileo* had stopped 600,000 kilometers from Target Zero, giving it a wider berth than *Capricorn* had while still being close enough to scan it. Direct flight time was four minutes, but she'd plotted an elliptical course, planning to keep an eye on their sensors in case the thing was as bothered by proximity as the relay had been. The drone had survived, but nobody—including Captain Lockwood—was keen on making assumptions when people were involved.

She powered up the shuttle and steered them out. Ahead, the stars began to disappear as Target Zero filled their viewscreen. Darkness Nataliya had expected, but she hadn't expected darkness so deep it was essentially nothing at all. She waited for their meager running lights to illuminate *something*—shape, texture, some visual indicator besides void. But although *Apate*'s schematic display still showed the gamma emissions, there was nothing else. As they grew closer, Foster had the shuttle render the object's shape, then frowned at the result, asking for a recalculation.

No change.

"*Galileo*," he said, "are you getting this?"

Jessica answered him. "If you're asking if we see a great big featureless rectangle," she said, "then yeah, we're getting it."

The shape *Apate* had rendered was precise: a rectangle, a little over 300 meters wide, a little over seventy meters high, hanging before them, unmoving. But there was nothing mundane in the non-responsiveness of the object. Gamma kept coming in the same regular, leisurely bursts; but there was nothing it could be radiating gamma *from*. Nataliya found herself hypnotized by the rhythm of its bursts, every pulse beating out the same word in her head: *danger danger danger...*

Her years of training had taught her what she did and didn't find frightening. This was wrong. "Do you feel that?" she asked Foster.

"Feel what?"

How to describe it? "Primal terror. The existential urge to get the fuck out of here. I don't think it's natural," she clarified. "Natural fear I've had since we left the Fourth Sector. This is more like...specters at night."

She focused on the schematic, gritting her teeth against the anxiety.

"I don't feel it," he said. That fucking careful tone of his was back, and even in her terror she wanted to choke him. "You think it's artificial?"

She nodded.

"Jess," he said, "it's emitting something. Something designed to push us away."

"To push *me* away." Fuck him for trying to protect her. "It's not affecting him."

There was a pause, and then Jessica said, "We're not reading anything here, Greg."

"It probably attenuates," Nataliya said. She shook her head; that didn't help. "It's not as bad if I look out the window."

Foster turned off the schematic and looked ahead, the black absence of stars growing larger before them. The pulse in the back of her head quieted, a predator lying in wait.

"One hundred meters," Nat said.

"You still got us, *Galileo*?" asked Greg.

"Loud and clear," said Jessica. "Can you see anything yet?"

There was nothing before them but all-absorbing blackness, untouched by their bright running lights. At 100 meters, they should have at least seen a faint pool of light. "Take it slow, Nat," Foster said. "Can we parallel the surface?"

Enough was enough. "The drone landed on it safely," she said.

A brief silence from *Galileo*; she could only imagine the discussion happening on the other end. "I'm thinking this is a good argument for live weapons," Jessica said at last.

*To shoot what?* But Nataliya activated the ship's defensive systems anyway.

She stopped their forward momentum, and sank the ship slowly, delicately; she managed to land without a jolt, but she felt something familiar, an unpleasant, uneven tug in her gut, like...

*Son of a bitch.* "We have gravity," she said. She looked up at Foster. "This thing's got a gravity field now. Are you getting this, *Galileo*?"

"We are. .005 within the gravity on your ship. Shit."

"Did it do that to the drone?"

"Hell, no."

It had sensed them and reacted to them, and the gravity field was as nonsensical as the gamma. "Anything else, *Galileo*?"

This time it was Shaw who spoke. "Not a thing. I think we're going to have to poke at it."

Captain Lockwood swore for a while, but when Nataliya looked over at Foster, he was grinning.

*Damn fool.*

Greg took a pair of mid-range handguns out of the armory cabinet and held one out to Nat. She stood unmoving, staring at him; through the rippled, clear fabric of her hood, he couldn't quite read her expression.

"Unless you'd rather have a plasma rifle," he said.

She took the gun.

He set the ship's gravity field by the door, leaving the oxygen generator running. They'd walk around, see what they could see; ten minutes, Jessica had ordered, and they'd be back and heading home. *Apate*'s field would preserve the shuttle's interior environment even if Target Zero relinquished its hold. The shuttle would be there when they returned, no matter what the object decided to do.

He opened the door, and stepped out into the dark.

The surface was unremarkable under his feet: solid, like any starship corridor. He crouched, bringing his helmet light close to the ground; at half a meter it was at last reflective, but it was still impressively dark. He reached out a hand and brushed his fingers against it, his glove transmitting the texture: slightly rough, like stone, but the fine sandy grain seemed too regular to be natural.

He straightened. Next to him, Nat stood with her fingers curled tightly around her gun. The glare of her hood light concealed her expression.

"Left or right?" he asked her.

"Left," she said.

"Keep your lights on," he told her. "And don't get out of my sight."

"Yes, Captain," she said, and it might have been sarcasm, but he didn't think so.

Greg stepped forward, his light illuminating a small patch before him. There was a ridge down the center of Target Zero; in the dim light he couldn't be sure if it ran the full length of the structure, never mind speculating about its purpose. After a few steps he wondered if the platform's uniformity would be the most remarkable thing they learned about it.

"Anything, Nat?" he asked.

He saw her light move as she shook her head. "Tried to take a surface sample," she said. "If I got anything it's microscopic. Whatever this material is, it's harder than anything we can currently etch."

"It's not getting any brighter over here," he told her. "If we—"

The shadows ahead of him shifted

"What?" There was an urgency in Nat's tone, and he remembered the last time they'd done this, when he'd fallen silent and she'd apparently yelled at him for ten minutes straight. He'd frightened her. He'd seen, since they met, so much of what made her vulnerable. He didn't think someone like Nat was accustomed to being exposed.

"It's okay. I'm okay. I just see something up ahead."

"Stop," she said, and it came out like an order. "I'll be right there."

"I'm just going to get a little closer." He kept walking.

Elena's voice in his ear. "What is it?"

"I'm not sure." It was a light, or a pocket of even darker darkness; he couldn't quite tell, against this strangely absorbent surface. "It's a variance, that's all I know. Are you seeing anything there?"

"I'm not—wait." Elena's voice grew urgent. "It's emitting now. It's growing. It's another wormhole, Greg. Same as the readings on the relay, but stronger."

"You've got my vid feed?"

"I do," Elena verified. She sounded tense, nervous. Excited. She should be here with him, seeing this at his side.

"Foster," said Nat. "*Wait*, for God's sake."

No gods out here, he wanted to tell her; but wherever this thing came from, he didn't think it was Shadow Ops or Ellis or anything remotely human. He could still see the original worm-hole in his memory, that strange snaking pattern; he'd been convinced it was going to be the last thing he saw in his life.

And there it was, up ahead: small, smaller than his hand, but whirling and twisting, still and dynamic all at once, hurting his eyes when he tried to focus on it, but so compelling, so *elegant*. Math come to life; Elena had called it *sideways matter* when they'd talked about it, and he'd laughed at her because that meant nothing, but here on this platform, this alien place—because it had to be alien; they'd been foolish to think otherwise—the phrase made sense, and he wondered that he'd ever tried to call it anything else. He stepped closer, and abruptly it was bigger, as big as his hand, or his head, or *Galileo* or all of space and time. No foreboding, no fear; all he felt was tranquility and longing, and something in the back of his mind said *snare* and it didn't matter, and he heard Nat shouting at him and a chaos of voices in his ear and he took a step forward and the surface beneath him dissolved into light.

Everything happened at once.

Foster moved forward, and she shouted at him to stop, and he mumbled platitudes at her. Bloody Corps captain. No matter what he resigned from he'd always be the same, stubborn and immovable and always knowing best. The ripple before him brightened, broke, opened like the maw of a sea monster from a horror vid; and it was everything she could do to run toward it and not screaming back to *Apate*, letting her terror pull her away from Foster and her assignment and abandon him on the surface of this absolutely *wrong* object hanging in the middle of galactic nowhere.

In her ear she heard Captain Lockwood shouting at him to

stop, to back away from it, to wait, for God's sake, what the fuck was he thinking?

"Commander!" Jessica shouted. "Stop him! Stop—"

His vid feed brightened, overloading her sensors, and she stopped, blinded, fumbling to cut off Foster's feed. She blinked against the afterimage and began moving forward again, and then she could focus on him, see him clearly...

...as he stepped forward into the ripple, and dropped, ramrod straight, into nothing.

Lockwood was shouting into her ear, possibly firing off orders, possibly looking for a sitrep; something professional. These people were nothing if not unflappable in a crisis. Even if Nataliya'd had a plan, she'd have had to scuttle it; Foster had looked mad, jumping in, but still heroic, still doing what they all wanted to do themselves. He might have actually done himself in without her help, on vid for his whole crew to see, stepping into a manufactured wormhole on an alien structure, being swallowed into—what? It had to be a door of some kind, and that meant he was probably still alive. Or possibly. Nataliya had never been any good at figuring the odds.

*If he dies here, like this, he looks like a hero.*

Exactly what she had been sent to prevent.

"I'm on it," she said. She was closing on the wormhole; she could see it better now, all glow, no depth, snaking off Target Zero's surface, huge and tiny all at once, but growing smaller with each step she took in the fickle artificial gravity. It might let her go at any second, let her drift off into the darkness to risk the precariousness of rescue; she still felt that pressure to turn away, to run from inevitable death, but she found something stronger beneath it, something old and solid that had been with her all her life, even before she'd become what she was.

All her foreboding vanished.

*Why this target?* she'd asked, when she'd received the mission.

*Our reasons don't concern you,* they'd said.

*With respect,* she had continued, *is it true? What he said about* Chryse?

It was a personal question for her, and they had to know it. They'd taken nearly five full seconds to respond.

*No. He is a liar.*

And she hadn't cared, anymore, why he was a target. He was hers, her mission, like a dozen before—no, sixteen. Precisely sixteen. There was no point in being an assassin if one was sloppy with numbers. All the others had been easy: dictators, kidnappers, political linchpins. All people whose loss improved everyone's lives. There was something she didn't know yet about Foster, something that made him part of that crowd as well. He would be seventeen.

But she'd have to catch him first.

"I'll bring him back," she said, and Jessica Lockwood was shouting *stop,* and she reached the closing wormhole and dove headfirst into its bright jaws.

# EIGHTEEN

*I PROMISED YOU*, Elena thought. And then: *You stupid son of a bitch.*

She nearly fell getting to her feet; she'd been sitting badly again. Her cane was on the floor next to her chair, and there was nothing for it but to sit down again to retrieve it. Jessica was shouting something at Nataliya Gritsenko, telling her to stop doing whatever it was she was doing, not that it mattered. Elena was back on her feet before Jessica started swearing.

Jessica was stalking out of the room, Bristol at her heels, ending up a step ahead of Elena. "Samaras, get me *something* out there, send a drone, use our sensors, I want some kind of vid feed *now*. Pair of functional adults, and they both end up doing something stupid."

"What do you mean?" Elena asked.

"She went after him," Jessica told her grimly. "He walks into a wormhole like some fucking ambulatory *fungus*, and she goes in after him. *Fuck.* What the fuck are we supposed to do with that?" Jessica stopped then, and turned. "Where the fuck are *you* going?"

Elena went around her; the damn cane was slowing her down. She collapsed it and held it in her fist. "I'm going after him," she said, limping heavily, pain in every step. *Damn this hip* —it was never going to heal anyway.

"You are *not*, Elena. Stop."

*Sparrow* was probably the best choice for a shuttle. She was small and maneuverable, and ready for remoting; Elena could reconfigure her for live piloting in a few minutes. Still, a few minutes was a delay. Better choice, maybe, to take *Unicinta*, unless Kali had reprogrammed everything. Yes, that was a better idea: no delays. She walked faster, steadier; she had a plan now.

"Commander."

There was no time to explain the details. "I'll be careful," she told Jessica, even knowing it was an impossible promise. "I'll get him out, and we'll figure out what to do next."

"You *stop*, Commander, right now. That's an order."

*Now* Jessica was choosing to stand on ceremony? This was ridiculous. "Think it through, Jess," she said. "We can't get him out with a drone, and I'm the only other person on this ship who—"

"Lieutenant Bristol, stop the commander, please."

Bristol was light on his feet for such a big man, and Elena stumbled as he appeared before her, blocking her progress. She glared. He quailed, but held his ground. Greg said Bristol was afraid of her because she was blunt, and he was never sure how she wanted him to respond. Well, fine; she could use that now.

"Get the fuck out of my way, Lieutenant," she said levelly.

He reddened. He might as well have written every feeling he had in large letters above his head. "I can't, Commander," he said.

*Never explain obeying an order.* "Jessica. Call him off."

She heard Jessica's footsteps behind her, but she kept looking at Bristol. He was the one she had to beat; he was the one between her and where she was going. "I'm not letting you go after him, Elena," Jessica said.

Elena replayed that in her head a few times, and then turned.

Jessica looked exhausted. She hadn't been sleeping much, Elena knew, since the discovery of Kali, having become fixated on figuring out how the CI had entered their ship. But she also looked pissed off, and worried, and frustrated, and hardline determined in a way Elena recognized. She'd faced off with enough officers in her career to know when she was running out of professional slack.

"Captain." Her reasoning was sound; it was just a matter of helping her superior officer understand. "All of our readings tell us that object he fell into is the same configuration as the wormhole on the relay, the same as the wormhole we found years ago. He and I have both survived traversing it. He's gone through, and Commander Gritsenko has followed him. There's no one else on this ship qualified to get them back." *I promised him.*

But Jessica was unmoved. "First of all, our data tells us that little tiny thing he fell into is *probably* built from the same technology as whatever blew that relay to bits, and did you forget about that? Second, you analyzed absolutely *fuck-all* when you traipsed through that wormhole two years ago—*also* being insubordinate, as I recall. There is nothing at all about you that makes you uniquely qualified to dive into some unstructured rescue, Commander, and you know it."

*She's not listening.* "I know how he thinks," Elena tried. "I know why he would have—"

"How he *thinks*?" Jessica interrupted, incredulous. "He wasn't *thinking*, Elena! That thing fucking grabbed him, just like it did before, and my big mistake here was letting him go and face it again!" She took a step forward, and Elena could feel cold, controlled anger coming off her. "I'm not going to handle this incident by sending officer after officer into that thing. We're going to deal with this like soldiers and scientists. You are not going anywhere, Commander, and that is a fucking order, you understand?"

A wave of panic shot through Elena, and it was everything

she could do not to push past Bristol, to run down the hallway, damn her hip, damn her orders, damn all of it. "You don't understand," she said. "I have to go after him, Jess. There's no time. I promised him. I can't go back on that. I can't." *Please.*

Elena could see it in Jessica's eyes: sympathy, grief, comprehension. Her friend understood.

Her captain had already made up her mind.

"Lieutenant Bristol," Jessica said, "please take the commander into custody. Commit her to Doctor Hastings' care; she's his patient. He's to look after her until I say otherwise."

"Yes, Captain." Bristol sounded almost relieved.

"If she resists," Jessica added, "knock her out."

"Yes, Captain." Less relieved.

"Jessica," Elena said. "Please. I have to."

"You don't, Lanie," Jessica said. "*I* have to. This isn't a thing you can do. When I figure out what is, I'll let you know."

And she turned on her heel and headed back into the machine room.

Elena kept her eyes on her friend's retreating figure. "I could take you," she said to Bristol.

She heard the soldier shift and clear his throat. "No, Commander," he said. "Maybe before you got hurt, if you surprised me and got lucky. Right now you can't. Please don't try."

Her panic turned to cold rage, and she turned to glare at him. Of course she could take him. She had her cane, which made a decent weapon, although it wasn't as strong as the training quarterstaves they used. He was weaponless, and he would be surprised, especially given his assessment of her health. She could knock him down; she didn't have to disable him, just get far enough ahead. Behind the knees might be best. That was a weak point for anyone, and if she could hurt him enough to keep him down for a minute, even just thirty seconds, she might be able to get to the landing bay and off the ship. Azevedo would let her through, surely, although he was curiously particular about regulations. She'd have to lie to him, come up with something that would at least make him drop his guard. Which meant she'd have to keep Bristol out of commission longer, so he wouldn't alert Jessica, so there'd be no alarms she'd have to explain away. She supposed she could hit Bristol on the head, and hope the resulting concussion wouldn't be too serious, but that kind of refinement with a blunt instrument was beyond her skill. She'd have to count on getting lucky, but if she wasn't lucky she might kill him.

She couldn't risk it. Not even for Greg.

Bristol relaxed a little; he'd seen it all on her face. "Let's go, Commander," he said, and she hated the kindness in his voice.

She fell into step next to him, using the cane again; he slowed his usual pace, and she thought even if she wasn't going to bash him unconscious it might be nice to at least punch him once. "I bet I could have," she said at last.

"When all this is over," he said, "and everybody's home safe, we can meet in the gym and you can try."

His kindness nearly undid her, and she spent the rest of the walk to Bob's office in silence.

Bob was reading when they arrived, feet up on his desk. Clearly nobody had told him what happened yet, and Elena felt annoyed for him. He should have been with them, watching. Instead he was here, in the infirmary, waiting for the consequences of this mess to be brought to him to fix.

He sat up as they walked in, instantly tense, worried, expecting the worse. "Elena?"

She opened her mouth, but Bristol spoke over her. "Excuse me, Commander Hastings. Commander Shaw is under arrest;

the Captain told me to put her in your custody. She's your charge until the Captain notifies you otherwise."

Bob's eyes never left Elena's. "What's happened?" he asked.

"He's gone into it," she said. "Target Zero."

She watched his face: denial, terror, anger—and then a sad sort of amusement. "Of course he has," he said. At last he met Bristol's eyes. "Why am I in charge of this soldier, Lieutenant?" he asked.

"Captain's orders," Bristol said simply. "She's grounded."

"Yes, she is." He studied Bristol a moment longer, then turned back to his desk. "You let the captain know I've taken responsibility," he said. "Thank you, Lieutenant. You can go."

Elena waited until Bristol was out of earshot, and then it all poured out of her in a rush. "I have to go after him, Bob. I promised him. I promised him I'd always go after him, and he's fallen into that thing while he's angry with me and Jessica is *not* thinking clearly."

Which was possibly projection, but also almost certainly the truth.

Bob had opened a drawer and was rummaging for something. "I need to start recycling some of these things," he said, half to himself. "Ninety percent of this junk I'll never—ah, there it is." He found what he was looking for and kept his back to her, studying whatever was in his hands.

"What are you doing?" she asked.

He turned around, strapping a set of medical instruments to his arm. "Coming with you," he said easily. "Although officially you're coming with me, since I'm in charge of you." He still sounded amused.

She shouldn't have been surprised. "Bob, no. I can't ask you to take that risk."

He let out a sigh. "Greg's right about you," he said. "You really do get stuck on irrelevant bullshit." Before she could ask what the hell that meant, he stepped forward and put a hand on her arm. "I met that boy when he was three months old. He is my family, as much as he is yours. You're not asking me to do anything. This is my choice, and you've no authority to stop me. And besides—if you want to help him, you need me. Jessica put me in charge of you. She didn't tell me what I could or couldn't do with you. Now." He dropped his hand. "Where are we going?"

Elena had no idea what to say to any of that. "Landing Bay One," she told him, and for the first time in the few minutes since Greg had vanished she felt a flare of hope.

They fell into step. Bob took it slow and casual, which somehow felt less insulting than Bristol doing the same, but she could explain Bob's actions by believing he was trying to draw less attention to them. And indeed it worked. Bob, who was genial with people without being especially personal, smiled and nodded at the few soldiers they passed; everyone was rushing around, focused on securing the ship, having no time to wonder where Bob and Elena might be going. They drew no unwanted attention at all.

She had to admit Bob had a pretty good instinct for prevarication.

"Which ship are we taking?" he asked as they approached the landing bay.

"*Unicinta*," she said. He looked over at her, and she added, "She's ready to go. The backup shuttle is configured for drone flight; it'd take me too long to make the changes."

"Why is *Unicinta* on deck?"

"That's where we put Kali. The CI."

Bob absorbed this news. "I had wondered," was all he said. "But wouldn't *Unicinta* be locked down?"

"We weren't really worried about Kali flying away."

He made a sound, and she supposed he disagreed. But when they walked through the open door and turned to Azevedo, Bob was all easygoing smiles.

"Afternoon, Lieutenant," he said. "We're here for *Unicinta*."

If Azevedo found the request strange, he said nothing. "Comm chips in the locker," he said. "Or incinerate them if you don't care what's on them."

Bob stripped off his chip and pressed it into the incineration slot, utterly unconcerned. Elena moved to do the same, but at the last instant she palmed it instead, the sticky dot clinging to the heel of her hand.

Kali would need to know what they were facing.

They climbed on board the ship, and as Bob turned to close the door, Kali said, "Hello, Commander Shaw." She sounded pleased.

"Hello, Kali," said Elena. "I've got a comm chip with me I'd like you to read." She peeled it off her hand and placed it behind her ear, reactivating it.

Less than a second passed before Kali said, "I see. Target Zero is not the same threat as the booster relay, Commander."

Bob settled himself into the copilot seat and began a pro forma pre-flight check. "That seems obvious," he said. "But I don't think the obvious differences are what you mean."

"It's nice to meet you, Doctor Hastings," Kali said.

He smiled, just a little, over his work. "Nice to meet you, too, Kali. We hadn't arrived at Target Zero when you were put in here, had we?"

"No. It's not an Ellis lab."

A shiver went up Elena's spine. "I didn't think so," she said. "It seems too different from what they've been doing."

"Ellis' technology is impressive," Kali said, a little dismissively, "but they build incrementally on what exists. The technology of Target Zero is different."

"You're familiar with it?"

"I am," Kali said.

Which confirmed a number of theories Elena didn't care about in the moment.

"But I don't think I know very much. We'll see if the little I've been allowed to retain is helpful. Lieutenant Azevedo appears unconcerned with our behavior so far. Shall we go?"

Elena half expected Kali to start the engine for her, until she remembered they'd restricted the CI's systems access. With a glance at Bob, she powered up the little ship and raised them a centimeter off the decking. *No hotrodding,* she told herself, although all she wanted to do was to full-throttle toward Target Zero and physically extricate Greg from whatever was holding him.

*You don't know what you'll have to do.*

*You don't even know if he's still alive.*

"Everything will be all right, Elena," Kali said gently.

Elena piloted them off *Galileo* and into the dark.

# NINETEEN

The machine room went quiet as soon as Jessica returned, and she bit down on annoyance. Elena had a lot of fans in the engine room, despite her time away from *Galileo*. It was hardly a surprise people were shocked to see Jessica have security take her away. Had Jessica not been captain, she'd have told them she didn't much care for it either, and reminded them they all knew Elena was emotionally involved and too willing to launch herself toward something she was utterly unprepared to handle.

There was no time for any of this.

"Samaras, Petrikoff," she commed, keeping her expression composed, "I need you on the booster relay data again. Not the stored messages, but anything else: incoming, automated, any activity. I want to know if something contacted it. I want a way to get in touch with that thing out there. Understood?"

"Yes, Captain," Samaras said. Crisp and solid. At least someone was keeping a level head.

She turned to Ted, who was gaping at her like the others. "Ted. I want you to remote *Apate* and get her to where Greg disappeared. I need eyes on that thing."

Ted had the good sense to immediately turn to his console

and pull up the shuttle remoting controls. "Yes, Captain," he said. At his compliance, the room's tension eased. Crisis averted, at least for now, but she'd seen enough of the politics of command to recognize when a situation had the potential to bite her in the ass.

She commed the landing bay. "Azevedo? Where's our drone?"

"In place halfway between us and Target Zero," Azevedo said. "Still picking up nothing."

Which was insane. Jessica was not a physicist, but living in space meant there were a few basic things she'd needed to learn for survival. One was that any change generated some sort of entropic effect, usually in the form of radiation. That Target Zero had apparently swallowed two of her people meant it should have given her *something*, even just a change in temperature. The wormhole itself had emitted a now-familiar jumble of changing energies—how could it be shut off so fast?

*Because something has shut it off.*

"Get that drone as close as you can," she said. "And I want a full scan when it gets there. That thing isn't inert. Whatever it's doing, it's able to hide it from our sensors."

"Captain." Ted was frowning at his console, his fingers busy. "*Apate*'s not responding to the remote."

*Of course it isn't.* "Why the fuck not, Ted?"

"It thinks it's docked," he said. "All the controls are locked, and when I try to unlock them, it tells me I need to release it first."

*Fuck.* "Can you override the shuttle's safeties?"

"If I can figure out why they're on in the first place," he said.

"Captain?" Samaras said in her ear. "One of the emissions we got from the relay when the wormhole opened up is structured like a comms signal. Standard, but scrambled."

"Can you decode it?"

It was Petrikoff who replied. "Of course." A flash of his familiar ego.

"Let me know when you can contact Target Zero," she told them. "Bonus points if we can learn anything about what's inside it."

She turned at familiar footsteps; Bristol had returned. He looked somber but relaxed, and she felt a hint of relief. No drama transferring Elena, at least. Which meant she could look forward to all the drama later.

"She's in the infirmary," Bristol said, without prompting. "She's safe."

Bristol's simple status report leeched the last of the animosity from the room. *Bless you, Lieutenant.* "Now," she said, loud enough for all of them to hear, "we just need to get everybody else safe as well." She turned to Ted's console. "*Galileo*, combine our readings with what Greg picked up on the surface, and replay his EVA."

The console morphed into a featureless rectangle representing Target Zero, and a small, orange-bright icon indicating *Apate*. For a few moments the image was motionless, and then two other bright spots—Greg and Commander Gritsenko— emerged from the icon and split up.

And then Apate's orange-tinted avatar faded to blue.

Cold. The shuttle went cold.

"Did they shut the heat off?" Jessica asked.

"Shuttle environmentals reverted to storage defaults," *Galileo* told her.

That wasn't standard procedure. "Is it still tethered to Target Zero by a gravity field?"

"Unknown," *Galileo* said. "Shuttle isn't responding to comms."

Bristol made a small sound, and she turned to look at him. "Cough it up, Lieutenant."

He looked away briefly. "It's obvious, I guess. But—it's

always comms, isn't it?" When she didn't interrupt, he went on. "The signal that Foster got back on Sochi, and the booster relay, and even how the CI got on *Galileo*. Setting storage defaults on a shuttle—that's over comms, too."

"It's just a data transfer," she said.

"Yeah," he agreed. "But there are lots of kinds of data transfers we use. Off-grids, streaming—they're different tech, aren't they? Comms is…basic, in a way. Old. Just a carrier. Easy to feed it a payload if you can get past security." He shrugged. "Like I said, it's obvious."

But there was something else in what he was saying, something she couldn't quite pin down. "It *is* basic," she agreed. "It's also supposed to be hard to hack." Too many mysteries. She hit her comm again. "Samaras, give me *something*," she snapped, and remembered how many times she'd heard Greg demand the same thing during a crisis, when he was frustrated with his own inability to act.

"I'm looking at the data from the Target Zero wormhole," Samaras said, steady in her ear. "There are some data chunks that resemble a comms signal, but they're incomplete, maybe encrypted, but with a different scheme than the booster relay data. Commander Petrikoff and I are working on it."

"Keep trying to contact that thing," she said. "Even if we're speaking gibberish, I want to know if it responds. Azevedo? Where's my drone?"

"We're seeing the same power drain we did at the booster," he told her, and his usual deadpan tone was touched with frustration. "Trying an oscillating orbit to see if we can pick up a complete picture. Maybe Doctor Hastings can get us some filler data."

*Damn.* Target Zero had decided to shove them off, just like the booster relay. "Keep up that oscillation," she said. It was a good thought, as was the filler data, and—

*What?*

"How is Doctor Hastings going to get us filler data?"

"He's just landed on Target Zero," Azevedo said, and if he was surprised she didn't know he didn't let on. "He and Commander Shaw took *Unicinta*."

Jessica was not, despite the persistent reputation of redheads, prone to anger. She could be passionate, of course—what person couldn't?—and she was aware, sometimes, that the intensity of her response was interpreted as displeasure when it was simply a reflection of what mattered to her. Even when she got angry, she rarely lost her temper; losing her temper meant losing control of the situation, and anger made her want to be in control more than any other feeling she ever had. Anger was usually a sign that something was very wrong, and that an adjustment was needed quickly before whatever situation she was in spiraled entirely out of control.

She couldn't remember ever feeling as angry as she did in this moment.

"I didn't tell him what to do with her, did I?" she asked, keeping her voice level.

"No, Captain," Bristol said.

She supposed she ought to have guessed. Bob's attachment to Greg was familial, even if it wasn't based on a biological tie, and Jessica should have known to order the doctor to keep his ass on the ship.

"Samaras," she asked, "is *Unicinta* still comms-locked?"

"Yes, Captain," he said. And then, after a pause, "I'm showing her off the ship. Is that correct?"

"Yeah," she told him, with a sigh. "Can you get through to anyone on board?"

A moment passed. "I'm getting a pingback from Commander Shaw's comm," he said.

*Of course he is.* Not only had she bolted the ship, she'd broken her own protocols for Kali's quarantine. "Give Petrikoff the reins on Target Zero for a minute," she told him. "Put me through to Elena."

"Yes, Captain." A moment later, he said, "Go ahead."

"*Unicinta*," she said, keeping her voice level, "this is Captain Lockwood. What's your current status?" *What the fuck do you think you're doing?*

There was a long pause before she heard Bob's voice. "We've just landed on Target Zero, Captain," he said, his tone as calm as hers.

"Ted," she asked, "can you use the comm link to get ahold of *Unicinta*'s controls?"

"Elena's turned off remoting,"

"Stop sounding like you admire her."

"You have to admit," Ted said, "she does think of everything."

"Except about actual people."

"We could move closer," he offered. "Snag the shuttle with a gravity field. But if you want to maintain distance we can't do a damn thing."

She thought about what she might say next. Threats wouldn't help; none of them had a career to burn anymore. Jessica's command of this ship was entirely at the indulgence of the crew, who so far were happy enough maintaining military hierarchies. Except for Elena and Bob, of course, who had both decided they didn't trust her to do the right thing.

"Hold that as a backup for now," she said. "Samaras, put me through again." Ideally this was not a comm she'd have sent in front of the entire machine room crew, but she didn't have to lose her temper. She could explain her perspective quietly, professionally, and with only one or two expletives. Probably.

"Captain," said Samaras.

"One-way is sufficient, Lieutenant," she said.

Samaras didn't answer. Ted looked up from his console; Bristol froze, abruptly alert.

"Lieutenant Samaras," she said. "Respond."

"Petrikoff here, Captain," said the PSI commander. "Lieutenant Samaras is busy at the moment."

*What the fuck is this?* "What's he busy with?" she asked him.

"He's indisposed. Perhaps you can help me instead."

She muted her comm. "Contact Emily," she told Bristol. "Tell her we've got a security situation." Reconnecting, she asked, "What is it you need help with?"

"That CI of yours. The pet you decided to keep."

She blinked. Did he know Kali was on *Unicinta*? Why was he concerned about the CI now? "Commander Petrikoff, I don't think now is the right time—"

"Now is exactly the right time, Captain," he said. This time his voice came over the shipboard intercom for them all to hear. The arrogance was back full force; he'd abandoned every effort to be charming. "You had the chance to do the right thing when it was discovered, but you didn't. I'm sorry about Captain Foster. I'm even sorry about Nataliya, although she wouldn't be sorry if our positions were reversed. But I know she agrees with me on this point: you're a danger to *Meridia*. The ideas you bring to us are corrupt, and built on lies. I have no desire to hurt anyone, Captain, not even your Lieutenant Samaras. But I can't tolerate the threat of that program. It's the same thing that destroyed *Chryse,* and we *will not* bring it home. Do you understand? Even if it means none of us gets home at all."

Jessica blinked. "You're commandeering my ship?" she asked. "From *comms?*"

"I'm telling you to delete that program, Captain," he said. "Or I'll kill your Lieutenant Samaras. And then I will destroy this ship, and none of your crew will be able to lie to PSI ever again."

# TARGET ZERO

transit: greg

*Greg hadn't lived by the ocean in years, decades, eons. They'd moved when he was seven, before his mother had re-enlisted, before his sister had lost her temper and never regained it, before his father had turned quiet and somber, waiting for a reunion that would never come. Greg hadn't missed the ocean when they left it—they'd moved north, by a lake, where it was cooler and dryer and lovely in an austere, other-worldly sort of way. His mother had always carped, just a little, about the move away from the ocean. She had been teasing, except not, and Greg's father had always reacted with gentle rigidity, never apolo-gizing for what he'd had to do to keep his children comfortable.*

*And then Greg's mother had died*

*[died]*

*and he had been happy they weren't by the ocean anymore, because he could pretend he didn't miss her, she'd never been here, the lake and his sister and his father were all he had ever known.*

*It smelled familiar, this ocean: overwhelmingly salt and seaweed, a hint of something that had crawled up on shore and become stranded there. Before him was nothing but sand, washed into flat, shiny plains, filling in his puddling footprints behind him. To his right were dunes, abrupt and high, obscuring his view of anything beyond the tall grasses that sprouted at the top. To his left, the ocean opened into expansive blueness.*

*Far ahead of him walked a woman. Her hair was jet-black and shiny, springs of unruly curls tugged by the sea breeze, the sun adding copper and bronze to her deep brown skin. He had her coloring, he knew: that skin tone so dark indoors, burnished and smooth and nearly jet, but highlighted with red and gold under sunlight. Everyone always told him he looked like her, but apart from her skin he could never see it. He kept his hair short and neat, but he suspected if he hadn't it would have grown dense like his father's long-cultivated locs instead of his mother's freewheeling curls, and although he'd been told, over and over, that he had his mother's beauty, he could never see her in his own face. Some of that was his eyes, gray and black, mottled and strange like his father's. His mother's eyes had been brown and full of good humor and intelligence, and sometimes—in flashes, here and there—deliberate cruelty.*

*Perhaps he was more like her than he thought.*

*She was barefoot, her trousers rolled up to her calves, a white shirt billowing around her body in the wind. She paused for a moment, sweeping her hair out of her face, to look out at the waves, and he caught her in profile. Pregnant, heavily, and it was him she was carrying, although he couldn't have said how he knew it.*

*"Kate!"*

*The word was nearly swallowed by the wind: a low voice, a man's, but mostly Greg heard the whistling of the reeds and the crashing surf. His mother turned her head, her contemplative look replaced by antic-ipation, joy; she knew who was calling her. She was pleased.*

*One hand strayed to her stomach, and he found his own hand resting on his abdomen. They had been one person once, he and she, except he had been dependent on her, autonomy evolving cell by cell over months, and in many ways he was still dependent on her and always would be.*

*A head appeared over the sand dunes. The light off the ocean waves blurred Greg's vision, but the man's eyes were unmistakable: bright blue, vivid; smart, like Greg's mother's, but cynical instead of cruel. In Greg's earliest real-life memories, Bob Hastings had already gone gray, already looked, to a child's eyes, like an old man, even though he was barely a decade older than Greg's father. Here, on this bright dream-beach, Bob was young, his hair yellow, his pale skin barely lined at all.*

*Bob slid down the dune, struggling to keep his footing in the dry sand. Greg's mother moved to intercept him, and when she caught him she put her arms around him and they held each other as if they hadn't seen each other in months.*

*Something soured in Greg's stomach.*

*Kate drew back first, and Bob's hands fell away from her. She caught his fingers in hers and smiled. "I told you," she said to Bob, chiding, "I'm fine."*

*Bob was studying her face, blue eyes wide, vulnerable, hungry. Oh, Greg knew that look. Greg knew what it was like to want someone, to find himself so starved for them the most casual contact would throw him off for days. He'd felt that way for...for... It couldn't have mattered so much, really, if he couldn't remember her, but his stomach turned over again and he felt strangely bereft.*

*A flash of sun caught his mother's hair, and this time it lit her curls blue.*

*"I hate this, Kate," Bob said, his hands in hers. "I don't know if I can do it." He paused, steadied himself. "I don't know that I want to."*

*She let go of his hands, turning to continue her walk down the beach. Bob, disconcerted, fell into step next to her, and Greg walked a little faster to catch up.*

*"He'd understand, Katie. You know he would."*

*"You don't even know him."*

*"I know he loves you," Bob said. "I know he wants you to be happy."*

*"I'm beginning to understand why you never got married." Her*

*words were light, but Greg caught the warning, the tone that meant Bob needed to back off, and quickly.*

*"Then come away with me," he said. "We could raise him out there. You said that's all you ever wanted, really, was to be out there. We could—"*

*He broke off when she laid her hand on his arm. They stopped and turned to each other, and Greg saw in her eyes what Bob had yet to understand: he had already lost.*

*"I don't want to come away with you, Bob." She said it with more gentleness than Greg had thought she would, but the shock in Bob's eyes was no easier to watch. "I love him, too. And with all this talk of your baby—have you forgotten Meg? Do you really think I'd leave her behind? Do you really think I'd leave Tom behind, and pretend I never built anything here?" She shook her head. "You can be a part of his life, Bob. That much I'll allow you. But that's all. He's to know nothing, you understand?"*

*"I could tell him anyway. I could force a test."*

*Her dark, cruel eyes softened, just a little, with pity. "And what would that accomplish?" she asked him. "I'd never go away with you. Even if Tom threw me out, I wouldn't be yours. And this child? He belongs to himself. Do you think you could be the one responsible for him being born into chaos, and still have him love you?"*

*Bob looked shocked, bewildered, lost, like a child, younger than Greg had been when his mother had died.*

*"I can't lose you, Katie," Bob said.*

*She smiled, the spider finally wrapping up the fly. "You don't have to lose me," she assured him, "if you say nothing, and allow my family to remain my family."*

*"I can never tell him?"*

*"You can never tell him."*

*His bewilderment turned to resignation. "All right, Katie. All right. But you need to—"*

*They started walking again, and Greg forgot to follow them, and the surf kicked up and the wind whistled loudly through the thick, stiff marsh grass. Greg tried to walk forward, only to find his feet wouldn't move. The sand had washed up to his ankles; he'd loved that, when he was little, the sand swallowing him feet-first, and he'd stood in the surf and cackled, watching his feet sink until his mother had taken him home. But now he wanted to run after her, drag her back, demand the truth from her; he wanted to push Bob away from her and save her from secrets.*

*The sand was up to his knees, and they were still walking, far ahead of him now, so far even if the surf had quieted he couldn't have heard them. "Hey!" he shouted, because whatever this was at least some of it was real, because he couldn't move his feet and the sand was creeping higher. "Wait!"*

*They turned a corner past the sand dune and disappeared from sight.*

*Greg looked down. The sand had reached his torso, his elbows resting on the beach; he was cold and wet, and he had the sensation of squeezing, as if something was trying to push the air from his lungs, as if he was trying to breathe air that wasn't breathable. "Hey!" he cried out again, this time with some desperation. And then his arms were under the surface and the sand was around his neck, and he thought he could taste it at the back of his throat. "Bob!" It made sense, some-how, to call to Bob and not to his mother, because she had left, hadn't she? She had left him after all, and she had left her daughter and her husband and she had gone*

    *[died]*

*unapologetically and without regret. What did she know of truth, of promises? Bob would know what to do. Bob would dig him out and give him a sardonic grin and Bob wouldn't be that helpless, lost young man, so vulnerable to this woman who had given more of herself to the stars than to any person she'd ever loved, and Greg was no different was he? Because he couldn't even stay with*

    *stay with*

    *dark eyes different eyes sweeter his and his and*

    *who*

*who*
*who was she*
*he was*
*he was*
*[alone]*

# TWENTY

He was standing in a windowless starship corridor, no sea or sand in sight, and he could breathe again.

Odd, how in his dreams his mother was always on the beach. He'd liked the feeling of sand under his feet, between his toes, but he had never much cared for the ocean. His mother had insisted he learn to swim, but he'd never enjoyed the cold, dark water, the impenetrable depths that never let him see how far he'd have to dive to find solid ground.

The dream was fading, the salt smell in his nostrils giving way to the faint astringent odor of recycled starship air, but the emotions clung: betrayal, abandonment, uncertainty, grief.

*Nothing new, then.*

Grim humor, his perennial fallback. His sister had always loathed him for it, and he'd been out of his childhood home for ten years before he'd realized that was one temperamental thing he'd inherited from his father, not his mother. That knowledge had thrown him at first. His teenaged falling-out with his father had extended into decades, but they'd reconciled, become friends again, and his father had been kind and forgiving since...

...since...

He caught a phantom whiff of surf and shook his head. *Grief and cobwebs.* He was in a hallway, on his feet, which argued he'd experienced a hallucination or illusion rather than a dream. Reality was this starship, and his familiar uniform. Not his dress uniform, so this wasn't some diplomatic nonsense on *Hephaestus* or *Aphrodite* or any of the other Corps ships assigned to the Fourth Sector with *Galileo*. Just his regular gray-and-black Corps uniform, the collar open to reveal his white undershirt beneath, cool and smooth as if he'd just put it on. He reached up to rub his head and felt the right amount of stubble. He'd shaved that morning, then, close but not smooth over his skull, entirely smooth over his jaw and lip.

A regular day. If this were *Galileo*, he'd go to his office, look at his agenda, assemble information until his scattered memory filled in the gaps.

But this wasn't *Galileo*. For one thing, *Galileo* had no corridors like this: dead end, square and nondescript, not even a token storage room tucked into the useless corners.

For another, this ship had been through a battle. The walls were scarred and dented with what had to be plasma fire; there was a hole in the wall to his left, the exposed nanocomposite edges burnt but burnished from wear. Weeks or months old, this damage, and he wondered why it hadn't been repaired yet.

No matter how vivid the hallucination, he couldn't believe he'd have blocked out a battle.

He moved forward, slowly, alert for sound, vibration, anything that might be threatening. Normal environmental noises—a different resonance than *Galileo*, lower and louder, but familiar enough. No drive hum, which meant they were not in the field; even the newer designs produced some melody, an artifact of the precise multipliers used to construct the faster-than-light encapsulation folds. But the sounds of the ship told him she was healthy, which meant he was not in imminent danger.

He found more damage further up the hallway. Some of it was severe: deep, burned-out pockets etched into the walls, holding barely-visible shadows that seemed to shift if he tried to focus on them. Strange, those shadows; perhaps he *had* been dreaming, and was still. Perhaps this was some kind of mental addendum: he had dreamt of his past, or something built on its bones, and now he was seeing his future.

Maybe it was a metaphor: stuck forever on a starship, every step forward the same as the one before it, no point in going back. Maybe whoever had made him dream thought it would trap him, unbalance him.

The question, of course, was: who would want to trap him?

He knew a few secrets he shouldn't, but that was hardly unique in the Corps. Even Admiral Herrod leaked intel to Greg now and then, and that man was as careful as any in the Admiralty. This was more likely a product of his spotty disciplinary record. Over the years he'd disobeyed orders, feigned ignorance, begged forgiveness after the fact—all in service of his mission, of course, but he'd still made enemies. So someone in the Admiralty might be trying to take him down, but he could imagine a dozen more efficient scenarios than allowing him to roam the halls of an ordinary starship. It was much more likely he'd learned something they wanted him to forget, and he'd been roped in to test some new memory-wipe drug. He couldn't even rule out the possibility he'd volunteered; it'd be like him to be willing to throw away his memories. So many of them were awful.

He stopped, frowning, and looked around again. Before him, the hallway ran straight, falling into shadow before he could make out a turn. Behind him, the battered hallway grew dark and hazy. Was the light following him?

"Why am I here?" he said aloud. His voice bounced off the walls, flat and dispassionate.

The salt returned, strong and tangy, touched with the

metallic fragrance of hot sand. Moments later it was replaced with the dense, oily smell of smoke. Not an electrical fire; there was no scent of charring, no auditory signal that any of the ship's quietly resonant systems were overloading. Familiar, though, and it took him a moment to place it: *plasma fire.*

He responded instinctively, flattening himself against the interior wall, acutely aware of the light over his head. No weapon, which was certainly a disadvantage; on the other hand, if the enemy had plasma rifles, there would be little he could do in this shelterless corridor no matter what he was carrying.

Why was there plasma fire on board a Corps starship?

He heard the voices a moment later: unintelligible, talking over one another, but organized. The easy chatter of Corps infantry. His anxiety eased. Whatever the circumstances, these were his people. And if he was stuck here, he could help them.

The infantry moved closer, still within the confines of the smoky shadows: three, maybe four soldiers, their cross-talk compact and precise. No rifle fire; whatever they'd been fighting, it hadn't followed them. The cloud lightened enough for him to make out shadows, but he didn't think they'd be able to see him yet.

Allowing them to stumble onto him abruptly was possibly not a great idea.

"Hey!" he called out. "Here! I'm unarmed!"

The soldiers stilled. A good squad, whoever they were; he'd barely registered their silence when a rush of footsteps brought the muzzle of a pulse rifle three centimeters from his forehead.

"Hands where I can see them."

Calm, professional, appropriately tense. Greg moved his arms slowly away from his body.

"Flagg, make sure he's alone." Greg heard soft footsteps fade down the hall behind him, and met the gunman's eyes. Tawny, almost yellow-brown, a shade lighter than his taupe-dark skin, bright under his black eyebrows. His hair was braided close to his scalp in precise rows. His wide mouth was set, no lines around it at all, and his uniform was clean but worn. He stood no more than two centimeters shorter than Greg, and not even his own breath disturbed his aim.

"I'm unarmed," Greg said again, keeping his voice as even as the soldier's.

"Turn around," the gunman said. "Hands against the wall."

Greg turned, and was body searched quickly and efficiently.

"Face me."

Greg turned back, his hands still up. The gunman had taken a few steps backward, but the weapon didn't waver. "It's all right, soldier," Greg said. "I'm not the enemy."

Which he couldn't know, not yet, but it seemed the wise thing to say.

"How long have you been here?" the soldier asked him.

Interesting. Not *How did you get here* or *What do you want.* "About five minutes," Greg said. "I woke up in the corridor and—"

The soldier took half a step forward, his arms on his weapon stiffening, and he shouted. "Where did you come from? Did you come from Level Four?"

"I don't know," Greg told him. Why was any of this relevant? "All I know is I'm here now, and I'm not your enemy." *I might be, though, if this keeps up.* "What's your name, soldier?"

"He stands like one of us, Eyenga," said the soldier to the gunman's right. She looked younger, less certain, but that might have been her slighter build.

"You assuming the enemy can't learn, Yarov?"

Yarov blinked, betraying an instant's frustration. "No, Commander. But they haven't so far."

*Who's 'they'?* "If you could take me to your superior officer," Greg said, "I'm sure we can straighten all this out."

"The Captain's got no time for—"

Flagg returned. "All clear," she said. Flagg was closer to

Eyenga's size, thick and sturdy, pale under a shock of short red hair. Even with Yarov's slightness, Greg didn't think he'd stand much of a chance against all three of them.

"What do you think, squad?" Eyenga's eyes were ice-cold. "Should we drop this off at an airlock before we report back?"

That was enough. "I don't know what's going on here, Commander," Greg said, letting some professional steel creep into his voice, "but when I was coming up, summary executions were frowned upon."

"When *I* was coming up," the young man told him, "war zone meant you shut the fuck up."

*War zone? On a starship?* Greg held the commander's gaze. The younger man was still in control, for the most part; but there was something seething there, something that spoke of battle and sleep deprivation and horrors that Greg didn't know about. Whatever had happened here—was happening here—it was bad.

*Best if you don't get yourself killed, Foster.*

"War zone also means chain of command," Greg said. "And I outrank every one of you."

"I said shut the fuck up."

Greg risked one step forward. "Under the circumstances," he said, "I'll let that go, Commander. Once." The muzzle of the gun was less than a centimeter from his forehead.

"I will take you out."

"Here or there, soldier," Greg told him, "makes no difference to me."

"Hey." Flagg spoke up. "Eyenga. Wait."

"Fuck off, Flagg."

"No, Commander, that's not what I mean. I think I know this guy."

"Fuck you, Flagg, you never had the balls for this kind of thing. Captain was clear. No prisoners."

Flagg stepped forward, one hand on the pulse rifle that hung at her side, until she was as close to Eyenga as his weapon was to Greg. "He's *not the enemy,* Commander. He's one of us. Captain Foster, off *Galileo.*"

"Bullshit. *Galileo* was in..."

The overwhelming scent of salt filled the air, burning Greg's eyes.

Eyenga trailed off into silence, his expression unfocused. Greg blinked away the sting and looked at Yarov and Flagg: they looked as dazed as Eyenga, as if all three minds had wandered in unison.

The sting of salt vanished, and Greg took a breath of plasma smoke and ozone. Eyenga was glaring at him again, marginally less hostile, substantially less murderous. After a beat he dropped the nose of his rifle and came to attention. "Captain," he said, throwing Greg a salute, "Commander Eyenga at your service."

Behind him, the other two followed suit, Flagg with a slight eyeroll Greg did not think was aimed at him.

"At ease, squad," Greg said. "Sitrep."

Flagg and Yarov relaxed a little; Eyenga remained stiff. Whatever had eased the suspicions of the others hadn't worked quite as effectively on their leader. "We have hostiles in possession of our engine room, Captain," he said. "We've been deploying around the ship to attack them from various angles, but they've done us a lot of damage. We're dead in the water until we take the engine room back."

"How many hostiles?"

"Indeterminate," Eyenga told him, "We're guessing eleven at this point, but we're hoping less. Started out as nineteen, but they've lost eight we know of. Six in just the last two weeks."

*Two weeks?* How long had this ship been under siege? "I'll need to talk to your captain," he told Eyenga. He could help, surely, if only as another foot soldier. "Who's in charge here?"

Eyenga turned, and Greg fell into step with the squad. The

corridor was lit down its length now, all the smoke dissipated. "That'd be Captain Niemann, sir," Eyenga told him. "Welcome aboard the CCSS *Capricorn*."

Salt and sulphur filled his nostrils again, but he could no longer remember why.

# TWENTY-ONE

*I will wring* Freja Taras' *neck with my bare hands.*

"Ted," she snapped, "cut the power to the comms center." Petrikoff's voice fell silent, and she turned and strode out of engineering, Bristol at her heels.

A moment later, Petrikoff commed her directly. "You restore power *now*," he shouted, "or your engineer comes out in pieces!"

Close to the edge. She didn't have much time. "Ted, can we—"

"Got you already." Ted had been following her thoughts. "Routing you through engineering. Should give you enough power to reach Bob and Lanie. Just don't get complicated."

She spoke as quickly as she could. "*Unicinta, Galileo.* No time. Petrikoff is trying to take the ship. Keep Kali away from here. Stay away, stay safe, rescue Greg, whatever you need—but *keep Kali away from here.* I'll deal with your fucking insubordination later, but stay the fuck away until you're ordered otherwise. And *do not* fucking acknowledge. As far as Petrikoff knows, I want you blind." Her next comm was for her crew. "All hands. Essential communications are to be over radio only. I want shipboard comms flooded with as much ordinary, non-privileged chatter as you can generate.

Bristol." He caught up with her, and they ran side by side. "I need a radio jammer at the comms center, and I need it two minutes ago."

"Acknowledged, Captain," Bristol said, as if she'd just asked him to bring her coffee. He turned back toward engineering.

They didn't carry a radio jammer. Jessica, who like most people had played with analog signals as a child, had long since lost the knowledge of how to build one. But she knew someone on board still had that knowledge, and Bristol would find them.

She hoped he'd find them fast enough.

Petrikoff commed her again. "I mean it, Lockwood! You have ten seconds!"

*Fuck.*

"Ted, restore power." She reached the comm center and leaned against the door in the futile hope of hearing something through the wall. "Petrikoff? You're back on line. Let me talk to Samaras."

"Fuck you, Lockwood," Petrikoff shouted. "I told you. He's—" He broke off, realizing he was back on the shipwide intercom. "Don't do that again, Captain," he said. "You know what I'll do to your lieutenant."

"How do I know you haven't done it already?"

"Don't panic." Acid in his tone; he had to know Samaras's health was the only reason she wasn't blasting through the door and personally dismembering him with one of Elena's nanospanners. "He's in one piece. You do what I want, he'll stay that way, and we can all go home safe."

Bristol reappeared, holding what looked like a stack of paintbrushes stuck together. When she nodded, he turned the device over, exposing raw circuitry; he nudged a small crystal into place. "Clear," he said. "It's relatively weak, but it's still got a radius. You want to radio someone, you'll need to be ten meters away."

She didn't want to leave that door, not without Samaras on

her side of it and Petrikoff's unconscious body on the other. Reluctantly she moved down the hall, and with a hiss and a squeal, her comm picked up the radio signal.

"Captain?" said Ted.

The hiss grew louder, more variegated; her crew coming on line. No, that wasn't right, was it? *Tuning in.* This was old-fashioned analog. Slow, simple, nearly useless given the scale humanity had built for itself. Thank all the gods for useless simplicity. "Hang on, Ted. Commander Broadmoor, you on?" she asked.

"Yes, Captain." Just like Bristol, cool and relaxed, as if nothing odd was happening at all.

"I need a strategy for breaking into comms."

"Sitrep?"

"Petrikoff has taken Samaras hostage. Petrikoff claims he's all right, but I haven't heard his voice, so he has to be at least restrained. No idea what Petrikoff has for weapons, but you know Samaras—for him to stay that quiet, I'm guessing Petrikoff has got at least a short-range handgun. And Petrikoff claims he can destroy us from in there, so we're likely talking about explosives."

"We should assume the door is wired," Emily said.

"Then get me around the door. I won't have this dragging on."

"Yes, Captain. Conferring with tactical."

She switched back Petrikoff. "What is it you want?" Her voice echoed throughout the corridor; he was piping her shipwide as well. Trying to frighten them, to make them comply with whatever madness had taken him. It wasn't like none of them had ever seen him volatile before.

*Should've paid more attention, Lockwood.*

Petrikoff's voice was a taut wire. "I want proof you've destroyed that thing," he told her. "And then I want an official, witnessed, signed statement from you disavowing your association with PSI."

Emily spoke in her ear. "Running strike scenarios," she said. "We'll have some choices for you within two minutes."

"First priority is keeping *Galileo* in one piece," Jessica told her. "Second priority is retrieving Samaras. Distant fucking third priority is keeping that rat bastard alive so we can turn him in to Taras and she can deal with him."

"Could use some intel on the first, Captain."

"Ted? Loop Emily in on the ship's condition, and how much damage we could live with." She returned to her conversation with Petrikoff. "Renouncing PSI is easy," she told him. She'd have no trouble drafting a document; nobody, not even the deeply diverse and opinionated PSI fleet, was going to hold her to anything signed under duress. "Eradicating the CI is more complicated."

"You said you had it isolated." His voice rose; she didn't think it would take much to make him panic. "If it's isolated, you can destroy it."

"You know how complex *Chryse* was." There was more truth in that statement than he knew. "It's not just a memory wipe. This thing has tentacles."

"Then maybe the best thing to do is blow the ship." He said it matter-of-factly, as if he'd been thinking about it, as if it had been his backup plan all along.

"You're telling me you have explosives in there?"

"I'm telling you," he said, "I can stop this ship in its tracks any time I want to. Can you destroy the CI, or can't you?"

"I can," she told him. "I'll need to concentrate, so I might not be as responsive to you, but let's keep talking, okay?"

"You better not be bullshitting me, Lockwood."

"If I could've hit the big delete button," she snapped, "don't you think I would have by now?"

She might have. Not precipitously, not without consulting

with Greg and Ted and Elena and Emily, and likely anyone else who would listen, but she had some sympathy for Petrikoff's view that Kali was a threat.

She just didn't believe Kali was only that.

"If you plot with your crew," Petrikoff told her, his panic ebbing, "I'll know it."

"I don't want to plot with anyone," she told him, and that was close enough to the truth. "I just want my people safe. I think we can both get what we want here, yes?"

"That's up to you, Captain Lockwood." He was back to the way he'd been at the start, only a hint of agitation in his voice. "I'll look forward to your update."

"Thank you, Petrikoff." *You fucking terrorist.*

Petrikoff's voice continued over comms, reciting a surprisingly organized list of *Galileo*'s perceived transgressions. Jessica paced in front of the comms center door. "Ted, Emily," she said, "I need that attack plan."

Emily answered her. "For a quick strike, either we go external, or blow the internal door. For external, we can keep the gravity on in that room to hold the air in, and blast through the bulkhead from the outside."

"How much precision can we get with that?"

"Not a lot," Emily admitted. "But we have more control over what happens to the hull. If he's wired the walls, this will allow us to contain the damage. But even spacewalking with hand weapons rather than using a shuttle—there are windows in that room. There's a good chance he'd be forewarned."

*Shit.* "Can we just gas the room?"

"Air systems changes show up as alarms," Ted said. "I've started work on an override, but it's going to take at least an hour."

Suddenly systems security seemed counterproductive. "What about an internal breach?"

"Simpler," Emily said. "But odds are good that's what he's

expecting, and he'll be able to do a lot of damage on the way out. And we're back to dealing with the wired door."

*Never any good answers.* Greg had said that to her once, early on in their time working together. He'd even smiled.

"External," she said. "A small group. Breach with targeted explosives, and bring close-quarters weapons only—I want minimum, controlled hull damage. And bring two extra env suits, in case our containment fails." She wanted to tell them to bring only one, to let Petrikoff suffocate. "I want that fucker alive, so I can be sure he gets what's coming to him, but Samaras has priority. Understood?"

"Yes, Captain."

"And I'm leading the mission."

Emily paused. "Permission to speak candidly, Captain."

*Oh, here we go.* "Of course."

"You're being sentimental," Emily said. "You want to rescue him because you feel responsible. You're not responsible."

"I am responsible for everything on this ship."

Jessica had a flashback of the years before her promotion, reporting to Emily, skirting the edge of insubordination far too often. "That doesn't mean you need to do everything yourself."

"I—" She thought of Elena. "If you have a better suggestion, Commander, I'll listen. But we are not losing comms, we are not losing Samaras, and we are not losing this ship. We need each other now. All of us. This isn't some bullshit assignment from the Admiralty. This is a complete—"

A high-pitched screeching interrupted Petrikoff's droning, and the room went dark.

# TWENTY-TWO



*Soldiers should be offered a better death.*

Captain Tauno Niemann sat at the table he'd co-opted for a desk and surveyed the cafeteria around him. This had once been *Capricorn*'s main socializing space: two levels high, 100 meters square, the perimeter lined with food preparation stations. Now half the food stations were closed in favor of medical aid and weapons repair, and the floor was covered in line after line of cots, set up in groups of six by squad. There had been forty-two cots at the beginning of this mission; now a third of those were unoccupied, inert reminders of what they'd all lost.

Niemann's crew astonished him, every day. Dedicated, focused, determined. Loyal to one another, and to him. Following orders without question, even when it became clear every single thing that was happening to them was a clusterfuck.

That was the job. They all knew this. Niemann had known this for forty years, since he'd first sat down to memorize the Corps rule book in hopes of enlisting. None of them were expected to understand everything that came down from on high. They were expected to shut up and implement what they were told to implement. They might never know why, and that had to be enough.

But this was a far less morally ambiguous threat. This was a set of POWs he never should have agreed to transport, murdering members of his crew and taking over his ship. This was *intolerable*, and some days, as he lay sleepless listening to the quiet breathing of his remaining crew, he thought it might be best to blow *Capricorn* to pieces and free the universe of these meddlesome terrorists.

No, not *terrorists*. *Terrorists* suggested a goal, a purpose. Some level of reason. These POWs were bitter, spiteful, unreasoning insects, and he needed to be rid of them.

*Soldiers should be offered a better death.* The thought wasn't quite right, was it? But it persisted in his head. When they got home, he was going to have words with the Admiralty. He was done letting his people be walked over and taken advantage of. Anything the Admiralty didn't like they could lay on Niemann, and he'd take whatever punishment they meted out. His career didn't matter. *He* didn't matter. Only these people, who'd served him without question, who'd been noble and strong in the face of...

The acrid odor of burning flesh hit his nose, and he closed his eyes before Hadley said, "You keep forgetting Anaxis."

Hadley was a persistent son of a bitch for an apparition. He was a solid one, too; Niemann would have thought he could take a swing at the man and have his fist connect with an eye socket, maybe with a satisfying *crack*. But Hadley was dead, had died... how long ago? Niemann couldn't remember. He couldn't even remember how it had happened. But Hadley was Niemann's companion now, not constant but frequent, heralded by the stench of recent death, swift and merciless. Niemann wouldn't have minded a useful ghost, but all Hadley did was tell him, over and over, they were all going to die. As if he hadn't already known.

"We did what we could," Niemann said under his breath. He'd tried not arguing with Hadley, but somehow that made things worse.

"And just look where that got us."

"We didn't make them take the engine room."

"I don't know, Tau. We took from them; now they're taking from us. From their perspective, it probably looks pretty fair."

The use of his given name was oddly steadying. Hadley had never used it when he was alive. Even during those brief times when Niemann and Hadley had been something resembling real friends, the engineer had never called Niemann anything but "Captain." This Hadley wasn't real. This Hadley was something in his head determined to fuck up what he was doing, to defeat him.

He might have thought it was guilt, had he had anything to feel guilty about.

"They'll get a fair trial just like anyone else," Niemann said. "If any of them survive us taking our ship back."

Hadley laughed at that. "You mean," he said, "if any of us gets out of this alive. Which we won't, Tau. You know that. You've known that for weeks."

Niemann's anger flared, and he turned in his chair, ready to dress down Hadley despite knowing he'd look like a madman to the others. That kind of thinking helped no one. That kind of thinking—

Hadley vanished.

The familiar rhythm of a squad marching in formation recaptured his attention, and he turned to the cafeteria entrance. Eyenga's squad, back nearly sixty minutes early. Something was wrong; he should have known it when Hadley had appeared. Hadley's appearance always meant change, or danger. He scanned the figures for someone limping or bleeding, and felt some relief when he saw no stretcher.

What he did see was an extra person.

Niemann recognized the new man right away. Greg Foster had, after all, one of the most famous faces in the Corps. The Admiralty had exploited that face for recruitment, although it was well known Foster didn't care for that use of his image. He was known to be serious, often to a fault, with a sharp mind and a good diplomatic sense. He was also fearless, and not shy about fighting alongside his infantry when it was called for. He was younger than Niemann by more than twenty years, which meant he had a great deal left to learn, but under the circumstances Niemann thought that was workable. Help was help, and he had Hadley to prove wrong.

He got to his feet, and Eyenga's squad stopped before him. "Captain Niemann," Eyenga said, and gave him a crisp salute.

Unflappable, Eyenga. The steadiest officer Niemann had ever had. Unconscionable he'd had to ask so much of the younger man already. "Commander Eyenga," Niemann replied, returning the salute. "What have you brought me?"

"We found him in the aft port corridor section, Captain," Eyenga said. "Level Twelve." The commander's eyes slid briefly toward Foster. "Captain Foster, off CCSS *Galileo*. He's been briefed."

True to protocol, Foster took a step forward, his eyes on the opposite wall. "Captain Niemann," he said. His deep voice carried throughout the big room.

"At ease, Captain." Foster shifted to parade rest, and Niemann sat down. "Commander Eyenga, you and your squad may return to patrol."

Eyenga spared one last glance for Foster—always watchful; Niemann approved—then led his people out of the cafeteria.

"Please, Captain Foster," Niemann said, "have a seat." Foster waited a polite moment before taking the chair opposite Niemann. "Commander Eyenga says you were briefed?"

"Yes, Captain," Foster said. "He says your engine room is

occupied. We didn't get to the part where he explained how it happened."

It was a fair question, but Niemann found himself swallowing a sharp retort. None of them knew how the POWs were holding the engine room, but who was this interloper to highlight their failure? "I know it seems unlikely," Niemann said instead. He allowed himself, just a little, to sound weary; an experienced commander like Foster would expect that. "You're aware of the colony of Anaxis, aren't you, Captain?"

"Of course."

"We were assigned to pick up their latest research for the Admiralty. They were...unwilling to give it up."

Burning flesh again, threatening to distract him. Out of the corner of his eye, he caught Hadley shifting.

"We tried diplomacy, but you know how it is with those people. Things got out of hand. Some of my crew were injured." He turned his head; Hadley's phantom had vanished again. "It was clear someone needed to renegotiate the terms with that place, but that's above my pay grade. We plucked the ringleaders, threw them in the brig, and took off for home.

"And they broke out, and took over our machine room."

Foster would know Niemann was leaving things out. Niemann waited for accusations of incompetence that might even have been justified, but Foster—as he should, on another captain's ship—kept his reservations to himself. "Only the machine room?" Foster asked.

"Access corridors as well," Niemann said, "including maintenance crawlspaces. We're not entirely sure *how* they're maintaining control, but we haven't been able to do more than contain them."

Foster frowned. "Can you cut off their oxygen?"

"Tried that first," Niemann told him with a grim smile. "They nearly blew the whole ship."

Niemann watched Foster digest this; a suicidal opponent

limited tactical solutions. "What are their demands?" Foster asked.

"They change every time we talk to them." Frustration got the better of Niemann, and he got to his feet to pace. "First they wanted us to take them home. Then they wanted us to surrender the ship to them. Then they asked for supplies, and threatened again to blow the ship if we didn't deliver."

"Did you?"

Niemann shook his head. "Drew the line there, but it didn't matter. They've been stealing. We catch one of them once in a while, but it hasn't slowed them down."

"How long has this been going on?" Foster asked.

Niemann stopped pacing. "Seven weeks."

Foster's expression closed. "Captain," he said, "you have a mole."

Losing his temper would help nothing, would only waste the potential assistance he'd just been handed. "Captain Foster," he said, "you're new here, so I'll let that go. But I will say this only once: My crew's loyalty is not in question. Ever. However the POWs are acquiring information, my crew is not involved. Are we clear on that, Captain?"

Foster hadn't moved, but Niemann knew exactly what he was thinking. He didn't believe Niemann, not for an instant, and he was weighing the consequences of saying so. They were equals in rank, but this was Niemann's ship. Foster could say whatever he wished, but he would never persuade Niemann's crew to turn on their own.

In Foster's shoes, Niemann would believe the same things. He'd point out the vagaries and discrepancies, wouldn't let another captain off the hook, no matter where they were.

He wondered if he'd have to call Eyenga back, if they'd have to put yet another person out the airlock. The odor of dead flesh in his nostrils was nearly unbearable.

But when Foster spoke, he spoke with respect. "Yes, Captain Niemann," he said. "We're clear."

# TWENTY-THREE

Not once in her eleven years in the Corps had Elena considered someone might try to take her ship.

As a mechanic, she had been trained to think of contingencies, but she couldn't do that without data. Jessica had given her entirely too little information to work with. Had Petrikoff stockpiled weapons? Kidnapped a pack of ensigns? Gassed half the infantry while they were assembling for one of his classes in the gym?

Had he killed anyone? Were her people all right?

*Fuck.*

"Well," Bob said at last, "at least she was clear about our orders."

They had landed moments before Jessica's message had come in. Bob had answered instead of Elena, hoping to keep the interaction calm. Elena had been preparing to add her own argument to his, fully expecting he'd advise her to keep her mouth shut. All her mental preparation had been in the wrong direction.

"You think it's the right thing?" Elena asked Bob. "For us to stay here, to ignore whatever is going on back there?"

"I think we're two people," Bob said. "The captain has 164."

He sounded short-tempered and irritable, and she couldn't blame him. None of this was good; none of their choices were workable. Everything in her was screaming to turn *Unicinta* around, to rush into whatever was happening and choke the daylights out of that perfidious bastard Petrikoff until he undid everything he'd done.

Which would mean abandoning Greg.

She'd been taught, years ago, that chain of command was important because there was never enough time to brief everyone on the complexities of a situation. Soldiers were there to act. Choice was left to the people who knew the nuances. She'd always thought that was bullshit. She had learned to parrot the correct responses on exams, but she'd never really believed following orders by rote was a good idea.

*Fuck.*

"This is a naive question," Kali put in, "but why doesn't Captain Lockwood just turn me over to this person?"

How could Kali have monitored their comms for so long and still not understand them? "He'd destroy you," Elena explained.

"Yes, I know. But I am one. And I'm not even human. Why value me over them?"

Elena met Bob's eyes at that, feeling the decision settle into her bones. "I don't think that's what she's doing," Elena said.

"If I know Jessica," Bob added, "she would resist the idea of a hierarchy of value. But mostly—"

"Mostly," Elena picked up, "it's about not giving in to threats."

"She believes destroying me would be unlikely to appease Petrikoff." Kali sounded so tranquil.

"In part." Bob shifted in his seat. "But also, you're leverage. As long as she can keep you hidden, she's buying time to figure out how to thwart her enemy."

Kali was silent a moment. "People are contradictory."

"You mean Jessica?"

"No," said Kali. "Captain Lockwood is consistent." She sounded approving. "But Commander Petrikoff…to threaten the ship over me. What I knew of him before—I wouldn't have said he wanted to die, and yet he threatens to kill everyone. Is he bluffing?"

"That's the problem," Bob told the CI. "We have to hope that he is, and behave as if he isn't." He didn't sound especially hopeful.

*Enough.* It would take them four minutes to fly back to *Galileo*, and there was no way they could do it with stealth. They'd expose Jessica's plan, they'd expose Kali, and they'd gain nothing at all. She met Bob's eyes; he looked tired, anxious, and as convinced of the right answer as she was.

Elena pushed herself to her feet and headed to the back of the cabin for their env suits. "It probably makes sense to recon first," she said. "We can split up like they did, if you want, but it's not a particularly large space. And I have no idea if it'll respond to us like—" She turned to find Bob hadn't moved. "Bob?"

It wasn't exhaustion on his face, she realized. That anxious look was one of barely-controlled panic. This was about more than Nikolai Petrikoff. "I think," he said, "I understand the unease Commander Gritsenko was reporting."

"You okay?"

"Not at all." Casual, matter-of-fact; he was fighting it. "I've got a very strong urge to take off and get as far away from this thing as possible."

Manipulating him, just as it had manipulated Nataliya. Why? And why only him? "Is there something that would help?"

"Besides getting the fuck out of here?" His fingers closed over the arms of his chair, and he looked through the window, unfocused. "I gather you're not having the same experience."

"I'm not." In fact, she was fighting the desire to rush her suit check and get outside as quickly as she could. "Adrenaline, sure, but mostly I'm eager to get going."

"Me and not you," Bob said tightly. "Like Gritsenko but not Greg. Why is it trying to separate us?"

"If I may," Kali said, "I think it might recognize you, Elena."

And wasn't that alarming? "Are you saying that thing out there is sentient?"

"It's not." Kali's reply was definitive. "But it can analyze its environment."

Elena was beginning to see what Kali was suggesting, and she didn't think it was going to do Bob's nerves any good. "We wondered," she said aloud, "if that wormhole in the booster relay didn't somehow recognize Greg from our mission two years ago. Are you suggesting Target Zero might recognize me for the same reason?"

"I don't think going through a similar wormhole has anything to do with it, with him or with you."

"So are you the common factor?" Elena asked. "The device I had on Indus Station, Bayandi, that thing out there...and you? You're all the same, after all."

"No, Elena." There was a sharpness to Kali's tone. "We are not the same. Our origins may be, but that object out there...it's not like me."

"But you know it."

"It's familiar. I don't know why."

"Can you get it to stop goosing my cortisol?" Bob asked. "Because that's getting tired really fast."

"I can't communicate with it. I can only tell you it isn't designed to cause permanent harm."

*How would it know?* "Kali, what *do* you know about this thing?"

"Well." Kali paused, and Elena recognized one of her own conversational tics. "As I said, it's not sentient. It's not a probe, either, at least not like ours are, but it can sense its immediate environment with some precision, including your biological reactions. It's capable of self-defense, but it's not a weapon."

Bob had pulled his eyes from the window, and was focusing on Elena again. "So what's its purpose?"

"That I don't know," Kali said, frustrated. "I think...it's not built to hurt anyone, but that doesn't mean damage isn't a side effect of what it's doing."

"Destructive analysis, perhaps," Bob ventured. "Like an archeologist."

Their off-the-cuff research seemed to be steadying him. "So in its destructive analysis," Elena said, "it's targeting Bob but not me."

"Something like that," Kali allowed.

"But why? Just to demonstrate it recognizes me?"

"I am guessing, you understand," Kali said. "But I think it's more that it recognizes your connection to Greg Foster."

Which didn't comfort Bob at all. "You're saying it understands we have different relationships with each other? How would it get that kind of data?"

"The same way I did, I suppose," Kali said.

Comms. The thing had always gone through comms. "But if we're not transmitting a comms signal," Elena said, "how is it tracking us?"

"That I don't know. But it's been doing it all along."

Bob's irritability had returned. "You say that thing is one of you, and you can't even guess how it's gathering data?"

Another piece fell into place. "Kali's limited by our hardware," Elena realized. "She may process data differently, but she can't learn anything we can't. We have no way of telling what that thing out there can do."

"I have," Kali said, with some hesitance, "a theory." She paused. "I think...if we assume the wormhole inside the booster relay and Target Zero are from the same source, it's fair to assume Greg was admitted because he was recognized there as well as here."

"What about Nataliya?"

"Data shows the wormhole's energy readings were dropping rapidly when she followed."

"You think it wouldn't open for Bob."

"I think," Kali said, "that's why it's targeting his cortisol levels. It doesn't want you to try, Bob. But it wants Elena to try very much."

Elena sealed her gloves and hood, and Bob double-checked her work. His hands on her wrists were trembling slightly; she peered at his face through her hood, but he wouldn't meet her eyes.

"I'm all right," he said.

"Still feeling it?"

"I'm all right."

He wasn't. She needed to get them out of here as much for him as *Galileo*. "I'll be quick," she said. "I'll drop the drone, and we'll figure out what we need to do. We'll get home as soon as we can."

"You are a terrible liar, Elena," he said, but there was a softness in his voice. "Thank you."

Elena turned to the shuttle's open door, and stepped out on to the surface of Target Zero.

It was an anticlimactic moment. The sensors in her boots read a nondescript, inert surface; apart from the preternatural darkness of the material, she might have been on the exterior of a hundred Corps starships or intercolony freighters, wandering along the hull in ordinary starlight.

After a few steps, the artificial gravity shifted, and she stopped, her stomach turning over. "Kali?" she asked.

"You still have gravity," Kali said. "But it's at half Earth normal now."

"It's accommodating your injury," Bob said in her ear. "Son of a bitch." This time there was more curiosity in his voice than tension, and she suspected whatever had been pushing him away had decided its job was done.

*Apate* sat in darkness, powered down and dark. Greg's wormhole had appeared less than seventy meters from his shuttle; a short walk, far shorter than it had seemed when she was listening in. When Greg was home and Jessica had spaced Nikolai Petrikoff, they should come back to this object, examine its whole surface, find out if it had more secrets to reveal.

Ahead of her, something shifted. She shined her light forward, futilely; but surely there was something moving there, a tiny motion against that aberrant darkness. "Do you see this?" she asked, but she wasn't really interested in their answer. Astonishing, really, that something like a wormhole could simply appear within a solid object, like a ray of afternoon light. Whatever had built Target Zero had managed something terribly clever.

The glow was brightening, and she turned off her light. She could make out the undulating surface, the strange blocky snakes of matter, shifting in mathematically impossible ways, still somehow flush with the surface. Smooth, iridescent, beautiful. Such a thing couldn't possibly harm anyone.

"Probe," Bob said in her ear.

She felt a prick of annoyance. The probe was a waste of time. She could drop through, and find Greg, and even Nataliya if she decided that mattered, and Kali was right, this thing wasn't going to hurt her at all.

Pulling the looped wire off her belt, she unraveled the probe and turned it on. It hovered for an instant, then obligingly disappeared into the wormhole. The cable stayed taut for a few seconds, and then went slack. Elena pulled it back, and was greeted with nothing but a severed wire.

"Well," said Bob.

Elena examined the join. Clean, like a spanner cut. Fifteen centimeters of cable and the probe, surgically removed.

"Don't like the idea of what that might do to a person," Bob said, but Elena had stopped listening.

Bob and Kali began to discuss the cut cable, and what they might do next, which seemed pointless, because Elena knew exactly what she would do next. Bob sounded annoyed now, which was better than scared. He didn't care for fear, although like most people who'd had to be brave in extraordinary circumstances, he generally recognized it as part of the deal. She should be feeling fear now, some distant part of herself realized. This mood, these thoughts were not her own, not really. She was being lured, but that was all right, because Greg had been lured and she'd promised him, just as Kali had promised her that everything would be all right. Easy, all of this. She couldn't remember why any of them had been afraid.

Bob's shout came as she lifted her right foot.

"Elena!"

She leaned forward.

"Elena," Kali said in her ear, "This is important. To accomplish its mission, it will lie to you. *It lies*, Elena. Remember that."

And she fell into the tangle of color and light.

transit: nataliya

*"Alice. Please put that down."*

*Alice set down the figurine, and laid her chisel on the table next to her other tools. They had been a gift from her mother three years earlier, on her sixth birthday: fine, precise, the most sensitive nanotechnology on the market at the time. They allowed her to make minuscule cuts and add the smallest details, things even Alice's young eyes couldn't see without a scope. She loved working at the suboptical level, carving in repeated patterns, fractals and birds and intertwined snakes. There was peace in the patterns: regularity, reliability, perfection. Nothing in the macro world was ever so trustworthy.*

*She nudged the chisel slightly so it lay in perfect parallel with the others, and stood.*

*The woman standing with her mother was a surprise. When she'd been told an official would be visiting, she'd expected someone older, more severe. Or someone with an entourage and expensive clothes, someone alien to the quiet, austere existence Alice's mother had carved out for them in the years since Alice had been chosen for the program. This woman was not much older than Alice's mother, and she was smiling, but something in that smile whispered caution to the back of Alice's mind.*

*"How do you do, Alice?" the woman said, and held out her hand.*

*Alice walked forward, aware of her mother's anxious gaze, taking in the woman's face. She was pale, nearly as pale as Alice herself, and her hair was blonde, or perhaps silver; it was difficult to tell. Alice took the woman's hand, and was surprised to find it warm. She gripped carefully, as her mother had taught her, and let go before the clasp went on too long.*

*She caught approval in the woman's ice-blue eyes.*

*"I'd like to talk to you a little, if you don't mind," the woman said.*

*"Of course," said Alice.*

*Alice's mother slipped from the room.*

*The silver-pale woman exhaled, as if she were relieved. "Now. Alice. Show me what you've been doing."*

*Alice brought the woman to her figurine shelf, and began describing her work. They were all creatures from her imagination: multiple limbs, enormous ears, absent noses; the tails of foxes and the hooves of cows; wings, sometimes; scales and exoskeletons, armor against the world. The woman seemed interested, and Alice went on longer than she generally did. Her mother found the figurines disturbing, found Alice's focus alien and strange. But this woman nodded encouragingly, asked questions, praised the precision of her work. When Alice showed her the nanocarvings, the silver-pale woman's entire face changed, and Alice felt the stirrings of pride. Somehow, she had impressed this person, not by being skilled "for her age," but by being skilled.*

Watch out for pride, *her mother had taught her.* Pride will make you drop your guard. Pride will ruin you.

*She forced herself into silence, and stood with her hands folded as the woman's eyes swept over her collection. "Alice," the woman said, "you know why I'm here."*

*"Yes."*

Don't answer any question they don't ask, *her mother had*

*said.* Volunteer nothing. Whatever they ask of you, whatever they teach you—you don't belong to them. Not ever. You belong to yourself, now and always.

*"We've been very pleased with your progress," the woman said, and smiled again. "We believe you will be very valuable to us."*

Will be. *Not* Are.

*"Thank you," Alice said.*

*The woman kept looking at her, perhaps expecting some kind of small-child enthusiasm, or fear, or curiosity. But Alice was not curious. She knew why she was going, what she would be trained to do. She knew how much of an honor it was. She knew how hard it would be. Her mother had told her this for years, had prepared her in every possible way.*

*Every night Alice lay awake, listening to her mother sob in her bed, and in the daylight never confessed she'd overheard. She was stronger than her mother. One day, she was certain, that strength would save her life.*

*After a moment the silver-pale woman's expression changed, and she became different: calculating, distant. That tickle in the back of Alice's mind again:* do not trust this one. *Which was a silly thing to think, of course, because Alice didn't trust anybody. Still, it was a shame. This woman had liked her nanodesigns. She'd even known what Alice's stylized birds were; Alice's mother always assumed they were frogs.*

*"We'll be leaving in a few minutes." The woman had once again found her maternal mask. "You may take one bag."*

*She waited by the door as Alice packed. One change of clothes only; she would be provided with what she needed. Her access terminal, a still picture of her mother, a drawing she'd done of a cat they'd had when she was very small. Her hands hesitated over the stuffed rabbit she slept with; she left him with a whispered apology. He'd been a baby gift, and she thought her mother might appreciate the memory.*

*She put her tools in her toolkit and stashed that in the bag, then turned to her figurines. Choosing was impossible. They were all little extensions of herself, each one a mood or a memory, something she wanted to keep, something she wanted to lose.*

*In the end she took one that was half-fox, half-child. She'd shown it to the woman, proud of the texture of the fur, the seamlessness of the joins. She hadn't shown the woman the nanocarving she'd done on its belly, an elaborate map of her colony's star system, curved and swooping and full of color and movement. It had been an experiment, a break from her usual repetitive patterns. Half of her loved it, and half of her found it unsettling. She thought, somehow, that dichotomy was important.*

*She closed her bag. "May I say goodbye to my mother?" she asked.*

*"No," the woman told her. "But we'll let her know you're all right."*

*Alice slung the bag over her shoulder. The woman held out a hand to her, and Alice stared at it for a moment, considering. The woman watched her, and that same look, that calculated realization that Alice was not an ordinary child, came over her face again.*

*"I'm sorry," she said at last, dropping her hand. Her tone of voice was different. She spoke the way grownups did when they were speaking to each other. "That was a mistake, wasn't it?"*

*"It's all right," Alice told her. "I can hold your hand if you want."*

*The woman's expression shifted again; Alice had surprised her. "No, thank you," she said. "It'll be part of your training, learning to do things you don't wish to do. But you don't have to with me, Alice. Not ever. I promise you."*

*Alice didn't like this woman. She was cold and uncomfortable and unfamiliar. She was also Alice's future, and Alice felt power coming off of her, dominance and surety. Liking was not required, only obedience. This promise she'd given meant something, and Alice decided this was a woman worth her loyalty.*

*"Thank you," Alice said.*

*She walked with the woman out of her room, and into her next life.*

# TWENTY-FOUR

NATALIYA BLINKED IN the diffuse light, faintly dizzy, the odor of sculptural nanopolymers melting with the dream. She wondered whether her own mind had produced the memory, or if something else had dredged it up for her. Years since she'd thought of her mother; she couldn't remember her face well, which was probably why so much of what she'd recalled had involved looking at other things.

Like that figurine. She'd sent it to *Chryse* with Viktor. For a long time it had been easier to be enraged by the loss of her artwork than her friend. Grief had always come at her in odd ways.

She remembered jumping in after Foster, despite that dread returning, shrieking in the back of her mind to stop, turn back, leave him to his fate. Odd, that. Another thought she was fairly certain something else had planted; but that something hadn't closed the wormhole against her, had it? Perhaps it couldn't. Perhaps the wormhole was open, all the time, on the surface of Target Zero, and the opacity was the illusion. That would make more sense than using energy to open and close it. It might even explain why Nataliya found herself here, in a suspiciously Corps-looking starship corridor.

More battered than any starship corridor she'd ever seen, of course. This corridor—a dead end, which was an odd architectural choice, splitting into left and right before her—had seen conflict, the walls scarred and dented. She could smell it, too: the chemical odor of melting composites, the electrical charge of weapons. Recent, this damage; hours, perhaps, but no more.

She let her eyes scan the ceiling, squinting at the too-bright light. Solid, undamaged. All the scarring here was along the walls. Another point in the hallucination column: surely a wormhole that had wrenched open a real starship would have left behind damage.

If none of this was real, she had nothing to fear.

She shook her head; the dizziness remained. An artifact of the trip, perhaps, but she'd have to be careful. Injury or no, she hadn't come here to sightsee. She was going to have to keep her head clear to do her job.

She tried her comm first. "*Galileo*?" she said; but there was nothing. Her signal was going out clean, but she had no completion, no response. Her hardware was fine, but her recipient was out of range.

Or gone.

She reached into her pockets for something to mark her location; only then did she realize that her env suit was gone, and she was wearing her PSI uniform. Her rank insignia, too. Not everybody on *Meridia* wore theirs, but Captain Taras had insisted she bring it with her to *Galileo*. "You know what the Corps is like," Taras had said, half-apologizing; but Nataliya liked wearing her insignia. It made her feel less like she was lying to everybody.

*Watch out for pride.*

She shook her mother out of her head, and for an instant she felt a sharp headache that faded before it took hold. *Damn.* It seemed jumping through a wormhole left one with a hangover. She wondered, once she figured out how to get back, if all the side effects would be magically undone.

*None of this is magic, Nataliya. Pay attention.*

She chose left and started walking. An ordinary hallway, apart from the damage; except there were no doors anywhere, nothing indicating there was anything at all on the other side of the polymer walls. The corridor branched, and as she was trying to figure out if the bend would take her back where she had come from, she heard voices. Their words were unintelligible, but the tone was calm, relaxed; she heard someone laugh, and a flurry of conversation afterward.

Human, at least.

The voices neared, and she began backing up. Her soft-soled shoes sounded absurdly loud on the floor, and she turned, running from the chatter. One bend in the hallway, two, three... more than four, surely, and she wasn't seeing her dead end. The corridors had become a maze somehow, and she felt lost and disoriented, the panic building as it had on Sochi, and this time she had no one to calm her.

She came around a corner and nearly crashed into to four startled-looking Corps soldiers.

They might have stood there gaping at each other for eternity, but out of instinct Nataliya reached toward her waist. The gun Foster had given her had vanished with her env suit, and abruptly she was staring down the barrels of four charged pulse rifles, four people shouting contradictory instructions at her.

The threats drove away her panic; she knew this drill. She put her hands behind her head and knelt on the floor, watching the feet of her captors. They all wore full combat boots, solid and weather-proof, the sort that would link up easily with an env suit if quick egress was required. And they all stood squarely on both feet, ready to move in an instant if they had to. These people were not fucking around.

Hallucination or not, this seemed the sort of situation she should take seriously.

She waited for the shouting to stop, then lifted her head to look into the eyes of the soldier closest to her. She couldn't see much of a face above the gun sight, but she did see two pale gray eyes set against light skin, the hair covered with a hard helmet. *What the fuck is falling on you in the middle of the hallway that you need a helmet?*

"I'm sorry," Nataliya said, "what was the question?"

"Just shoot her," said one of the others. "You know what Niemann said. No prisoners."

*Niemann?* She was hallucinating *Capricorn?*

"Look," she said. "I don't know who you're fighting, but I just got here, and as we've just established I have no weapon. You want to repeat the question, or do you folks generally just execute people you find in the hall?"

Those gray eyes didn't waver, and Nataliya realized yes, they probably did just execute people they found in the hall.

"Kelson." This was a voice from the back, still tense, but not quite as close to murder. "None of them have been in PSI uniforms, have they?"

*Them.* An enemy lurking. No wonder they were trigger happy.

"PSI's a bunch of fucking traitors, too," said one of the others.

The traitor accusation was an old, familiar argument, and she wasn't feeling patient. "Traitor to what? We've never pledged an oath to your government. Or is that your problem with us? If we don't agree with the way you've organized your outsized bureaucracy, we're—"

"Shut up." Kelson had a flat, angry voice, but like the man in the back seemed in control. "What the fuck are you doing here?"

Her dream came back in a flood, the feel of the figurine in her hand, the verdant scent of her mother's ubiquitous house plants, and for one moment she was genuinely thrown. Surely how she'd appeared was the more interesting question. It was also the only one she couldn't answer. Kelson's rigid expression suggested his question held deadly importance.

She inhaled ordinary starship air and said, "I'm looking for someone."

Kelson scoffed. "Come on."

"He would have arrived a few minutes ago," she persisted. "If I can find him, we'll leave you to whatever this is."

One of the others spoke. "A few minutes? The only one who—"

"Shut up," Kelson said, but he took a step backward, his weapon unwavering. "Get on your feet."

She rose. Her head came up to Kelson's shoulder.

"Put your hands against the wall."

Now she was just pissed off. Someone knew something, and she'd get nowhere rolling over for these over-armed idiots. "Fuck you," she said. "You want to shoot me? Look me in the eye when you do it. You know I'm not armed."

"We don't know shit," one of the others said.

Arrogant children. They could have used her mother's advice. She kept her eyes on Kelson, and let every moment of her training, every successful mission, every shot she'd fired sure and true color her tone. "You know I'm not armed," she said clearly, "because if I were, all four of you would be on the floor." She dropped her hands. "I need to talk to whoever's in charge here," she told them. "I'm looking for someone, and I don't have the time to educate a pack of boots itching to justify shooting anything that twitches."

She'd found, over the years, her slightness was an advantage: if she widened her eyes and let her lip tremble, she became instantly vulnerable, something to protect, like a baby animal. It had worked so well with Foster, that veneer of vulnerability, even if she hadn't planned to use it on him. But if she let just a hint of her real self show, she transformed into something dangerous, to be respected: a predator, small and wily, who didn't need stature to hunt.

She faced her enemies as herself, watched Kelson absorb the reality of her.

He didn't lower his weapon. "Jomard. Bassir. You two take point. Shoot first, questions later. Tengan, you're with me. You. PSI." He took a step backward. "Follow Jomard and Bassir, one pace behind." He knew, somehow, she'd understand the instruction. "You deviate at all, even one foot, and I will shoot you in the back. Are we clear?"

The threat hadn't changed, not really. He was still jumpy, overly tense, reacting to some situation of which she was unaware. But he was speaking with respect, acknowledging her competency, and for now that was enough.

*Pride will ruin you*, the dream whispered in the back of her head, and then faded from her memory.

# TWENTY-FIVE

THE EMERGENCY LIGHTS glowed blue along the floor, the ship eerily quiet. "What the fuck?" Jessica said. Her voice echoed flatly off the walls. No environmental hiss at all; their primary power was down.

Petrikoff would panic. She considered panicking with him.

"Everything's off-line, Captain," Bristol said, one hand on his comm, the dim light casting worried shadows on his face. "Including our radio. Did Petrikoff do this?"

"Not from comms he didn't."

Jessica heard banging on the comms center door. "I warned you, Captain," Petrikoff shouted.

"This wasn't us this time, Petrikoff," she shouted. "We've got no power out here either."

"I will kill your man. You think I won't?"

*Fuck, fuck, fuck.* She ran up the hall to the door and laid her palm against it. What had Emily said about the windows in the room? "Look outside," she said, willing him to believe her. "Are our running lights on?"

There was a moment of silence. "You could have shut them down," he said.

"They're hooked into the main grid. It's the same on *Meridia*, isn't it?".

His next words were calmer. "You better not cut off the airflow."

Oxygen would become an issue eventually; but if it got to the point of him noticing, they were all doomed anyway. "Nobody's cutting off anything," she promised. "We're trying to figure out what's going on. Please, just *wait*."

She heard murmurs, and for the first time a second voice: unintelligible, but deep and resonant, its rhythms familiar. She indulged in one relieved breath: Samaras was still alive.

But she was running out of ways to buy him time.

She stepped back from the door. "Bristol," she said, keeping her voice low, "I need everyone in emergency suits." Assuming there had been no hull breaches, *Galileo* held enough oxygen to keep the crew going for days before the air quality began to degrade, but she had no intention of taking chances. "Spread the word. Go, now."

He fled, and she turned back to the door. "Petrikoff. I have to go down to engineering to find out what's going on. I want your word you won't hurt Samaras."

More low voices, and then Petrikoff said, clearly: "If I hear from you within ten minutes, he'll be all right."

She should thank him. She should keep the dialog between them as cordial as she could. Some things were beyond her. "I'll be back," she promised, and fled.

Her arrival in engineering was entirely ignored. All around her, Ted's team huddled over dead consoles and open access panels, comm lights illuminating the surfaces before them. Next to an ensign half inside a maintenance crawlspace, Ted crouched before a panel in the wall. He glanced up, the only one to notice her. "I'm trying to see what's blocking our reserve," he explained. "This should all have kicked in with the emergency lights, but—"

As abruptly as it had cut off, the power returned.

Jessica blinked against the light and hit her comm. "Petrikoff?"

"Well done, Captain." Over the intercom again, and she suspected she wasn't the only one paradoxically relieved to hear him. "And thank you. You've encouraged me to consider a time-frame. I will wait one hour for proof of the CI's eradication. I will give you an additional ten minutes after that to produce the renunciation document."

One hour? When she had no idea what the hell was happening? "Petrikoff, I—"

"One hour, Captain. That's all." And he cut her off.

She closed her eyes. No time for worry, for thinking of Samaras, alone in there with a lunatic, undoubtedly trying to come up with ways to escape. An hour was a respite of sorts; she had time, now, to work out the kinks with Emily and figure out how to break into that room.

Assuming the ship stopped breaking under her hands.

"Ted," she said, "what the fuck just happened?"

"Funny you should ask." She opened her eyes to find him on his feet, a detailed schematic of *Galileo*'s hull displayed on the console before him. "You know that elevated gamma? That we've been so clever about avoiding? Well, we just got hit with a big wave of it."

"Is that what killed the power?"

"No, Captain. I have no idea what killed the power. But it sure fucked up our batteries. And...wait. Come look at this."

He waved her over. The schematic was zoomed in on the hull, exposing its microscopic structure. "What am I looking at?" she asked.

He zoomed in further, diving deep into the nanolattice, and finally stopped. "There," he said. And then swore.

Jessica recognized the familiar structure of her ship's hull, nanocomposite structures and metals dovetailed cleanly, ready to shift and reinforce as the ship required.

And then a break.

Two molecules, perhaps three, a flash of energy from atoms torn to pieces. No surrounding damage, no path in or out. Just a tiny, impossible exploded section in the ship's protection from the vacuum.

"Is that as bad as it looks?" she asked.

"At the moment?" he said. "We're green across the board. We're seeing this in scattered places, including on our shuttles, but nothing mission-critical has been hit, not yet. But if it keeps happening we could be in real trouble."

Jessica supposed she should be grateful it had stuck to their machines, and then realized she'd have no way of knowing it had. "What could cause that sort of destruction?"

"It's pretty classic gamma damage," he said. "There are a few other possibilities, but everything else I know of would linger. This is familiar, even ordinary, except there's no entry path."

Jessica looked up at him. He was alert, focused, but she knew him well. His jaw was set against exhaustion, and—if he had any sense at all—more than a little fear.

"Do we have the technology," she asked him, "to insert gamma particles—or anything else—inside of a hull lattice without leaving a path?"

"Nobody does," he said.

"Ted, it's right here."

"*Nobody does,*" he repeated. "It's not possible. This isn't a thing that happens. This is not physics, Jess. Not as we know it."

He didn't say it, but he was leaving her with only one conclusion.

"I need to talk to *Unicinta*," she said.

"You want to comm from engineering again, Captain, we'll be depleting batteries. Not keen on that until our assessment is done."

"If we beamed a radio broadcast at *Unicinta*, would she pick it up?"

"She'd get washed with radio waves," he told her. "Which aren't exactly uncommon out here, but their sensors might flag the concentration."

"A pattern, then," she said. "Something simple." Something to make Kali recognize an incoming message.

Ted swept the hull schematic aside and pulled up a generic command console. "I need a frequency."

"99.7," she said immediately.

Ted entered a series of commands. "Okay," he said. "I've got a pattern firing in a loop. If they're receiving—"

Jessica's comm crackled with analog static. "Captain?"

An entirely unearned wave of relief washed over her. "Ensign Kali," she said, "Sitrep."

A pause: radio delay. About four seconds, if Jessica's math was right. "We're on the surface of Target Zero, Captain," Kali said. "Commander Shaw has dropped through a wormhole with readings identical to the one that ate Greg Foster."

*Of course she did.* Apparently Jessica still had enough energy to be annoyed. "Is Bob there? Is he all right?"

The pause felt longer this time. "I'm fine, Jess," Bob said, but he sounded exhausted.

"Target Zero has been targeting him with cortisol," Kali explained. "It's backing off now, but he's still feeling its effects."

"As you can hear," Bob said dryly, "I'm being well looked after by our newest medical student."

Still himself, then, and Jessica's worry abated.

"Captain," Kali asked, "why are you on radio?"

"That's a long story," Jessica said. "But no comms, not unless I order it. Understood?"

"Understood, Captain."

"What's your system status?"

"Normal. The only environmental change we've had is the radio waves of your message." Her voice was curious. "Captain. What's happened?"

Jessica opened her mouth to say *You can't be reading biometrics off my comm* before she remembered the last message she'd sent. "Petrikoff's taken Samaras hostage in comms. We're pretty sure he's wired the room with explosives. And we just got hit by a wave of *something* from that thing you're sitting on. Did it damage you at all?"

"We've experienced no wave, Captain."

She met Ted's eyes, and he shrugged. "If it targeted us specifically? Sure. No weirder than any of this other stuff."

"Check your logs," Jessica told Kali "There should have been some traces coming off that platform. A power surge. Something."

"From here, Captain, it's been inert," Kali said, curious again. "Just as we detected no mechanism for raising Doctor Hastings' cortisol."

Same story, every time. "How *are* you doing, Bob?"

"It's not as bad as it was," he said. "I think it just wanted to make sure I didn't follow her."

"You're saying that thing has a plan?" Ted asked.

"I don't think so," Kali told him. "I think it's just reacting."

"By picking and choosing who it eats."

"Yes," she said.

"Can we choose a different metaphor?" Jessica said irritably. "Kali, what are you basing your conclusions on?"

The silence this time was longer than four seconds, and it was Bob who answered her. "Kali is theorizing she and Target Zero may share origins."

Jessica's first reaction was a visceral desire to haul Bob off the shuttle and blow the living daylights out of both Kali and that platform.

Her second reaction was *Of course.*

1,000 years, give or take, since humanity had started seriously exploring the stars, and they'd never found anything suggesting alien intelligence. For *Galileo* to abruptly run across two pieces of technology from two distinct alien species was extraordinarily unlikely. Their origins had to be the same.

And if Kali was the same as Target Zero, *Chryse* had been as well. And Bayandi, *Chryse*'s CI captain, had saved the lives of an awful lot of people, including Jessica.

*Individuals, then. Not a hive mind.*

If they were lucky.

"Can you talk to it?" Jessica asked Kali.

"No," Kali replied, subdued. "My knowledge of it is limited. And even if I did know how to connect to it, it's unlikely any of our hardware would be compatible."

"It seems compatible enough with *Galileo*'s."

"It does, doesn't it? It's crude, but its purpose seems to involve some kind of low-level connection, or synchronization."

"Do you have any idea what it wants?"

"It's not sentient, Captain," Kali said. "That I'm sure of. So it doesn't *want* anything. And I don't believe it's a weapon."

"Sure as fuck is acting like one."

"Yes, Captain." Damned if she didn't sound patient. "But that's a cultural bias, isn't it?"

"It ate *three people*, Ensign."

"Yes, Captain. Nevertheless." Kali, perhaps aware she'd annoyed her command chain enough already, changed the subject. "You mentioned a wave. Were you able to pinpoint the reason for it?"

"You think there's a reason for it?"

"I don't think Target Zero would expend energy like that,

especially directed energy, for no reason at all. Tell me: what happened before the wave?"

Jessica thought back. "Petrikoff had already grabbed Samaras," she said grimly. "I'd commed Elena, and we'd switched everyone to radio."

"How did you ensure your comm to Commander Shaw wouldn't be intercepted?"

"I shut off ship-level comms and sent it through engineering," Jessica told her. And before the CI's response reached her, she understood.

"It was answering you, Captain," Kali said. "At least—that seems a plausible assumption. If it's like me, if it's like the pieces of Bayandi that preceded me, comms are its primary conduit. An abrupt comms drop might have caused it to send some kind of query or keep-alive signal."

"Nice keep-alive," Jessica said, "when it whacks our power."

"I'm only speculating," Kali said again. "But if Target Zero shares attributes with me, it's very possible its knowledge of us is crude. It's designed with a purpose, yes; but it's reactive. It doesn't know anything about nuance."

"So if we cut comms again," Jessica said, "it hits us again?"

"That's a reasonable assumption, Captain."

She swore. "Ted, I need to know how many more whacks like that we could survive."

"Yes, Captain." He headed for the battery room in the back of the floor.

"Emily? You on?"

"Here, Captain," said Emily in her ear.

"Hold on the breach for now," Jessica told her. "That thing out there is likely to hit us again if we lose comms in the process. Putting together a risk assessment."

"Yes, Captain. Standing by."

Her comm flashed with a narrow-banded signal: a sparse construct, uncomplex. The kind of thing that might have come from a system status notification, or an automated alert of some kind. Nothing urgent.

Except it was encrypted.

Nobody bothered to encrypt uncomplex comms. Most people never even bothered to learn how. Unless they were a comms expert and a recreational hacker, someone who enjoyed the process as a strange, hyperfocused art form.

She and Samaras had been trading notes on encryption schemes for more than a year.

She waved Ted over and looped him in, decoding the comm.

"—not going to be a deterrent," Samaras was saying.

He sounded out of breath, his voice tight; he'd been injured.

"I'm one person in a crew of 167. Keeping me here won't keep you alive."

"She's sentimental, your captain," Petrikoff said. He didn't sound smug or sneering; he was calm, collected, deliberate. "She won't waste your life unless she has to."

"She'll have to," Samaras said. "The way you've wired this room, she can't afford to try to take you alive."

*Fuck.*

"She doesn't know how I've wired the room," Petrikoff said dismissively. "And she won't, at least not until that thing has been destroyed."

"You don't care about your diplomatic document?"

"That's hardly going to matter. The ship will be destroyed, and *Meridia* will know I've saved them. Don't worry, Lieutenant. Your life won't be wasted, whatever your captain manages to do. You're helping to save my people. I'm sorry there's nothing you can do to save your own life, but sometimes it's too late."

Jessica heard a sound: low, more vibration than audio, as if something was brushing against Samaras' comm chip, likely too quiet for Petrikoff to detect. It took her a moment to recognize the pattern: a simple tap cipher. This one was basic, and he'd kept the message short: *Defusing. 35 minutes.*

"It doesn't have to go that way, you know," Samaras said. Under his voice, Jessica heard a quiet tone: a safety signal. He'd restored something...or disabled something. Disabling the explosives, right under Petrikoff's nose. "You know none of us have any loyalty to the Corps. If you talked to people, you might find more of us support you than you think."

"It doesn't matter." Bleakness crept into Petrikoff's tone. Suicidal or not, he'd been walking this path for a long time. "My life ended when Nataliya made us come out here. Fucking traitor. Taras trusted her. *I* trusted her. And now here we are, and I'll never get home." He stopped; Jessica could hear his breathing. "But at least I can save the people I love. At least I can—"

The message ended.

*Shit.*

"Emily," Jessica said, "Petrikoff is going to blow the comms center no matter what we do. But Samaras is trying to disable the explosives. I still want a strategy, but I want to give Samaras as much time as we can."

"Yes, Captain."

She turned to find Ted emerging from the battery room. "Small cause for optimism," she told him, "but I'll take it." She caught the look on his face, and her stomach dropped. "What have you got?"

"What I've got," he said grimly, "is banks of batteries draining faster than we can charge them. Between these gamma pocks and whatever took out our power, we've lost more than eighty percent of our capacity. We can't jump, Jess. And if we get hit again with another pulse, even a weaker one, we're not even going to be able to go sublight. Petrikoff or no Petrikoff, we're stuck here."

# TWENTY-SIX

"Squad Seven return to base. Acknowledge."

Greg held up a hand, halting his squad's advance, and met Eyenga's eyes. The younger man raised his eyebrows, for once without the thinly-veiled antipathy he'd carried for Greg for weeks. Greg couldn't really hold Eyenga's attitude against him; Niemann had given Eyenga's command to Greg without comment, deferring to tradition and rank. At Eyenga's age, Greg wouldn't have taken it well either. He felt fortunate all Eyenga did was roll his eyes and occasionally snark at an order.

But Eyenga's reaction to Niemann's message was unencumbered by disrespect: he didn't know either why Niemann would call them back early from patrol, nor why the captain sounded so tense.

Not that Greg could fault Niemann for any level of tension. Greg's three weeks on board *Capricorn* had given him a much clearer picture of the debacle Niemann was facing. How the POWs had secured the engine room in the first place was still a mystery, but how they were maintaining their stranglehold was frustratingly clear: they had a small piece of territory to defend, and absolutely nothing to lose.

Gen Naude's team was supposed to be on the other side of the ship, eyes on engineering, gathering intelligence on the enemy's strategy and capabilities. As far as Greg knew, she'd never filed a single report. Greg had asked Niemann, with some care, if he could talk with *Capricorn*'s first officer the next time she and her team checked in; while Niemann hadn't lost his temper, his negative had been crisp.

Now and then, when Greg lay awake during his sleep watch, listening to the steady breathing of the others, he wondered if Gen and her people had been killed, if Niemann was covering her fate to preserve the morale of his overextended crew. But out here, playing hurry-up-and-wait with the enemy, it seemed increasingly strange that Niemann wasn't just storming the room and shooting at everything they could until they got their ship back, damn the casualties.

He'd grumbled just that to Eyenga on their last meal break, and the commander had eyed him without humor. "You know," Eyenga said, "that'd be a war crime."

Given the circumstances Greg wasn't sure Eyenga was right about that, but he took the caution in the spirit in which it had been given. Niemann's people had been in this mess much longer than Greg had; he had no business second-guessing their strategy. Destructiveness was unlikely to resolve this situation to anyone's satisfaction.

And yet something had made Niemann pull them away from purportedly vital surveillance duty. Whatever his reason, it wouldn't be trivial.

Greg motioned to his people. "Squad Seven on our way, Captain. Move out," he told the others, and the squad headed down the hall.

"The fuck?" Yarov asked as they walked.

"Foster's pissed him off," Eyenga explained.

Yarov snorted. "Your famous charm at work," she said, and they all laughed.

*Making friends as always,* someone whispered in Greg's head, but he lost the memory before it could coalesce.

He laughed with them. There was always an edge to Eyenga's humor, but in most cases it made sense to ignore it. He wouldn't have to worry about Eyenga's attitude much longer. They'd make a breakthrough any day now, and then he could get back home to *Galileo.*

The cafeteria was more crowded than usual, and it took Greg a moment to notice why: Squad Nine, under Kelson, was there as well. He frowned. Nine had been on Level Twelve this morning, the same level where Eyenga had found him. His heartbeat quickened; had they found someone else? Someone he knew?

An image flashed in his mind: dark hair streaked with blue, sandstone skin; the odor of industrial soap touched with citrus; the sound of a voice he could almost conjure, melodic and affectionate and amused. A bubble of emotion burst in his gut, and he felt, suddenly, anguished and angry and in desperate need of escape from this place, this ship that was not his own, where nothing made sense and nobody asked any questions.

The back of his throat tasted of salt, and the emotion faded.

Kelson's squad parted as Greg approached Niemann's table, and he saw who they'd found—or rather, who they were keeping prisoner.

Not at all the woman who'd appeared in his imagination. This woman's hair was shorter, and yellow, like Caroline's. He thought her skin tone might be warmer than his wife's, but she was blushing so brightly he couldn't tell. Her eyes, too, might have been Caroline's, had they been blue instead of dark: wide and round and expressive. She was small, but he took in the lean, tense muscles of her arms and legs and suspected she often used her stature to deceive. Her physical presence seemed designed to make her appear weak or innocent, but at this moment she seemed neither. He was pretty sure, had she not been surrounded by people with live weapons, she'd be taking a swing at someone. If he was any judge of body language, this woman was absolutely furious.

She wore the familiar uniform of a PSI officer, the unrelieved black striking against her bright coloring; but even beyond that recognition, he knew her. He couldn't quite remember her name, but he remembered sarcasm, intellect, impatience. And a vulnerability over…something. Something awful had happened, and he'd been with her, and she had taken it badly. Or was that not quite right? He could almost—

A flash out of the corner of his eye, like bright sun on sand, and he was focused again. Before he could address Niemann, the woman interrupted.

"About fucking time, Foster," she said. Furious, but also relieved. Relaxed with him. "You want to get these goons off me?"

Greg could have told her she was better off with Kelson's goons than most of the rest of the crew, but she was not, at the moment, his primary concern. He met Niemann's eyes and came to attention. "Reporting as ordered, Captain," he said.

Niemann's expression was watchful, and Greg wondered what sort of experiences *Capricorn* had had with PSI. "Foster," Niemann said, "this woman says she knows you."

"Yes, Captain," Greg said.

"She's PSI."

Details began returning to him. "Yes, Captain," he said. "Her name's Gritsenko. She's a commander off *Meridia*. We've worked with them from time to time."

The woman—Nadiya, Greg thought, or possibly Nataliya—gaped at him. "Seriously, Foster? Did you fucking hit your head down here?" She frowned at him, studying his chin, and he was abruptly aware he hadn't shaved in a few days. When she asked again, her voice was quieter. "Did you?"

Freja Taras had introduced Greg to Commander Gritsenko, although he couldn't remember when. *Nataliya.* It was Nataliya.

He called her Nat, and he wasn't sure she liked it, but perhaps Taras had suggested the nickname. Taras excelled at all the mandated social niceties; more than that, she seemed to perform them with sincerity. She was an expansive, outgoing woman with many friends, and she liked all her friends to know each other. That she trusted almost no one was something of a surprise to people who weren't close to her. That she trusted Greg was something he'd taken as a great compliment. If Taras trusted Nat, Greg could trust her as well.

"So you work ops with PSI?" Niemann asked.

This was one of the schisms in the Corps, one of the discussions he'd had with other captains that sometimes grew contentious. Hundreds of years of history had led to PSI being secretive with Central, and Central in return being deeply mistrustful. Greg had dealt with *Meridia* for some years, and was comfortable with their culture; but he'd run into PSI ships in other sectors that had been completely opaque. *Meridia*'s sister ship, *Chryse*, was a cipher, preferring to have no diplomatic relationship with Central at all; but Greg had the impression even Taras found *Chryse* mysterious.

None of which mattered to Tau Niemann, and Greg couldn't blame him. If a PSI officer had shown up on *Galileo* in the middle of a crisis, Greg's first concern would have been divided loyalties.

He chose his words carefully. "We've done some rescue operations in coordination with *Meridia*," he said. "They've helped us with distribution, and in one case evacuation."

"You see any distribution and evacuation needed here?"

At that, Nat spoke up. "I told you," she said to Niemann. "I'm here for Foster. I don't give a damn what else is happening to you."

Her eyes on Niemann's were unequivocally hostile; she should have been afraid, because why wouldn't she be, in the face of a man who might at any point decide he was tired of listening to her and toss her out an airlock? But she showed no fear, nor did she seem to comprehend her jeopardy. She was outraged at Niemann's behavior, and annoyed with Greg's, although he couldn't imagine why. She should have seen enough of life outside PSI to know all of this was expected.

"What do you mean," he asked her, "you're here for me?"

Her expression shifted into incredulity. "You *jumped into this thing*," she told him. "I'm supposed to just say *fine* and head back to the ship?"

She said it as if the words would make sense to him, and he remembered his dream, the wind and the sand. Nat hadn't been in that dream. Maybe she knew where it had come from, but he didn't think this was the time to ask her.

"I'm here to assist Captain Niemann," he told her, "at his discretion."

She blinked at him, baffled, and he had another, brief, gut-wrenching memory of citrus and sandstone. "What," she said, "do you think you can assist him with?"

"That's classified," he told her.

"Are you—" She sputtered into silence, and her gaze sharpened, boring into his head and into everything that had happened over the last three weeks. She looked down at his chin again; self-consciously he raised a hand to run it along the stubble. Why did her focus on his nascent beard fill him with unease? "Foster," she asked, "how long have you been here?"

"Three weeks, six days, and seventeen hours."

Her face went blank. "You haven't though." For the first time she sounded less than confident. "Foster. I just left you."

Niemann exhaled impatiently. "Your PSI friend is a liability, Foster. You know it as well as I do. Give me a reason why I should permit her to consume our resources."

This was easier territory. "She's not a threat, Captain."

Niemann looked at Nat, his pale eyes like ice. "That the truth, Commander Gritsenko?"

"You've got a pack of goons with guns on me," Nat retorted. "How am I a threat to anyone?"

Niemann and Nat locked eyes for a moment, hers defiant and fearless, and Greg felt a wave of admiration. Damn fool, this woman, but it was impossible to dislike her.

Niemann apparently agreed. Something almost like a smile played over his lips. "Too bad you're not Corps," he said to her, and Greg thought he meant it. "We could use someone who takes no bullshit." He looked back at Greg. "We don't have room to keep anybody in the brig. She's your responsibility, Foster. Your squad, your sleep pod. You are joined at the hip with her twenty-four seven. If she gets caught stealing, or sneaking, or just looking at somebody wrong? She's out of here. We get to rationing, she loses first. We get to picking each other off, she's at the front of the line." His gaze went from Greg to Nat and back again, all his good humor gone. "Do we understand each other?"

The PSI commander opened her mouth, and for one terrible instant Greg thought she might say something foolish. He didn't remember her being impulsive, but she seemed irritable and out of balance. But all she said was, "Yes, Captain Niemann. I understand."

Niemann turned back to Greg. "Squad Seven can stand down for now, but I want you back on Storage Twelve tomorrow. At 0515, you, me, and Eyenga are going to sit down and review strategy. I'm tired of getting jerked around by fucking civilians."

Greg snapped to attention again. "Yes, Captain."

"Show this PSI officer the ropes, Foster. And don't let her out of your sight."

"Yes, Captain."

"Dismissed."

Greg led Nat toward the cooking station in the back of the room. She turned back toward the gunners who'd been guarding her and waved at them.

"Fuck me, Foster," she said, "you might have been faster with that. For a minute there I thought he was going to space us both."

"We're under siege," he said to her. He felt annoyed, unsettled; she wasn't comprehending, and he wasn't sure if that was deliberate or not. "He's entitled to space anyone he needs to."

She snorted. "He gets pretty snippy for someone who probably isn't real," she remarked.

He found himself suddenly ravenous. "There's not a lot of variety," he told her, grabbing a plate and opening a pot of protein stew, redolent of red curry and raisins, "but what we have is hot and restorative. Even kind of tasty, once you get used to it." He scooped up a generous portion, but she hadn't taken a dish. "You should eat now," he told her. "You don't know when you'll have a chance later."

He felt her eyes on him, and turned to her.

"What is it?" he said. Something was wrong with her. She had no business being this cavalier when she might have been killed just a few minutes earlier.

But her look was, speculative; something calculating in it, something he knew as well as he knew her, maybe better. "He can't be real, Foster."

"Did you have a dream on your way here?" That was the only thing that made sense. "I did, too. You'll get over it soon."

"You don't remember anything, do you?"

"Niemann's as real as I am," he assured her, but somehow she didn't look any happier. "Commander. We have a mission here. Stick with me and I'll keep you safe until we can fulfill it, and then we'll see where we all are, all right?"

She watched him in silence, and he turned away again.

Eventually she said to him, "You really have been here four weeks."

"My hair doesn't grow like this overnight."

She swore, quietly. Still unafraid; she wasn't a stupid woman, but he was beginning to think of her as a foolish one. "Okay," she said at last. "I'll work the mission with you. Tell me what's up, and we'll get through it together. And then we can go home."

He looked down at her. Her eyes were almost kind, although he suspected those clever eyes never quite crossed into kindness. She was his responsibility, and he would keep her alive along with the rest of them. "I promise you," he told her, "I'll keep you safe."

She scoffed, and picked up a dish.

transit: elena

*Elena had never understood why the afternoon sun bothered her so much. It wasn't like the light was brighter. It wasn't even that the long shadows got under her skin, although that might have been a part of it; they seemed inhuman at this hour, narrow and furtive, as if they knew things she did not. She should have liked afternoons. Afternoons meant night was close, and she would be able to exhale and look up at the stars and everything around her would feel whole. But here, an hour before sunset, her nerves were frayed and loud in her head, and she wanted to be somewhere else.*

*The house was just as she remembered it: squat, gray, nondescript, differentiated from every other house on the street by the neat rows of flowers and vegetables in the front yard. Her mother's work. Most days they ate from the garden, supplementing with soy and barley from the big community fields, and the same neighbors who pretended not to see her mother's friendly waves were always happy to take proffered leftovers. It was a small house for three of them, Elena and her mother and her grandmother, but she hadn't known that at the time. Even now, living on a starship with plenty of room allocated for personnel, she preferred a smaller room.*

*Her mother was shouting. That was unusual.*

*The door opened silently, recognizing her, which was odd, given how long it had been since she'd been home. She'd tried moving back a year ago, when she'd first quit the Corps. It had been devastating, enervating, dragging her down into a darkness that didn't bear close inspection. It had been her mother, two weeks into her stay, who had taken her aside and said, with great love, that she needed to get the fuck out of the house before it killed her.*

*Elena heard another voice, low and familiar: her uncle Mike. Her stomach twisted. She'd been close to Mike until her teens, and although she'd long since chosen to forgive him, the rift had never healed. That her mother—who never shouted at anyone—was yelling at Mike, of all people, was concerning.*

*"You have to do it, Maggie!" Mike shouted.*

*"I don't have to do anything of the sort," Elena's mother retorted. "If you want to crush her dreams, you do it herself."*

*"What kind of mother are you?" Elena walked into the room to see Mike, taller and wider than her mother, looming over her, tense and angry. "They'll eviscerate her, and you know it. How can you let her walk into that?"*

*"She wants to try," Maggie said. "I'm not going to take that away from her."*

*"No. You'll just let the professionals do it, when she has nothing to fall back on, and nowhere to start over."*

*"And whose fault is that?" Maggie Shaw, short and slight and resembling Elena not at all, had no trouble standing up to her much bigger sibling. "You encouraged her in this from the time she was a baby. You gave her all those tools to play with because you were too annoyed to actually look after the children."*

*Elena had spent her childhood in Mike's machine shop along with his four sons, her cousins. Mike had given them tools and bits and pieces of engines and machine bodies to entertain them while he worked. The boys had been disinterested; she'd been riveted from the start, had figured out how to piece things together, had started building machines and never looked back.*

*Were they saying that had all been a lie?*

*"It's one thing to help me fix some tourist kid's skidder on the weekends," Mike was saying. "But the Corps? They won't take her, Maggie. We both know it. And you need to tell her before they break her heart and ruin her life."*

*"Absolutely not."*

*"I've stayed out of your parenting," Mike told her. "All those years you let her walk into anything at all, and never even warned her. You picked her up and dusted her off and sent her off again. And it's irresponsible, Mags." His voice softened. "You know I love her. I know you love her, too. We need to protect her. I don't think she'll recover if she doesn't learn the truth now."*

*But Maggie was unmoving. "You want to tell her?" she said. "You tell her yourself. I'm having nothing to do with it."*

*It didn't go that way, Elena tried to say. Mike. It didn't. I was a Corps mechanic. For years. And now I'm...what am I? I'm not. I'm not anymore. They took it away from me. They moved me away from it. They...was this why? Why wouldn't you tell me? Why wouldn't Mama tell me?*

*Mama?*

*Elena's vision broke character, and Maggie Shaw looked directly into her eyes. "This isn't real, Elena," her mother said.*

*And it wasn't.*

# TWENTY-SEVEN

There was something wrong with the ship.

Elena noticed before she opened her eyes: the environmentals straining a little too much, the thrum of the vibration through her feet, as if everything was slightly misaligned. Had the ship been in the field she'd have panicked at those sensations, but she heard no FTL harmonics. The ship she was on was idled, doing nothing but unnecessarily wearing down its own parts.

*I should find out why they haven't shut down.*

And then she remembered, and her eyes flew open.

She was in a Corps starship corridor, the standard blue-gray composite walls declaring the ship's provenance. For a moment the air had smelled like Mike's old machine shop, all fresh lubricants and inefficient civilian engines, but that was just the dregs of her dream. This air smelled of battle: electricity, sweat, distant plasma fire. A combat area, then, wherever she was. She blinked once and looked around: typical iron-gray floor, diffuse white light from the ceilings, periodic seams in the walls indicating maintenance access. The corridor led away from her on either side, but no doors, no windows, no other branches, just long, empty halls fading into darkness, and the odors of war.

She took a step, and a whisper of pain telegraphed from her hip. There was a reason for that, and she couldn't quite recall what it was, but in the moment it was irrelevant. What mattered was there was no visible wormhole here, as there had been on the surface of Target Zero; she'd been deposited somewhere, and the wormhole had gone about its business. No way of telling if it had deposited Greg in the same place. No way of telling where he was at all.

It was possible her strategy had been poorly thought through.

Resisting the urge to call out, she started to her left. Her shoes made no sound on the honed flooring, and she abruptly remembered that a moment ago—before that odd memory/dream, and what had her mother said? *This isn't real, Elena*— she had been in a full env suit and gravity boots. She looked down at herself and found an orange jumpsuit over soft-soled machine-room shoes: a civilian mechanic's uniform. She'd lived in clothes like this for most of the last year, but she hadn't even seen a civilian for the last eight weeks. Eight weeks ago, she'd—

That powerful smell of the machine shop again, so pungent her eyes watered. Persistent, that dream.

Whatever had happened eight weeks ago couldn't possibly matter in the face of all this. The only important thing was the task before her. Which was...the environmental systems whined again. *Fixing this ship*. That was it. She needed to find the engineers and make sure they checked the alignment on every system, no matter how small. Something was knocking this ship off-kilter, and she could help them with repairs. Never in her career had she encountered anything she couldn't fix with enough time and parts.

As she progressed, the battle damage became more severe:

misaligned wall panels, dents in the floor, smudges that might have been plasma fire burns. And no doors, still, even thirty meters down the hall. Corps ships weren't built like this, not even the older ones.

That dream of hers, the conversation that had never happened. Was this corridor just another hallucination? Was any of this real?

"Is any of this real?" she tried aloud. Her voice sounded familiar, echoed normally. She'd had hallucinations, and fairly recently; they hadn't felt like this. They'd felt like—

She shook her head. Fuzzy, like right after her injury, that injury she'd received...somewhere. Had she hit her head? Again? She needed to focus, she needed to—

"Greg." She said his name out loud. "I am here to find Greg."

Abruptly she heard voices. Close, maybe thirty meters, talking over each other, unintelligible. Nowhere for her to turn, or to hide. Wherever she was, she was an interloper.

"Hello?" she called out, trying to sound non-threatening. "Who's there?"

The voices fell silent, and she heard the single squeak of a shoe before a military team of five appeared around the corner, shouting at her all at once: *get down, hands on your head, shut up, don't make a sound, what are you doing here.* Elena lowered herself to her knees, and her hip twinged again; persistent, this injury she couldn't remember. The shouting continued, and she took the time to examine her captors: all in Corps uniforms, the familiar black and gray, every fold and seam crisp and straight. But their equipment was less robust: their weapons were worn, held together with field tape, pieces missing. One, right at the edge of her peripheral vision, she was fairly certain wouldn't fire at all.

Not that four wouldn't be just as effective as five at melting her into her component chemicals.

One voice rose above the others: "She's a civilian. She's one of them."

Everyone fell silent. That didn't seem good.

"She's not a *civilian*." This other voice seemed less belligerent, less inclined to blast her into atoms. "She's a mechanic. You seen them with any mechanics, Brixa?"

*Them.* Who was *them*?

The first voice again, this time derisive. "Fuck you, Miro. It's an orange jumpsuit. That doesn't make her a mechanic any more than your pretty eyes make you a vid star."

Snickers in the crowd. Elena began to feel like she might not be summarily executed.

"Can it," said a sharp voice, and the group fell silent again. One of the rifles moved closer as its bearer took a step forward. "What are you doing here?"

Elena looked up. She could make out little past the weapon: an armored headpiece, the face shield open; dark, gold-brown skin, not as dark as Greg's—*you are here for Greg*—one deep brown eye under a furrowed eyebrow. A thoughtful eyebrow, Elena thought. Not the sort of eyebrow that would kill her without satisfying its curiosity.

"I'm looking for someone," she said.

"One of your fellow POWs?" Brixa asked..

"I'm not a POW," she said. "I came in here alone."

"If you're alone, how could you be looking for someone?"

"I—"

"Commander," Brixa interrupted, "she's lying. We need to take care of her and move on."

The commander, the one with the curious eyebrow, never stopped staring at Elena. "Wait," she said, and the furrow deepened, as if she were searching deeply into her memory. "I think... do I know you?"

"I don't know," Elena said pointedly. "I can't see your face past the barrel of that thing."

The rifle moved aside, giving Elena a clear view. The woman was short, around Jessica's height, but much broader-shouldered. Infantry, or infantry-trained, the powerful muscles of her arms and legs emphasized by her uniform's elastic fabric. She had a flat nose and full lips, and those curious eyebrows arched away from her eyes in an almost elfin curve. Her face was nearly unlined, but her bearing suggested she was Elena's age, or older: this was a woman who knew effortlessly how to take charge, to brush off defiance. Elena knew the self-assurance in that stance. If this woman wasn't a captain, she was highly ranked, and probably had been for most of her career.

She was entirely unfamiliar.

"I don't think we've met," Elena said, regretfully.

But the woman kept frowning, her eyes searching Elena's face. "No," she agreed thoughtfully. "But I know you. You're Foster's mechanic. Shaw. The one who quit the Corps."

"You know Greg?" Abruptly the weapons pointed at her ceased to matter. "Is he here?"

But the confusion on the woman's face told Elena all she needed to know. "Why would he be here?"

*Fuck.* She felt abruptly exhausted, her muscles aching; her annoying hip poked at her sharply. She flexed her fingers. "I don't suppose I could stand for this conversation," she said.

"Commander." It was Brixa again, but the commander just waved a hand.

"It's all right, Brixa," she said. "I'll take responsibility. Let her up."

Four rifle noses pointed at the floor. Elena kept her hands on her head, and got to her feet. Eye to eye the commander looked competent, relaxed, professional. Nearly friendly, although Elena figured that was due to their mutual acquaintance with Greg.

"Can I put my hands down?"

"Of course."

Elena lowered her hands, and noticed every pulse rifle pointed at the floor was still armed. "You have me at a disadvantage," she said to the commander, doing her best to ignore the tension from the others.

But the woman had chosen to trust her, and flashed a quick smile. "Sorry. Don't encounter many new people these days. I'm Commander Naude, first officer here, and in charge of these assholes. That's Brixa, Miro, Hoang, and Nkosi."

Elena's eyes went from face to face. Brixa was a redhead whose pale skin was blotchy from annoyance; Miro was tall and reedy, with short, thick black hair and rough, desert-brown skin; Hoang, wide and solid like Naude but taller, eyes black and unreadable, ruddy dark skin visible under the stubble of his shaved scalp; Nkosi, about Elena's height, all legs like Greg, relaxed but not blinking, not even once.

"Commander Naude." Elena turned back to the first officer. She knew that name. "You've known Greg a long time."

"Fifteen years," she said. "Since he was a dumbass first year ensign. Surprised he lived this long."

"But..." There was something strange about this, and Elena blinked against machine-shop-scented cobwebs. "Something's wrong here."

"Damn straight," Naude said. "Our ship is occupied. Which explains your warm reception."

Elena let her eyes stray over the others once more. "No. That's not it. It's—"

And she remembered.

"Gen Naude," she said aloud. "*Capricorn*. Is this *Capricorn*?"

"Of course." Naude nodded to her squad, and apart from exchanging a quick glance with each other, they fell into formation without objection. "You in the habit of dropping in on random warships?"

Elena stood still, her eyes on Gen. She had destroyed

*Capricorn* herself. That strange ship, powered but drifting, as fragile as snowy lace.

Had it been a fake? The ident, the makeup, the configuration...no. It *couldn't* have been. *This* had to be a fake. This tactile, breathing corridor with actual people in it had to be a fake.

Didn't it?

"I...don't know how I got in here," she began. If this was a hallucination, referencing the wormhole might not be the best start. "But I followed Greg. I don't know that he ended up in the same place I did, but I need to find him."

"He may be with the Captain," Gen said to her. Elena fell into step with her. The others marched behind them: synchronous footsteps, following their commander but still on alert. *Why would I hallucinate trained combat soldiers?*

Even as her dream had hurt her, on some level she'd known it wasn't real. This was different.

"Last we were able to check in," Gen said, "Captain Niemann was on Level Five, on the other side of the machine room." Her lips grew thin. "We hear fire now and then, but they haven't been able to break through any better than we have. If Foster's with the captain, he'll be put to work. Don't worry. We've been making headway; we should be able to hack a comms connection in two or three days."

*Two or three days?* "Break through where?" Elena stopped; behind her the footsteps stopped with her, and she heard more than one hand shift on a rifle barrel.

"Into our engine room," Gen told her. "Those fuckers took it over. But we're close to getting it back."

"We should never have brought them on board." Brixa's voice was bitter, and Elena wondered that she hadn't seen before how utterly exhausted all these people were.

"Orders are orders, Lieutenant," Gen said shortly. Elena heard Brixa shift behind her, but the woman said nothing else.

Here was something Elena was familiar with: a problem. The

ship was under siege, but the enemy was isolated. Comms were disrupted, rendering their strategy insufficient. *This is why I'm here,* she thought. *I can do this.*

"You know," she said, starting to walk again, "I might be able to help."

Gen grinned again, and fell into step beside her. "Music to my ears, Foster's Mechanic. Let's get those assholes off my ship."

# TWENTY-EIGHT

"That's not an acceptable conclusion," Jessica said.

Ted glanced around the machine room and lowered his voice. "I can't change physics."

"That thing out there can."

"Apparently. But we are not it."

"Don't patronize me." She was becoming annoyed. How long had it been since Petrikoff grabbed that room? Five minutes? Ten? How much longer did Samaras have? "I need a different answer. Maybe we *are* fucked. But I'll be damned if we're going to sit here and roll over without analyzing every possibility, no matter how nuts it might seem." Reflexively she clenched her fists. "And that thing *doesn't* change physics. It just knows more than we do. So fucking *use* that, Chief Shimada, and figure it out. Are we clear?"

"I—" Ted straightened. "Yes, Captain."

"While you're saving our asses," she said, "I want to know what we can do with the status quo. If we're going to limp home sublight, I want to know how close we can get to an object that might have minerals we can mine." She knew better than to ask how long it would take to get back to the booster relay, never mind all the way to the Fourth. "One way or another, we're getting out of this, even if it's a long fucking trip home."

She thought Ted might get angry with her, tell her she was out of her mind; or worse, just salute and turn away, another subordinate sent off to do the impossible by a delusional superior officer. But they'd known each other too long for that, and as she glared, his face relaxed into a genuine smile.

"Never did like the idea of going down quietly," he said to her. "Okay. I'll squeeze the daylights out of the battery array and get you a report stat."

He turned and headed back to the battery room, and she closed her eyes against a wave of relief. If Ted didn't find a solution, she'd know there was none.

"Kali. Are you still on?"

"I'm continuously monitoring, Captain," Kali said smoothly.

"How much gamma damage have you got on *Unicinta*?"

"We have no gamma damage," Kali said. "We've seen no waves since we landed here."

*It's protecting her.* That tingle ran up her spine again; maybe Kali's kinship with Target Zero wasn't all bad. "Kali. Do you think we could comm with you without triggering a backlash?"

"It'd be an additional comm signal, not an interruption," Kali said, "so yes, that's a reasonable assumption."

*To fix a four-second delay.* Four seconds could mean everything, and if she was wrong, they would be no more dead in the water than they were already. "Switch to comms," Jessica said, "direct to me. We can't risk Petrikoff hacking in on a public line."

"Yes, Captain," Kali commed.

"What's the condition of your batteries?"

"97.54% charged, Captain." Another pause. "I don't think they're big enough to power *Galileo*."

"If we could start a fold initiation," Jessica clarified, "could you stabilize it enough for us to escape?"

"We could stabilize the field briefly," Kali told her, "but we couldn't hold it unilaterally. And we'd need to be closer."

"How much closer?"

"102,309 kilometers."

Still nearly 500,000 kilometers from *Galileo*. They might be able to fold *Unicinta* into the field with them at that distance, although they'd need to calculate how much extra power that would take. Either way, though, it would mean abandoning Greg and Elena, and Captain Taras' strange, spiky training pilot. "How fast could you get that close?" she asked.

"At full speed," Kali told her, "50.22 seconds."

"Ted, did you get that?"

From the battery room, Ted said, "Possible stabilization with shitty troop ship batteries, full speed 50 seconds. Yes, Captain." Caustically familiar. They still had a chance.

"Commander Broadmoor," she radioed. "I want your people in the aft landing bay and breach-ready, but I'm gonna give Samaras as much time as I can to defuse those explosives."

"Yes, Captain."

"Bristol? Where are you?"

"Distributing env suits, Captain," he said.

"Delegate that. I want more information on what's in that room. I want to know what he's using for explosives, and how Samaras is shutting them down."

"Yes, Captain."

"Kali?"

"Eighty seconds since we started using comms," Kali told her. "I think you're safe from another backlash."

A weak definition of *safe*, but for now she'd take it. "Emily," she said again, "switch to 89.7." She changed her frequency, and the cacophony of the crew ceased. "There's a good chance Samaras won't be able to disable everything," Jessica said.

"We have protocols for breaching wired rooms, Captain."

"Even with an exterior breach, an explosion will clobber the corridor."

"If I may suggest," Emily said, entirely calm, "we should seal the internal bulkheads before we breach."

Isolating the strike team.

It was the right answer. It was their best shot at keeping the ship intact, and the rest of the crew safe.

It also increased the risk that Emily—and her entire breach team—would be lost, along with Samaras, and that asshole Petrikoff.

*I should have let Lanie clock him in the head.*

"We'll set it to auto-seal on containment loss," Emily continued. "Shouldn't take more than a few minutes to set that up."

"Rope in anyone you need. And Emily?"

"Yes, Captain?"

"Don't die. That's an order."

"We'll do our best, Captain."

She should take that back. If Emily had to die, the last thing Jessica wanted was for the woman's final thought to be that she was disobeying orders. For a moment, she allowed herself to be angry with Greg and Elena again. Primarily Greg, of course; in recent years he'd become a good deal more reckless. He had the feel, sometimes, of a man who'd lived his whole life in a box, attracted to a sliver of sunshine he had no real context to understand. Elena was different: she had always charged ahead without looking, box be damned. Jessica was never sure if they were good for each other or absolutely terrible, but this had not been a good moment for their personality flaws to coincide.

She wasn't abandoning them. Of course she wasn't. They'd come back for them. They'd figure out how to dodge Target Zero's weaponry, and they'd—

"Captain!"

Ted was calling out behind her; she turned, half grateful, half resentful for the interruption, to see him animated, energized, and…hopeful? Was it possible he'd make all these horrific decisions unnecessary?

"I may have something, Captain," he said. "It's a longshot, though. Kali? You still on?"

"Of course, Commander Shimada."

In his hands he had a battery brick, one of the photovoltaics that lay quietly arrayed in *Galileo*'s power banks. Small, efficient, easy to charge, arranged in stacks rising a full level, so redundant they should never have had to worry about running out of power. She could see the damage: the surface was mostly black, unreflective, indicating the areas that couldn't hold a charge anymore. But the mottled surface glowed blue here and there, in some spots very brightly. Like a damaged battery shouldn't have been able to glow.

"What am I looking at?" she asked him.

"You are looking," Ted told her, "at the ugliest, riskiest solution to an engineering problem I have ever conceived of in my life."

# TWENTY-NINE

NATALIYA GLOWERED AT Foster. "I am not," she said firmly, "going out there again without a weapon."

Frustration played over his face, and she waited for him to make up his mind.

She'd been patrolling with Squad Seven for two weeks, hauling their ammunition, repairing damaged weapons, doing recon without betraying their location. Once Eyenga had thought it would be funny to send her, unarmed, ahead into the line of fire. He'd thought she'd refuse, but instead she'd inched her way around the curve in the corridor, never letting that asshole see how desperately she wished she were holding a gun. And not on the enemy.

Hallucination or no, she wasn't going to let someone like Eyenga fuck with her.

Foster had been handling all this absurdity with that irritating equanimity of his, but even he had to be fraying at the edges. He'd been doing more than fighting; he'd been doing half the personnel work Niemann should have been doing. When *Capricorn*'s captain told the crew about the most recent casualties—three dead via a trap in one of the maintenance crawlspaces—Yarov had gone into one corner of the cavernous cafeteria to weep. Foster had waited out Niemann's announcement, then excused himself to sit with the young ensign. He said nothing to her, but eventually she leaned against him, and he put an arm around her.

The sight had provoked a twist of jealousy, which had startled her. She'd been long-hardened by Yarov's age, and she wouldn't have been open enough to take an embrace from anyone, never mind a captain she barely knew.

Which was another thing: they thought he was a captain. *He* thought he was a captain. When she tried to correct him, he didn't believe her. All her attempts to shake him out of his intellectual torpor had failed.

"We've got to find a way out of here, Foster," she'd urged him a few days earlier, because he had to understand he was in some kind of cage.

He'd taken a sip of coffee—not even tea in this place; whoever had stocked this simulation hadn't bothered with proper supplies—and nodded grimly, agreeing with her. "Fixing the engines will be the second part of this," he said. "Niemann's worried, but he doesn't want to let on how much. The POWs have had possession of the engine room for a long time now. Even if they're not technicians, they have to be pretty close to figuring out how to sabotage the environmentals while protecting themselves."

"That's not what I mean."

He'd looked at her, frowning slightly, as if she weren't terribly bright. "Nothing happens until we're back in control," he'd said, and despite his look his tone was instructive, respectful. As if he were teaching a recalcitrant child. "That's our priority: getting the POWs out of the engine room. Once that happens, we can go back to *Galileo*, and everything will be fine."

She supposed she should have been grateful he remembered the name of his ship at all.

But facing yet another patrol where hallucinatory plasma fire seemed pretty fucking realistic, she had reached her limit. "Look," she told him, "you all can play whatever war games you want. I don't care. But if I'm part of this squad, I'm not going to be the only one going out defenseless. Seriously, Foster. What the fuck?"

His lips tightened, but she caught some sympathy in his gray eyes. "It's not my call, Nat."

*Fucking nickname.* Of all the things he remembered. "That's some bullshit, Foster. You're the hero of the hour around here. Get me a fucking weapon. I don't care if it's a pulse rifle or a butter knife, I am *not* going out again with nothing."

For a moment his eyes bored into hers, and she was struck by the certainty that he could see right into her mind, read her thoughts. An artifact of the color of his eyes, she thought. She remembered their conversation in *Galileo*'s atrium, and felt her face warm. *Power.* The man had power, and it was an utter and complete fucking waste that he didn't understand how much.

"Okay," he said after a moment, and she had to remind herself what they'd been talking about. "Let me see what I can do. But you stay here, Nat. Within everybody's line of sight, yes? Because if I'm across the room talking to Niemann, I can't be here saving your damn neck."

She didn't bother telling him how many of them she could take out before they'd have a chance at killing her. She watched him walk away from her—effortlessly, enragingly graceful— then sat down on her bunk.

The other inhabitants of the massive cafeteria had dispersed to the edges, grabbing a handful of calories before heading out on patrol. Eat, sleep, fight, all in the same small groups, too small for real squads, too small for any kind of strategic effectiveness. Military rigor for the hell of it: habits to keep people moving in a hopeless situation. Surely Niemann knew the truth of it. Didn't he?

*Trapped.* They were trapped in here, and she felt abruptly like she had on Sochi, when something invisible was coming to kill her, something she couldn't control at all.

Wasn't that why she'd stayed in this business? Because it kept her in control? People handed her names and told her to take lives, and she was good at her job and it satisfied because she didn't need to know *why*, just that it was her responsibility. She'd always chosen the place and time, and usually the method.

Foster should have been an easy job. She'd let her ego get in the way.

"Fuck," she whispered, and put her hands over her face. Panic served no purpose. She took one deliberate breath, and then another, counting carefully as she exhaled; wherever she was, she was not trapped, not running out of air or space or anything else. The danger she was in wasn't from this place, whatever it was, however it was formed. The danger she was in, as always, was from the people around her. Not her doubts. She had no doubts. Curiosity, intrigue, even attraction—none of those feelings were doubts.

She kept breathing evenly, drawing on her old lessons to calm herself, until she heard a step. She looked up; Foster was approaching, his lips set, annoyed. In his belt was tucked a tiny, snub-nosed handgun: lethal at close range, little more than an irritant past four meters. He met her eyes, and she thought his annoyance didn't have anything to do with her at all.

"Best I could do," he told her, handing the gun to her grip first. "It's charged for two shots."

"You are fucking kidding me." But she took it, the grip settling easily into her hand. More heft than she would have assumed given the size, and designed for easy manipulation. Not a bad close quarters weapon. Entirely useless for the sorts of skirmishes they tended to have around here.

"That was all he'd agree to," Greg told her. "So if you decide to fuck everybody over, remember: if you can't get it done in two shots, you're better off not trying at all."

"Fine," she said, and tucked the weapon into her belt, climbing to her feet. And then, because she realized it was expected: "Thank you, Foster." It was indeed better than nothing.

And he had no idea what she could do with two shots.

After traversing two stairwells and three hallways crossing the widest parts of the ship, the team's formation had relaxed. Eyenga and Flagg took point; every once in a while Nataliya saw Flagg flash a quick, sunny grin in the commander's direction. A private conversation over silent comms; discouraged in most military units, but she couldn't see Foster pushing that point. Yarov, looking worried, walked on her own: an easy, even step, but she was the most vulnerable, the closest thing the team had to a weak point.

*She's a good soldier,* Foster commed silently to Nataliya, reading her damn mind again. *The best shot of all of them, apart from Eyenga, maybe. She doesn't panic in the moment; she sublimates it, and it all comes out later.*

Nataliya wondered how much sublimation a person could do before they broke. *That's lovely,* she replied. *Why are we doing this?*

*This is one of the only predictable ways we can lure them out.*

*And what does luring them to their deaths get us?*

*If we can take someone alive,* he told her, *we might be able to get a better picture of their capabilities.*

Now this was interesting. *You remember, of course,* she said to him, *Niemann's order of no prisoners.*

*If we can bring someone back,* he said, *he'll recognize the importance of intelligence.*

He might, she thought. What he'd do with any prisoner afterward was clear. What he'd do with Foster for disobeying orders was less clear, but she didn't think it would be anything good.

Abruptly Foster stopped. "Right-hand corridor, 700 feet ahead." The others before him halted.

That was another thing: the reconfigurations. The ship changed and shifted, like the never-ending spiral she'd encountered at the start, but Foster and the others always saw it before it happened. She'd asked him how, and he'd mumbled something incomprehensible about salt. Incomprehensible or not, she was the only one who was never forewarned, and none of them had ever been wrong. Almost as bad as lacking their precognition was realizing they took the reconfigurations as ordinary, something the ship somehow just *did*.

*Has a reconfiguration ever hurt anyone?* she asked Foster.

He shook his head. *And yeah*, he told her, *before you ask, that's surprised me, too. You'd think if they can do this, they'd just build what they need to kill us.*

*What do you conclude from that?*

*That they'd rather intimidate us than destroy us.*

*Or they're manipulating us.*

*How do you mean?*

This was the worst of it: dealing with his entire absence of critical thought. *We're going to follow that change, right? Like we always do. They can lead us by the nose and tell us exactly where to go.*

He turned to her, those gray eyes abruptly focused, and for one instant she allowed for the possibility that she might not be in this on her own. But then the cobwebs returned, and he looked away. *That doesn't matter. We've got to get to engineering. All reconfiguration means is that they're trying to stop us.*

Her fists clenched in frustration. *So we walk right into their trap? What kind of battle strategy is that? You've been trying this for two and a half months. What makes you think it's going to work today?*

*Because things have changed,* he told her. *You're here.*

Before she could remark on the utter absurdity of that, they were ambushed.

The sound of a rifle shot filled the corridor, and Flagg went down, making enough noise that Nataliya knew she was not dead, at least not yet. Before the others could do more than raise their weapons, two people came out of the newly-formed corridor. One of them grabbed Yarov, an arm around her neck, a handgun at her head; the other pinned Eyenga to the wall, the nose of a pulse rifle under the commander's chin. Next to her, Foster stopped, and together they raised their guns.

"Weapons down!" one of the enemy yelled. "Disarm or we kill them! Now!"

In Nataliya's head, the whole scene slowed down.

Two enemies, then. The one holding Yarov looked shakiest: pale skin, nervous dark eyes, slight build, thinning hair. Dressed in gray, like a lab tech, no armor, nothing combat-related except the handgun. A small one, too: smaller than Nataliya's. Not a distance weapon, but it would put a hole through Yarov's head without any trouble.

The one pinning Eyenga was a bigger problem. He was taller, broader, which explained both the larger weapon he was carrying and his attack strategy. But he was older, too, possibly twice as old as Eyenga, and likely slower. He wasn't dressed in gray, but in shades of brown and black: civilian clothes, which made more sense. His legs were armored, but his boots were thin and soft-soled, the sort someone would wear someplace corporate.

His head was uncovered, and that was where she shot him.

Yarov's assailant was partially protected by the ensign's body, but Foster had been right about Yarov: she kept her wits. As soon as Nataliya aimed at Eyenga's captor, Yarov jerked away from hers; she didn't escape, but she moved a few centimeters away from the POW's body. Nataliya would have to remember, later, to tell her she hadn't needed to do that. Nataliya had always been a very good shot. Yarov had never been in any danger at all.

Her second shot met its target before Eyenga's attacker even had time to slump. The two POWs slid to the floor nearly in unison, eyes open. Nataliya's small weapon left nothing but neat holes, and she decided she liked it all right after all.

They all stood in silence for a moment.

"Fuck me," said Eyenga.

Nataliya tucked the gun back into her waistband and walked up to the body of Eyenga's attacker. She leaned down and pulled the pulse rifle off of him, handing it to Eyenga. "You should be glad," she told him, turning to Yarov's attacker and retrieving the little handgun, "there were only two of them. Because some *asshole* only gave me two shots." She turned to Foster, extending the enemy's weapon to him grip first. "Orders, Captain?"

He was looking at her, and for a moment his eyes held that clarity again, the knowledge of who he was and where he was and exactly what he was looking at. He should have been afraid of her. He should have seen everything she was capable of, and been fucking terrified.

About time he learned to be terrified of her.

In the end all he did was take the enemy's gun from her and thumb the cartridge open. He pulled the ammunition pack, then tucked the empty weapon into his belt. Extending the pack to her, he said, "There are five charges left on that cartridge."

She took it, never dropping his eyes, and loaded her gun. For the first time since she'd arrived, she felt like herself again.

Behind her, Eyenga was attending Flagg; from their chatter, she gathered the injury was superficial, although it must have hurt like a son of a bitch. A quick field dressing and they'd be able to keep going, pushing forward yet again toward the engineering deck, and what moments earlier had seemed eternally and mysteriously inaccessible now seemed vulnerable.

She was beginning to remember why she liked her work.

"Come on," she said to Foster. "Let's follow the salt, or whatever-the-fuck, and root these bastards out." She turned on her heel and strode down the corridor. They would follow her. They would all follow her. One way or another, people always did.

# THIRTY

Throughout Squad Seven's relation of the story, Tau Niemann kept an eye on Foster.

Yarov spoke with enthusiasm, a theatrical embellishment of the incident. Unprofessional, but she was young, and still filled with adrenaline. He could forgive her. Eyenga was quieter, more circumspect, as Niemann would have expected. He would be more suspicious, not less, of Nataliya Gritsenko, no matter whose life she'd saved. Eyenga would wonder where she'd learned to shoot so well, would have more questions about her ties to Foster.

Or perhaps Niemann was projecting.

Foster hung back, letting his people speak for themselves. Appropriate, but Eyenga would find that suspicious, too. Despite Foster's silence, though, he wasn't exactly composed. It had taken Niemann only a few moments to deduce his fellow captain's mood: Foster was annoyed. He saw the incident as a failure, likely a personal one.

Now why would he feel like that?

Fifteen years ago, when Niemann had started hearing Greg Foster's name with more frequency, he'd been as dismissive as his fellow officers, assuming Foster would be leaning on his mother's notoriety. Instead, Foster had focused on listening, learning, and uncompromising hard work. Niemann approved of the hard work, and the lack of assumptions. He approved less of the man's humorlessness. Perhaps that was all he was reacting to. Perhaps it was only that.

"Do you suppose he knows a few things you don't, Tau?"

He ignored Hadley.

Yarov ended the story with a flourish: "Two dead shots. Perfect fucking aim. She saved our lives."

Eyenga tightened his lips at that, and Niemann felt a wave of affection for the commander. Always a cynic, even after his life had just been saved. Eyenga was the sort of soldier Niemann needed to get them through this, however they managed to get through it. Never stop being suspicious. Never acknowledge a loss. Never, ever give up, not until they take you out.

Foster shifted, and Niemann met his eyes.

"Captain," Foster said. "This was my failure. We knew something was up, but we didn't regroup and replan."

*There* it was. "I don't see a failure here, Captain. I see two dead enemy, and a healthy squad."

Foster looked away, and Niemann resisted snapping at him. He was going to have to talk to the man about his fatalism, which would involve revealing more of himself than he preferred to reveal. But this wasn't the time. This was the time to give his soldiers room to celebrate. He turned back to Eyenga and Yarov.

"You've done well," he told them. "Take a meal, get some rest. Flagg will be fully recovered tomorrow; we'll hit them again. You're dismissed. Foster, Gritsenko, a moment please."

Niemann almost missed the quick glance between Eyenga and Yarov before they turned to leave.

The two strangers waited before him at parade rest. He wondered if Gritsenko was aware she was standing like that; as far as he knew, PSI didn't have the same protocols as the Corps on such things, although he had to allow different ships might have different standards. He knew little of *Meridia* apart from her captain's reputation as an expansive, friendly woman who was expert at extracting far more from her Corps counterparts than she offered in return. Still, *Meridia* wasn't known for disrupting shipping routes or getting involved in politics. That kind of thing was reserved for *Chryse*, her sister ship, whose captain was far more reserved and far more likely to fuck up a well-constructed Central op.

That ship would have suited Commander Gritsenko much better, had she been what she said she was.

Niemann stood, his body a constant complaint of old wounds, and rounded the table to stand before Foster. The man was two, possibly three centimeters taller than Niemann, but Niemann was broader, and older. So much older. Foster waited, still annoyed, still turning it all on himself.

"I understand your thinking, Captain," Niemann said to him, and it was almost the truth. "They got the jump on you, and you're not used to that. But you've been here long enough to know *that's what they do*. You can expend energy kicking yourself over it, or you can learn what you can, accept what was out of your control, and move forward." He tried to make the words sound compassionate, but even to his own ears they were harsh. "You brought your squad home, Captain, and without serious injury. Take the victory. Do better moving forward. Dismissed."

Foster snapped to attention, saluted, and walked away.

Gritsenko waited, hands clasped behind her back, but she was far less controlled than Foster. Her expression held puzzlement, along with irritation he suspected had been building for at least a week.

"That's because," Hadley said in his ear, "she's noticed nothing about this makes sense."

"I see you made the most of those two shots," he said.

She stayed silent.

"Where did you learn to shoot like that, Commander?"

Her eyebrows twitched in annoyance. "Do you think PSI doesn't train?"

Not an answer to his question. "I think PSI does whatever it needs to survive," he said, "including emulating the military organization it claims to hate."

"Being independent from Central doesn't mean hate."

"And how independent are you from Central," he said, "when you willingly walk into a den of vipers after a Central Corps captain?"

Puzzlement again. Well-timed. Always well-timed. "I told you," she said. "I was working with him, and we got separated."

"What would a starship captain be working on with a PSI sharpshooter?"

Her expression shifted at that. Subtly, momentarily; a less observant person wouldn't have noticed. "We were on an exploratory, Captain," she said. Polite now, all her irritation swallowed. She could control herself when she wanted to.

"And what were you exploring?"

"The same thing you were, I expect. When you arrived here." Her eyes never left his.

"You won't tell me."

"It's not for me to tell."

"And if I ask Foster?"

A flash of irritation again. "He doesn't remember," she said. "Just like you don't remember how you ended up here with your engine room in the hands of a pack of civilians."

He almost answered her. She was good at that, he realized. He'd had a handful of conversations with her since she'd arrived —all of them short—and she still knew, somehow, how to deflect in a way nearly guaranteed to get under his skin.

Smart. Observant. A dead shot. What kind of mission could Foster have been working that required such a partner? Foster was watchful, careful, decisive when he needed to be; he'd fought hard to arm this woman, and the first thing she'd done with her weapon was kill civilians.

One of them was leaving something out.

He'd been in the Corps for forty years, twice as long as the average officer. *Capricorn* was a combat ship, used almost exclusively for top secret missions. Some of them were, strictly speaking, illegal, but Niemann had never given much credence to strictness. He trusted his chain of command. They'd kept the Six Sectors safe for hundreds of years, kept trade going over those vast distances, and lost very few colonies to conflict. Niemann drew no lines between the official Admiralty and Shadow Ops; he knew the importance of burying certain types of operations under misdirecting paperwork. All he had to know was they all had the same goal: keep people safe, keep people fed, and don't let them think too much about the absolute madness of their civilizations depending on ships that could vaporize an entire city with half a battery bank.

He'd killed people. Civilians. Always under orders, but the fact remained. The deliberate killing of civilians changed you, made you something you hadn't been before. He'd had to do it, and no regrets.

Foster wouldn't kill civilians; Niemann would bet his life on that. But Nataliya Gritsenko would.

"Let me say this clearly, Commander," he began. Standing over her, he was struck by how much shorter than him she was; she never seemed small. "What you were doing before you came here is irrelevant. Up to a point."

And now he had to let her know what it all meant: that he was unimportant, that she was unimportant. That Central itself was unimportant. Nothing was important anymore outside of his crew, these people who'd pledged themselves to him and put their lives in his hands.

He let his voice go icy. "But if anything about your or your mission interferes with the operation of my ship, with taking back control, I will have you both killed. Is that clear?"

Her eyes never left his. She had pretty eyes, he supposed, if you liked that sort of thing. Undoubtedly trained to use them; in her line of work, she'd have been taught to exploit every advantage. To her credit, she seemed to recognize her pretty eyes made no difference to him. "You don't remember how you got here," she said conversationally. "Do you?"

He turned away from her. Hadley was standing behind his chair, smirking, but for once he didn't have anything to add to the discussion. "It's not personal, you understand," Niemann told her. "I am genuinely grateful you saved my people. But right now I have one priority, and you and Foster are not a part of it. You help me? You'll have my thanks. But that calculus changes moment to moment. I do not have the luxury of sentiment, so please understand, there will be no sentiment spared for you."

She should have been frightened, or at least feigned it. Instead, her face relaxed, just briefly, into something that looked like sadness. Pity, perhaps. He could imagine she'd pity him. This young woman, this instinctive killer, would see him as an old man who'd lost everything he'd ever built. She'd be right about most of it. But he hadn't lost everything yet.

"Thank you for your candor, Captain," she said smoothly. "I have no intention of interfering with your mission."

He took note of her phrasing: *I*, not *we*. Careful with words, this one. "Go with the others," he said. "If you're going to help us, you might as well get fed and rested."

He watched her walk away. Her stride was compact, brisk. She could move through a crowd, he realized. Disappear into one. Even her appearance—beautiful, but strangely unmemorable. It might indeed be a coincidence that she'd randomly shown up mere weeks after the Corps' most recognizable captain had appeared in one of his ship's dark hallways.

"You know that's bullshit," Hadley said. "You know why they're here."

Niemann had been a soldier two-thirds of his life. The work was all he knew, all he cared about, but it hadn't made him blind. He'd seen cracks in his command structure; they came and went, because people were people, and not everyone could be strong when they had to be. For decades, he'd been able to ignore it all. But of late, their missteps had affected him more directly. They'd hurt his people. These POWs, these rebels they'd been forced to carry—that was the Admiralty's mistake. They'd wanted him to believe Anaxis was an anomaly, that what had happened there was unimportant.

He wondered if they'd known what was likely to happen. He wondered if Foster and Gritsenko had been sent after him, to make sure he would never be able to challenge the Admiralty's version of events.

"Why would the Admiralty lie, Tau?" Hadley asked him. "Why would they have to? The truth condemns you well enough."

He hesitated a moment before hitting his comm. "Commander Eyenga," he said, "when you've eaten, I'd like a moment of your time."

He hadn't brought his crew this far to have his command chain take him down with a Shadow Ops assassin.

# THIRTY-ONE

Elena frowned at *Capricorn*'s schematic. "This should be easy," she said, half to herself. "Why has this not been easy?"

She was in a small kitchen, its tables removed and replaced with two dozen cots, neat bins filled with personal items beneath about half of them. There were plentiful food stations still in operation along the walls, along with a few tables that had been preserved for socializing, and for work. She might have been on *Galileo*, in one of their smaller kitchens, like the one outside the gym that always ended up with massive lines, even though there was a bigger kitchen one level above. People liked their routines, even if they had to wait for them.

*Capricorn* was so like *Galileo*, in so many ways, and yet not.

The schematic, for example, revealed *Capricorn* as a ship of fairly unsophisticated construction, assembled from the same mass-produced sheets of nanolatticed composite as every other starship, including *Galileo*. Where the two ships differed were their interiors: *Capricorn*'s were made of unreinforced panels, which struck her as a short-sighted attempt at some sort of easy reconfigurability. *Capricorn* was built for power and agility, but not for self-defense, an omission Elena found inexplicable. Optimizing for offense made a backhanded sort of sense for a warship, but ignoring internal integrity went a long way toward explaining why a group of civilian POWs had been able to barricade themselves in the ship's engine room for what Gen said had been more than two months.

There was something in these plans, something that could tell her what was wrong, if she could only see from the right angle.

Gen was seated next to her, leaning back in her chair, legs extended under the table. She'd arranged her wiry form to look relaxed, but Elena had been a soldier long enough to recognize how on alert Gen really was. The commander's eyes moved constantly, scanning the room, checking the exits on either side. And watching her people, always. Elena couldn't help but notice there were far more bunks than soldiers. She'd been expecting another team to return, for Gen to comm someone, for any evidence that these dozen people had once been twice that. There had been nothing.

But if there had been loss, Gen wasn't going to betray any of that to Elena.

"Every time," Gen said, "it's been something different." She leaned toward the schematic. "We tried here, here, and here," she said, indicating the main entrance to engineering, as well as two well-hidden maintenance access crawlspaces. "They had those covered, and we didn't bother persisting, because after they blew the hell out of our front-line drone we figured out we weren't dealing with bullshit paper pushers after all." Her lips thinned. "We knew we weren't getting in the easy way. So we've been working around the problem."

*Working around the problem* had meant a variety of thwarted attempts at ingress. Some were longshots—burning through bulkheads, bypassing alert systems that were easily restored via the consoles in engineering—but most were solid strategies.

One of them—cutting off the environmentals to the engineering floor so the POWs would have to leave—seemed tailor-made for success, but Gen's records, rendered as red spotlights on the schematic, showed seventeen attempts and seventeen failures.

"What the fuck is this, then?" Elena asked, too confused to be circumspect.

Gen arched an eyebrow at her, but she seemed more amused than anything else. "That's Brixa's favorite plan," she said. "And every time we try it we hit a power outage, or our tools fail, or some other random bullshit. Last week Ventikov got food poisoning and kept throwing up while we were trying to bypass the air handlers."

*Last week?* Why had they persisted with a plan that had long outlived its usefulness? *Capricorn* was a warship, and yet none of this suggested sound military planning. "Have you tipped your hand with that one, do you think?"

Gen ignored the incredulity in her voice. "Good question," she said easily. "At this point? They've been entrenched for so long, I'm guessing they've figured out as many possibilities as we have, and they have less territory to cover. Which is where you come in." Gen's gaze sharpened. "You're an outsider. You don't see this ship the way we do."

There was something to that, as well, but that strange, recurring smell of Mike's machine shop arrived to distract her, and the thought vanished. "Being out of the Corps for a year didn't make me a different mechanic," she said, but Gen waved a hand at her.

"That's not what I mean." The commander stood then, lending some of her nervous energy to pacing back and forth. "We've been at this problem for months now," she said, her voice quieter. "We try the same things, variations on the same solutions. We know this ship, down to every join and repair. I think..." She broke off, and her gaze grew introspective. "When you know something so well," she said, half to herself, "you stop seeing it." Abruptly her dark eyes snapped to Elena's face. "Don't you find?"

Elena kept her eyes on the schematic. This wasn't the first time Gen had shown signs of being conscious that all of this was inexplicably strange, that the battle was stacked against them with a sort of personal prejudice. For a moment Elena thought of confronting her, of asking her how this had begun, how the POWs had acquired weapons, how long they had been...where? She frowned, fighting her own mind's blank spots. Exhaustion, perhaps; she hadn't been sleeping well, not for weeks, because pain and stress and all the changes she'd been going through, because there had been a lot, hadn't there?

Hadn't there?

"You feel it too," Gen said quietly. "Don't you?"

Gen's voice was soft, too soft for the others to hear it, as if she were trying to keep secrets from her squad or the terrorists or the ship itself. "There's more going on here than coincidence," Elena said, nodding at the schematic.

Gen nodded. "Someone's listening."

*No,* Elena thought. *It's something.* Why did she know that? What was it? Why was she...*Greg. You are here for Greg. Hang on to that.* "So we proceed as if they're going to know all our plans." Elena returned her mind to the engineering problem, the one she might be able to solve. "How many people have we got?"

"You've met them."

Twelve, then. Half the people there were beds for. "It's been that bad?" she asked.

A shadow passed over Gen's face, and she turned away. "Most of them we lost at the start," she said. "Hadley—our engineering chief—he went first. He got shot during..." She frowned. "It all blurs together, you know? I remember it was fast, at least. Wouldn't even have known what hit him. The rest—most we lost in battle. A few just lost their grip. If I had to guess, I'd say that's more likely to be our ultimate fate."

The despair in that statement. But Gen's tone of voice was relaxed, neutral, accepting. Whatever had been happening here, Gen had given up hope of being able to change it. It was the same coping mechanism Greg used: accept the things you cannot change, even if they enrage you.

*Greg.* Why was she bothering with a schematic? She wasn't here for *Capricorn.* She was here for Greg. Something kept trying to pull her away from him. *It lies, Elena.* Who had said that? For a moment she saw the place clearly: wrong, damaged, a danger to all of them. A thing she had to escape.

She wasn't sure how dense Gen's own cobwebs were. "When did you last talk to Captain Niemann?"

Gen frowned in concentration, then shook her head, rueful. "Damn, this place is getting to me. I can't remember. We have a radio frequency, but lately he hasn't responded."

So if Greg was with Niemann, Gen would have no way of knowing. Absurdly, the thought gave Elena hope. "We need to get comms back up," she said. "We need to get through to Niemann, and find out if he has Greg."

"Keep forgetting about him." Gen laughed a little, unamused. "Yeah, depending on how long he's been here, there's no way we'd have heard. If he's here, he's with Niemann."

*Or he got grabbed by the terrorists.* "So our primary objective of this mission," Elena said, "should be to restore comms."

Gen shook her head. "We've got to go for all of it. We've got to root them out."

Which went against all of Elena's training. "With you being short-staffed, we've got to aim for objectives we can meet," she explained. "With comms restored we can coordinate with Niemann, and we should—"

"It's got to be all or nothing," Gen insisted. "Gonna have to make that an order, Shaw, if it comes down to it. We've been pushing at this too long. And now we've got you, which gives us the element of surprise, but only once. We get you to the comms center, you work that piece, and we'll take care of the rest of them. If we fail this time?" She exhaled sharply. "They've seen every trick we've got. It's do or die, Shaw. You get Foster, we get our ship back, or we all go down together."

# THIRTY-TWO

Nataliya passed Eyenga as she walked away from Niemann. She expected one of Eyenga's self-important glares, letting her know he didn't trust her, as if that was big news to her. But he didn't look at her as he passed her, didn't acknowledge her at all. She turned, and watched long enough to see him salute Niemann.

The captain met her eyes, expressionless, and she turned away again.

Not great.

The adrenaline from the attack was finally deserting her. She'd gone over the events in her head, as she'd been taught: the attack, her assessment, her actions. Her killer instinct kicking in, except not for anyone she'd actually been tasked to kill. A failure, her teachers would have told her; not only had she not achieved her objective, she'd attracted scrutiny, jeopardized her cover. She'd been trained—six years, all day and all night, and hard supervision for another six after that—to be mindful of her environment, but agnostic about anything that might be happening outside of her mission. She should have let those POWs—damn, she'd even adopted their terminology—kill Foster's people. Certainly it would have made him look a fool. She could easily have taken out both him and Eyenga once the enemy had killed the others, and arranged the evidence to suit any story she might have wanted to concoct.

But she hadn't been thinking like an assassin. She'd been thinking like a soldier, and her team had been under threat, and she'd been pissed off at Eyenga and wanting to show off. It had felt *good*, doing what she knew how to do, defending people in an unambiguous situation, becoming something other than an object of suspicion. And now Niemann—who saw too fucking much about everything other than his ship—was discussing his suspicions of her with Eyenga, and everything had become exponentially more complicated.

*I need to get Foster out of here.*

Foster was sitting over a bowl of that rancid stew, taking an occasional bite, but mostly watching it drip off his spoon. Niemann was right about him: he needed to let shit like this go. Their team had survived, hadn't it? They'd been defending themselves against an enemy that would absolutely have killed them. It was possible, of course, he was only angry because the other side had gotten the drop on them, but she didn't think so.

She scooped herself some stew and settled into the chair next to him. Across the kitchen, Eyenga had sat down with Niemann, and the two men were talking quietly.

*Safety first, Nataliya.*

She nudged Foster with her elbow, nodding at Niemann and Eyenga. "That's probably not good," she said conversationally.

He focused, briefly, then lowered his eyes to his food again. "Niemann's security conscious," he said. "Has to be, in a situation like this. He can't afford to take us at face value." He took a more substantive bite.

"You realize Captain Security Conscious could have us chucked out an airlock any second he wanted."

"The way you can shoot?" A hint of amusement in his voice. "He's not throwing you out of anything."

Why did she always want to hit him when he lightened up? "Are you just not paying attention, or are you deliberately ignoring that we're in imminent fucking danger here?"

If she weren't sitting practically on top of him, she wouldn't have heard him sigh. "Of course we're in danger," he said, and put down his spoon, finally defeated by his lunch. "We've been in danger since we got here."

"This is not the fucking same, Foster! This is the captain of this ship deciding if we're worth keeping around!" She said it hoarsely, under her breath, but she wanted to scream it in his ear.

Foster abruptly remembered what commanders were supposed to do. "I need you to *calm down*, soldier," he said sharply. "We have a situation here, and the state of our own skins is only one piece of it. I don't know what the fuck you did on *Meridia*, but you're not stupid, and you're not two steps out of the Academy. Look the fuck around."

He was close to her again, his face centimeters from her, but instead of that vague background heat she usually felt, she found her wasteful self-recriminations giving way to long-ago training. *Sitrep, soldier.* She looked around the room, first where Niemann and Eyenga still whispered to each other. Definitely a covert conversation, but Eyenga's pulse rifle was slung carelessly across his back, and Niemann wasn't armed at all. No incipient violence in their postures; Niemann could hide it from her, but Eyenga couldn't.

She let her eyes drift to the outside walls. All squads were in, which meant twenty-eight people, including her and Foster. To a one, they were exhausted. Some hid it better than others— Flagg, having her wound healed by another soldier with a med kit, was laughing and cracking jokes, likely driven by pain and adrenaline. Some were eating, mostly with the same lack of enthusiasm as Foster, but the rest were on alert, weapons easily accessible, their eyes darting among the room's exits in unending circles.

None of them were looking at her and Foster.

"That doesn't mean he's not setting us up," she said, assuming Foster would follow her train of thought.

"It means if he is," Foster said, conversational again, "he hasn't yet clued in the rest of the crew."

"Except maybe Eyenga."

"Eyenga isn't going to kill me." He said it dismissively, and her hackles went up again.

"Christ, Foster, I have no idea how you lived this long," she told him, and he laughed.

She saw Eyenga and Niemann stand. Eyenga saluted, but then stood at attention before his captain, and Nataliya tensed.

"Crew," Niemann called, his booming voice echoing throughout the room. "At attention."

"Here we go," Nataliya said. Foster took her bowl along with his to the recycler, then fell into step with her as she headed back to Niemann's table.

There had to be some way out of this. There was always a way out.

Foster instinctively took the front row with Eyenga, and Nataliya positioned herself between them. Eyenga wouldn't like that, wouldn't like her implied protectiveness of Foster, or her assumption of equality. But to his credit he kept his eyes forward, his annoyance showing only in a single twitch of his eyebrows.

Whatever he'd been told to do to them, he would know that she, at least, was ready.

"This last salvo from the enemy," Niemann said, "was sloppy of them. It was a direct threat, and they underestimated us badly. They're making mistakes they haven't made before."

No one moved.

"It's time," he said, "to *stop fucking around.*"

Murmurs of assent from the crowd.

"The time has come for a direct assault. This time it's all of us. And this time we push until they're dead, or we are."

"Yeah," someone said, and the murmurs grew louder. Nataliya resisted the urge to look around.

"Team leaders," he said, "with me. Everyone else—" He straightened, and Nataliya caught herself straightening with him. Like Foster, Niemann had power. As with Foster, Nataliya wondered what had taken him so long to use it.

"Get ready. Arm yourselves, and get in formation. You are the best crew in this fleet, and it's time to show these fuckers why. It's time to take our ship back, soldiers!"

At that, the cheers became unrestrained, and Nataliya snuck a glance at Foster. He remained at attention, awaiting Niemann's command, as the rest of the soldiers milled around, energized, enthusiastic. Abruptly she wondered if she could have misread him, if his confidence had nothing to do with stupidity. If he could, perhaps, against all evidence, have seen this coming as easily as she had.

Niemann startled her out of her focus. "Commander Gritsenko, with me as well."

She waited with the others as Niemann divided the teams into two groups. Less than a platoon each, but still: solid firepower. Why hadn't he tried this before?

*Because he knows he will fail.*

Niemann outlined a fairly straightforward two-tiered plan, and Nataliya had to believe they all saw its biggest flaw: he was depending on Commander Naude's team to back them up on the other side. She watched the team leads; not one of them looked doubtful. Perhaps they believed Niemann's fairy tale about talking to Naude on a regular basis. She knew Foster didn't; he'd pushed the point as far as he'd dared with Niemann, and learned nothing. Which in a situation like this meant there was nothing to learn.

Was Niemann setting them *all* up?

"Any questions?" Niemann asked when he was finished. Nataliya had to restrain herself from putting up her hand and asking *Are you completely out of your mind?*

"We deploy in five minutes. Foster, you're in charge of First Platoon. I'll take Second. Dismissed. Commander Gritsenko, not you."

The others fell away. Foster stood still, waiting; she caught his eye and shook her head. With some reluctance he left her alone with *Capricorn*'s captain.

She stood at parade rest, and waited him out.

"With our impending operation, Commander, it's become necessary for me to know what you're doing here."

Angrier than he'd been earlier. She wondered what Eyenga had said. "I've already told you," she said. "I'm here to take Captain Foster home."

His lips tightened. "What is your mission?" he clarified.

A large part of her training had been on what to do if she were captured; this was familiar ground. "I can't elaborate on that, Captain."

"This is my ship." He said it conversationally. "I could make you elaborate."

He couldn't. That had been another part of her training. But she didn't think she'd enjoy it much if he tried.

"I know what you are, Commander."

Which was either true, or a bluff. If it were true, he had to know better than to push her. If he were bluffing...if he were bluffing, she was in much more serious trouble.

"Foster isn't your mission."

Bluffing, then. She was almost disappointed. If he knew what she was, he'd know who she was after. Unless...how much did he remember? Did he remember the Admiralty sending his ship into exile?

Did he think she was after *him*?

"I'm sorry, Captain," she said. "I can't discuss my mission. It doesn't matter that this is your ship, or what you could do to me. I'm not permitted. I'm sorry."

A flash in his eyes: rage, betrayal, and—was that despair? It vanished before she could be certain, and he became a level-headed commander again. "I can respect that, Commander. What I can't do is trust it." He waved a hand, and Eyenga appeared, quiet as a wraith. "Commander Eyenga," he said, "Commander Gritsenko is to be directly under your command for this operation."

Eyenga didn't react at all; this had to be what he'd discussed with Niemann earlier. "Yes, Captain."

"See that she's issued a weapon. Not a pulse rifle," he said clearly. "A handgun. Four charges."

Nataliya waited until Eyenga was at the weapons table, too far away to overhear. "Respectfully, Captain," she said, "maybe you should just shoot me yourself."

"You can't take out your entire team with a handgun, and I suggest you don't try."

The time for taking out Niemann's people was long gone. "Captain, I have no intention—"

"In any other circumstance I'd leave you behind, under guard," he said. "But this is our last stand. We're getting out now, or we're not, and I'm not giving you the chance to sabotage everything we've been working for."

"I wouldn't do that."

"Depending on your mission, I believe you absolutely would."

*Fair point.*

"When this is over," he said, "I'm going to have you put off this ship. In one piece, but as far away as I can get you, as fast as possible. And I'll thank you to never appear before me ever again, for the rest of your life. Understood?"

"Understood, Captain. Captain—"

Nothing to lose now, after all.

"You're deploying twenty-eight people—and whoever's still alive on Naude's team, if anyone—against what is, to the best of the intelligence I've seen, no more than nine at this point. Why?"

"You're questioning my strategy?"

"I'm questioning everybody's strategy, Captain. We're going into a situation heavily armed, outnumbering the enemy, and you're acting like we're all doomed. Why are you doing this now? Why have they been able to keep the engineering deck for so long?"

He just stared at her, and she thought, for one moment, he looked confused.

"Hasn't it occurred to you," she said, hating the note of desperation in her voice, "that none of this is what it seems to be?"

But he'd succumbed again to the miasma that permeated this ship. "That's enough. You will go with Commander Eyenga, and you will fight your best alongside these people, every one of whom is worth more than you, than everyone you work for. You will save lives, and if you die, I'll see you're remembered well. But if you put one foot out of place, Eyenga will shoot you down and step over you like you're rotted fruit. Do you understand?"

She'd kill Eyenga first, but he was right: she wouldn't be able to kill them all. Defeated, she nodded.

Eyenga returned with her handgun, and she checked the charge and the safeties as she always did. The commander was watching her closely, something hungry in his eyes: vengeance, suspicion, anger, bloodlust. She didn't know anymore. She only knew she'd made a mistake, probably weeks ago, and this time she might not be able to maneuver herself out of it.

# THIRTY-THREE

"THIS BATTERY IS one of the older ones," Ted said, pulling the casing apart so Jessica could see the interior. "It wouldn't charge more than about eighty-eight, eighty-nine percent, which is about average for a battery more than five years old. The backlash hammered it—left it with five percent, if that—but for a few seconds before it burned out, it held 112 percent of its original capacity."

Jessica looked up at him. "Why does that sound like you're excited that nuking your house turned the lights on the instant before you were vaporized?"

He ignored her. "Initiating a fold takes just shy of seven seconds."

"6.3589113 repeating," Kali put in, and Ted closed his lips against a smile.

"Okay. Initiating a fold takes just shy of six and a half seconds. With our current battery capacity, we could get a fold that's about seventy percent complete, and *maybe* be able to enter it and not get pulled apart. I'd place our odds at survival pretty low, and no, Kali, I don't need anything more exact."

"Understood, Commander," Kali said tranquilly.

"Most of the power usage isn't the fold itself, though," Ted went on. "It's extending the fold around the ship. Eighty-nine percent—shut up, Kali—of the power is used sealing the encapsulation properly. And that happens in the last..." This time he paused to look it up. "0.4899 seconds of the initiation sequence. Which means we've got less than six seconds between when we commit to the fold and the moment we need a power boost to complete it and get out of here." He paused. "It's okay this time, Kali."

"That leaves us 5.869 seconds between initiating the fold and needing the battery boost."

"That doesn't sound like eternity, Ted." But Jessica started to feel lighter, more focused: this was hope. "What was the interval between the comms outage and the backlash last time?" she asked.

"Seventy-two seconds," Ted told her.

"Captain," Kali put in, "we only have a single data point on the backlash. And my hunch."

"It's not a hunch, Ensign," Jessica corrected automatically. "It's an evidence-based guess. Do you think, based on what you maybe, sort of, possibly, tangentially, vaguely know of this thing, another comms outage will trigger another backlash?"

"I do," Kali said. "But without other measurements, I can't tell you if the time interval will be the same, or the strength of the pulse. It might be too weak to get *Galileo* through. It might be strong enough to destroy you."

It always came down to guessing. Jessica supposed that shouldn't have been a shock; she'd watched Greg do it for years. She'd just assumed he was particularly good at it. It was turning out most things were just luck.

"Ted," she asked, "if we took another hit now, without setting up to siphon off energy, where would that leave us?"

"With too many batteries completely dead to pull this off," he said. "So no, Jess, I don't think we can test this theory, which is one reason why, like I said, it's ludicrously risky." His expression was grim. "There's one other issue. Coming out on the other side might be a little rough."

It had been some decades since a ship had been lost in a field failure, and even field entry accidents were rare. But ships tripping, falling, going to pieces when exiting the field was far more common than Jessica liked to think about. She'd said as much to Lanie once, who'd said, "If I had a centime for all the civilian cruisers I had to reassemble because somebody fucked up the exit balance manifolds, I'd buy my own shipyard." She hadn't talked about fatalities. Lanie tended to assume anyone who died abusing their hardware had it coming.

"Define 'a little rough,'" Jessica said.

"Apart from the obvious? If we make it out in one piece, we're likely to be on low to no power for a few days, and that's assuming we've got anything left in the battery banks to charge. Our best bet is going to be to jump as close to civilization as we can, and send a distress signal."

"So what you're telling me," she said, "is getting into the field is a longshot, getting out is a bigger longshot, and if we don't get within the range of Hemera Relay, we're dead anyway?"

"That about covers it."

"And if we end up with a big hole in the hull if Petrikoff blows the comms center?"

His answer to that, oddly enough, was optimistic. "We won't be able to seal the breach," he said, "but with the inner corridor sealed she should travel all right once we're in."

"Okay." How much time would she be able to give Samaras? "How long can we put off this scheme?"

"You mean how long until our current batteries are too depleted to take any charge at all?" He thought. "Twenty-eight minutes, maybe twenty-nine."

*Damn.* "All right," she said. "Set it up. Let me know when

you've got a configuration you think will work, and we'll time the backlash." But there was one other contingency she had to cover. "If we lose comms early because of Petrikoff," she said, "we're going to have to ride whatever backlash we get, no matter how little you've got set up. Bob?"

The old man's voice in her ear was as calm and relaxed as always. "You'd have to leave us behind."

"If we make it home," she told him, "we'll come back for you."

"Not particularly smart," he remarked, "since getting this far nearly took *Galileo* to pieces. I'll wait for Greg and Elena and leave as soon as possible. You can meet us halfway."

"It won't come to that," she said decisively. "Emily. Where are we with the comms breach?"

"My strike team is assembled in the landing bay, Captain. Eight minutes to finish sorting weapons and supplies, and then we're a go whenever you get here."

Samaras had nearly another half-hour left on his estimate. She'd have to hope he finished early. "Ted?"

"We'll make it happen by then."

She left Ted's team to their work and headed back toward comms, wondering if she should stop for a weapon. *Galileo* never armed people on board, not even security, because weapons were never needed there. The enemy was always from the outside. Always.

Maybe she could order someone to hold Petrikoff down while she stabbed him through the heart with a dried paintbrush.

"Where are we on environmentals?" she snapped into her radio. "Bristol? What's in that room?"

"Partial data, Captain," he said. "We're reading trace polymer degradation, suggesting surface adhesive. Best guess is he's mocked up something crude, probably from maintenance scrap and the food supplies. Likely he's had to use multiple detonators."

Low tech. The worst to disarm. No wonder Samaras asked for so much time. "Emily? I need all your people with plasma fire off. We can't risk triggering something that'll—"

"Captain?" Kali broke in, her voice high and uncertain. "Captain, something's happening to Target Zero."

*Fuck. Fuck all of this.* "Be more specific, Ensign."

"It's—the artificial gravity has gone off, Captain, and it's beginning to radiate energy. You may not—I'd advise not waiting for a pulse, Captain. I think you should get the ship away from Target Zero now, as quickly as you can."

"We can't move, Jess," Ted said definitively. "If we move, we are dead in three days."

Jessica clenched her fists to keep her hands still. "Best guess, Ensign Kali. What's going on?"

"It's a state change, Captain. I don't know what's happening. But it—"

The ship was plunged into darkness again, and Kali was cut off.

# THIRTY-FOUR

ELENA SPOKE ACROSS the projected map of *Capricorn*'s engineering section. "We've broken the task into two teams," she told Gen's people.

They held the briefing in the corridor, a hundred meters away from their home base. Gen allowed it wasn't perfect insulation against spying—nothing was—but she hoped they'd be able to deploy their plan quickly enough to surprise even an eavesdropping enemy. Elena kept her own suspicions to herself. If they were being watched by a larger entity, worrying about the element of surprise was moot; but if Gen's precautions made her people more watchful, Elena wasn't inclined to interfere.

They were watchful already, of course, but mostly of Elena.

Gen stood next to her to back her up, which Elena considered entirely insufficient. Gen should have been giving this briefing; too many of the others took their cue from Brixa, who had been unambiguous about her suspicions. Elena had said as much to Gen, who'd handwaved it away with that cavalier attitude she never seemed to shed. "They need to hear it from you because you're different," Gen had said, as if that made any sense at all. Elena had the distinct impression apart from Gen no one thought her being different was a good thing, and few of them would be grieving much if she didn't make it back from this mission.

"Alpha Team gets the main frontal assault. Based on previous behaviors we can expect the enemy to defend efficiently, but the purpose isn't to break through there. It's to cover for Beta Team. Given how many times this assault has been tried, we need to assume they're going to know it's a distraction. So we have to fight to win."

It wasn't quite a suicide mission. They had armor; they had weapons. They had solid cover and easy retreat. If their intel was anywhere near correct, Elena wouldn't need more than three minutes to get their comms back on line.

"Beta Team will take the crawlspace," she said. "They might have it blocked, but given the size it's unlikely they're expecting us to break through there. While this is happening, Commander Naude, Lieutenant Brixa, and I will make the comms repairs, and contact Captain Niemann for reinforcements." She looked around the group, meeting each set of eyes one at a time. "Both teams are likely to be taking fire, but given the enemy's numbers, we should be able to hold them off long enough. Any questions?"

Nothing, just the clear-eyed patience of an experienced group of soldiers. They would be wanting to get started, feeling exactly what she was: the planning was done, and the battle would hold surprises, as battles always did. Elena dismissed the schematic, trying to ignore the itch between her shoulder blades.

Brixa's presence in her escort hadn't been her choice. She'd watched from a distance as Gen spoke with Brixa, letting the lieutenant vent at some length. Phrases like "stranger" and "anomaly" and "taken enough chances" kept reaching her ears. Gen never wavered, but neither did she bring the hammer down on the other officer. Gen was persistently calm, friendly, casual;

but Elena saw the tension through her shoulders, the way her hand never strayed far from her gun.

As soon as Gen had said Brixa would be accompanying them to fix the comms, Elena had said, "Then I get a weapon."

The handgun settled at her hip was no match for Brixa's multiple armaments—or even, she suspected, Brixa's arms—if Brixa decided to take Elena down. But despite the trigger-happy lieutenant, Elena's biggest fear was not *Capricorn*'s soldiers. Elena's biggest fears were a pack of civilian POWs who had managed to keep the crew of the Corps' best warship at bay for weeks, and the extremely vague information she'd been given about the state of the comms system. There was a familiarity to that, to not understanding what she was getting into, to suspecting her main source of information was somehow unreliable. Her hip ached, and she shifted. This was different, surely; but what had happened then? It had gone badly, she remembered that much, but why? How had she survived? What could she—

She inhaled gently, trying to ease the tightness in her chest. None of this was important, not now. She'd get rid of the cobwebs soon enough. She would reconnect their comms, find Greg, and get the hell off this ship, and if she didn't know just now how that would happen, she was certain Greg would be able to help. They'd solved so many problems together over the years, even the ones they'd caused themselves.

"This is the same as any other two-pronged raid," Gen told the team, her calm voice easing some of the tension. "Strike, hold your ground, wait for orders. Radio only. You need reinforcements, you radio, or better yet, don't need them. You get the all clear from me, you regroup back here." She straightened. "Let's get these bastards."

Enthusiastic shouting in response: they were ready for a fight. Why was it all Elena could feel was dread? The plan was overly elaborate. They should have won this battle weeks ago.

Every plan they'd had should have worked. There was something else going on here, and she couldn't clear her head enough to see it.

Greg would see it. Whenever she was blinded, his perspective always showed her the truth. Get comms back, find Greg. Then she would understand.

*This is a setup,* Nat sent.

They were making their way to the engineering level, Greg and Eyenga marching together, Nat and the rest of the group behind. Niemann's group was three precise meters behind them, but Greg's attention was on his own people. Eyenga had been quiet since the mission briefing, to the point where Flagg had started needling him about it, which meant Flagg didn't know what Niemann might have said to him. Yarov suspected something, because she wasn't stupid. Greg was fairly sure he'd have her support, should it come down to choosing between him and Eyenga, but he didn't know the rest of the soldiers well enough. If Eyenga had Niemann's backing, Greg could count on no one at all besides Nat.

*You've said that,* he sent back to her, *fourteen times now.*

*Setup,* she sent. *That's fifteen. You listening any better?*

*If we break through this time it won't matter.*

*If we break through this time, it'll be* Foster died in service of the mission *and you get to be a hero. Won't be any less dead.*

Amazing how exasperation could come through without sound. *I didn't know you cared,* he returned.

*Fuck you, Foster. I don't know how you stayed captain all those years. Your crew must have wanted to fucking murder you.*

*One of them tried once,* he told her.

*I missed that story.*

*Yeah. It was—*

He broke off. It hadn't been that long ago, had it? He had no business having a foggy brain, not now, not when they were headed for a final assault.

*Maybe I saw it in a vid,* he sent.

Nat replied as if he'd never stuttered. *When your crew is making vids about killing you off, you know you're in trouble.* Then: *I'll keep an eye on Eyenga, as much as I can. God knows I'd love a chance to kneecap that smug fucker. But if Niemann really has sent him after you, this battle gets far more complicated. Assuming there's really a battle here.*

*If Niemann wanted me dead,* he pointed out, *he'd just have me spaced. They'd never protest, not one of them. Not even Yarov.* They were approaching the access corridor; Greg raised a hand, signaling the squad to slow. *I take everything seriously,* he told her. *But I'm also banking on Niemann wanting his engine room back more than he wants Eyenga to shoot me in the head.*

*Didn't have you pegged as a man of faith.*

*Then you haven't been paying attention.*

They came to a stop before a wide foyer, an unadorned entryway one sharp bend before *Capricorn*'s engine room. He'd never seen this part of the ship except on the schematics; it had been Gen's crew, he'd been told, who'd cleared the way for this battle. He couldn't quite manage to believe that; Niemann had never shared Gen's messages with any of them, even Eyenga. Greg was fairly certain she was dead, and if that were the case, he had far more to worry about on this mission than Niemann's assassins targeting him. Without Gen's backup, none of this would matter anyway.

Niemann sent silently over the general frequency. *Foster. Your squad, take point here. Keep the enemy from moving forward. Everyone else with me.*

Niemann's people turned down a side corridor, their footsteps fading.

And Greg was left to keep his people alive, whether or not any of them were trying to kill him.

*Wait for it,* Greg sent to his squad. *Whatever you see or hear, you wait for the signal to shoot. We don't know what they've got in there, what they might have rigged, how much firepower they might have. We get exactly one chance at this, and we are not fucking it up. Understood?*

*Yes, Captain.* All in unison, even Eyenga.

He signaled Nat, who led Flagg and Yarov off to the right to flatten themselves against the wall. The hallway hadn't always had a bend in it; he could see along the ceiling the rough, unprofessional joins, more and more common across the ship. Strange technology that would be able to reconfigure their hallways but do such a bad job of it. There was something about that, but he kept forgetting it, kept getting distracted, and he didn't have time for distraction now, but so often before a battle his mind went on overdrive, and his mother had always taught him—

He shook his head and turned to Eyenga, who glared at him, but took point on Greg's left as he always did.

*On three,* Greg sent to them all.

He counted down, and together they moved around the corner and began firing down the long hallway.

Elena followed Gen and Brixa, her eyes darting around the narrow corridor. She was used to ship schematics having only a tangential relationship with reality, but *Capricorn*'s schematics were wildly off, and in inexplicable ways. This corridor should have been twice as wide, and indeed when she looked at the ceiling she could see it had been. The wall to her right bifurcated the original space, dovetailing clumsily with the lighting in the ceiling. Some kind of temporary traffic flow need would have driven a change like that, a short-term solution to a longer-term

problem the crew had no faith the Corps was ever going to
bother fixing.

Which was fair enough, but Elena would have eviscerated
anyone on her team who'd been anything near this sloppy. It
was puzzling. *Capricorn* was a battleship, for sure; but her engineers were known to be meticulous and efficient. Elena couldn't
imagine Chief Hadley approving work like this, not based on
what she'd known of him. Rumor, perhaps; part of the ship's
mythos. That was always a possibility. She knew *Galileo*—and
Greg in particular—was still the subject of some outrageous
apocryphal legends.

But in her experience, mechanical sloppiness was a canary in
a coalmine on a ship like this. Shoddy work installing a temporary bulkhead would have been an indicator of something far
deeper wrong: something disciplinary, something cultural. None
of it fit with Gen's laconic, clear-eyed leadership, or the suspicions the others had about Elena herself.

They reached the end of the hallway, and Gen waved them
against the temporary wall. Elena flattened herself between Gen
and Brixa; Gen slung her pulse rifle off her shoulder and held it
against her chest, leaning carefully forward to peer around the
corner.

Elena, useless, held her breath.

After a moment Gen turned back, more relaxed. "We're
clear," she said quietly. "Let's go."

Without waiting for Brixa, Elena stepped away from the wall
and around Gen into the comms maintenance station.

And saw something far worse than a sloppy bulkhead.

The comms panel itself looked undamaged, recessed and lit
dimly in green and blue. But the wall around it—the original
bulkhead, not some makeshift piece of temporary junk—was
warped and cracked, as if it had been pressed too long from
above. The ceiling above them had collapsed in places, leaving
massive gaps revealing the inter-level machinery and crawl-

spaces. The enemy might even have been able to come in from above, had they known about the damage.

Why hadn't they known?

"Commander," Elena began; but Gen was already at the console, opening the maintenance interfaces, ignoring the ceiling.

"You can see here," Gen said, "where they've severed the main transmission line. *Capricorn* should have been able to reroute it, but they've jammed the system somehow. They shouldn't be able to do that, not without command codes." She looked over her shoulder, and met Elena's eyes. "Any chance you can unjam this shit, Shaw?"

*Comms first, then Greg,* then *figure out why this place is falling apart.* "I'll do what I can," she said, as she'd said at the start of a thousand other jobs. She took Gen's place in front of the console and began assessing the damage.

The ship-wide comms break was the simplest, most effective thing the terrorists had done. It had required no passwords, nothing but physical access: they'd snapped the main power feed to the comms system. *Capricorn*, like most modern ships, was designed with one central system and a series of decentralized backups; the idea was that the central system, easier to observe and maintenance, would rarely require defense, and then not for very long.

Gen had been mostly right: the bulk of the backup routes had been burned out. Crude, but effective; routing around them was fiddly, but workable.

But the other half of the redundancies were still intact. And every single one of them had been access-locked.

Because the redundant systems had never been used, there were no access logs. Elena found a faint memory shadow on one, a meaningless maintenance trail that should have at least required a Corps validation. And indeed there was a series of numbers, unbroken identifiers that would match up to various members of *Capricorn*'s crew, but none were important except for the point at which the access had been locked. Elena magnified the shadow terminus, and—

"Shit." She straightened, blinking her strained eyes, and looked over at Gen. "It's been bio-keyed. We're gonna have to build a bridge."

Annoyance flashed in Gen's eyes; but she nodded. "How long will that take?"

A bio-key was an entirely different problem. She couldn't route around it; she'd need to construct an entirely new decentralized line. "Longer than we planed," Elena told her. "Ten minutes. Optimistically."

"Fast as you can, Commander."

Elena was used to close work under pressure, but here, on this strange ship, every touch, every twist of her spanner seemed to go awry. She felt clumsy, incompetent, her uncle lurking in the back of her mind, slowing her down. But even manufactured memories couldn't keep her from wondering how a pack of civilian POWs from a planet nobody ever visited could have bio-keyed the comms systems on a Central Corps warship.

Elena was sure there were people who might have that ability, probably in Shadow Ops. Jessica might know. But Elena was fairly sure none of them were research scientists on Anaxis.

Elena heard the enemy's footsteps, a hundred yards off, just before Brixa spoke. "Ten o'clock," the lieutenant said. "I make multiple targets."

Far more than nine. They'd miscounted the enemy.

"How the fuck did they get this far?" Gen asked. She hit her comm. "Squad A. Squad B. Sitrep. Acknowledge."

Gen was greeted with silence, and Elena watched her set her jaw.

"We need more cover," she told Elena. "Any chance we could move that starboard bulkhead?"

*Is that a serious question?* "However it started its life, it's structural now. Even if we didn't have to blast it to move it, it's holding up half the ceiling."

Gen swore again. "Take cover, then," she said, and Elena lowered herself to the floor, pulling the console controls down with her. Her hip complained loudly, and she huddled close to the wall, hoping to stay invisible.

Gen and Brixa stood, weapons brandished, eyes down the hallway to the right.

The rifle fire began.

Greg had forgotten how much smoke pulse rifles could kick out. He had not forgotten the noxious fumes they caused when their output mixed with the vaporization of bulkheads carrying power conduit and memory striping. The hardware on these ships burned low and slow—easier to contain, and later to repair—but despite decades of attempts at cleaner materials, the fumes were toxic. It occurred to him too late they should have had masks of some kind, environmental suits, and surely that's something they should have worn for every battle on this strange, morphing ship, which wasn't a thing ships did, was it? Why would Niemann treat it as normal if it wasn't?

*Nat*, he sent, *what—*

He felt the heat of plasma fire speed past his ear, and pressed himself against the wall. Eyenga had dropped to a crouch, shooting low; Greg shot high, aiming as well as he could toward the smoke-obscured source of the assault. The smoke lit up like flame filling the hallway, his squad's shots covering a wide swath; but they didn't know the enemy's defenses, didn't know where they might be barricaded. This might all be a waste of energy and batteries, but it was the closest they'd come to taking the ship back.

"Advance!" he shouted, and Eyenga was at his side as if

they'd never had an argument. The corridor was filled with the sound of ejected plasma and the odor of burning composites, and it was in his eyes and he blinked, unable to see, unable to even know how far they were from the machine room anymore. But the enemy fire was thinning, dissipating; he heard the other side shouting to each other, too garbled for him to make out words, but as sharp and staccato as any orders he'd given his own team. Organized, these terrorists. Maybe trained. Once they were through this—

*Focus, Foster.*

"Cover!" he shouted, and he heard his people's footsteps scrambling for the walls. "Cease fire!"

The enemy's plasma shots kept speeding down the hall, but every stream streaked past them, attenuating into oily, tepid liquid against the far walls.

The enemy wasn't hitting them.

Brixa dropped to a crouch, Gen firing over her head for cover. Elena kept her eyes on the console; she caught, now and then, the flash of an enemy round flying past in her peripheral vision. Familiar, in so many ways; she'd spent a lot of battles fixing hardware her comrades didn't understand. Constructing a decentralized bridge was easy, and she was close, so close, just a few minutes more, just—

The firing stopped.

Elena heard Brixa shift, and Gen hissed under her breath: "This is a trap. Don't you drop your guard."

*Reroute, Elena.* Another junction, another block; they'd done an impressive job, the POWs, even before the impossible bio-key. *Capricorn*'s comms systems were a tangle, and once they had control of the ship back she would recommend a complete stem-to-stern overhaul. Someone had known enough to disable without crippling; it would have taken a few hours before it became obvious all their messages were getting localized and looped back. She wondered when this work had been done. She wondered how the POWs had held off *Capricorn*'s crew while they sabotaged the systems. Could they have done it from the brig, before they broke out? Could they have done something this elaborate, this complete, under the radar of a trained Corps battle crew? They weren't engineers, after all, Gen's people; they were fighters, and good ones. They took orders, went where they were told, neutralized situations without asking why. *Capricorn's crew* was renowned for its efficiency. They were—

*Pawns*, said her mother. *They are all pawns.*

The last junction fell, and Elena stopped, flexing her fingers. "I'm through," she shouted. "I just need to—"

She smelled it first: plasma smoke and burning wire, coming from the direction of the enemy, growing stronger and stronger until her eyes started watering. Chemical warfare? She pushed herself to her feet; her hip twisted, collapsed, and she fell against the wall, pushing up with splayed fingers, just as she had when—

"Commander Naude?" Brixa asked. The soldier was peering into the smoke, her finger on her rifle's trigger, waiting for a word from Gen. But Gen didn't respond, and Elena drew her own small weapon. If the enemy was approaching, she wouldn't go quietly, wouldn't go at all, wouldn't—

She began to hear voices, low, sharp, angry, but no fire, no flash; the acrid smell of the smoke kept her mind foggy, and she closed her eyes, shaking her head. They would have detected Elena's work, known she was trying to build a new connection. Why weren't they firing? Were they waiting for Gen to betray their numbers? Were they concealing their own weaknesses? How weak could they be when they'd already broken through Gen's second squad, and had Elena and Brixa pinned against a dead-end corridor?

The voices grew more distinct. One of them, deep and sonorous, tickled something in her mind: a memory, a feeling, a *reason*. Something she had lost.

Elena's thoughts abruptly stilled.

Greg heard Eyenga murmuring to himself—"we need to *go* what the *fuck* we're *close* let's *get* these mother*fuckers*—" but he let it go; a big part of Greg agreed with the commander, felt that urgency, that drive to keep shooting, to press on, to finish it, to finish them. Odd, that. He'd been in as many battles these last months as he'd been in his entire career, and he couldn't remember feeling before that powerful compulsion to use violence as a first resort rather than a last. That had never been his training, never been his reputation. Surely this place hadn't worn him down so quickly. After all, these POWs had information. Greg still, after all these weeks, didn't understand how they'd managed to take the engine room, never mind keep it. He suspected it was tied to whatever research Niemann had been tasked with picking up, but if they all died, he'd learn nothing about that, either. Why the hell had Niemann planned it like this?

He couldn't rule out Niemann wanting to destroy evidence. Which left Greg with a conundrum: defy orders and take at least one of the enemy alive, or let a potentially catastrophic command failure remain hidden.

The shouting and firing from the other side went on for a few seconds longer, and then everything fell silent. All that separated them from the enemy was a stretch of corridor, and a choking amount of plasma smoke and burning residue.

A shout came through the fog. "Stand the fuck down! Surrender your weapons!"

"Fuck you!" shouted Eyenga, and Greg should have admonished him, but there was something in that voice.

"You're outflanked," he shouted in return. "Drop your weapons and we'll take you alive."

The response was immediate: "Stand down or we start firing again! You have five seconds."

He knew that voice. Didn't he know that voice?

"They've got nothing," Eyenga insisted. "It's a trick."

"Doesn't matter if it is or isn't," he said, but something was off, *different*. Maybe he could convince this person. Maybe, if he agreed to a truce in front of all of them, he could persuade Eyenga not to fire.

"Wait." It was Nat. He turned to look at her; she was peering through the smoke, the expression on her face something between fear and hope. "Foster. Look."

In the depths of the smoke he could make out a shadow, vaguely human-sized, moving slowly toward them. Eyenga lifted his rifle again, and Greg could hear the whine of the power circuit; he held up a hand, and hoped that would be enough. The shadow moved slowly, and not much like a soldier; he caught the rhythm of steps, but it was uneven, every other step short. He began to make out color and shape: the person was dressed in orange, not in uniform at all, not one of them, and he raised his rifle again. Taking someone alive was one thing; stupidity was something else. "Eyes sharp," he told his team. "Hold your fire."

The fog began to thin. Tall, this person, not as tall as he was, but taller than Nat, taller than Yarov, maybe even taller than Eyenga, but he'd have to stand them side by side to be sure. The orange mechanic's suit was ill-fitting; she'd tucked it into her boots for safety and tied off the sleeves. She'd pulled back her dark hair, but it was ill-fitting as well, grown longer on one side, the other hanging in her eyes; sloppy, for someone who'd otherwise been so careful about maintenance-proofing her uniform.

She was limping a little, one hand skimming the wall as if she expected to have to lean against it, and as she emerged from the fog, he noticed streaks of deep blue in her hair.

She was staring at him as if she knew him.

They were too far away for Elena to make out words, and she was probably wrong, because none of this made sense and where had they come from? But she found herself making her way around Brixa, her gun still in her hand, ignoring Brixa's whispered command to stop. She balanced one hand on the wall, moving slowly, as if she could dodge if the enemy decided to open fire. Which they'd do, of course, because she had to be wrong, and even if she wasn't there was all this smoke, these puzzling odors short-circuiting her thoughts, and were all of them experiencing this, or just her?

Hadn't she just been wondering how much of this was real?

She peered uselessly into the fog. Nothing, nothing, and nothing; the voices were still garbled, although this close she should be able to understand them, or at least pick out a language. But the syllables were broken, scrambled, like comms interference, and all this fog, all this fog…

The voices broke off, and Elena stopped.

Footsteps, one set only, slow and hesitant, and after a moment Elena could make out a shape: tall, armored, a pulse rifle aimed steadily forward but not firing at her, not yet. No one else joined the figure; no other footsteps echoed in the corridor. Alone, this person, and did she recognize something in how he moved, something familiar in the mundane act of brandishing a weapon?

She began walking again. The line of his shoulders, even in armor. Bare head, dark hair, dark skin. She could not make out his features yet, but the fog was sinking to the floor, puddling at her feet, and her eyesight cleared more moment to moment, and could it be? Aiming a rifle at her, no recognition in his face—could this be Greg, found just like this, in the corridor of a dead starship among the crew that had perished with it, in this impossible place they'd found at the other end of a wormhole?

Those bright, strange eyes on hers were hard, and his hair had somehow grown long, tight curls promising imminent unruliness, a beard sprouting over his chin. He betrayed no recognition, never lowered his weapon, and she knew that look on his face, the grim focus; he'd do his duty, even if that duty was to take her down, and if he loathed himself afterward it would make no difference, and she'd never felt so entirely whole ever before in her life.

"You stupid son of a bitch," she snapped, and flung herself at him.

Nataliya's relief was almost immediately replaced by the absolute certainty this wasn't going to go well at all.

"What is this bullshit?" Eyenga asked. He was standing next to Nataliya, armed plasma rifle still in his hands. "She's one of them. Look how she's dressed. She's—"

"Captain Foster." Yarov talked over him, nervous. "We've got a mission here. What are you doing?"

But Foster, as always when Shaw was around, entirely failed to notice the imminent fucking danger he was in. The mechanic had embraced him, and he'd taken only a moment before embracing her in return. His pulse rifle was trapped between them; uncomfortable, certainly, but they didn't seem to care. Nataliya wanted to look away, but instead focused on keeping her palm on her handgun's safety. She didn't want to kill any of them, not really, not even Eyenga; but maybe Shaw's presence would clear some of the rot in Foster's head, and they could get the fuck out of here so she could take her life back.

Foster pulled away from Shaw and looked her up and down as if he were examining her for injuries. "Is Gen with you?" he asked.

She nodded and turned. "Commander Naude!" she shouted.

Nobody answered.

*Of course.* Nataliya heard Eyenga's feet shift behind her. Whether Naude had been with Shaw and was now trapped behind a shifting wall, or whether Shaw had been provided with some sort of vivid hallucination with Naude's face, she couldn't guess.

Shaw was still clueless enough to be annoyed. "I was fixing comms," she said. "The walls were damaged, and the ceilings. I wonder if—"

"That's enough." Eyenga moved up next to Nataliya, his weapon still live. He hit the radio at his ear. "Captain Niemann? We've got a prisoner."

That caught Foster's attention. He turned irritably, still misreading the room. *Love apparently makes you stupid.* "She's not a prisoner, Eyenga. She's *Galileo*'s mechanic."

"Working with the POWs?" At that, Eyenga's rifle came up. "I don't think so, Foster."

"I told you." Shaw's tone had gone wary; she was quicker than Foster at recognizing how bad it was about to get, which would do her no good whatsoever. "I was on the other side, with Commander Naude, when—"

"Eyenga." Niemann had arrived with his squad, and Eyenga and Yarov both came to attention. Doom, then; there was no way Foster was going to split this crew, no matter how he'd acquitted himself for the last month and a half. She could die with him, or she could die afterward, when Niemann decided she was in the way.

She fantasized one last time about delivering Foster a

painful, horrible death, and raised her weapon, placing herself between him and Niemann.

*You don't need to do that,* Foster sent to her.

*Fuck you,* she replied, her finger still on the weapon's trigger.

Niemann's eyes landed on Shaw, still sheltered under Foster's arm. The captain's eyes narrowed; he would probably recognize her, Nataliya realized, out in the real world, but in here it was anybody's guess.

"Sitrep," Niemann snapped.

"She came out of the smoke," Eyenga said. "From the other side. Claims she's working with Commander Naude, but Commander Naude isn't here."

At the mention of his second-in-command, Niemann's lips thinned, a wave of something Nataliya was fairly certain was grief pulsing through his eyes before he became cold and calculating again. "Commander Naude," he said, "is MIA. At this point we need to presume she's dead."

"Captain," Shaw tried, "she's not. She—"

"*Shut. Up.*"

Niemann didn't speak loudly, but he didn't have to. Shaw fell silent. His eyes met Nataliya's.

"Commander Gritsenko. Deactivate your weapon and disarm. Foster, you do the same."

Behind her, she heard Foster shift his gun; she heard a similar sound from where Shaw was standing, although the mechanic's weapon was smaller, like Nataliya's, fatal only if her aim was good. Nataliya wondered if Shaw's aim would be good enough, if she'd be less encumbered with sentiment than Nataliya was.

"It's not his fault," Shaw said, as if she'd been reading Nataliya's mind. "There's something about this place. It takes pieces of them."

"Captain." Foster spoke in that quiet tone of his, the one he'd used when she was panicking on Sochi, the one she thought would work on Tau Niemann not at all. "Think this through. If she were the enemy, why did they stop firing?"

"They ran, as all cowards do," Niemann said seriously. "Yarov. Pick a side, Lieutenant, and do it now. That's an order."

Yarov looked vaguely green as her gaze went from Nataliya to Foster and back again. With an agonized look, she brought up her weapon, and aimed it at Nataliya's midsection.

*Well,* Nataliya thought. *Not everyone can manage to be brave.*

"Drop your weapons," Niemann said, "all three of you."

"Or what?" All the nuance was gone from Foster's tone; he'd remembered, and he was done with this shit, damn the consequences. "You're going to space us anyway."

"If you drop your weapons," Niemann said, "it'll be quick. You cooperate, tell us why you're here, what you've been doing, and—"

"You know why we're here!" Foster shouted.

"None of us know why we're here," Nataliya reminded him.

"Captain Niemann," Shaw tried, "if you could listen for a moment, I have information about your internal comms system. It seems someone—"

"Shut up!" Eyenga shouted. "Captain," he said, and his hand on his weapon was trembling. Nataliya set her jaw and held up her handgun; he was close enough she'd have no trouble getting him between the eyes, and with some luck he wouldn't be able to get a shot off at all.

"Nat," Foster said behind her. "Don't—"

And all the lights went off.

Jessica stopped in the middle of the corridor. "Ted?" she said, but the power was dead again.

The lights came back up, fluctuating along the way, and she swore.

"Ted, what the fuck?"

"It hit us again," he said in her ear. "I don't know why this time, but it—"

"Petrikoff?" Jessica ran the last few meters toward the comms center. "That wasn't us! That was that thing again! Don't—"

"Jessie." Ted's voice in her ear was tense, quiet, alien. "We have company."

"The fuck does *that* mean?"

"It means," Ted said, "another ship just appeared, hanging above Target Zero. It's *Capricorn*, Jessie. She's here."

Thirty meters away, on the other side of the sealed door, the comms center blew up.

# EVENT HORIZON

# THIRTY-FIVE

The darkness swallowed everything: light, sound, the smell of smoke and plasma, the solid floor beneath Elena's feet. No breath, no heartbeat; nothing but void, and the unshakeable sense of being watched.

After an eternity, she felt the brush of Greg's hip against hers, their shoulders touching as they held their weapons steady. Relief swept away the void's eerie sentience: he was here, with her, alive and whole and well; her mission had been successful; he would explain everything, and then they would go home.

Relief, it turned out, was a liar.

The lights came up to warning-blue, and *Capricorn*'s smooth baritone said, "Attention. Time to reset: thirty minutes eighteen point nine seven six seconds."

Tau Niemann, who looked exactly as he had moments ago, had become a different person. He dropped the nose of his rifle as if he hadn't been about to kill all three of them, and turned away. "All hands," he said into the radio, "reset protocols."

At his words, most of the infantry, alert and with purpose, broke ranks to run down various hallways. Eyenga slumped against the wall, eyes closing. Flagg put her hand under his elbow; he sank slowly to the floor, and she crouched next to him. Yarov, watching the pair of them, blinked, something suspiciously like tears in her eyes.

"Captain," Greg said.

"Wait," Niemann said tersely, and crouched next to Flagg, all his attention on Eyenga. "Commander," he said, and his voice was different: kind, gentle, all belligerence wiped away. "Carlo. You're all right. We're out. We're safe."

Eyenga didn't seem to hear this. The commander's eyes were fixed on the ceiling, the blue light washing him with an underwater glow. Tears traced rivers through the sheen of plasma smoke on his skin. "I thought for sure it would kill me this time," he said, to no one in particular. "Why didn't it kill me?"

"You're all right, Carlo," Niemann said, and Elena wondered why it wasn't something else, some reassurance that everything was fine, that Niemann was glad Eyenga had survived. "Go with Flagg. I can take your reset duties. You rest, get something to eat."

That, of all things, seemed to focus the soldier. He blinked his eyes clear, then turned to Niemann. "No, Captain," he said. "I'd rather—I'd like to do my duty, if it's all right with you."

"Of course, Commander. Let Flagg take you for food, then you can get to work." Niemann's eyes had brightened, but of course that had to be wrong. Before the lights went out, he'd been about to shoot her, to shoot all three of them, for the sin of being inexplicable. He'd been collected and dispassionate. Nobody changed that fast.

Niemann got to his feet, and Flagg tightened her hold on Eyenga's elbow. Elena half expected Eyenga to shake off the help, but instead he leaned on his squad mate and let her pull him to his feet. He rolled his shoulders, lifted his head: a soldier again, worn out but sure-footed and calm, unrecognizable from the paranoid man Elena had faced less than a minute earlier.

Before Elena, Nataliya's arms, still holding her weapon, were beginning to tremble. "Captain Niemann," she said, something like a warning in her voice.

Niemann didn't acknowledge her at all, turning to Yarov as Flagg led Eyenga away. "Ensign," he said, "you with us?"

Yarov blinked, her expression uncertain. "I...Yes, Captain. I think..." She closed her eyes and shook her head. "I'm back," she said, more steady. Her eyes met Elena's, then swept Greg and Nataliya. "Captain. What does it mean, that they're here?"

Niemann smiled faintly. "I'll brief the crew when I find out," he said to the ensign. "Attend your station, Yarov. You've done well."

Yarov's lips set. "Yes, Captain. Thank you, Captain." She snapped to attention, then turned to run down the corridor after her comrades.

Niemann faced them, holding up a finger. "Gen?" he said into his comm. "You still in one piece?"

A voice came over the radio, and that duplicitous relief found Elena again. "Here, Tau," Gen said. "Fucking thing reconfigured on us right before reset. We've picked up Dixx's crew and are headed back to the caf."

Niemann's eyes on Elena were intelligent, speculative, restive. Difficult to read. "I've got your missing mechanic. And a few of her friends."

Gen swore with some eloquence. "You've got Foster as well, then?"

"And a PSI officer."

"Damn, I was sure Shaw was an illusion. You still there, Foster's Mechanic?"

Greg shifted next to her, and Elena said, "In one piece, Commander. Waiting for someone to tell us what the fuck is going on."

At that, Gen laughed, with that combination of genuine humor and fatalism most soldiers cultivated after enough experience, and Elena realized nothing here was what she'd thought it was. "If we knew that," Gen said, "we'd be long gone. Tau. It's a short one. We'd better check weapons, and fast."

"Put your people on that," Niemann told her. "I'll meet you in the caf. And Gen—" He sobered. "Tell Dixx I'm sorry."

All the good humor left Gen's voice. "I will," she said. "But you know he already knows."

That was enough for Nataliya. "All right, Niemann, you tell us what's going on *right now* or I swear to God I will shoot you in the head!"

Niemann stared down Nataliya's gun, entirely unafraid. "Fine," he said. "But can you shoot me while we're walking? We don't have a lot of time, and I need to get back to the command center."

And he turned his back to them again and headed down the hallway.

For a moment, Elena wondered if Nataliya would shoot him in the back. Greg stirred, slipping his hand into Elena's, squeezing it gently. Warm and alive, and everything she'd been seeking for the last three days. Even in the midst of this surreal confusion, he felt like coming home.

"You heard him," Greg said, his tone deliberately light. "If we want to hear what he has to say, we'd better keep up."

Not worried about Nataliya at all.

He moved, and Elena fell into step with him, and together they walked around the PSI officer as if she weren't holding a fully-charged weapon in her hands. And then they were between Nataliya and her target, and Greg was walking with some confidence, and Elena felt her shoulder blades twitch and wondered if perhaps she shouldn't be so sanguine about following a man who two minutes ago had forgotten he'd known her for nine years. She didn't know Nataliya Gritsenko well, but she thought the woman's threat had been genuine.

But then Nataliya swore—not as expansively as Gen had, but

teaching Elena a few words she hadn't known—and followed them.

They caught up with Niemann, who didn't bother turning around. "Where's *Galileo*?" he asked.

"I don't even know where *we* are," Greg replied.

Niemann barked out a laugh. "Fair point. You're on board *Capricorn*, in the Seventh Sector, in proximity to an alien-built structure coded Target Zero by the Admiralty. Our coordinates are probably still 992.43.1189.18. Haven't checked yet this time, but we haven't moved since we got here."

That made no sense. "Captain," Elena said, "we didn't detect any ships near Target Zero."

"So you *are* nearby."

Which was still not an answer. "We were when I left," she said. "But—"

"Who are you?"

He hadn't slowed or broken stride, and her hip was starting to complain more loudly. "Elena Shaw, Captain. I'm a mechanic aboard *Galileo*."

"Of course. You're the one who quit the Corps."

"I came back," she said simply. There was no time to explain more thoroughly.

"And do you know *Galileo*'s precise location?"

His directness was throwing her. Had she really been out of the military so long? "When I left her," she said, "she was 600,000 kilometers from Target Zero, and about half a million kilometers from your coordinates. But Captain—"

"Tell me later, when we're out of all this."

Nataliya spoke up. "What's *all this*?"

"Like Genicka said," he said, turning a corner, "if we knew that, we'd have been out of it eighteen months ago."

*Eighteen months?* "So there's a time skew," Elena said aloud, glancing at Greg's long hair.

"Only in sim," Niemann told her. "Out here? It's been a few weeks. But out here doesn't matter, not to us."

The corridor opened into something that had once been a cafeteria, although the ceiling was at least three levels above their heads. Elena could see equipment mounted on the walls, all the way up. Like the small room Gen's team had repurposed, the floor was covered in line after line of cots, many with gear stowed underneath.

In one corner of the room, two soldiers were rapidly disassembling and reassembling weapons. Niemann stopped and turned around. "Surrender your guns," he said.

"Respectfully, Captain," Nataliya said, "fuck you."

Nataliya still held her weapon in her hands, safety off, thumb close to the trigger. Elena shifted closer to Greg. He nudged her with his elbow: *Let it play out.*

Niemann took a step toward Nataliya, staying in her line of fire; if he was annoyed, he kept it to himself. "Respectfully, Commander," he said patiently, "sometimes the sim makes us sabotage our weapons. We've found it's more efficient to check the integrity of our equipment than to accidentally blow ourselves up."

Nataliya kept her eyes on Niemann's, defiant; but after a moment she palmed her gun's safety back on and handed it over. Elena followed up with her own handgun, and Greg surrendered his pulse rifle. Niemann carried them to the weapons table.

Elena looked at Greg, who was watching Nataliya with something akin to pride. They'd been through something together, and it had taken more than three days. "Greg," she asked, "how long have you been here?"

"Almost eight weeks," he said.

Nataliya was still scowling, eyes following her gun as if she'd surrendered a small child. "I've been here two. When did you arrive?"

"Day before yesterday," Elena said.

"And how long had we been gone when you jumped?"

"Fifteen minutes," Elena told her. "Probably less. Listen. There are—"

Niemann returned, speaking as if he'd never left. "The main thing we need to do is get a message to *Galileo*," he told them. "We can't use comms, so this is going to depend on how likely she is to detect a radio sweep. Your ship needs to get the hell out of here before she gets caught like we're caught. It's imperative they get back to the Six Sectors and let people know about that thing out there."

"Actually, Captain," Elena volunteered, "I was pretty close to getting your comms systems back on line. If you give me a few more minutes—"

She broke off. Niemann had frozen, the color draining from his ruddy complexion. "You didn't get through, did you?"

"No." She frowned; was he *upset* with her? "I'd been about to finish the bridge over the bio-key and test the new route when the shooting stopped, and I heard Greg. But—"

It all fell into place, and if she hadn't been muddled by the sim, she'd have realized it sooner.

"*You* bio-keyed the comms."

"In the sim," he said, "we all forget what that thing can do."

"It uses comms to travel."

"It broke in before we knew what was happening," he said. "We can keep it out—mostly—with radio, but that doesn't stop it responding to us if we so much as twitch."

"You keep saying 'sim'," Nataliya pointed out. "So none of this has been real?"

"All of this is real," Niemann said. "It's creating a situation, and arming us. It takes our memories and replaces them with nonsense. Our memories are simulated. The fighting is real. Death is real. And we're all real."

"Meaning," Nataliya said, "I murdered two of your people." She sounded more angry than sorry. Elena might have felt the same.

"Not mine," Niemann told her. "But that was real, too. I'm sorry, Commander." That compassionate note in his voice again, like he'd used with Eyenga. "It's not your fault. You got caught, just like us. If it's any comfort, they'd absolutely have killed my people if you hadn't shot them first. There's been a fair amount of mutual murder over the months, and we've had to learn to let it go. Nobody's responsible except that thing out there."

Elena couldn't remember ever seeing the PSI commander's complexion quite so gray.

"But what are they doing here?" Greg asked. He let go of her hand and slipped his arm around her waist; he was more shaken up than he was letting on. "Why did you end up out here with a ship full of POWs from Anaxis?"

And that, of all things, finally deflated Niemann's mood. His lips set, and the lines around his eyes grew deeper. "There are no POWs from Anaxis," he told them. "There never were. When we left Anaxis, everyone on that planet was dead."

# THIRTY-SIX

"Hull breach in comms," *Galileo* announced. "Breach sealed. Atmosphere intact."

Jessica ran for the comms center door and started banging. "Petrikoff. Petrikoff!" Her comm link to him was still active; not everything in the room had been obliterated. "Petrikoff, dammit, we didn't do this, you know we didn't, you know what's out there, you—"

"Why is there a warship off our bow, Captain?"

His voice still held that note of paranoia, but for reasons unknown he seemed more sedate, more in control. Apparently blowing shit up calmed him down. "Fuck you, Petrikoff, I want to talk to Samaras. I'm giving you nothing until—"

"Here, Captain."

She closed her eyes against crashing relief. Still alive. Still talking. She still had time.

"Sitrep, Lieutenant," she said.

"Big bang," he told her. "Field up. I'm good. Little singed."

*He's hurt.* Rage backfilled all the adrenaline she'd just lost.

"And now you answer my question, Captain," Petrikoff said. "Why is there a warship off our bow? And remember: it would be trivially easy for me to shove your friend through the gravity shielding into space."

Another tickle through her comm: *40% detonated 21 minutes to disarm.*

*You better survive, Samaras,* she thought, *because I'm going to promote you so high the rest of us are going to look like little ants.*

She moved down the hall until her radio kicked in, and caught Ted mid-sentence. "—getting an official ident." He sounded fascinated. "The mods, the config, the engine signature —it's the same ship, Jess, or someone's gone to absolutely insane lengths to mock it up."

The insanity of *Capricorn*'s appearance didn't change her fundamental problem: she needed to buy time. And only one even remotely plausible lie came to mind.

"It's there, Petrikoff," she said, assembling the story as she spoke. "The CI. It's on the warship. We sent it ahead when we found it; you really think we'd have kept it here? You're right, it's Central tech, but once it was detected we couldn't keep it on board, we were bringing it here for study, so we sent it ahead and they've got it. I need to make contact with them, and—"

"You're bullshitting me. I recognize that ship. That's the one that you shot down over Sochi." His voice was growing shaky again.

"Come on, Petrikoff," she said, trying to sound derisive, "you think we couldn't have faked an explosion like that? We had to camouflage the ship so we could use it to hide contraband. It's standard Corps procedure."

One of the first things Jessica had learned from Captain Taras was that PSI, despite centuries of observation and spying, knew very little about standard Corps procedure. It surprised Jessica, every time, even remembering how much bullshit detail she'd had to memorize at the Academy. When *Galileo* had first left the Corps, she'd learned she and Taras had less of a common vocabulary than she'd assumed. A staggering percentage of PSI's assumptions about Shadow Ops and Corps intelligence work were flat-out wrong. PSI had been unsurprised at the degree of corruption *Galileo* had uncovered within the Admiralty's ranks, but PSI's estimate of the Corps' ability to throw something complex together with little to no notice was way, way off.

In the Corps, you got two of three: complexity, effectiveness, or speed. And in space, where your only protection was a meter or two of nanolattice bulkhead, complexity was always the criterion that got tossed.

She was hoping Petrikoff hadn't figured that out yet.

"How will you convince them to destroy it?" he asked.

"Destruction was always on the table," she told him. "It won't be a problem."

"It might have escaped," he said.

"Not with their containment procedures."

"It might—"

"Petrikoff." She dug her fingernails into her palms; she could lose her temper later, when everyone was safe and they were on their way home. "If that thing is loose on their ship, we will absolutely destroy her. That's protocol as well, and her crew knows it. You get your wish either way."

*Please*, she thought. *Please.*

"All right," he said at last. "I'll give you fifteen minutes to contact them. If you don't give me an update at that point, your man goes through that gravity barrier out into space. Understand?"

"I understand." She terminated the comm. "Nobody comms that ship," she said over radio. "Kali. How much of a radio delay have you got to *Capricorn*?"

"One point eight zero three seconds," Kali replied.

Nearly four seconds round-trip. "Send a signal," Jessica said. "Rotate the frequency. If they're listening at all, I want to get through. We need a line to that ship, whatever it is. Bob? You still there?"

"Here, Jess." He answered her unspoken question. "No sign of them. But no further changes to Target Zero, either, so I guess we're status quo, at least for now."

"When you get back here," she said conversationally, "I'm going to strangle all three of you." Four, she reminded herself. Nataliya Gritsenko wasn't officially her problem, but she thought she might spare a little ire for the PSI officer anyway.

"Hoping that's soon," Bob said. "Gotta say, I'm not feeling all that great sitting alone in a little shuttle with a warship hovering over my head."

"But you're not alone," Kali said, with some surprise.

"We're all alone," Jessica told her. "Ted. Drop to 99.1" She changed frequencies. "What did that last flash do to our batteries?"

"Was able to siphon off a little power," he said. "Bought us some time, if we have to go sublight, but given the additional damage, not as much as I would have liked. We lost some capacity. There's no way we can sustain a field now, with or without *Unicinta*'s batteries."

At least she wouldn't have to leave Elena and Greg without a shuttle. "Can we initiate?"

"Possibly," he said. "But only if we abandon every single failsafe. That'd mean protecting the comms center is off the table. But Jess, it doesn't matter. Even if we could get in, we don't have enough power to stabilize. We'd fall out— hard—and that would be that."

"Would a transfer of energy from another ship help?"

"Even if that warship is friendly, they're not showing much production. I wouldn't count on them having enough left to transfer us anything."

That was not the hopeful response she'd wanted. "Get me numbers," she said. "I want to know what to ask for."

"Assuming there's anybody there to ask."

She hadn't let herself think about survivors. "Ted. They can't both be *Capricorn*."

"That's a thing, isn't it?" He sounded almost cheerful, the way he did when he got fatalistic. "That ship back in the Fourth? Same ident. Not sure I want to think about it if Ellis, or Shadow Ops, or whoever-the-fuck is able to fake something that well. And the one in the Fourth had a flight recorder, unless you think Captain Reed was bullshitting you."

"So this one has to be the fake."

"Fits the facts," he agreed. "But it doesn't fit our readings."

"If we believe our readings, there are two of them."

"So it seems." Ted paused. "Seems like a weird thing to do, duplicating a whole-ass warship. What's the point?"

"Who's to say there's a point?"

"Kali says Target Zero is a machine," he reminded her. "Machines always have a point, even if it's only decoration or distraction."

"We're certainly distracted, aren't we?"

They were both silent a moment. "So what's the plan?" he asked her quietly.

She blew out a puff of air. "I've fabricated some bullshit to keep Petrikoff from spacing Samaras," she said. "Kali is trying to contact that ship, but either way, we need to regroup and take the comms center. With holes in the wall, and Petrikoff on high alert? Not quite so easy."

"You could let Samaras go, you know," Ted said. "He'd understand."

She said nothing. Ted knew her history. He knew how she felt about death and duty, and how much she needed to believe she could save people.

"It's the job, Jess. We know it when we sign up."

"He's a good officer. He'd die for us. He'd die for me, and he wouldn't even ask why. That means I owe it to him to make sure there are no other options."

"You can't work miracles."

"I can at least find out if there's anything useful on that *Capricorn*-not-*Capricorn* out there before I choose to sacrifice him."

"Fair enough," he said. "And here's your base number: if they've got sixty-two extra stellar batteries with sixty percent or higher charge, we could take enough of an energy dump to form a field and at least get some distance between us and that thing."

"One jump?"

"One jump."

"Just us, I assume."

"Jessie. We couldn't even rope in *Unicinta* at this point. It'd be just us, and we'd still have to scrape the low-power cells along the way."

A ludicrous conversation, in the end. If this *Capricorn* were abandoned, if they could cannibalize what was there, if they had the right parts, if, if, if...

"Captain."

Kali sounded excited, and vaguely disbelieving. "Ensign."

"I'm picking up radio from *Capricorn*, Captain," the CI said. "It's short-range—internal-only, I suspect at this point."

"Can you tune us in?"

"I'll have to amplify it, Captain, but I can simulcast it over comms."

A burst of static sounded in Jessica's ear, and then she heard footsteps, shouts, and occasional unidentified thuds. The voices were too indistinct for her to make out words, but she thought there were thirty or more people on the line, all sounding urgent but unpanicked.

And then she heard a low, even baritone: a classic Corps starship voice interface. "Reset in twenty-six minutes four point one eight two repeating seconds."

*Reset?*

"*Galileo,*" Jessica asked her ship, "does that chit-chat sound like *Capricorn?*"

"Eighty-four point nine nine seven percent certainty, Captain," *Galileo* told her.

*Not good enough.* She checked her timer: eleven minutes before she had to get back to Petrikoff. She straightened, remembered who she was, and commed Kali again.

"Ensign Kali," she said, "redirect our signal to their busiest radio frequency. Identify us, and ask for Captain Niemann."

"Yes, Captain. Sending now."

"And I want you to put together a comms mockup," Jessica told her. "Chatter between our crew and theirs, professional and casual, as if we're negotiating the return of something."

"Yes, Captain."

In Jessica's ear, the manufactured voices of artificial bureaucrats began droning about coordinating shipping schedules and filling out forms. It was a shame, in a way, that *Galileo* had left the Corps; something like Kali would have saved a lot of officers a lot of irritation.

For now, she'd settle for the CI saving her ship.

# THIRTY-SEVEN



"We were all there," Niemann began. "We were all involved. But let me be clear: what happened was my fault. No one else's."

Elena knew all about ops gone bad. It was impossible, if you were in the Corps more than a month and kept your eyes open, to miss them. The Admiralty liked to tut at unstable colonies and chains of information that turned out to be too slow, but now and then they were behind the bad decisions to begin with. She'd watched Greg, over the years, reinterpret and flat-out blockade orders from above that were clearly counterproductive; because his outcomes had been good, they'd let most of that go. Or maybe the outcomes hadn't been the issue: maybe he'd gotten away with it because *Galileo* had been far from home, and the Admiralty had no way to quickly deploy the sort of counter-measures that would have worked on a soldier like Greg.

Those countermeasures had worked on her, of course, but she'd always been more gullible than he was. She'd always wanted to believe in justice, that her government's ultimate goals were always benign, even if their implementation involved missteps. She'd wondered, in the months since her last, disas-trous mission, if it was the scant five years Greg had on her that made him more savvy about such things, but she didn't think so. She'd been blinded by the idea of self-sacrifice, of saving the people she loved, her ego buying into all the heroic stories she'd heard since childhood.

Tauno Niemann was twenty years older than Greg, at least. She wondered if he'd been blinded by the same things she had.

"We'd been out seven months. Too long, no matter what duty you've been given, but we'd just come off putting down the rebellion on Loki 7."

*Putting down.* Elena bristled. Beside her, Nataliya Gritsenko took a step away from Niemann, as if distance could shield her from his story. Elena wanted very much to do the same.

"We were six weeks overdue for liberty when Shadow Ops asked us to pick up research on Anaxis. I figured it was a small enough job, but our briefing left out the part about Anaxis refusing to deliver. S-O didn't tell us until we'd arrived. Admiral Waris commed me personally." Niemann gave a mirthless laugh. "Always a bad sign, isn't it, when they comm you personally? She said we needed to get that research, no matter the cost. She was very specific about that." He fell silent a moment, his eyes straying to his busy crew. "Should have paid more attention to that. But we were *Capricorn*. Nobody was going to fuck with us."

Such bitterness in his voice. Whatever had happened, then and since, had burned something out of him.

"We'd picked up from Anaxis before. But the people I usually spoke to weren't talking, and the ones who were told us to come and take it, if we thought we could.

"So I sent a squad."

Greg stirred. "A military squad."

Elena looked over at him; he'd become stiff and expressionless. It was a look she'd learned to recognize, over the years, as nascent rage. She shifted closer to him, letting her elbow brush his; comfort, whether he'd accept it or not.

Niemann's blue eyes flashed. "We're a warship, Foster," he said brusquely. "We're not in it to make nice."

Greg kept silent.

After a moment Niemann looked away. "Waris knew we were overdue for liberty," he went on, defensiveness gone. "I figured she was paying us a compliment, believing we could do the job properly, despite that deficit." He looked back at Greg. "They do that," he said. "They use us for what we can seem to be, as often as for what we are."

And didn't that hit Elena right in the gut?

"Turns out," Niemann went on, "Waris left out one other thing: the scientists on Anaxis were armed. And if I'm any judge of either scientists or soldiers, they'd been training. Not only did they not intend to give up their research, they were ready to kill for it."

"And die."

Elena hadn't even been sure she'd said it aloud, but Niemann nodded.

"What the hell were you picking up?" Greg asked him. "Why didn't they just destroy it before you got there?"

"No idea. We didn't even get a close look at it." He smiled, but it was all bleakness. "Not our job."

Nataliya had moved away from their group entirely, and Elena couldn't blame her. Some stories were worse when you already knew the ending.

"And it was your job to destroy the whole colony?"

Niemann's eyes flashed again. "You think that was us?" He shook his head. "We'd have had to do that from orbit, and we didn't. The op, though, was a mess. One of our people was killed. A stray shot, I think; they were just a bunch of scientists, and Hadley never was any good at covering his ass. But that set my people off, and they started shooting on sight." His lips thinned; this was the part he held on to, the part he felt he should have foreseen. "Gen put a lid on it as soon as she could, but there was no resistance left by then. We retrieved the research and headed home.

"And as the team was leaving, the whole place went up. Percussion wave caught the shuttle; we had to tow them back." He looked back and forth between Elena and Greg. "I sent an overworked military crew on a mission they weren't suited for, and civilians died. I own that. Those lives are on my conscience. But the rest of the colony? *That wasn't us.* Something blew those reactors one after another, as if they'd been daisy-chained. And we had nothing to do with it."

Which made no sense at all. "Nobody daisy-chains reactors," Elena said.

Nataliya reappeared at her elbow, her color slightly better. "Had to be sabotage." She sounded brittle, and Elena wondered what nightmares this story had dredged up for her. Joined PSI at fifteen, Jessica had said. People rarely joined PSI that young without some horror in their history.

"Ellis," said Greg. "They've already used environmental tech to destroy colonies. This would have been easy for them."

"You'd think." Niemann gave his grim smile again. "But those passengers we have, those people the sim keeps telling us are POWs from Anaxis? Those are Ellis workers. Ellis contacted Central right after the explosion, and *they* were accusing *us.*"

Niemann didn't have the experience Elena did with Ellis. "They're liars," she told him. "Covering their tracks."

"That was my first thought," Niemann admitted. "But they convinced the Admiralty. Shadow Ops authorized nineteen Ellis researchers on my ship for this expedition. And they weren't what we expected. Yes, at the start, we did, after a fashion, make them prisoners, restricting which parts of the ship they could access. But on the way here...you can't live on a ship this small and not socialize. We got to know each other. And we learned that Ellis employees are not a monolith, nor do they all approve of what their corporation is doing."

Elena thought of the Ellis employees she'd met: ordinary, even likable. The same as people she'd known all her life, just dedicating their lives to duplicity and death. "Still enabling them," she said shortly.

Niemann was unoffended. "We had plenty of time to talk about that, too. But the one indisputable thing we learned? They didn't blow Anaxis. They don't have that tech. They're not even *working* on that tech. The weapons tech they've been developing —it's all around stealth. That's their goal. Daisy-chaining a pack of reactors is both too dangerous and too fucking obvious for them."

She scoffed. "Too obvious for Ellis? Who hid all their work in plain sight? Who—" She stopped, paging in her memories of all the times they'd dealt with the weapons manufacturer. She met Greg's eyes. "People watch reactors for this very reason. Even if Ellis could have masked the sabotage, making it undetectable would have been a hellish job, without any obvious return."

"Exactly," Niemann said. "There'd be no profit in it." He looked down at her. "We've endured the sim alongside these people for eighteen months. They've proven themselves to us. I suspect, if you had the time to discuss with them their current views of their command chain, you'd find they were largely in agreement with you. It all changes out here."

"People revisit their motivations," she said. "Change their actions. I don't think that's quite the same thing."

If Niemann felt insulted, he kept it to himself. "Shadow Ops knew Target Zero was out here," he said, "even if they didn't know precisely what it was. And I could understand sending us here, especially wanting to get us out of the Six Sectors when the news broke. Punishing us for Anaxis, because the public was going to demand punishment. But you? Who did *Galileo* piss off?"

"Actually," Greg began, "We didn't—"

And then a familiar voice came over their radio connection.

"*Capricorn*, this is Captain Jessica Lockwood of the starship *Galileo*. Are you receiving?"

Niemann froze, his thoughts comically obvious. For a moment they might have been back in the sim, Elena, Greg, and Nataliya an existential threat to his crew.

"You're not *Galileo*'s captain any longer," Niemann said to Greg.

Greg looked resigned. "No."

"And is she no longer a Corps starship?"

Elena was trying to figure out how to explain concisely, when Nataliya spoke up, sounding more like herself. "After *Capricorn* left the Six Sectors, Central destroyed Athena Relay and fucked comms for half the colonies, *Galileo* raided an Ellis think-tank and leaked their data to the public, Foster resigned so he could rescue some fucking useless Ellis scientists, and *Galileo*'s whole crew voted to fuck off and join PSI. Any questions?"

For a moment Niemann stood frozen, frowning down at Nataliya, as if she'd abruptly started clucking like a chicken. And then the big man threw back his head and laughed, loud and genuine, the sound echoing throughout the cavernous space. The crew all stopped what they were doing to look, some cautiously; but apparently something in Niemann's affect reassured them. Some of them laughed as well, and when the crew went back to their tasks, the whole room felt lighter.

A small glimpse of why there had been so little turnover on *Capricorn* over the years.

"About time somebody called those fuckers on their shit," he said. He looked from Greg to Elena. "You really joined PSI? The whole ship?"

"They took a *vote*," Nataliya said, and Niemann guffawed again.

"Captain Lockwood," Niemann said into his radio, still chuckling, "this is *Capricorn*. It's good to hear your voice, but you need to get out of here. This thing is going to cycle in a little over twenty minutes, and trust me, you don't want to get caught."

There was a pause of several seconds. Radio lag, Elena realized. Why were they on radio? "Thank you for the warning," Lockwood said, with an edge of sarcasm. "We're not able to maneuver right now."

The last of Elena's self-pity vanished. What was wrong with her ship?

"Captain, what's the state of your ship? Because we could use a little help here, and maybe we could help you in return."

Niemann's lips set. "I'm not sure there's much we can do for you Captain Lockwood," he said. "We can't maneuver—any movement triggers an energy pulse from Target Zero, and our shuttles have been out of commission since we got here."

Elena couldn't keep quiet. "With your permission, Captain?" When Niemann nodded, she touched her comm. "Jess. We're here. Me, Greg, Commander Gritsenko. Why can't you maneuver?"

The pause this time was longer than what would have been caused by the slow signal. "Fucking *hell*, Lanie, what the *fuck* were you thinking? You're alive? Fuck all of you. Petrikoff blew a fucking hole in our hull, and Ted is working magic to see if we can get out of here at all, never mind FTL. Target Zero has hit us with two energy pulses, and our batteries are losing charge every fucking second. Connect with Ted, and the two of you figure out how to fix this. That's a fucking *order*, you understand me, Commander? Because I've had a fucking *day*, and I'm not arguing with you anymore. Greg. You there?"

Greg was smiling, and Elena wondered if Niemann's good humor had cheered him as well. "Here, Jess."

"You're fucking lucky you don't work for me," Jessica said.

"Good to hear your voice too."

"Fuck you. Don't be nice." She inhaled, exhaled. "You okay?"

"Bumps and bruises." A lie, but it was the same sort of lie Elena would have told. "We're all okay."

"And you're on *Capricorn*? For real?"

He opened his mouth to answer, and Elena saw the calculation on his face: Niemann didn't know they'd destroyed *Capricorn*, or some version of *Capricorn*, three weeks ago. Or eleven weeks, or eighteen months, or a day and a half; time, it seemed, had lost all meaning.

"Far as I can tell, Jess," Greg said, and only someone who knew him well would have noticed the care he took choosing those words. "Been working with Tau Niemann for the last eight weeks. Seems like himself."

"*Eight weeks?*" Jessica said, incredulous.

"Kind of a long story," he told her. "In the meantime, Niemann's right. You need to get *Galileo* out of here."

"Yeah, well, I have a feeling this is going to be an all-or-none kind of thing." She paused. "Eight weeks? Time travel?"

"Dilation, at least."

"That doesn't—" She stopped herself. "There has to be more to it than that."

Over the intercom, *Capricorn* said "Reset in nineteen minutes zero zero zero seconds."

"If there is," Niemann said, "we can have a nice long talk about it in nineteen minutes."

Reading over Ted's damage report, sent in agonizing minutes via *Unicinta*'s radio, Elena was nearly overwhelmed by the desire to get back to her crippled ship, and by near panic when she remembered that was impossible.

All the damage *Galileo* had taken was explicable, except for the gamma pocks. Elena, like most mechanics, knew only as much physics as was absolutely required to get her work done, but she'd seen enough radiation damage to understand particles didn't just appear without leaving some kind of trail. She'd encountered a lot of cutting-edge research over the last two months—much of it explicitly designed to be deadly—but none of it suggested even a theoretical path to something so fundamentally impossible.

She thought of the cortisol in Bob's brain, and shuddered.

All she said aloud was, "How fast are you losing power?"

Ted's tone was brash and cheerful; they must be in grave danger indeed. "If absolutely nothing else happens to us, and we keep the environmentals to a minimum, and nobody else blows a fucking hole in the hull, we could *maybe* get to about ninety-eight percent lightspeed and stay there for a year or so. If nothing else damages our batteries, which are dropping like proverbial flies."

"FTL?"

"Status quo? Not a chance in hell."

"And your answer to this is to poke that thing until it hits you again."

"You got a better idea, Lanie, I will be over here jumping for joy."

She reviewed the battery data: more than half of *Galileo*'s battery banks no longer held a charge at all, and most of the rest of them were leaking. "Five percent undamaged," she said aloud.

As always, Ted followed her thinking. "We're probably past the point where contingency planning makes much sense."

Elena looked up and scanned the room. *Capricorn* had lost forty-five percent of her crew. On *Galileo*—when she'd been fully staffed—that would have been a hundred people Elena knew, worked with, cared for. How did *Capricorn*'s losses affect such a small crew? And how many had been killed while they were attacking a peaceful colony of three million? They would have thought of it as war, she realized; to the Corps, Anaxis had no right to refuse to surrender their research. The Corps justified murder during war—used the blameless word *casualties*—but she'd found, for herself, killing was killing, no matter what the reason.

It occurred to her feeling guilty might mean she had actually retained her humanity.

"How much shielding can you strip from the batteries that can still take a charge?" she asked.

"Less now than I could when I thought I had more time," he said. "But I'll start with the fresh ones. They'll take a stronger boost, and if we don't make it, it won't matter if they're dead afterward. Any chance we can get any juice from that bird you're on?"

"I don't think she's got a hell of a lot."

"We don't need much. Seriously, Lanie. Before Petrikoff blew a hole in the wall, it was a longshot. Now we've got nothing, even if we can properly time a jolt from Target Zero." He paused; he knew her so well. "What's bothering you?"

It had nothing to do with the problem at hand; they'd make it work, or they wouldn't, and handwringing over it was a waste of time. "Ted," she asked, "if you were trapped on *Galileo* for a year and a half with some alien fucking with your memories and picking your ship to pieces, what would you do?"

"I'd kick that fucker as hard and as often as I had to until I got away," he said easily. "You thinking *Capricorn* is stuck on purpose?"

She looked up at the crew rushing around her. All the activity was exactly what she would have expected: triage equipment, check the ship's capabilities, repair if possible. "No," she said. "They're doing all the right things. But Ted. I don't know how much cumulative time they've had between sims, but if they've been stuck a year and a half, it's got to be days, at least. Probably weeks. And the situation has gotten worse, not better." Niemann wasn't wrong; *Capricorn* could take at most another half-dozen of Target Zero's energy pulses before her internal systems would simply give up the ghost.

"Are you telling me you think there's no way to get away?"

"I'm asking what you'd do if you *believed* there was no way to get away."

"If it were just me," he said, "I'd drink. A lot. Maybe kill myself that way, although I don't think that's the most pleasant way to go."

"They're not drinking, though. They're still fighting."

"I'd always heard Niemann was charismatic."

Elena glanced over at *Capricorn*'s captain. He looked old, tired, resigned. Determined, but not in a way she would have found inspiring if she'd been serving under him. "He's loyal to his people," she said. "Maybe more than they deserve."

"That sounds judgmental. I wish we had time to gossip properly. You have a point here, Lanie? Because you and me, we've got to start saving backsides here."

"No point, Ted. At least not yet." There was something still nagging at her, but she knew from experience letting it rest in the back of her mind would be the best way to get it to emerge. "I'm gonna see about a power transfer. Maybe we can get everybody home after all. Whatever we've got to give, we can give more of it if we get *Unicinta* closer and funnel it through her. How much damage has she taken?"

"None."

She blinked. "*None?*"

"Not a ding, not a pock."

"Well isn't *that* interesting."

"Nice choice of words. Scares the shit out of me."

"If *Unicinta* can maneuver..." She headed for Niemann. "I've got to talk to some people. I'll ping you back in a few."

"We don't have a whole lot of 'few' left, you know," he said, but let her go.

"Captain Niemann." He turned as she approached, his eyes

lasering into hers. Maybe that was what people meant by *charismatic*. "I think the shuttle I took to Target Zero can move without drawing fire. I believe she can send and receive comms, too—Captain Lockwood is already routing through her. Not only could we get rid of the radio lag, but we'd improve attenuation of the signal. We could get more power to *Galileo*. Enough to take *Capricorn* with us as well."

Niemann's eyes narrowed. "Why would your shuttle be exempt?"

And here was where she'd learn exactly how flexible a Corps warship captain could be. "We've stored some technology in her systems," Elena told him. "Technology we think has the same origins as Target Zero."

"You have a piece of that thing?"

"No. We—" How the hell could she explain? "*Unicinta* is running software that we believe may have been originally designed by the same civilization. A CI. But regardless of where it came from, it's native. It's ours."

The explanation sounded convoluted to her ears, but he followed her. "Would have to be," he said, half to himself, "running on our hardware. An autonomous CI? Truly? You have control over it?"

"It's already saved lives here, Captain," Jessica put in. "*Unicinta* is solid, and if our little bit of alien tech makes her resistant to the poking and prodding of that thing out there, I say we use her. Unless you have better options."

For a moment Niemann remained motionless, and Elena felt a tingle on the back of her neck. But then he barked out a laugh. "No better ideas here, Captain. How big is that shuttle? Can we offload my crew?"

"Bob?" Jessica prompted.

"It'll be SRO," Bob said, "but yes, we can take everyone."

Greg, who had been talking with Nataliya, had grown abruptly attentive at the sound of Bob's voice. Elena caught his eye, twitched her eyebrows; he smiled a little, reassuring her. *Later*, his expression said. They were leaving so much for later.

Niemann still had questions. "Captain Lockwood, how sure are you that shuttle isn't going to trigger a backlash?"

"Not at all," Jessica said candidly. "But statistically speaking, it should have taken *some* damage, given the distribution across the rest of the ship, and it's untouched. Whether it's worth the risk or not is your call."

Elena watched the calculus play over Niemann's face: the possibility of evacuating his crew from his crippled ship, the possibility the shuttle would invite destruction, the possibility they'd be no better off on *Galileo* than they were here.

He made the same choice she would have.

"All hands," he said, his voice coming over the ship's intercom, "report to Landing Bay Two for evacuation. We're getting out of here, people. All of us together."

Elena waited for protests, formal and informal. But after a moment of silence, she heard a cheer, and then the whole cafeteria was filled with sound: victory whoops, laughter, delighted tears. He'd handed them hope.

"Sounds like we'd better not fuck up," Ted said in her ear.

Elena kept her eyes on Tau Niemann, who was watching his crew, his expression one of open affection and pride. And then his eyes filled, and he blinked away evidence of a very different emotion.

"I think," she said to Ted, "it's not entirely on us."

# THIRTY-EIGHT

Jessica muted Kali's fake comms traffic as Tau Niemann, over radio, gave her the rundown on what his ship could—and couldn't—provide.

"Out of range of any kind of comms booster, our options for transferring power are limited," he said. "Even with full privileges to your systems, what we can do is going to be very crude. And I'd advise you not to grant *Capricorn* full privileges to your systems."

Without a first-hand hardware evaluation from Elena, Jessica didn't even want to guess how inefficient the power transfer might be. Engaging their logic systems could smooth out the redistribution, but there was no reason *Galileo* couldn't handle the battery feed—especially boosted through *Unicinta*, which would provide something of a checkpoint—directly. Either way, she was willing to grant whatever privileges *Capricorn* needed; Niemann's damaged warship was the only hope they had left.

"Do you think your ship has been compromised?" she asked him.

"I don't know, Captain Lockwood. But you must protect yourselves. The most important thing is getting word back to Central about Target Zero and what it's capable of." He paused. "This CI you've got on your shuttle. If it's really the same tech as Target Zero—"

"Kali was sitting in our systems for six weeks before we discovered her," Jessica told him. "If she's malevolent, it's too late for us anyway. But as far as we can tell, she never integrated with the rest of the ship's functions, and her autonomous operations, to date, have been nothing but helpful."

"You're just as suspicious as I am."

"With 167 crew? You bet I am, Captain. But without Kali in the mix, none of this is going to work, and we're all dead anyway."

He huffed out a laugh, and Jessica had the disconcerting impression that if she'd spent time with him, she'd have liked this cold-blooded warship captain. That was the thing about Central Gov, she reflected; so much of what it did was good, it was sometimes hard to remember what it did that was indefensible.

She heard footsteps; he was walking. "It's unlikely," Niemann told her, "we'd have the time to do more than open up a standard non-privileged distance conduit anyway."

*Non-privileged.* Sixty percent attenuation at a minimum, even if *Capricorn* were in good repair. For a moment she fought panic, thinking of all the power that would be dissipating, useless, into nothingness, a bit of energy that might put them over the top, save all their lives, get them home. She took a breath. That was Ted and Lanie's problem, and if the two of them couldn't figure out how to save her ship, they were lost anyway. "I'll tell Kali to expect the access request," she said. "You have an ETA on getting this set up?"

"Ask me again in five minutes," he said. "Captain. Can you drop to 101.9 for a moment?"

*Unicinta* altered the frequency for her, and the shared radio chatter fell silent. "Captain?"

"I need you to promise me," he said, "to treat *Capricorn* as expendable."

"We're balancing the system for both ships, Captain," she said. "I'm not sure I can—"

"Captain Lockwood. You and I took the same oath. We're here not for Central, not for the Corps, but for humanity as a whole."

"You *are* compromised."

"I can't know the answer to that," he said, and she heard some of the frustration he'd shown in his message to Admiral Waris. "But the things that come up in the sim...there's no way for Target Zero to know them. The ways it's altered our memories, the things it manufactures about our perceived enemies. The ways we behave. Without knowing the mechanism I don't think it's safe for *anything* to be communicating with *Capricorn*."

She almost told him, then, that *Capricorn* had been destroyed, that her flight recorder had been picked up, its contents shared with all of the Corps and Jessica's own little renegade ship. If *Capricorn* had been compromised, it was far too late to prevent contamination.

But that was assuming the two *Capricorn*s were the same. Greg and Elena seemed to believe Target Zero could manipulate time; certainly Greg's experience with the booster relay was evidence in that direction. But time dilation and moving backward were two different concepts. The former was theoretically possible, although as far as Jessica knew, no organization— corporate, military, or academic—had yet to find a practical way of making it happen to objects not in motion.

Going back in time, on the other hand, broke every bit of cosmological theory Jessica had ever learned. If that ship she'd seen in the Fourth Sector was the same as the ship before her, the universe was not what any of them thought it was.

"We'll do our best to isolate her once we get home," Jessica promised him. "But we need the physical fact of her. Even your word, Captain, might not be enough for Gov. They're so bogged down in their petty political squabbling they're likely to summarily fire on us as soon as we show up, even if we bring you back in one fully operational piece."

"That bad, is it?"

"You surprised?"

"Eighteen months ago I'd have dressed you down and defended them, Captain, never mind you're PSI. But even then I wouldn't have been surprised." He paused. "It occur to you they're squabbling over the wrong things?"

"That," she told him, "is the biggest reason we need to bring *Capricorn* home."

"Very well. But she still needs to be last on the list. If she puts the plan at risk, even a little? You're to drop her."

She almost reminded him he couldn't give her orders. "Let's hope we don't face that, Captain," she said.

He made a small sound to let her know he recognized the dodge, and signed off.

She tuned back into *Galileo*'s general radio frequency. "Bristol. Where are we with the explosives in that room?"

"We've figured out what he's using," Bristol told her, and rattled off a list of organics. Volatile, vulnerable to plasma fire, but not as unstable as she'd feared. "Based on the air quality in that room, he detonated about forty percent of them. Lucky he only blew out the wall."

*Shit.* "And how much of the wall did we lose?"

"Too much. Shielding has added another .07% drain to our batteries."

"Is it at least a constant drain?"

"So far, Captain. But they're telling me if the edges of the hole are too frayed, initiating the fold is going to make the drain unpredictable."

Which wouldn't bode well for it holding well enough to get them into the field, never mind out of it again. *Dammit.* "Emily. We'll be heading out to some ragged edges. Warn your people. I don't want anyone who's not Petrikoff hurt out there, and we may have to do this very fast. I'll be there in a few minutes."

"Yes, Captain."

"Bob?" she said, via *Unicinta*'s secure comms channel. "You there?"

"Hanging on every ragged edge, Captain."

"How close are you to *Capricorn*?"

"About forty seconds to landing," he said. "Getting a good look at her exterior. Happy to be in here with Kali."

"Bob." There was no simple way to articulate her unease. "I get the strong impression Greg and Elena haven't told Niemann we blew the fuck out of his ship."

"No reason he needs to know that, is there?"

"It doesn't bother you at all?" she pressed. "The idea of a time loop?"

"At my age, Jess? All I know is I don't know a damn thing about the universe."

"If it is a time loop, why didn't we emerge in the Fourth when *Capricorn* did?"

"I suspect it's the nature of time loops," he replied, "that we won't know until it's happened. Captain. As I'm de facto skipper of this shuttle, do you have any orders for me?"

*Besides 'don't die'?* "Nothing you can't figure out for yourself," she told him. "But Bob. If anything there feels off, if anyone behaves strangely, if you get an itch behind your ear making you worry they're going to sabotage us, you let me know, yes?"

"I'm a little worried," Bob said easily, "that you're thinking someone's going to sabotage this mission. Especially when it's their only chance to escape."

She told him what Niemann had said. "Just watch him, Bob," she repeated. "Eighteen months in some fucked-up quasi-military sim isn't going to make anyone a good decision maker. I don't want him to be our single point of failure."

At that, Bob chuckled. "It's charming," he said to her, "that you think we have a choice."

# THIRTY-NINE

"THAT'S A HELL of a longshot," Niemann said.

"Yes, Captain," said Elena, and waited.

Greg studied her face, the planes and shadows, the familiar set of her lips, the loose lock of hair touching one eyebrow. That would be annoying her; she'd had some of her hair burned off on that last, disastrous mission, and it was taking its time growing back. That lock of hair would be a constant reminder of an op she considered a failure, even though she'd never told him why. She'd saved lives, maybe millions, but inexplicably she believed she'd done it the wrong way.

How could he have forgotten her?

When she'd thrown her arms around him, all his memories had come flooding back, like a comm signal that had finally locked on true. He'd remembered every bitter conversation they'd had before he left, every hurt and resentment fresh as if eight weeks hadn't passed, and he felt as if he'd never been alive before that moment. He was still angry with her, still uncertain what their future held; but without her he'd been a husk, and now he was not.

It was disconcerting.

Niemann's eyes on Elena held a less personal sort of energy, and after a moment the captain nodded. "All right," he said, with the resignation of a man who knew his only shot was a dire one, "let's get everything in place. Shaw, since you've already compromised our comms systems, maybe you could come with me to finish the job." He hit his comm. "Commander Eyenga."

"Here, Captain." Eyenga sounded considerably more steady than he had when Greg had last seen him.

"I need you to reconfigure our battery output so we can siphon power to *Galileo*'s shuttle."

The line was briefly silent. "I'll have to pause my other work, Captain," Eyenga said at last.

"If we succeed," Niemann told him, "that work won't be necessary."

Greg wondered if Eyenga knew how big that *if* was.

"Acknowledged, Captain," Eyenga said.

Niemann turned to Greg. "Foster, I need you to check *Unicinta*'s field stabilizers, and make sure *Capricorn* is configured to match. You still have your command codes?"

"They're out of date now."

Niemann smiled grimly. "Not here they're not. Commander Gritsenko? Go with him. Help Commander Naude get the crew on board and secured. This plan is fragile enough; we don't need last-minute disruptions settling the wounded."

Nat started, as if her mind had wandered. "Yes, Captain."

"Okay," Niemann said. "Everyone—report back to me the instant you know something, good or bad." He clapped his hands as if he were dismissing a football team. "Let's get to it."

Niemann left the cafeteria, and before Elena followed him out, she met Greg's eyes. Her lips twitched and her expression warmed, and then she was gone, marching after the ship's commander. Greg fought a powerful desire to run after her, to keep her in sight, just to make sure that empty existence never returned.

At his side, Nat stirred. "Come on, Foster," she said. "One way or another, we're gonna have to get this done."

He pulled his eyes away from the exit and looked down. Nat looked exhausted and shaken, worse than she had on Sochi when she'd been convinced they were about to be blown to bits. *She just found out she killed civilians.* But he remembered her now, and he knew it was more than that.

"You okay?" he asked her, because it seemed the thing to ask.

A flare of rage in her expression. "None of your fucking business," she snapped, and turned away. "We don't have time for any of that shit. Come on."

He followed her toward *Capricorn*'s landing bay.

Greg watched *Unicinta*'s approach in silence.

Curiously, the bay was untouched by Target Zero's internal ministrations, the three-level-high walls and office partitions as clean and square as if they'd just come off the manufacturing floor. Three pristine troop shuttles, each sized for no more than two squads, were neatly lined up against one wall. They'd tried once, Gen had told Greg, to evacuate using those shuttles, but the barrage of power hits the ship took had threatened to pull her to pieces, and the shuttles found themselves with batteries that could no longer hold a charge. In sim, they'd never had any reason to access the landing bay, except to dispose of the dead, and that wouldn't have been a time any of them would have been thinking about shuttle damage.

Greg wondered at the violence of Target Zero's response to the shuttles. The alien structure was clearly powerful enough to destroy *Capricorn* if it chose, but all evidence suggested it was more concerned with keeping them immobile, under its control, until it was finished. With what, he couldn't know.

Gen was monitoring the ship's sensor readings—crude,

initially, but becoming more detailed as *Unicinta* approached—and had left her radio on. Somewhere, in one of *Capricorn*'s forward weapons turrets, someone was tracking *Unicinta* with something swift and destructive. At the first sign of backlash from Target Zero, Gen would order *Unicinta* blown to pieces.

On his other side, Nat stood, tense and vibrating, more self-contained than Gen was. Fighting another panic attack, he suspected. Her panic attack on Sochi had seemed different, down to lacking control over the outcome more than anything else. This time, inaction made her more frustrated than afraid. Lack of knowledge rather than helplessness. Endgames, he realized. She grew restless as events approached, and her particular brand of sharp-tongued cynicism wouldn't help her right now. For a woman who could be tremendously patient, she had a lot of trouble waiting.

One way or another, he was going to have to deal with her, or she'd throw them all off at a time when they very much needed to be on. More than he wanted to handle just now, but since when had he been able to choose?

When *Unicinta* crossed the shield barrier into the landing bay, Target Zero remaining undisturbed, Gen relaxed into a smile, and Greg felt something that might actually have been hope. Nat shifted, unwinding a little: another step, one way or another, toward their fate.

He wished he could be sure what result she was hoping for.

"Soldiers!" Gen called. *Capricorn*'s crew were already gathering at the landing bay entrance. "There's a doctor on board that shuttle. Anyone requiring emergency attention goes first, then the immobile, then the injured. If you're able-bodied and clear-headed, help the others. There's room for everyone. No fucking panic or I'll space the lot of you." The crew laughed, and Gen broke into another grin. "You know what, Foster?"

"What?"

"I think we might survive this."

Nat scoffed, but he didn't think Gen heard her.

Seeing Bob Hastings appear at *Unicinta*'s door finally shook the last of the memory cobwebs from Greg's head. He'd known Bob all his life, every feature of his face as familiar as his own father's, and he wondered how he could have entertained the idea they were biologically related. It wasn't just the skin tone, but the shape of his face, his eyebrows, his jawline. Greg mostly took after his mother, but only mostly: his eyes were his father's, in color and shape, and while had his mother's expressive mouth, his wide, rounded nose was all Tom Foster. Even when his relationship with his father had been at its worst, he'd never doubted their kinship.

Target Zero had unearthed a very personal vulnerability, and fabricated a scenario convincing enough to throw him off stride for weeks. As with the nature of that Fourth Sector *Capricorn*, he'd have to deal with that at some point.

Bob's half-smile held both relief and anger. "You keep doing this," Bob said, "without caring that you're stripping years off my life."

*I'm sorry.* The words came reflexively, but Greg didn't say them aloud. He wasn't sorry, and he wouldn't lie, not even to comfort Bob. The last eight weeks had been hideous. Stressful. Strange, and astonishing. And now they had a chance to save all these people they thought had been lost.

"You can get back at me later," Greg said, "when we're home." He turned to check on Nat, who was helping Gen settle the worst of the wounded into seats that weren't designed to accommodate injury. She caught his eye and scowled, and he let her be. "I need to look at your field stabilizers," he told Bob.

"I'll keep folks out of your way as long as I can." Bob moved past Greg to attend the wounded.

Greg made his way up to the front of the ship and got on the floor under the main console. Cursing his long legs, he curled himself out of the way of the growing crowd of soldiers and began linking *Unicinta*'s stabilizers to *Capricorn*.

"Greg Foster." Kali spoke in his ear, on a private line.

"I'm here," he said.

"I have a concern."

*Only one?* "Go ahead," he said.

"The wormhole you jumped into, on the surface of Target Zero. I am trying to figure out what it did with you."

"It brought me here," he said.

"That's not what I mean." She sounded frustrated. "At the relay...your perceptions were changed. To you, that ten minutes passed quickly, but you were physically present for it. This time... you are eight weeks older. It's in your biometrics."

*Unicinta* had a solid tolerance profile for such a small ship, but Niemann had been right: he was going to have to modify *Capricorn*'s stabilizers to avoid an overload. "I'm not sure this is the time," he began, but Kali interrupted.

"You were moved, both physically and temporally. Sideways. Somewhere else. That's a fundamentally different technological achievement than changing your perceptions at the relay."

"And?"

"Time and space are not the universe, Greg Foster," she said earnestly. "They are side effects in which we happen to exist. We're trapped by them, but it seems Target Zero is not. This may have implications for our plans."

"But we're in normal space right now," he said. "Aren't we?"

"You are assuming where we are right now affects what it can do to us."

Perhaps the question of *Capricorn* couldn't be left until later. "Kali," he asked, "that ship we destroyed. Is it the same as this one?"

"Are you asking me if we are in a time loop?"

"I'm asking if this is physically the same ship we blew to pieces outside Sochi."

"I'd need molecular data to make a precise comparison," she told him, "and the flight recorder didn't give us that. This *Capricorn* is in better shape than that one was when it was destroyed, but I can't tell you it's impossible."

*Does that mean we fail?* he thought. *Does that mean we loop again, and again, until* Capricorn *is too damaged for that thing to make use of her?*

"We need to get the fuck out of here," he said, to no one in particular.

"Yes," Kali said, her pleasant calmness reminding him, as always, of Elena. "We do."

Greg clambered gracelessly to his feet. The ship was filling quickly; it was going to be an uncomfortable trip. At the back of the cabin Nat was strapping in an absurdly young-looking officer who was cradling their hand; Nat looked ashen and twitchy.

She was one thing he could take care of, one way or another.

Gen stood in the shuttle's doorway, checking names and moving people in. "Commander Naude," he asked her, "can you spare Commander Gritsenko?"

Nat froze, but Gen kept up her task, her eyes flicking between the faces entering the ship and the crowd beyond. "We've settled the worst," she said. "I'm good on my own."

Greg met Nat's eyes. "Need your hands, Commander," he said, and stepped out of the shuttle. A moment later, he heard her footsteps behind him.

# FORTY

"How far did you get?" Niemann asked.

Elena was able to keep up with him, but her hip made it clear it would punish her later. Perhaps that would be the eventual steady state of her life: an injury just loud enough to make itself heard, reminding her she needed to slow down once in a while. Something she'd get used to, sometime in the future.

Optimistic of her, believing she had a future.

"I bridged around it," she said. "I had one more connection to go before I could shift the power."

He made a broken sound that might have been a laugh. "I'm surprised Target Zero didn't make it easier for you."

"You mean by stopping you all from shooting at each other over my head?"

"Yes."

Elena hadn't had as much time to think about the sim as Niemann had, but she hadn't been as entrenched in it, either. "Do you think it has that level of control over you?" she asked him. "Or do you think it sets things in motion, and sees how they play out?"

He took several steps before replying, and instead of

answering her question, said, "The Corps was stupid to let you go."

They hadn't let her go. They'd pushed her until she'd felt she had no other choice but to leave. *Just like pushing Niemann to attack on Anaxis.* Something about the analogy made her deeply uncomfortable. "They were trying to get at Greg," she told him. "I was incidental."

That brittle laugh again. "I don't expect anyone who's ever worked with you directly would call you incidental." He looked down at her as they walked, and she recognized something in his eyes: that reflexive authority, the weight of responsibility that seemed to settle tangibly on starship captains. Greg had had it when she met him; Jessica had acquired it gradually, subtly, over the last few weeks.

They were still in step when they reached the damaged comm center, and she headed for the console as Niemann's eyes took in the collapsing ceiling. He inhaled, nearly silently, and she wondered how much worse the place had become since he'd been here last.

He crouched down next to her as she resumed the work she'd been doing less than half an hour earlier. Sophistication was less important now; what she needed was connectivity to the ship's power array, and the ability to trigger a transfer. "Gen could have done this," he remarked, and she nodded.

"Probably faster, if she'd thought of it," Elena said. "She was focused on breaking into engineering. She didn't give a shit about comms."

"It didn't let her."

He was beginning to figure it out, and she wished she had the time to discuss it with him. She removed a coolant condenser and set it gently on the deck. "Here," she said. "I need this one opened."

He worked quietly, handing her back the condenser in two pieces. She took them and extended the rerouted connection;

with a little luck, they wouldn't have any blockages between here and the battery controllers in engineering.

"That bridge isn't going to last long," he remarked.

"You want it more robust?" she told him, in the tradition of every engineer ever born. "Talk that monster out there into giving us more time."

Niemann was unfazed. "If your Chief got his numbers right, it'll be enough." He looked down at her again. "Is he as good as you were? Your Chief?"

He knew her background, of course. The Corps was small; *everybody* knew her background. Niemann was likely one of those officers who assumed she'd left *Galileo* in some kind of snit, and would have nothing good to say about her successor. Not a one of them, she reflected, understood engineers. "He's excellent," she told him truthfully. "He's the best mechanic I've ever worked with."

"Besides yourself."

Testing her honesty. "Yes," she said. "And the nice thing about me working for him instead of him working for me is that I get less managerial bullshit and more hands-on." She pulled out a feedback balancer, discolored by plasma smoke and old-fashioned dust. "Wins all around."

"You really see it that way? Even now?"

She met his eyes. Blue eyes were beautiful, but they often struck her as cold, unfiltered and unveiled. Cruel. Greg's eyes were gray, flecked with black and white; they seemed light all the time, full of energy and optimism. Which was strange, given what she knew of him; but it was hard, looking into Greg's eyes, not to get pulled into whatever madness he had on his mind in the moment. Niemann's eyes usually looked mechanical—aggressively logical—and she suspected he'd taken advantage of that for most of his career.

But here, with the maintenance panel open before them, he

looked crestfallen, more lost than anything else. And still, underneath it all, cruel.

"Like you," she said, nudging the balancer's main circuit back into alignment, "I have not been a starry-eyed cadet in some time. The structures, traditions, constraints of the Corps? I don't miss them, and neither should you. The mission of the Corps is what matters, and just because they've lost their way doesn't mean we have to follow them." She turned to replace the unit.

"That's a curious perspective for a military professional."

She felt, under her fingers, the familiar snick of the part sliding into place, and waited for the power indicator to show her the battery controllers were connected. "The same people you think wouldn't call me incidental," she told him, "would tell you my perspective is the entirety of my problem." She waited for the dull flare of blue, the scent of electricity, the faint subdermal vibration under her fingers, and kept waiting.

She frowned, and pulled the circuit. Her magnifier yielded nothing; she put it away and set the unit back in place again.

Nothing.

"What is it?" he asked.

She pushed at the balancer. It didn't shift; the connection was clean. "There's something blocking the power."

He bent his head over the panel again. "You're sure that connector is good?" he asked.

"Tested it twice," she told him. "Look for yourself if you want."

But instead of reaching for the circuit, Niemann hit his comm. "Eyenga," he said. "We're not seeing power flow from the engine room."

Silence.

"Eyenga, acknowledge." Some urgency in his voice now. "That's an order." More silence, and Niemann switched frequencies. "Commander Naude, have you heard from Commander Eyenga?"

Why had he needed to switch frequencies to talk to Gen?

"Not a peep, Captain." Gen sounded out of breath, but cheerful. Elena wished she knew the woman well enough to know if that was good or bad.

"What's your situation there?"

"Almost loaded," she said. "Amazing how getting the fuck out of here is motivating people."

"Meet me in engineering," he said, and signed off.

He no longer looked crestfallen, or even angry. Elena would have expected, at the very least, for him to look annoyed.

He looked worried. And, if she was any judge, very, very afraid.

"Perhaps he's hurt," she suggested. Eyenga had been physically healthy when he'd left the battlefield, but his emotional state had been more than a little precarious.

Niemann looked down at her. "Are you done here?"

She nodded.

Something rippled over his expression, but she didn't know him well enough to identify it. "Come on," he said, holding out a hand. "Let's check the engine room."

She let him help her to her feet, and they set off down the hall in search of his errant commander.

# FORTY-ONE

Nataliya Gritsenko had had quite enough of trailing after Greg Foster.

She had always done her best to avoid killing civilians, but sometimes it was unavoidable. There had been one assassination—not her first, but early in her career, before she'd learned to compartmentalize properly—where one of her target's assistants, a young woman who'd treated her with friendly good humor, had managed to be in the way at precisely the wrong time. Nataliya hadn't hesitated, but afterward she'd returned to *Meridia* and sequestered herself in her room with large amounts of liquor most of her crewmates believed her still too young to drink. No guilt—never guilt—but the regret had been briefly overwhelming. She'd been more careful, after that, about getting tangled in the lives of her targets.

Until now, of course. Until now.

*Shadow Ops won't care. They were Ellis employees. The enemy. And Niemann was right: they were trying to kill us. Better them than us. Self-defense.*

Every moment was a battle against uncontrollable shaking,

and hiding that was threatening to preoccupy her beyond all usefulness.

Innocents. They'd been innocents.

Like Viktor.

Helping Gen Naude deal with the injured had been surreal. Naude was the sort of officer Nataliya had always liked: cheerful, professional, economical. Never wasting anyone's time, but also not seeing the need to propagate misery, even in the face of this godforsaken suicide op. Nataliya's mind produced an image of Naude, stuck between Nataliya's gun and Foster, and she closed her eyes, briefly dizzy.

A hand gripped her elbow. "Steady, Commander," Foster said, that infuriating gentle patience in his voice. "We're close, and then we can all get some rest."

He thought she was tired. She wanted to laugh in his face.

They had stopped in the corridor beyond the landing bay, and she braced one hand against the wall. The surface felt damp; her heart was racing. Another fucking panic attack. All the years she'd spent training them away, and here she was, alone in a hallway with the man who'd triggered two of them in as many months.

Hell or high water, it was past time to get this over with.

She pushed herself off the wall and shook off his elbow. "I'm fine," she said. "Where are these fucking stabilizers?"

He led her around a corner, and she recognized the door. It had been resisting them for weeks, but this time it opened smoothly at their approach. The room was an aux chamber under *Capricorn*'s engine room; they'd hoped to dismantle the ceiling, but they'd never been able to get through. The room itself was ordinary: a small square space without windows, ceilings low, access panels around the perimeter easily accessed by one person.

On the floor was a dead man, and she flinched.

Next to her, Foster stared down at the corpse. He was

dressed like the POWs—no, the Ellis crew—in simple civilian neutrals. From the look of his skin he'd been gone several weeks already; the room was dry, but even dryness couldn't prevent decay. She had no idea how old he'd been, if he'd been handsome, if he'd died smiling, how he'd died at all.

"You okay, Nat?"

Foster was watching her again, but she didn't have the energy for witty banter anymore. "We should get him out of the way," she said, and without another word Foster leaned over to help her pull the dead man out of the little room.

They settled the corpse against the wall, gently, respectfully, as if he might, from some shadow dimension, care about his mortal remains. Foster put a hand briefly on her arm before heading back to the room.

Nat kept looking at the dead man.

Ellis wasn't innocent. Nothing it touched could be innocent. But a death sentence? For working with Central on an approved op? Or had they been sent as an experiment, as Niemann suspected? Had these Ellis people, including the two men she'd killed, been set up by the Admiralty? By Shadow Ops? By the same people who'd sent her to kill Greg Foster?

*Stop it.* She knew who she worked for. She'd always known. Justice was not her purview. Her purview was execution, in all senses of the word. Beyond the assignment, none of this was her business.

*Which is why you never told Viktor what you are.*

"Nat."

She nearly jumped. Foster was watching her steadily.

"Grieve later," he said, and this time she took it as an order, and shoved aside the past in favor of the present.

The room was small for the two of them, but when Foster opened the access panels, Nataliya understood why he'd asked for her help: the room held row after row of stabilizers, easily several hundred, set in neat rows from floor to ceiling. He reached up to slide the top bank of controls down to his eye level. "We need to check every connection," he told her. "Pull anything dead; we don't have time to replace them. The settings change takes time, but we can shave it down to about a minute if we only have to propagate it once."

If checking every connection was the faster method, they were completely screwed, but she turned to the opposite wall and did what he'd done: began at the top.

Every third unit was bad, and it took less than a minute for a substantial pile of junk to accumulate at her feet. Foster was having better luck on his side, but even so, they'd be buried in useless starship bits before they were anything close to finished. The work took on a rhythm, a heartbeat in the back of her head: *Viktor. Viktor. Viktor.* This would be her last chance at Foster, her last time alone with him. If they both made it back to the Fourth Sector intact, the job of making him look incompetent would become impossible.

It had to be now. Somehow, some way, it had to be now. Niemann would believe whatever story she made up; the others would be more difficult, would be unlikely to buy anything that didn't make Foster look like a fucking hero. Shaw would work in her favor. Everybody knew she was biased, and any protests from her would be put down to grief, even by her close friends. Those friends would be messy, of course, especially Lockwood; but Nataliya could do it, could finish this mission and escape back to *Meridia.*

She thought she might retire. Maybe, with time, she'd be able to forge new connections, find some friends to fill in the void Viktor had left. Maybe she could manage to live a normal life.

The voice of a cold-eyed woman filled her head: *That was taken from you years ago, Nataliya.*

*Stop it.*

Now or never.

"This is fucking futile!" she shouted, throwing a broken unit to the floor. Foster turned to look at her, and she glared at him.

*Closer. Come closer.*

"This entire ship is broken, and we're pretending that we can pull one intact thread through this whole mess and find our way home."

He turned back to his work. "You have a better idea," he said, "I'm listening."

*Damn* his equanimity, but it was helping, was making her angry, was reminding her who she was and what she could do. "Oh, fuck you, Foster," she snapped. "I am so tired of your sanctimonious let's-be-a-good-leader bullshit. You're not a leader anymore. You fucking *abdicated*, remember?"

That should have angered him, because no matter what she'd been told, he hadn't abdicated, had he? He'd followed his conscience, like an *absolute fucking idiot*. Nataliya's conscience had never led her anywhere useful, wasn't suggesting anything useful now.

"If you'd rather go back to the shuttle," he said, "I can finish this myself."

Which would take up precious time, but probably not enough to further doom their already doomed mission. "And your sideways bullshit. God damn it, I'm amazed it was only your second-in-command who tried to kill you. You're so fucking logical, Foster, except it's not logic, it's fucking denial."

Had it been logical to ask for her help with the stabilizers, when she wasn't going to make a difference?

He kept his back to her. "My ex-wife used to say that," he remarked, as if they were sitting back in *Capricorn*'s cafeteria, having coffee. "It seemed to piss her off, sometimes, when I wouldn't get pissed off."

They'd told her that much about him, at least: that he'd been married, that he'd been faithful, that it had taken a dozen years of nearly constant separation before the union had fallen apart.

She hadn't believed the fidelity part until she met him. Even then, seeing him with Shaw should have made it seem unrealistic, but the two of them were going about it so badly, tripping over their own feet trying to get to each other, it had to be new. That was part of his attraction: he could be so effortlessly in command, but on a personal level, he was as clumsy and vulnerable as anyone else. You wanted to follow him. You wanted to protect him. You'd die for him, and kill for him, and it was all the same thing.

*Stop it.*

How was she going to do this?

She could try to reroute the power into his bank of stabilizers. If she were quick, and lucky, that might give him a shock, or even burns, but such an injury was unlikely to seem like a plausible cause of death. She'd had it in her head that she could break his neck, or just suffocate him, but neither of those scenarios could be easily explained away. She could flame the whole room and barely escape with her life, but that would scuttle their escape plan entirely, and she'd die with the rest of them.

That idea didn't horrify her as much as it should have, and maybe in that thought was her answer: maybe this would be her last assignment for another reason. Maybe his foolishness would have been to trust her, to pull her away from everyone else for this critical operation that he could easily have done on his own.

Why hadn't he done it on his own?

And then he made up her mind for her.

"Is that why they sent you?" he asked. "Because you look so much like Caroline?"

*Well, hell.*

She pulled her little snub-nosed handgun, the weapon he'd fought for her to have, that she'd taken off Niemann's repair table while the captain was baring his poisoned, irredeemable soul to Foster and Shaw. It had served her well in battle less than half an hour ago, the battle where they'd all thought they were fighting POWs and a shooting war was about to begin. Only a fool would run around this place disarmed, and she'd been a fool long enough.

He stopped what he was doing and turned to her, taking in her gun, and she felt something like relief.

"They sent me," she told him, "because they knew I could do the job." Her voice was calm and even. *She* was calm and even. This was her training, her life; this was what she knew how to do. What she'd tell the others wasn't important, not yet, maybe not ever.

What was important was she'd finally be finished.

# FORTY-TWO

Ted was getting exasperated with her. "I'm just saying, Captain, that leaves us with no margin. A flat power transfer, with no way of modulating one way or another? We'll have no way to tweak anything while we're initiating. We'll have to automate the triggers now, based on *Capricorn*'s historic data on Target Zero's reset power shifts, and if *Capricorn* doesn't get us the juice we need, we're fucked."

*What the fuck do* you *think we should do?* Jessica wanted to shout. "Kali will be able to modulate the power, either toward us or toward *Capricorn*."

"Yeah. A little. Not enough for anything serious. Not enough to make a difference one way or another."

Jessica had her env suit hood in her hand. Bristol was crouching by her feet, checking her boot seals. She could have had Emily do all this in the landing bay as they prepared for the external breach, but she couldn't bring herself to leave the comms corridor just yet. Superstitious, sentimental, foolish: she wanted to stay as close to Samaras as she could, as if her force of will could keep him safe.

It crossed her mind that one of the reasons Greg had been

such an asshole sometimes was that he'd had years of this kind of irrational protectiveness. Emotionally, it was unsustainable without a decent dose of cynicism, and sometimes just being a jerk.

She didn't want to be a jerk.

"If Niemann's right," Jessica said, "this is our one and only chance to get away from that thing. And if Elena's right, *not* getting away from it has killed nearly half their crew, and brought a few others to the brink of suicide." Her fist tightened on her hood. "If we ditch *Capricorn*, does that improve our chances?"

"Not much," Ted admitted. "Like I said, it's getting back out of the field that's the bigger problem. Getting her in with us won't make enough of a difference if we're going to crash out; we might have a slightly better chance, but it'll still be small. It's just—"

He stopped, and Jessica waited.

"If that's the same ship," he said at last, "we know it's in for some damage before it gets to the Fourth. And I'm not sure it's a great idea for *Galileo* to stay that close to her."

"You think it's a time loop."

"There's no such thing as time loops," he said to her, in the same tone he'd used to tell her the gamma pocks were impossible. "But it's either that, or one of those ships isn't *Capricorn*. And neither of those answers makes me happy."

She let the silence linger between them.

"I think you're right," he said at last, "to lock them out of our systems. And maybe that other *Capricorn* was an echo, or an alternate something, or some bit of weirdness that doesn't mean she's doomed. But we're handing our fate over to an awful lot of variables."

"I know, Ted," she told him. "I hate it, too. And I know it's not the same; Lanie always says mechanics can never believe there isn't some way they could improve the odds if they just poked at shit a little longer." That earned her a quiet laugh. "This may kill some of us. Or all of us. Or we may get back to the Fourth and get blown away by our old comrades anyway."

"Well when you put it *that* way," he said, and this time she was the one who laughed. She heard him exhale. "I've set the triggers, Captain. When that thing out there starts changing, we're in motion. And if we don't get through this...no regrets, Jessie. Not for one second of it."

She blinked the corridor back into focus. "Same, Ted. Also, fuck you. Survive. That's an order."

"You're getting full of yourself, aren't you?"

"I'm the boss. It's my job."

Bristol straightened. She met his eyes behind his hood, and he nodded his readiness.

"Stay on the line, Ted," she said, and he laughed again.

"Where do you think I'd go?"

# FORTY-THREE

"So why," Greg asked, "haven't you done your job yet?" He took one step toward her.

So much of the last eight weeks had been spent living moment to moment, patrol to patrol; watching Niemann, watching Eyenga, watching Nat, knowing he wasn't safe with either enemy or ally, focusing only on his squad, his people, the ones he was tasked to protect. Nat had been one of them, and even in sim he'd known there was something strange about her, but she'd been his to look after and he'd have given his life for her, and it seemed he still would.

"Don't move," she snapped.

"Why not? Will that keep you from killing me?"

He took another step toward her, and she steadied her arm, bracing her other hand underneath it. "I told you to stop," she said.

Her hand was shaking. He thought back to the ambush, when she'd dropped the enemy—and they had been the enemy, in that moment—with the ease of swatting a fly. He'd never seen anything like it, although he hadn't dwelled on that thought; anything involving older memories had been shoved from his head fairly quickly. He'd had the momentary impression of an animal, not a predator hunting for food, but a casual, unconcerned killer, clearing the way for some unknowable purpose. It had seemed a non-sequitur, based on what he knew of her; but he'd realized, even then, it wasn't a non-sequitur at all. That killer was a piece of her, part of her mosaic, just as his own temper, his ability to strategize under pressure, his rage at his mother, his unreasonable love for Elena were part of him.

It had to be miserable, living with a killer inside of you.

He took another step forward in the small space. "It's all right," he said. "I know what it's like, when you have to do a job."

"You don't know shit, Foster," she said. Her voice was trembling now. "You don't even know why they want you dead."

There were so many possibilities, he'd have no hope of guessing which reason had driven them to call on a professional assassin. He'd been hunted in various ways his whole life, even before his mother had been killed; she was an officer of high achievement, and he'd been Corps royalty from the crib. He supposed his resignation was the most likely trigger, but there were so many times over the years he'd told them to fuck off. Even the most bloodless leaders got tired of that eventually. He couldn't even say he hadn't expected it.

"You do what you need, Nat," he said to her. "I know I can count on you to finish this job. I know I can count on you to get the others out of here, no matter what you have to do to me."

"They are never getting out of here, Foster! You and your false hope, that's a bigger crime than anything else you've done! They're innocents in this!"

The gun wavered, but not enough. "We're none of us innocents, Nat."

*"Stop calling me that!"*

He was half a meter away from her, and no matter how much her hand shook, she wouldn't miss at this range. "I'm sorry," he said to her. "I should have asked what you liked to be called when we met."

"You'll kill them," she said to him. "You'll kill them, just like you did *Chryse*."

She knew he hadn't. "Who did you have on *Chryse*?" he asked her, and her fingers twitched, her thumb threatening to brush the gun's trigger.

"We all had someone," she said.

But the response was automatic, and he didn't believe her. She'd lost something critical, and it had broken her, and he knew all about being broken. He stepped forward again, and the muzzle of the handgun rested against his chest. "It's all right, Nat. You do what you have to. I forgive you."

And it was the truth.

He'd faced mortal danger many times in his career, but somehow, in the moment, he'd never felt at risk, not really. He'd been too busy fighting, planning, giving orders, making decisions; he'd been lucky, he knew, that his decisions had usually turned out to be good ones. But here, looking down at Nat's red face, her dark eyes, bright hair so familiar, this woman he'd taken under his wing knowing she loathed him, knowing she meant to do him harm—he might really die this time, he realized. The lights would go out, and he'd leave behind anger and grief. Jessica, he suspected, would never forgive him. Elena would; she'd understand. He felt a pang for his father, who'd already lost too much; but his father would understand too, even through his pain.

And Nat would finish their task, reconfigure the stabilizers, do what she could to save every other life on *Capricorn*, and on *Galileo*. He knew what she was, even if she didn't.

He stood before death, and he was not afraid.

"Fuck you, Foster," she said. She glared at him, but her eyes were brightening, and the nose of the gun shook against him.

One heartbeat, then two: still alive. "I forgive you, Nataliya," he said again, and her eyes spilled over. He reached up and laid his hand gently over hers, over the gun.

"Fuck you," she said again. "Fuck you, fuck you." She started to weep, and he pulled the gun away from her and tossed it to the floor with the useless stabilizers, and put his arms around her as she started to sob. After a moment, her hands snaked around his waist, and she leaned against him, hanging on as if she'd be sucked into vacuum without him.

"They were innocent," she said, and she might have meant the Ellis people she had killed, or *Chryse*.

"Sometimes the innocent get caught," he told her.

"It's not fair."

He put a hand on her hair, patted it gently. "It's not." He asked again: "Who did you lose?"

She sniffed, pulling herself together. "My brother," she said. "Or as good as."

"I'm sorry."

"I was angry with him. He left me for some woman over there. He fell hard, and I didn't forgive him." She inhaled with a shudder. "I can't fix it now."

"I hated my mother for years," he told her. There were a dozen platitudes he could have fed her instead. "For dying, at first, but then for leaving me in the first place. I was seven when she re-enlisted. My sister's five years older, and I hated her for having had more of my mother than I had."

Nat sniffed. "Does it go away?"

"The rage?" He wished he knew how to lie to her. "No," he said. "But you learn to live with it."

She shifted her weight away from him and he took the cue, taking a step backward. She wouldn't meet his eyes, just brushed her face with her sleeve and looked past him at the stabilization matrices. "If we focus," she said, "I bet we can get the rest pretty fucking fast."

He was so busy being proud of her he nearly forgot she'd almost killed him. "Let's get to it."

They turned back to the matrices. "Set them all to receptive when you're done," he told her, reaching for the last few rows. "I've got *Unicinta*'s settings, and we can—"

*Capricorn*'s lights flashed blue, and the ship's baritone filled the room. "Attention," the ship said calmly. "Recalculation. Five minutes to reset. Repeating. Five minutes to reset."

Nataliya glared at him as if it were his fault. "It said we had nineteen minutes!"

"I guess," he said, starting in on the units again, "we get to find out if *pretty fucking fast* is fast enough."

# FORTY-FOUR

Bristol handed Jessica a pistol. Long-barreled and top-heavy, the weapon fired narrow, efficient charges that attenuated rapidly after about two meters. Designed for close-in fighting, for shipboard conflict. Less likely to trigger Petrikoff's organic explosives. Less likely to blow giant holes in the hull, of which they already had one more than she liked.

"Do you think I'm a violent person, Lieutenant?" she asked Bristol.

He was long used to her conversational randomness. "No more than most."

"Back home," she said, her thumb hovering over the gun's trigger lock, "they think I'm some kind of aberration for joining the Corps at all. Like there's something wrong with me because I'll kill to keep people safe." Which was a stinging judgement from a culture that let children die in the name of science, but somehow that never came up in her terse conversations with family on Tengri.

"Be fair, Captain," he said. "The Corps kills for more reasons than that."

"I don't."

"You don't," he agreed. "So you're less violent than most of the Corps."

"Hooray, I guess?"

"You wanting me to lie to you, Captain?"

At that, she laughed. "Not ever, Bristol. But if it comes down to it..." She took the time for a breath. "Maybe don't let me dismember Petrikoff with my bare hands, even if he deserves it. He gets proper justice."

"Captain Taras will space him, won't she?"

"There's no actual evidence she does that." Jessica still got a queasy feeling when she thought about it. Perhaps that meant she wasn't too far gone after all.

And then Kali's voice came over her comm, and broke everything.

"It's starting early, Captain!" The CI was shouting. "Reset's starting in five minutes. We're out of time."

"Ted," Jessica said.

"We automated everything based on energy levels," he told her. "Five minutes means *Galileo*'s going to cut comms in—"

Comms went dead, and along with it the radio.

Eyenga stood before Elena and Niemann, blocking the entrance to the battery room, pulse rifle aimed at them steadily. His muscles were tense, his eyes wide; he was overdone, broken, and she didn't think she could count on him staying in control. In an ideal situation he'd have been too shaky to be much of a threat; she wasn't particularly agile in her current state, but she had no doubt Niemann could have disarmed a distracted Eyenga with little trouble.

But Eyenga wasn't distracted. He wasn't blinking much, either. He was staring at his captain, something between despairing and determined.

"You didn't do as I said," Niemann said, still gentle.

Eyenga swallowed. "No, Captain."

"Why not?"

"I remembered what you told me at the start," Eyenga said. "That this was important. That whatever else happened, whatever else you told me, we couldn't let that thing near anybody else."

"And we won't," Niemann told him. He took a step forward, stopped when Eyenga stiffened. "Carlo. We have a chance here. We have a chance to get home."

Eyenga's eyes brightened. "We're never getting home, Captain," he said. "You know that. You've known it for a year. We all have." His face crumpled. "I'm not going in again. I *can't*."

"You won't, Carlo. We'll get you to *Galileo*, and—"

"It'll get them too, don't you see?" Tears were streaming freely down Eyenga's face. "It *knows* them, just like it knew us. It's not going to let any of us go, and I can't, Captain. I can't." He sniffed deeply, then composed himself. "And I won't let it get anyone else either."

"Commander Eyenga."

Elena hadn't heard Gen approach. She wanted to turn, but she wasn't going to take her eyes off that pulse rifle.

"Soldier," Gen snapped, "what the fuck to you think you're doing?"

Eyenga became abruptly military. "My duty, Commander," he said.

"Your duty involves holding a civilian mechanic at gunpoint?"

"She's not a civilian mechanic," Eyenga said, and for an instant Elena liked him very much. "She's Corps as much as you or me, Gen. You know it."

"What I *know*, Commander," Gen said, taking an authoritative step forward, "is that you're impeding a critical military operation. We are getting the fuck out of here, soldier. Why are you holding us up?"

*Capricorn* spoke over Eyenga's reply: "Attention. Recalculation. Five minutes to reset. Repeating. Five minutes to reset."

Niemann took a moment to regain control over his expression, but not before Elena saw something in his face that might have been understanding. "Shaw, Naude, get out of here," he snapped.

Gen never took her eyes off Eyenga. "Respectfully, Tau, fuck you. We're all going, or none of us."

"Captain," Elena said, "we still need the battery dump. Five minutes is cutting it very close, even with two of us."

He glared down at her, as bad as the worst look she'd ever had from Greg when he was her commanding officer. "I've given you an order, Commander."

"We don't have time for this!" Gen shouted. "Carlo. I've worked with you for seven years. Every fucking day. Don't you trust me?"

That seemed to get through to him. "I don't—" His eyes went to Niemann's. "Captain. Tell her."

Niemann kept glaring at Elena. "I've been having Carlo rig us for self-destruct," he told her. "A little at a time, during every reset. If we couldn't get away, we could destroy that thing, and our lives would be worth something. We'd save others."

*Now* that, Elena thought, *is what I would have done.*

"You *have* saved others," she told Eyenga. "You've saved all of my crew, Commander. My family. And your family—they're waiting for you. They want you to come with them."

"We can't let it survive."

Next to her Niemann shifted, and the cold-eyed captain she'd first met returned. "Commander Eyenga. You trust Commander Naude. Do you trust me?"

Eyenga looked scandalized. "Of course, Captain. With my life. With all our lives."

Niemann positioned himself between Eyenga's rifle and Gen. "I need you to go with the others. If *Capricorn* doesn't make it home—they'll need all our stories, yours most of all. They have more resources than we do. If we tell them what they're up against, they can destroy it."

Elena watched their standoff, seconds ticking loudly in her head, and just as she was wondering if she could tackle Eyenga and get to the battery room, the commander lowered his pulse rifle. Gen swore with her usual eloquence, and Niemann relaxed, reaching out a hand to clap Eyenga on the shoulder. "I'll take care of everything, Carlo," he said, and it sounded like an oath. "You go with Commander Naude. I haven't forgotten my promise to you. It's time for you to remember yours to me."

However Elena thought Eyenga might have reacted, she didn't expect his panic and desperation to fall away, for him to grow calm, collected, and more military than she'd seen him since the sim had ended. He stood at attention, and gave his captain a salute. "Yes, Captain Niemann," he said. "I remember."

It was Niemann whose eyes brightened at that, but he returned the salute easily. "I'll see you on the other side, Commander," he said.

Gen couldn't keep silent any longer. "Tau, we need to go *now*."

Eyenga stepped around his captain and joined Gen. "I'll be right behind you," Elena promised, and although Gen frowned, she led Eyenga away.

Elena headed into the battery room. So few of the batteries held any charge at all; they could finish quickly. "Two sets of hands, Captain," she said, and started the work she knew how to do.

"Reset in three minutes zero seconds," *Capricorn* told them.

Getting through the last of the stabilization units took Greg and Nat less than a minute, which he would have found impressive had it not been twenty percent of the time they had left.

"Take a step back," he told Nat when the connections were completed, and she gave him a wary look.

"Why?"

He shot her a grin; every moment of his life had become a miracle. "In case I fuck up and blow us to pieces."

She retreated into the hallway, watching through the open door.

He turned back to the panel and entered his command code. Learned a year ago, at the regular changeover time, revoked when he'd resigned. He had to hope *Capricorn*'s booster relay had failed early enough to prevent the warship from getting the update and locking him out.

He swept one finger across the display, and the stabilization matrices lit up with row after row of green lights.

One of them flickered.

Detonation wasn't the biggest worry, he realized. Getting *Unicinta* away before the whole matrix failed would be the challenge.

"Go!" he shouted at Nat, and together they ran out of engineering. He hit his radio. "Stabilizers are synched," he said, "but they're not gonna keep. We're inbound, probably forty seconds. We ready to go?"

There was a pause before Bob replied. "Down four," he said tersely. "Eyenga and Naude, and the engineering crew."

Greg swore. *Every goddamn time.*

"Elena," he said, keeping his voice as calm as he could, "I need an ETA." *Do not do this to me,* he thought at her. *Not fucking again.*

She was silent far too many seconds for his liking. "Give me a bit, Greg," she said, at last. And her radio went dead.

She had shut him out.

A wave of visceral anger went through him, and he let it flood his limbs, speeding his progress. He needed to get past the rage. This wasn't, after all, the same as her lying about Kali. She was an engineer, working with Niemann, doing something she knew how to do. "Prep for launch without them," he told Bob.

They rounded the corner into the landing bay. *Unicinta*'s doors were still open, a few soldiers milling around the outside, waiting for space. "Everyone," he shouted, and they all turned. "We're on a hard timer here. We've got some stragglers, so let's make sure we've got everything on this bird secure for when they get here. Get the wounded strapped in, and find yourself a handhold in case we lose gravity in the field. Go."

*Capricorn* interrupted with a helpful message. "Attention. Reset in two minutes thirty seconds."

A flurry of activity. He watched Niemann's crew for a moment. He could turn around, find the battery room, pull her out bodily. The hell with Niemann, and *Capricorn*—and their plan, of course. He was reacting emotionally. Nat stood by the shuttle door, staring at him. Her skin had lost its redness; she was as cool and composed as he'd ever seen her. He wondered if she was regretting not murdering him after all.

She held out her hand to him.

After a moment he took it, and climbed on to the shuttle.

There was no time to disable the explosive triggers, which made Elena very unhappy. It was easy enough to route the power around them, but one mistake, one hiccup in power transfer, and the whole ship could go up.

"He did this on your order," she accused.

"Of course he did." Niemann crouched next to her, pulled up an access console, and began methodically disengaging safety locks ahead of her reroutes. "After what that thing had done? I had to make sure it didn't survive us."

Which explained why they hadn't enabled a simple self-destruct. "A proximity trigger," she deduced, and he nodded.

"Apart from this," he told her, "all our reset protocols have been around attempts at escape."

"Which has been impossible for a while."

There was not a hint of regret on his face "My people were going to die fighting, like soldiers. It was my job to make sure we took the enemy with us."

"And you didn't know if you could pull it off on your own, so you stuck all of it on Eyenga's head."

His lips tightened, his hands still working swiftly. "You see him now," he said, "after everything. He's the strongest I've got. Which should tell you what he's been through." Something flashed on his console. "You can disable the second level now," he told her, and kept at his work.

Elena had to remove a thin panel for this; she tossed it onto the deck. "His work is thorough," she said. "Especially since most of it was done on a timer."

"We didn't know how to figure it at first," he told her. "Timing in between sims seemed random. It took *Capricorn* three iterations before she found a pattern. It's related to our power levels, our personnel, our hull integrity, and some massive prime number that's pretty much the only constant. But it was inevitable we'd get it wrong eventually. There's your third level open." He swept aside the lock and started on the next.

"Target Zero disabled you immediately," she said, "didn't it?" She felt him glance at her, but kept at her work.

"In retrospect? It was never going to let us escape. The only reason *Galileo* has a chance is because you've apparently got a piece of that thing with you."

"Kali's not a piece of that thing," she said reflexively. She needed to slow down; she'd almost missed a branch structure. "Kali's a piece of a PSI starship captain that died when he couldn't save his crew."

"You believe that."

There was no time to explain to him how Kali had found her way on board *Galileo*. "I *know* it, Captain. I was there for most of it." She made quick work of the branch. "Three more to go."

Niemann worked in silence for a moment. "Just realized," he said, "you're telling me there have been aliens around for a while now. Centuries, maybe."

"About 800 years, we think." He swore, and she smiled. "Yeah. Makes the odd wormhole seem like yesterday's gossip, doesn't it?"

"Attention," *Capricorn* said. "Reset in ninety seconds."

"That's it." Niemann stopped his work and took her arm, pulling her bodily from the access panel. "I'll finish it, Commander. You go. Now."

This was ridiculous; she was almost done. "Captain, I—"

"That is an *order*, Commander, and this is my ship. Get out of here and back to the shuttle, right now!"

"I'm faster than you."

His eyes flashed, but she thought he was amused. "You really think you're the only one who can do this?"

He didn't understand. None of them understood. "No, Captain. But I have to save them. I have to—"

"I know." His words were gentle, the way he'd spoken to Eyenga. "But it's not your place to take on a suicide mission for my ship."

He knew, then, the odds that *Capricorn* would survive a trip through the fold. "Captain Niemann."

"Go, Commander. You may already be out of time." Gently but decisively, he elbowed her aside, and picked up where she'd left off. "Tell Genicka I'm sorry. She'll know I couldn't have it any other way."

"Shuttle launch in forty-five seconds," *Capricorn* said calmly.

"I don't know if you can, on that bad hip of yours," Niemann said, "but you need to run."

He was wrong. She could help him. She had to stay here, to watch over the power transfer, to make sure the engines did everything they could in their crippled state to transfer the ship into the FTL fold. She knew what to do, what to look for, how to compensate if things went wrong. She knew how it would all look as it fell apart, too weak and too late to hold the ship together.

Niemann knew all of it as well, and he knew it better.

"Run, Commander!" he shouted.

She ran.

Greg's relief at seeing Gen and Eyenga come around the corner into the landing bay evaporated when Elena failed to appear after them.

Eyenga stepped on to the shuttle, walking past him as if they'd never met. Gen followed, looking tense and unhappy. Something had gone wrong, and she was far from certain it could be put right.

"They're right behind me," Gen told him, but she didn't sound convinced.

He turned to Bob. "We have to delay launch."

"We need to be within 500,000 kilometers of *Galileo* by the time the backlash hits," Kali said.

"So how long can we delay?"

"Forty-five seconds," Kali said.

Niemann's radio was still active. "Captain, you need to get back here *now*."

Niemann's response was composed. "I understand the time-line," he said. "I've sent your engineer back, and I'll be right behind her. You'll be in position for the energy dump in a minute, and then—"

"There's no *then*," he broke in. With Nat protesting behind him, he stepped out of the ship, heading for the corridor, listening for Elena's uneven step. "There's no time for anything else. We've lost any slack we might have had."

"Thank you, Captain Foster," Niemann said evenly. "I can do the math."

And he cut off Greg just as Elena had.

"God *dammit*."

Greg turned. Gen stood in the shuttle doorway, eyes on the empty corridor.

"That *bastard*," she said.

His stomach dropped. "Gen?"

She met his eyes. "He's not coming."

Greg hit his radio again. "Captain Niemann?" No answer.

"No!" Gen was shouting into dead air. "Dammit, Tau, I won't leave you here on your own. You understand?"

Niemann's next words came over *Capricorn*'s intercom. "This is Captain Niemann. You're all to stay on that shuttle and get off this ship. That's an order. I'm staying with *Capricorn,* and she'll protect me through the journey. I'll see you all on the other side."

Gen jumped off the shuttle and moved for the corridor opening, but just as Greg reached out to grab her arm someone shot forward from within the cabin and snagged her around the waist, hauling her off her feet.

Eyenga.

Gen struggled. "Let me go, Commander, or I swear to God I will pull your heart out of your chest with my *teeth!*" She was furious, desperate, her trained hands working to get beneath Eyenga's arm, her fighter's muscles countering every move he made.

Eyenga tightened his grip. "He gave me an order, Commander," the young man told her. There were tears on his face again, just as there had been when the sim broke, but he was calm this time, certain, and Greg felt a wash of uneasiness.

Gen kept pounding at Eyenga's arm. "Let me go! Yarov, Flagg —get this asshole off of me! Tau! You can't *do* this!"

Niemann would be able to handle *Capricorn* alone. But with their automated triggers, *Capricorn* wouldn't require any crew at all. Why was Niemann bothering to stay?

What would he have done, in Niemann's shoes?

"Twenty seconds, Greg Foster," Kali said.

Elena wasn't going to make it.

"Bristol!" Jessica shouted.

"Here, Captain," he said, centimeters behind her.

"We don't have time for the external breach."

"Understood." He took position opposite her, on the other side of the door. "Ready for manual override," he said.

Waiting for her to open the door. Waiting for her to decide that the two of them—a precipitously-promoted systems hacker and a brawn-over-brains infantry soldier—had a chance against an angry, experienced guerrilla fighter who had her ship wired with explosives.

No choice.

"On three," she said. "One—two—three!"

She kicked the door release and rushed forward, shoulder to shoulder with Bristol.

"Liftoff in five," Kali counted. "Four. Three."

Elena came around the corner, and Greg dashed toward her.

"One." The engines fired, and *Unicinta* rose half a meter off the floor.

Elena wasn't moving fast enough. "Kali!" Greg shouted.

"I can keep the door open until we hit space," she said.

Elena was limping, and badly. He reached her, and she met his eyes, and before she could speak he swept an arm around her waist and hauled her off her feet. Slinging her over his shoulder would have let him move more quickly, but there was no time for that, and she pulled up her knees and curled against him to keep from tripping him.

He ran.

The shuttle moved toward the landing bay opening, nothing but a gravity shield between all of them and freezing vacuum, between this doomed and crippled ship and a last-ditch shot at survival.

Elena managed to lock her arms around his neck, and he ran faster.

He got close enough to see the people at the door: Yarov. Brixa. Bob was there, leaving the piloting to Kali. They all had their arms out, all reaching for Greg and Elena. "Take her!" he shouted. She let go of his neck, and with one swing he threw her toward those outstretched hands.

The shuttle moved forward without him.

Samaras was on the floor, eyes on Jessica, hands shackled to something inside a maintenance panel. "Take Samaras!" Jessica shouted to Bristol, and brandished her weapon; but Petrikoff was reaching for his comm, ready to trigger the explosives he'd lined up around the room, a neat and clean circle broken by the gaping absence of wall where some of the charges had gone off. He was grinning at her, manic, resolved; no hope now of talking him down, and if she shot him he'd certainly have time to detonate the charges, to take all of them out into space. She launched herself at his arm, and he screamed as she pulled at him, wrestling him toward the open door, toward the safe, warm, protected corridor, and out of the corner of one eye she saw Bristol free Samaras, haul the big man to safety, and it was all right then, whatever happened now was all right, and Samaras was safe and Bristol was safe and—

"Let it go, Petrikoff!" she shouted. "You've lost!"

She was strong. She always trained hard. But he was half again as large as she was, and he had nothing left to lose. He braced himself against what was left of the room's back wall and shook her off his arm as if she were a fly. She slid along the floor and hit the wall by the doorway, her leg twisting in an unnatural direction.

She aimed her weapon, but there was no time.

"We've all lost," Petrikoff said to her, and it was the most despairing sound she had ever heard, and he reached up to his comm and triggered the explosives.

Elena scrambled to her knees, ignoring the shriek of pain that shot down her right leg, and crawled under Yarov's outstretched arm. "Greg!" she shouted.

Throwing her had lost him precious seconds. She could see the darkness creeping in from her peripheral vision now, and she would be outside, with Greg left inside. *No,* she thought. *Not after all this.*

"*Run,* you asshole!" she shouted at him.

He was tall, but not tall enough, those long legs, those hardened muscles would never get him far enough, not with *Unicinta* accelerating, not with them seconds away from space, two seconds, one second, less than—

He grabbed her wrist, and her hands closed over his arm, and she pulled as he jumped.

There was less of a flash than Jessica would have thought, which meant she could watch Petrikoff's face as he fell away from her, pulled out into vacuum. He looked surprised, as she supposed one would be; but she thought, in those few moments before he was pulled too far away, that perhaps he looked at peace as well.

And then she realized she wasn't being pulled out after him.

All the loose equipment had been sucked out with Petrikoff. Conduit and paneling from the smashed bulkheads flapped furiously, making a hideous noise as it fought against the rush of oxygen headed for the opening. They couldn't seal it, of course. Sealing it would mean they were over their energy usage, and none of them would get home.

The tug came at last, but from the wrong direction, and she realized someone had hold of the fabric of her env suit. She scrambled for a foothold on the meter or so of flooring left by the open door, managed to grab the lower edge of a damaged monitoring console; she pushed against the rush, and someone pulled her, and she managed to get back into the corridor.

The door stayed open, its mechanism blown to pieces with the rest of the room, but the hallway gravity seal held. They'd lose it once they entered the field, but for now, at least, she could take a breath.

"I tried to save him," she said to Bristol. His fist was still clutching the fabric of her suit.

"I know, Captain. I saw."

"Samaras?"

"Safe."

She glanced behind them. "The bulkhead got sealed."

"Yes, Captain."

He seemed so calm.

"We're on the wrong side," she pointed out.

"I know, Captain."

They were going to die, and he sounded so steady about it. "Thank you." It seemed vitally important that she say it, even if she had time to tell him nothing else. "For saving Samaras. For saving me."

He laughed at that. "My job, Captain. All I ever wanted to do."

The lights dimmed, *Galileo* initiated the fold, and everything fell silent.

Nataliya grabbed Foster's other arm, and together with Shaw pulled him on to the shuttle. She let him go, and watched as he wrapped his arms around Shaw, the two of them breathless. Safe, then, all of them. Or as many as they were going to get.

Eyenga released Gen Naude, and Nataliya backed out of the way as the woman rounded on him, all fury. "Explain to me," the commander said icily, "why I shouldn't break your fucking neck right here."

A flash of familiar fire in Eyenga. "Because I was following orders, just like you were!" he shouted. "I should be staying behind to help him! But you just *had* to haul me out of there, didn't you? I could be back there, making sure you all get away, but instead I'm here being fucking *useless* because he wanted to save *your* fucking neck, Naude, and if you want to murder me over that, go the fuck ahead!"

Naude stared at him for a long moment, then lowered her rifle. A palpable wave of relief went through the cabin, but Naude wasn't relieved at all. "You don't know what you've done," she said quietly.

"I do." Eyenga watched her steadily.

Nataliya had worked with Eyenga long enough to know that look. *What the hell is going on?*

"Receiving power transfer from *Capricorn*," Kali said. "Transfer to *Galileo* initiated...and...complete. She's 85% in the field. Initiating FTL fold."

The window was behind Nataliya, but the distant brightness of *Galileo*'s fold flared enough to illuminate the cabin. She never took her eyes off Naude, waiting for their own polarizers to kick in.

Seconds passed, the fold incomplete.

Something was wrong.

"*Capricorn*?" Kali sounded mildly concerned. "You're in motion. Correct your course 4.77 degrees in our direction."

Naude smiled, all sadness. In that instant Nataliya knew, but it was Shaw who said it aloud.

"He's not coming," Shaw said. "He's...*damn*. He thinks he's going to destroy Target Zero."

On the floor, his arms around Elena, Greg watched through *Unicinta*'s open door as *Capricorn* moved away from them. Niemann had to know he was jeopardizing their escape, the lives of all these people who had meant everything to him.

Greg wondered what the sim had done to Niemann's memory, if it had warped his history the same way it had distorted Greg's memories of his mother. Greg imagined Niemann living with a torturous ghost for eighteen months, possibilities leeching away moment by moment, leaving him nothing to live for but the morale of his crew. Greg would have surrendered the hope of escape, too.

Getting his people home, making sure Central understood the threat—that, as far as Niemann was concerned, had only ever been Plan B. Plan A was—had always been—destroying the threat entirely.

Greg wasn't entirely sure Niemann was wrong.

"Do we have enough power to pull them in anyway?" he asked Elena.

"As far away as he is? We'd be right at power tolerance. Anything at all goes wrong—"

"*Galileo* has a hull breach," Kali interrupted. "Two people on the wrong side of it. Shielding's holding for now, but the field will break it."

*Unicinta*'s automated voice broke in. "Field completion in three seconds."

"Captain Lockwood?" Kali commed. "Captain Lockwood, come in. I need to redirect power. Tell me what to do, Captain, *Galileo* or—"

The light was too bright, and the polarizer lagged, and they all turned away from the flare.

transit


*"You never know the life you're going to lead," Elena's mother told her. "And the rest of us? The ones who love you? We know even less." She reached out—up; decades since Elena hadn't been taller than her mother—and brushed at a lock of Elena's hair. "I would choose for you, my love, if I thought I could make your life better than you could yourself. But it's yours, and all I can do is watch, and hope you remember you're never alone in any of it, not ever."*

*Elena reached for her mother, and the light flared, and—*


*—the tide had receded, and Greg could see his mother in the distance, still strolling, the wind pulling at her dark hair. Bob had stayed behind, and become the age he was now, his familiar face traced with deep lines.*

*"She's lost," Bob said. "But you're not. You never were." He smiled, that crooked smile that was nothing like Greg's, and how could he have thought it was? "What you find in life is so much more important than what you lose, don't you think?"*

*Greg opened his mouth to reply, and the waves came up and caught the sun and the flash hit his eyes and—*

*—"We chose you," the woman said, "because you were efficient."*

*But Nataliya knew the lie for what it was. "You tried to make me the same as you. I am not. I will do as you ask for as long as it serves me. After that?" She turned her back on the ice-haired woman. "The galaxy is full of people who will perform atrocities for pay. Find another."*

*She awaited the kill shot between her shoulder blades, but instead the light flared, brighter than the woman's hair, and her hands before her turned bright-white, blurred by the flash, and she wondered if it should be hot or cold and it was neither, it was nothing, and this was right, this was—*

—She will forgive me, *Tau Niemann thought, as everything grew* dark. She always forgives me.

*When the night fell, he still wasn't sure it was the truth.*

# FORTY-FIVE

Certain death was taking its own sweet time.

Jessica leaned against Bristol, half balancing on an elbow, half in his lap, squeezing her eyes shut against the fold. No polarizer here, nothing of *Galileo*'s protective bubble around them. Just this small bit of floor, and the gaping wound in the hull that would at any moment usher them out into whatever odd death the FTL field might offer them.

"Bristol?"

"Yes, Captain."

"We're not dead."

"Noticed that, Captain."

Jessica wanted, against all reason, to open her eyes and look out past the wreckage into the field. She'd seen mathematical models of it since she'd first started learning close-field physics, but every ship she'd traveled in had either been windowless, or had automated polarizers. The unfiltered field could blind you, but she figured that didn't really matter now.

More seconds passed, and they continued to be not dead.

"Lieutenant," she asked, "Why are we alive?"

He seemed to take it as a quiz. "Gravity field?"

"That's a thought," she told him. "But we didn't have enough power to seal this breach. That was the whole point."

"Then I don't know," he told her sincerely. "But we are. Unless I'm hallucinating *you*, which I guess is possible but if I were hallucinating you I like to think I'd have managed to get you to the other side of the wall."

"You seem to have saved my life," she told him. "Again."

"It's good to have a purpose, Captain."

She laughed. She felt strangely free of worry, here in the protracted final moments of her life. "Comms?" she asked.

She felt him shake his head. "Nothing," he told her. "Radio is static. Ship's comms were routed through the bits Petrikoff blasted into pieces."

"Fucking Petrikoff," she said.

"Yeah. Captain?"

"Yes, Lieutenant?"

"I know he was, you know, under undue influence or something like that. But if he was, I guess we all were. How come he was the only one to go over the edge?"

She'd had so little time to wonder about that. She'd had no time at all to care. "I think," she said, "situations like this can only warp us in ways we were already warped."

"So he was always this guy?"

"On some level? Yeah, I expect so."

"You think Target Zero affected him like it did Commander Gritsenko and the doctor?"

"I think there's a good chance."

He was quiet a moment. "Hell of a weapon," he said at last.

"I really hate that idea, Lieutenant." She was sorry she'd never get to hear Greg and Elena try to dissuade her from that conclusion.

"Hey," Bristol said, quietly. "Hey, Captain. This is—Look, Captain. Just look."

With nothing left to lose, she opened her eyes.

The first thing she noticed was how close they were to the ragged, torn edge of the ship's hull, cracked and fractured, darkened by heat. They had less than a meter of floor before the ship opened up; Petrikoff's explosives had come close to blowing past the interior bulkhead safety. *Shore that up*, she thought to herself, hoping her muddled mind would remember. Hoping she'd have a future to remember it in.

The space beyond the torn hull was impossible.

Polarized FTL fields revealed little about their construction: streaks of bright and dark, subtle behind the shielding, always straight lines, sometimes thin, sometimes thick. But nothing here was straight. Nor was it bright: the color, constantly shifting, kept tricking her eyes into thinking it was blue or green or black, but what struck her most was the constant motion. They were engulfed in a mass of tunnels, all somehow both round and warped, knotting into each other and pulling loose, drawing her eye into infinity and blocking her vision a meter before her face.

It was beautiful.

"I would really like to not die before I can tell someone about this," she said.

Bristol laughed again. "Yeah. It's pretty, isn't it?"

"What the fuck is it?"

"Got me," he told her. "I barely passed first-year Academy physics."

"You must've been pretty good at hand-to-hand for them to not throw you out."

"I was," he said. "They also said I was good at reading people. I think they were just giving me an excuse to stay."

The Academy had been right, though. Bristol was never going to be a physicist, but he could spot a threat in a crowd like nobody else. "You're a good soldier, Lieutenant," she said, seriously.

"Thank you, Captain. If we're gonna die, that's not the worst thing I could hear in my last moments."

She took his hand, and watched space warp beautifully around her damaged ship.

Jessica didn't know how long they sat there in silence, watching the impossible geometry. Everything felt vivid, acute—the enormity of the universe, Bristol's warmth against her back, the pulsing ache of the wound in her leg, the strangely dry heat of the air behind the gravity field.

It might be all right to sit here for eternity.

But just as she was thinking that—after her thousandth breath, or her first—the tunnels changed, drawing together, growing narrow and wide until there was only one, squeezing the ship into a singularity, opening out into a wide, expansive, and decidedly familiar starfield.

She swept her eyes over the stars. "Bristol?"

"Yeah," he said. "We're back in the Fourth."

As he said that the radio in her comm engaged, and a cacophony of sound assailed her. She squeezed her eyes shut, wincing; everyone was shouting, talking over each other, in crisis mode. "Shut the fuck up, all of you!" she shouted.

They fell immediately silent, and she felt a wave of affection for her crew.

Ted spoke first. "Captain!" He sounded elated. "We thought you were dead."

"No," she said. She shifted; Bristol moved away from her, and she turned to look at him. His blue eyes were clouded with concern, and she wanted to pat him on the head and assure him she was fine. He must have seen that in her eyes, because he smiled, and she found herself smiling back. "Not dead," she said. "Bristol's here too."

"Lieutenant Bristol." This was Emily, with her usual brisk efficiency. "If we were still in the Corps, I'd get you a medal."

"Yes, Commander."

There had to be some PSI equivalent to commendations. Jessica would have to ask Taras. She shifted to her knees; Bristol climbed to his feet and reached an arm out to her. She took his hand and got to her feet, and very nearly passed out. He caught her around the waist.

"You need me to carry you, Captain?"

Gingerly she put weight on her leg again, and the pain was just as intense. "*Fuck*," she said. "Yes, Lieutenant. If you wouldn't mind."

Bristol palmed the emergency bulkhead open, and they left the ruined comms center.

And so it was that Captain Jessica Lockwood, at the conclusion of her renegade ship's first mission, greeted her crew being carried by a steady-eyed and faithful infantry soldier, her leg aching, her thoughts fuzzy with adrenaline; and when they all cheered at the sight of her, there was nothing in her heart but love.

# FORTY-SIX

Elena gradually became aware of Greg's arms still around her, the breathing and shifting of other people, cautious inquiries about where they were. She was still on the floor—the artificial gravity had held; that was a surprise—her hip alerting her with a throb that her body was still intact.

Someone sobbed, and she opened her eyes.

They were in normal space, stars shifting slowly around them as they rolled. Their regular engines hadn't kicked in, which could mean they'd taken damage; she'd have to get herself off the floor to check. Bob was leaning against the now-closed door, and *Capricorn*'s people were clumped together in seats and against the walls, some stunned, some weeping.

Gen was on the floor next to Bob, one palm on shuttle door. Her eyes were closed, traces of tears on her cheeks. She made no sound.

Greg helped Elena sit up, and she squeezed his hand, letting him know she was all right. He let her go and walked over to Gen. He leaned over *Capricorn*'s second-in-command, speaking in a low voice, holding out his hand; a moment later she clasped his arm and got to her feet. Elena watched her straighten, pulling her military training over herself like a shield, and look around at her people, her lips set in a grim line. *Back to normal,* Elena thought; but before Gen moved away from Greg she squeezed his arm, just for an instant.

"Soldiers," Gen called out, all authority. "Sound off."

They recited names, one after another. Elena stood as well—somewhat to her surprise, her complaining hip held her weight—and met Greg's eyes. Such sadness there, but not for himself.

Bob stumbled back to the pilot's seat, and she pushed past the regrouping soldiers to sit next to him. "How are we doing?" she asked him.

He kept his eyes on the console. "Not getting anything on ship-to-ship comms," he told her. "I'm getting *Galileo*'s ident, but not *Capricorn*'s."

She closed her eyes and swore.

"We knew it was a possibility," he said.

"Not like this," she reminded him. "Niemann didn't tell us what he was going to do."

"I should have guessed it."

Elena looked up; Gen was standing there, grim and angry, her hands in fists.

"I am a fucking fool," she said. "It was right in front of me, and I never saw it. He never had any intention of leaving Target Zero intact, no matter what the cost."

Elena had seen the determination in him too, hadn't known the man well enough to understand what it was. "I don't under-stand," she said, "how what happened on Anaxis led to this."

Gen's voice was brittle. "Simple. Tau believed Central was shipping us out of the way, sending us out here to be some sort of guinea pig for that thing out there, whoever discovered it. He never saw the inconsistencies in that. Because he felt guilty." She looked away. "He was, I suppose. But no more so than the rest of us."

"He's your captain," Elena said, with more forgiveness than

she'd thought she could manage. "He's responsible for all of you."

"We're not children. We could have stopped before we massacred all those scientists. We didn't, because in the moment we didn't want to." She met Elena's eyes again. "But I don't believe we destroyed that colony, either. Something else happened."

"It's going to get out," Elena told her. "It may have already. The rumors were starting before we left home. And it's been—" She shook her head. "Damn. How long has it been?"

"Six weeks, seven days, twenty minutes," Bob said.

"How do you know?"

"Because," he told her, looking up, "we've received a sync. We're back in the Fourth Sector, 8,000 light years from where we programmed the jump."

It took them seventeen hours to rendezvous with *Galileo*.

The *Capricorn* survivors seemed caught in an oscillating wave of relief and shock. Brixa stubbornly maintained that *Capricorn* might have survived the trip—"we haven't seen any debris, either, or picked up a beacon"—but Gen refused to speculate, and most of the crew knew what that meant. Elena wanted to say something to Gen, to assure her she'd done her duty, that Niemann chose to save her because he valued her, but she knew the woman wouldn't listen.

*Galileo* had contacted them half an hour after they'd emerged, and she'd received a terse, exhausted report from Jessica: the ship was safe, albeit damaged, and the only casualty was Petrikoff. Elena couldn't bring herself to feel bad about that, but when she told Nataliya, she was surprised at the sorrow on the woman's face. Nataliya had brought him to them; perhaps the look was merely regret.

It took her about four hours to make what repairs she could to *Unicinta*. The little ship had weathered the FTL run better than she'd expected: they'd lost none of their interior electricals, and although the FTL engine was completely burned out, she'd been able to repair their standard thrust in just a few minutes. She'd suggested to Jessica *Galileo* stay put, that *Unicinta* would come to them, but Jessica was looking at it from a different perspective.

"We all need you home," the captain said.

Jessica knew the same thing Elena did: it wasn't just Niemann they'd lost. They'd lost any evidence they might have used to gain *Galileo*'s freedom. And losing a captain they hadn't had to lose seemed bitterly unfair after everything they'd survived.

Kali wasn't speaking.

She was still functioning as a subsystem, spending all of her processing time, as far as Elena could tell, sorting through data. In addition to dump after dump of analysis on *Capricorn*, *Galileo*, and the jump, she was writing up long analyses on what might have gone wrong, what measurements might have been missed, where *Capricorn* might be. Every analysis sought to justify the hope that *Capricorn* had not been destroyed.

Elena knew survivor's guilt when she saw it.

She took to hiding from the others, lying on the floor with her head under the dash so they'd think she was fixing something. She'd watch the telltale flashes and sparks of energy use that made up Kali's thinking, and she'd say, under her breath, "Everything will be all right."

The analyses came faster, and eventually Elena pulled herself to her feet and left Kali alone.

Bob had returned to tending the injured, and Elena took the pilot's seat, fairly certain her suspension had become irrelevant. Gen sat next to her, a medical blanket draped over her shoulders. "You okay?" Elena asked.

Gen considered before answering. "I think," she said at last, "I'm not going to be able to answer that question for a while. I expected Foster to drop a load of judgement on my head, but he didn't. You up for the job?"

Elena tried and failed to imagine what it would be like to have done what Gen and the others had done. "Would it help?" she asked.

Gen huffed out a laugh, then grew solemn. "We fucked up," she said. "We knew it in the moment. There are reasons, and none of them are good enough."

"You didn't know what Ellis had done to the reactors."

Gen paused. "It wasn't them. I know what you're thinking, and I can't tell you your experience isn't valid—but it wasn't them."

Elena glanced back into the cabin at the nine Ellis employees huddled together in a corner; had it not been for their lack of uniforms, they'd have blended in with the worn and tired *Capricorn* crew.

"I know them. We've been through hell together. When they say Ellis wouldn't nuke a whole planet just to shield their research, I believe them."

Elena, who knew more of Ellis than Gen did, let that pass. "It doesn't matter now," she said. "You didn't mean to destroy the colony. You wouldn't have, even if given the chance. But intention makes no difference at all. Those people are still dead." She waited a moment. "Will you expose what happened?"

"I think I have to, don't you? Tau did what he did in part so I could blame him for it all, get our people off the hook. I think we've had enough martyrs."

"You could always join PSI," Elena suggested, and at that Gen laughed.

"I'll keep it in mind," she said. "But I'm pretty sure any self-respecting PSI captain would space me for having been part of *Capricorn* at all."

Elena had known a few PSI captains, and she couldn't tell Gen she was wrong.

Jessica, a bandage around one leg and a cane much like Elena's in her hand, met them in *Galileo*'s landing bay with half a dozen infantry and Nurse Redlaw.

Redlaw helped Bob unload the wounded; the rest emerged on their own, looking around *Galileo*'s larger landing bay, staying close to their injured comrades. The Ellis crew mixed with the others. Elena watched Jessica make note of each one of them. The captain stopped Bob long enough to say something brief Elena couldn't hear; Bob's response was an affectionate smile. Jessica tried to glare, but Elena thought Bob had been forgiven, mostly.

She suspected her reception would be different.

Greg reached Jessica first, and the captain flung her arms around him. "You stupid son of a bitch," she said into his shoulder.

Greg laughed, hugging her back. "That's exactly what Elena said."

"I thought we'd never see you again."

"Same."

Greg let her go, and her eyes strayed past him to Elena. "I don't even know what to say to you," she said. But when Elena took a few steps forward, Jessica flung her arms around her, too.

Elena hugged her back awkwardly, half guilty, half angry, entirely relieved. "I'm glad you're okay," she settled for in the end, because it was the only true thing she could say. She let go of Jessica, straightened, and saluted; then she asked, "Any sign of *Capricorn*?"

Sadness passed over Jessica's face. "No," she said. "Field analysis says we lost our grip on her before we completed. It's possible she's still back there, but if we caught her at all, she would have come apart in the field."

Elena tried not to shudder. There were a lot of theories on what such a death would be like, and none of them were comforting. "At least he agreed to save his crew," she said.

"Niemann was a stubborn jackass," Jessica declared. "I can't decide if he was an utter coward, or the bravest man I've ever met."

*Neither,* Elena thought. *He was neither. He was a man tired of carrying a debt, willing to do literally anything to pay it.*

Elena heard the now-familiar steps of Nataliya Gritsenko behind her. Jessica's expression shuttered. "Commander," Jessica said, all politeness.

"Captain Lockwood."

The two women were silent, waiting each other out. Nataliya won.

"Greg tells me you saved lives over there," Jessica said.

"Only by chance."

At that Jessica's lips twitched; she'd always approved of bluntness. "Did you know what Petrikoff was planning?"

Nataliya shook her head. "Just that he was an idiot. But I imagine you'd figured that out for yourself."

Jessica nodded, not entirely satisfied. "Later, once you've had a chance to shake some of this off, you and I can talk. For now—you're free to wander the ship, just like before."

Nataliya was transparently surprised. "Why?"

"Because I trust Greg, and he trusts you," Jessica said. "But Commander—that's the only reason."

"I trust him too, Captain," Nataliya said. "So...thank you for this. Whatever happens next." She glanced at Greg, then left the landing bay.

Jessica turned back to them. "I told Bob I'd send you directly to the infirmary. You want to do that?"

"Absolutely not," Greg said.

Jessica looked him up and down. "You look kind of malnour-ished, to be honest," she said. "Why don't you go eat and get some sleep. Maybe check in with Bob in the morning."

"Thank you, Captain."

"Do not thank me," Jessica said severely. "The only reason I'm doing this is that I'm mad enough at Bob he won't dare get on my case for it." She reached out and took each of their hands in her own. "Please," she said. "A small request. No insubordina-tion for a while, yes? Maybe at least until all of this plays out?"

Elena caught herself smiling. "I'll see what I can do," she told her old friend.

Her room was as she'd left it two days ago, or just hours ago. Greg moved to the window, his eyes seeking the stars, their distant light slowly charging the ship's bruised batteries. He seemed stiff, out of place; months, for him, since he'd been here. Months since he'd been in anything but survival mode.

"I forgot," he said at last, looking over at her, "that I don't live here anymore."

"That was your choice," she told him. "Not mine."

Even with the stubble and the long hair, his gaze was the same, strong and energized and centered. He always seemed to have his feet under him. She never stopped tripping over herself. She wanted to put her arms around him and fold him against her, squeezing him so compact she could carry him in her pocket.

"Stay," she said. "For a while, at least."

His eyes warmed, and he nodded. "I—do you mind if I clean up? It's been a long time since I haven't been on alert."

He took a long shower, and from the steam coming from the bathroom he was running it warm rather than cold for once. When he got out he shaved; she watched him from behind the book she was half-reading as he expertly smoothed his chin, then buzzed his scalp short. He emerged looking more or less like himself. Looks, she knew, were often deceiving.

She brushed her book aside and stood up. Jessica was right: he did look malnourished. He'd always been wiry, but now he was flirting with real thinness. His body was covered in cuts and recent scars, bruises that had been too deep for med scanners to heal. He stared at her as if she were the only thing keeping him from dissolving. She reached up to touch his chin with the back of her fingers.

"Welcome home," she said softly.

"You know," he said, "I'm not really all that hungry."

She could feel it ebbing out of her: the tension, the fear, the worry that had consumed her from the moment he'd vanished from her vid feed. The fight they'd had seemed an eternity ago; trivial, something they could easily iron out in sighs and whispers. "I could use a shower myself," she told him. "But you know, my hip's been bothering me a bit. I wouldn't mind a little help."

She waited for him to turn solicitous, to make her an invalid again.

But instead he took her hand, and for a little while, all their battle scars were forgotten.

Some time later, Greg got up to sit on the sofa, facing her where she was curled up in bed, in one of the few positions that didn't aggravate her hip.

"There's something I need to tell you," he said, "about Nataliya Gritsenko."

And it wasn't what she thought it would be at all.

# EPILOGUE

# GALILEO

No one came after them.

Jessica kept the crew on high alert for seven hours after they reappeared in the Fourth Sector, but by the time they'd caught up with the streaming news, it was clear why they weren't being pursued. The news about Anaxis had broken, along with vids showing *Capricorn* fleeing the planet as the generators exploded, and Central was too busy handling the fallout to chase down Jessica's little starship.

The streamers, official and unofficial, were making a meal of it all, and people were listening. Any attempt the Admiralty had made to spin *Galileo* as an aggressor against a peaceful Corps starship was lost in the cacophony of demands for accountability for Anaxis' three million residents. Some colonies— generally the self-sufficient ones—were proposing withdrawal from Central entirely. The others, still dependent on Central's distribution infrastructure, were staging boycotts and demanding transparency.

A few streamers were floating the idea that *Galileo* had destroyed *Capricorn* to save the innocent residents of Sochi Station. Jessica's crew had become folk heroes. Familiar with the nature of gossip, Jessica chose a handful of level-headed reporters to leak *Galileo*'s records of the incident. They'd still be venerated—at least as long as everyone was angry with Central —but the truth would be out there as well.

She waited a full day before reaching out to Admiral Overton.

Overton was one of the more thoughtful—and less reflexively secretive—members of Shadow Ops, and Jessica had hoped the woman would at least listen. But the call had begun with a lot of shouting, culminating in open derision at Jessica's lack of tangible evidence. "What do you expect us to do with this information?" she'd asked. "Shrug off the destruction of a starship and let you all run off?"

So Jessica transmitted their reports, including all the readings Kali had taken from Target Zero, and how they'd timed their escape. She transferred Greg's medical report, which included evidence he'd genuinely aged eight weeks. She saved Niemann's revelations for last, including the message they had found from him to Admiral Waris, which had likely never reached the disgraced Admiral. Jessica thought Niemann's rage at Waris had been what convinced Overton.

"I'll try for you, Captain Lockwood," she said at last, significantly subdued. "I can't make promises."

Which left *Galileo* in limbo while Jessica negotiated with Central for *Capricorn*'s remaining crew.

"They're all war criminals." This came from Admiral Isah, one of the only officials left Jessica thought might *not* be involved in Shadow Ops. "Even PSI must recognize that."

That was the first time anyone in Central had explicitly acknowledged *Galileo* as a PSI ship, and it gave her a bit of hope. "Commander Naude has agreed to stand trial for her people," Jessica told Isah calmly. "Perhaps we can come to some sort of understanding until you've had a chance to hear what she has to say."

In the end, deeply unhappy, Isah had agreed to let her shelter the soldiers.

Jessica had done her best to talk Gen out of throwing herself on her sword for the Admiralty. "They set you up," Jessica reminded her, "and then they sent you off to be food for that *thing* out there."

"It's not for me to condemn them." Gen spoke with no anger, and no shame; eighteen months in hell had, it seemed, given her some perspective. "What I did—what we did—it's not forgivable. Orders or no orders. You know this, Captain Lockwood, and so did Tau. He's paid for it. The rest of us? It's not enough. No matter how harrowing it was. None of it pays for murder."

Her eyes, when they met Jessica's again, were full of fierce protectiveness. "I have my own opinions, Captain Lockwood, and you know they're not objective. If it were your crew, you wouldn't be objective either. I can't say they deserve mercy; I'll leave that up to you. But I won't throw them to the wolves. I will take whatever punishment the Admiralty gives me. But before I do that, it all goes public. I will stream every single detail of what I remember, and every experience my people have shared with me. I will stream everything Niemann said and did, including why he sacrificed *Capricorn*. The Admiralty can throw me in a hole. They can even execute me if they want. But people will know, not just of our failure, but of Central's." She sat back, as if the declaration had exhausted her. "I trust you to mete out justice to my people, Captain Lockwood. If it's within your power, once that's been done...please. Look after them."

*If they let me*, Jessica thought. Fully half of the *Capricorn* survivors were openly repulsed by *Galileo*'s status as a PSI starship. She felt certain many of them would go back to the Corps and take their chances with a court martial. For the others...she had yet to figure out how to evaluate anyone who might ask to stay.

Jessica was aware her own lines in the sand were not always

consistent, but she'd seen too much mass murder lately to make her feel charitable. She wanted desperately to talk to Greg about it, but he was still reeling from his own experiences, and mending careful fences with Elena.

So she talked to Ted.

"What do you think Taras would tell you to do?" he asked, when she'd finished explaining her dilemma.

"Taras is a whole different problem," she said. "I still have to have a conversation with her about sending us a fucking *assassin* and a guy so unstable he very nearly blew us all up."

Greg had told her, after she'd taken them off alert, why Nataliya Gritsenko had come aboard *Galileo*. He'd also insisted Gritsenko was reformed, and no longer a threat. She'd yelled at him a lot, and the bastard had been immovable, but he hadn't fought her when she'd told him Gritsenko was being put off the ship at the first opportunity. When she found out later Gritsenko wanted to go back to *Meridia* anyway, she'd been vaguely shocked. Home was apparently home, one way or another.

"Honestly?" Jessica added. "She'd probably hear out the whole crew one by one, decide based on her instincts, and space the people she didn't like. I can't do that."

"Not going to make much of a PSI captain if you can't space anybody."

He was kidding, she knew, but only to a point. "It's different," she confessed, "without regulations backing us up. We're reliant on a shared sense of decency here, and I'm afraid of what happens when that's tested."

"You could try them publicly," he told her. "Just like Taras would. But you don't have to space the guilty. Just put them off on Sochi, or Aleph Twelve, or some planet in the Third needing more hands to build shelters. Hell, turn them in to Central if it comes to that. If anybody's redeemable? We've got room."

It wasn't a terrible idea. Even Taras would respect their sovereignty on that, although *Meridia*'s captain would roll her eyes. "Democracy is for when dictatorships go wrong," Taras had told her. "If you're just, if you're proactive, if you keep your people thriving, you don't need to bother with complex government."

PSI's charters were deliberately loose; Taras could run *Meridia* however she chose. If Jessica wanted *Galileo* to have a democracy, they would have one, and Taras couldn't do a thing about it.

Two days later a message from Captain Reed arrived, piggybacked on a commercial packet. "The official inquest into *Capricorn*'s fate has been closed," Reed said tersely. "Make sure you look at the supporting data. Tell me if I'm out of my mind."

Reed had encoded a weeks' worth of news and testimony, but it came down to this: *Capricorn*'s engines had been rigged to go off when the ship approached a large object, and *Galileo*'s shearing off of her weapons had been concomitant with the warship approaching Sochi. Prior to the explosion *Capricorn* had had no nav and no external comms; no one had figured out why her comms weren't working, but her nav had simply been corroded, as if the ship had been far older than it was.

Jessica, who knew the other side of it, found herself grieving anew for Niemann. *Capricorn* had been destroyed by her captain's desire to spare other ships his own terrible fate. She tried not to think about the implications of *Galileo* being the instrument of throwing *Capricorn* back in time six weeks. It felt uncomfortably like predestination. Jessica had always believed people chose their own fates, but the evidence here suggested nothing they'd done had made any difference at all.

*Look at the supporting data.*

There was very little. Scans of hull scraps, analyses of engine remains. Most unofficial logs had been wiped; whether they were a casualty of one of Target Zero's pulses or Niemann's foresight, she'd never know. Almost as an afterthought, she triggered the associated audio of *Capricorn*'s original sighting, which would include the radio message Greg had received on Sochi, routed through *Galileo* and intercepted by a half-dozen radio telescopes in the sector.

"—promised me! Don't you forget, not now, not after...us down, Captain! We can't control her! You need to destroy—"

But that was wrong.

The voice wasn't Gen's. It was Niemann's.

And the message wasn't routed to Greg, but to Jessica.

Jessica unapologetically held on to a handful of superstitions, not because she believed in the supernatural, but because there was far too much of the universe that was still not understood. Physics won in the end, she knew; but there was still so much of physics of which they were ignorant.

She pulled up her own records, finding Greg's original message. She still had it: Gen's voice exhorting Greg to shoot the ship down. Sending *Capricorn* back hadn't altered everything... but how could both realities exist together?

*Time and space are side effects*, Kali had told Greg.

She closed Reed's message, deciding she'd worry later about who to share it with. The only detail that was important in this moment was the exoneration of *Galileo*. Central could try to hang something else on the rebel starship, but not this. For the moment, *Capricorn*'s fate wasn't going to blow back on them. For the moment, they could have some peace.

It wasn't until nearly a week later that she read the rest of the report, and learned they'd found no human remains in *Capricorn*'s debris at all.

◆

*Elena.*

She opened her eyes.

Greg lay with his back to her, his breathing steady, undisturbed; the word hadn't come from him. She reached out, brushed her fingers against his back. During the week they'd been home that small gesture had become a mantra for her, a whisper of quiet in her soul, tethering her to what really mattered. He never woke when she did it, or never said so; when he slept, he slept deep and heavy, his own defense against the world.

*Elena.*

Not a dream, then.

She slipped carefully out of bed, easing herself to her feet, her hip stiff from inactivity. Bracing a hand against the wall she limped into the bathroom, and closed the door.

"Kali?"

*Yes.*

A wave of relief hit her. Since they'd returned, the CI had written up detailed reports, integrated massive amounts of information and interpolations into *Galileo*'s systems, but she'd reached out personally to no one. Jessica had accused her of sulking. Elena knew better.

"Are you all right?" Elena asked.

It was a long time before Kali answered: *No.*

Just a whisper in Elena's ear, as she had been in the beginning. "Can I help?"

Another long pause. *Nobody can help.*

And yet she had reached out.

"It wasn't your fault, you know," Elena said.

*I should have known reset would be early.*

"How?"

*It knew me. I should have known it.*

"Kali," Elena said gently, "you *did* know it. You gave us information that let us escape."

*Not* Capricorn.

She sighed. "You didn't know Niemann. You couldn't have known what he'd choose, what he'd risk for it."

*Dead is dead.*

Elena wondered, for a moment, what sort of thoughts the CI might have on *dead*. "We all did what we could with the information we had," Elena told her. "Including you."

*It's obvious now. That reset would be shorter.*

Was that what Kali was thinking? That if she'd had more time, she would have figured out Niemann's scheme, would have stopped him? "Maybe it was obvious it might be *different*," Elena said. "But with a more complex system? Why would we have thought it would be shorter?"

*When confronted with unexpected complexity, sometimes the right answer is a reset to defaults. I should have known.*

"Kali. Even if you had known—Niemann was a wild card." Humans, Elena realized, would always be wild cards to Kali.

*I had to choose. I wanted Captain Lockwood to give me an order, but I didn't know she couldn't. I chose the two people on* Galileo. *I didn't even know who they were. I chose to let Captain Niemann die.*

"You made the best decision you could with the data you had. And Kali? I would have chosen the same."

Maybe that wasn't a coincidence.

The pause was longer this time. *How long does it take before it stops hurting?*

*Oh.* "I'm not sure it ever does," she said. Her mind went back to Indus Station. All those people, just doing a job, dead at her hands. "Not every choice we're offered is good. Not every problem has a solution. And sometimes, no matter how much we fight, we lose."

Kali digested that. *Bayandi makes sense,* she said at length.

"I know." Elena swallowed. "I would ask you, though, to stay with us, at least for a while. Because it doesn't stop hurting, Kali. Not for any of us, not ever. But you learn how to live with it, sometimes. And you're not alone here."

Kali didn't answer that time, but Elena stayed awake, sitting in the small room, lending comfort to the alien subsystem that had saved her life.

The next morning, fifteen minutes before her scheduled shift in engineering, she reported to Jessica's office.

She'd woken up to the message, a terse meeting invitation with no content. Greg, dressing for the gym while she read it, seemed unconcerned. "She's got to yell at you, sweetheart," he said. "It's just part of the process."

He kissed her then, and she forgot about it for a little while, but as soon as he left the room she read and re-read the message. She wondered if Kali would answer if she asked if Jessica was still angry.

She had been insubordinate. Bob's loophole notwithstanding, she'd known full well Jessica would never have let her leave, in Bob's custody or otherwise. That her side trip had turned out to be helpful was nothing but a fortunate coincidence; it didn't change the import of her behavior. She'd disobeyed a direct order. Probably more than one, if she thought back. Had they still been in the Corps she could have expected a reprimand, even a demotion. Even discharge from the Corps.

She didn't think Jessica would throw her out of PSI, but she could imagine the captain shipping her off to *Meridia* as part of some horrific exchange program. Elena was sure *Meridia* was lovely, but she'd just come home. She'd just begun having real conversations with Greg. She was making plans. Hoping for a future. She didn't want to do any of it from afar.

Jessica had given in and taken an office: a small sitting room off the pub, originally designed for dignitaries who felt the need for some kind of VIP treatment. As a practical matter it had been used mostly for drunken poker, where everyone stopped gambling real money and made stratospheric virtual bets, laughing and joking and throwing cards, never actually finishing a hand. Elena, who couldn't drink, had attended one or two games, and had emerged with a sort of bemused affection for the players. There were a handful of mean drunks on *Galileo*—Greg was one of them; he'd had the good sense to quit the stuff years ago—but most people simply became some variant of silly.

Jessica was not looking at all silly.

Instinctively, Elena came to attention, not meeting Jessica's glaring eyes. "Reporting as ordered, Captain."

Jessica said nothing, and Elena waited.

Eventually, the captain sighed, and waved at the chair in front of her. "At ease, Lanie. For fuck's sake. Sit down."

Elena sat. Her captain—her friend—had her hands folded before her, leaning over the desk. Her eyes on Elena's were annoyed, but there was also familiarity there, and affection.

"You know why you're here."

Elena sighed. "Jess, I told you. I promised him I'd go after him. I—"

Jessica held up a hand, and Elena fell silent, miserable. "Let's get that out of the way up front," Jessica said. "I know why you did it. I know why you felt you had to. What I don't know is why you assumed I was going to huddle in a corner and bite my fucking fingernails instead of going after him myself."

"I—" Elena sat back, and looked away. "I wasn't thinking," she said.

"I'm sorry," said Jessica pointedly. "I didn't hear you."

"I *wasn't thinking*, Jess. I was terrified and angry and desperate."

"And you thought I'd abandon him."

"I didn't." What *had* she thought? "I thought you were the captain and you had other things to do and I could do this *one thing*."

"Because otherwise it wouldn't get done."

Now she was getting annoyed. "Don't put words in my mouth."

Jessica tilted her head. "I don't think I am, Lanie. But don't think I take it personally. It's not like this isn't something you've done before."

Elena tried to think of an answer to that. Jessica wasn't wrong, but she wasn't right, either. Everything Elena did was for the people she loved, to protect them, to do the hard things so they didn't have to.

The night before she'd said something like that to Greg, who'd had his arms around her, keeping her warm and safe and honest. "Love," he'd said, "why do you always think that's your decision?"

When she'd pointed out his behavior around Nataliya Gritsenko, he'd just laughed and told her hypocrisy didn't make him wrong.

She looked Jessica in the eye. "Do you want me to leave?" she asked.

Jessica blinked once, and it struck Elena in that moment how different her leadership style was from Greg's. He would have either immediately confirmed her fear, or grown so irritable at the question the conversation would have turned into a fight. But Jessica had always been more even-tempered than Greg—and far less pragmatic.

"You keep insulting me," Jessica said, but she didn't sound angry. "Lanie, honey. We're family here. That doesn't change just because you've got some insane martyr complex that's complicating my life in ways it doesn't need to be complicated right now. You stay here until you decide you don't want to be here anymore. Those are the rules."

Elena knew other PSI ships had exceptions to those rules, sometimes extensive ones. Taras had tribunals that could shove people off *Meridia* for more or less any reason her captain sanctioned; other PSI captains she'd known had used everything from meticulous lists of offenses that would lead to banishment, to the fuzzy and mercurial act of public shunning. Jessica would come up with methods of her own in time, based on need, but for now it seemed she was going to let Elena stay.

Elena laced her fingers together to keep herself from fidgeting. "I'm sorry I assumed you wouldn't help him," she said, and meant it. "Although it wasn't really that. I just thought—"

"You thought I wouldn't do it the right way."

"You make me sound arrogant."

"You are, Lanie. So am I. We all are here. Usually for good reason, but you went over the top this time. For what it's worth, I forgive you. I know you love him. I know, for whatever reason, that fucking terrifies you. But please understand me, Lanie. I love him, too. He is my family, as much as you are, or Ted, or anybody else on this ship. That was my life, growing up: families were links. Boundaries were artificial. I would have gone after him, maybe even risked the lives of everyone on this ship to save him. Which is actually what happened, except we saved you, too."

Elena hadn't been prepared for having the same conversation twice in a day. "I'm not sure what to do," she told Jessica honestly. "I understand what you're saying. It's not that I don't trust you. I just—" She hadn't been able to put it into words for Greg, but he'd understood anyway. "I was taught to always do everything I could. To know my limitations, but not to be afraid of pushing them." She'd been alone most of her childhood; her mother had been her champion, but she'd had no one who thought as she did, who wanted the same things she did. "If I *can* do something, I feel I *must*."

Jessica gave her a considering look. "That makes you kind of a lousy soldier," she said, and when Elena huffed out a laugh, she smiled. "When I was first assigned to *Galileo*, I thought Greg let you get away with shit because he was in love with you. Now I understand it was just damage control. A commanding officer has to pick their battles with a soldier like you. Either you figure out how much insubordination you're going to put up with, or you just toss them out of the service."

That felt a little unfair, but she was beginning to recognize Jessica was asking for help. "I can't change my nature, Jess," she said. "But I can try to be better. Include people in my thinking."

"So they're not blindsided when you steal a shuttle and take on a giant alien artifact."

Elena threw up her hands. "I can't regret what I did," she said honestly. "I can't tell you I wouldn't do it again, given those exact circumstances. What do you want me to do?"

"And *that's* the right question." Jessica straightened, looking suspiciously pleased with herself. "Nobody's throwing you off this ship, Lanie. And I'm not pulling you out of the engine room. That would be stupid, and Ted would campaign so relentlessly I'd never get a wink of sleep again. But I *am* formally disciplining you for this."

Elena should have felt insulted, or at least concerned. Instead, she was curious.

"After sifting through a pack of really interesting personalities," Jessica said, "I'm left with seven of *Capricorn*'s crew I'm willing to allow to stay aboard." Shadows fell over her eyes, and Elena realized Jessica would have interviewed each of them, ferreting out their part in Anaxis, making the decision whether to give them shelter or abandon them to the legal systems of the Six Sectors.

"They're all on probation. I've assigned Emily to evaluate them. She gets to decide if they'll fit in here permanently or not. She's doing this by putting all of them through six weeks of basic training. And you're going to join them."

Elena's first reaction was surprise, and even a little pleasure. Basic training—the physical and regulatory rigors demanded of every applicant the Corps accepted—was integrated into Central's larger curriculum, along with leadership training and specializations. Basic consisted primarily of physical and mental drills designed to teach soldiers to react before they thought, to streamline operations in active situations. Elena remembered it as incredibly demanding physically, and she'd been in good shape when she'd entered the Academy. But she'd enjoyed it, in an odd way: her physical progress was clear and measurable, and it kept her on a rigorous schedule that forced her to be laser-focused on her academics. She'd never slept better in her life.

She'd also been twenty-two years old, and without injury.

"My hip," she began, and stopped when Jessica shook her head.

"Bob tells me you'll be back to normal in about six days," she said.

Another jolt of surprise. Bob hadn't mentioned that.

"You know Bob. He's not going to stop hovering over you, so if you're not up to it he'll stop you before you hurt yourself again. But for now he agrees you should be able to start along with the others." Jessica sat back. "That's my condition. You go through Basic with these *Capricorn* assholes, Emily tells me you know how to behave yourself, and we're square. Fair?"

None of this was fair. The destruction of Anaxis wasn't fair. The loss of *Capricorn* wasn't fair. The need to leave the Corps just to remain on the right side of the fight wasn't fair.

She was here with her friends—her family—and they loved her and weren't going to make her leave.

She would never need another thing ever again in her life.

"Yes, Captain," she said. "That's fair."

# SVOBODAN TECHNICAL MINISTRY, OQQU 4

The receptionist at the Svobodan Technical Ministry was an artificial.

Ilona Waris regarded the object, annoyed. The Ministry knew she didn't approve of artificials in security positions. They were outlawed on most colonies, formally or informally; AIs in human form, when they were deployed too widely, always led to a rise in violent crime and an absolute plummeting of anything resembling social cohesion. Once people got used to abusing something that looked human, it seemed they stopped caring whether or not it actually was.

This one was well-designed, at least. Ilona hadn't recognized it was a fake until it stood and began leading her toward the secure back room. It had the form of a man of about twenty-five, the skin warm and tan and realistic, the features individual enough to be considered blandly handsome, but not so unusual as to make the object stand out.

She had been fooled until she saw it walking, and being fooled annoyed her as much as anything else. But if she were to be completely honest with herself—and she strove always to be honest with herself, whatever she had to be with everyone else —her annoyance was mostly due to having to be here at all.

They had abandoned her, the Admiralty, even the ones who'd been in on all of it. She'd known when they began this phase they'd need scapegoats should anything go wrong, but she hadn't expected quite so many things to go wrong. They'd squandered every advantage they had, and now they were back to handwringing and apologizing and making easy targets of themselves. Not a spine among them. Herrod had had a spine, but he'd tempered it too much with his heart and gotten himself killed.

Now it was only Ilona, and she had to make the whole thing work on her own.

The artificial turned into a corridor at the back of the room and led her to an elevator. It entered, touched something on the wall, and stepped out again, standing to one side.

"Thank you for visiting the Svobodan Technical Ministry," it said smoothly, and Ilona very nearly thanked it. She got into the elevator and the door slid shut, the car dropping toward its destination.

It was a long drop, and she felt her nerves quieting. They'd taken her security exhortations seriously, at least. Not that security would be needed much longer, if she was lucky; but secrecy had been critical up until now, and would likely remain so until she could regroup. The Admiralty knew too much already, even if they were too disorganized to know what to do with what they had. Whatever her contempt for their morals, she knew they were, in aggregate at least, not stupid. They'd figure it out eventually: the polyhedron acquired from Anaxis, the "corruption" rendering it useless, its convenient disappearance.

She would need to be far ahead of them when they did.

The door slid open, and Nikita stood before her. It took a supreme act of will for her not to flinch at the sight of him, his long, spidery limbs confined in an old-fashioned white lab coat, his pale eyes and pale skin and pale, unkempt hair giving him the look of an animated corpse. Nikita was one of the sharpest minds Ilona had ever encountered, but you wouldn't think it looking at him. His appearance was calculated misdirection.

He reached out without asking and grasped her hand, shaking it vigorously. "Admiral," he said, with expansive sincerity. "How lovely to see you again. I trust your trip was uneventful?"

Ilona withdrew her hand and scowled at him. Not that her expression made an impact; this was his side of their dance, the carefully curated public face of his personalty. His brilliance made her willing to put up with his eccentricities—that, and knowing once his purpose was complete, she could easily have him taken care of.

Even now, without the Admiralty behind her, she had resources.

She fell into step with him as he headed down the hall. "Your message said it was urgent," she reminded him. "I hope this is more than another data transfer milestone."

"Oh, I think you'll be pleased this time," Nikita said.

The corridor was dark here, lit only by cold emergency lights in the floor. No wasted resources: everything was the program. Ilona approved.

She saw the glow before they turned the corner into a large room, dimly illuminated by daylight-spectrum light in a small glass enclosure. Four of Nikita's team stood around the enclosure, studying output displays; a fifth was crouched by a panel on the floor. Maintenance of some kind, she suspected. It was important to keep an eye on the program's environment. One shadow fluctuation, one capacitor surge, and they would lose all their work.

In the precise center of the enclosure, resting on the floor, was a small gray polyhedron.

The destruction of Indus Station had annoyed Ilona for

many reasons, but her loss of rank and subsequent fugitive status had been the least of it. She had known throughout her career the Admiralty was full of weak-minded people. She had known her colleagues in Shadow Ops lacked the will to do what was really necessary.

Anaxis had been a surprise. She hadn't thought civilian researchers would have been able to find anything in what Shadow Ops had given them to work with: a small fragment of something pulled from the PSI ship *Chryse*, months before her destruction. Ilona had given it to them almost reluctantly, convinced it would go nowhere, a conceptual dead end.

Today, she had hope she'd been wrong.

Nikita was talking at her. "We couldn't think of a reason it wouldn't communicate with us," he said. "It knew all our grammar and syntax. And then it occurred to us we'd never shown it examples of ordinary conversation. We gave it some of the early readers used for the small children here. Turns out we didn't have to give it any more."

Ilona very nearly reprimanded Nikita. The experimental protocols had been clear: no unapproved inputs, no interactions that hadn't been explicitly outlined in the specs. Ten thousand words describing limitations, but it all came down to one thing: don't feed it unless it stops growing.

For this result, she forgave him. "It's talking?"

His grin widened. "Come and see," he said.

He led her over to one of the monitors, brushing the hovering scientist aside. Ilona's eyes went to the display.

She watched for nearly one full minute as the words scrolled, incessant. Not even a pause.

"Are you sure this isn't a glitch?" she asked.

"We cycled its power," he told her. "It started up again as soon as it was brought on line. It's *talking* to us, Admiral. We can do so much more with it now."

"This is excellent, Nikita," she said. "I'm pleased."

Nikita beamed.

"I want a proposal for next steps by the end of the day. Don't rush it. Let it grow on its own. But I want to see movement. Is that clear?"

"Of course, Admiral." He looked like she had just presented him with a prize. "We've already been discussing options. I'll send you the summaries in a few hours."

That would give her time to reach her new flat, shake off the long trip, maybe get some rest. Her body had held up well over the decades, but time hit everyone. She'd had so few opportunities, in the last two months, for a proper respite.

"You've done a very good job, Nikita," she told him. "I'll look forward to watching this experiment more closely." And perhaps she wouldn't need to have him taken care of after all.

She turned to head back toward the elevators, but in her mind she could still see the words, scrolling over and over on the display, the program's first cry into the outside world, to people Ilona had forbidden to answer:

WHO AM I?

WHO AM I?

WHO AM I?

# ACKNOWLEDGMENTS

With thanks to:

- Patrick Foster, Patrick Foster Design, for the layout and cover treatment
- Seth Rutledge, illustrator, for the cover illustration, in particular my lovely *Galileo*
- Gary Gibson at Jericho Writers
- Judi Hardin
- JJ Litke
- Nancy Matuszak
- Richard Tunley
- Margot Harrison
- Sylvia Johnson
- The crew at Absolute Write
- Nick Bonesteel, occasional physics fact-checker and forgiver of fictional science
- Steve and Emily, who still hang around despite me being, well, me

Mostly, though, this book is for my parents, who can't read it. I will miss you both forever.

# ABOUT THE AUTHOR

**Elizabeth H. Bonesteel** began making up stories at the age of five, in an attempt to battle insomnia. Thanks to a family connection to the space program, she has been reading science fiction since she was a child. She currently lives in central Massachusetts with her husband, her daughter, and various cats.